Praise f

THE WATER O

One of the Best Books of the Year—*Book Riot, Vulture, Polygon,* Goodreads, Amazon, *Gizmodo, Ms., Autostraddle,* IGN, *The Mary Sue*
Finalist for the American Library Association Andrew Carnegie Medal

"An addictive action-adventure novel and one of the most straightforwardly utopian books in ages . . . Huang's sensitive exploration of the conflict between law and justice is as exciting as the most spectacular airborne kick." —*The Washington Post*

"At once a boisterous martial arts epic, an intricate heist story, and an all too timely tale of resistance against tyrannical institutions, *The Water Outlaws* is also unusually engrossing. . . . In addition to being a Hugo Award winner, polymath Huang is a Hollywood stunt performer and armorer, able to write scenes of intricate combat with effortless clarity and breathless pacing. This novel reads like a movie in the best way." —*Vulture*

"In this addictive, queer, feminist epic fantasy, Huang brilliantly retells the fourteenth-century Chinese classic *Water Margin* for a twenty-first-century audience. . . . The author's background as a Hollywood stunt performer enriches the kinetic action sequences, which are both easy to follow and thrilling to read. This wuxia eat-the-rich tale is a knockout." —*Publishers Weekly* (starred review)

"Huang's new epic fantasy moves at a breakneck, adrenaline-filled pace that makes it difficult to put down, and the convincing, broad cast of characters powers the plot forward amidst cunning turns of strategy and shocking, dark twists. . . . Fans of *Iron Widow* by Xiran Jay Zhao and *She Who Became the Sun* by Shelley Parker-Chan will eat up this new adventure about justified anger and fierce female warriors." —*Booklist* (starred review)

"Nonstop action that will thrill you with its feminist heart. This tale's legendary gathering is the birth of true heroes: those with the imagination to understand how the world could be different for the downtrodden, and the courage to make it so. What skill it takes to turn a cornerstone of the canon upside down and yet have it feel so convincingly classic! S. L. Huang doesn't put a foot wrong in this magisterial epic."

—Shelley Parker-Chan, *Sunday Times* bestselling author of *She Who Became the Sun*

"This queer retelling of a Chinese classic is a fantastic and entertaining blend of action, humor, profanity, social justice, delightfully larger-than-life characters, and so many magnificent fight scenes!" —Kate Elliott, bestselling author of *Unconquerable Sun*

"Rogues with hearts of gold, the motley rebels of Liangshan will warm your heart as quickly as they'll cause it to race, thump, and break. Huang's writing is a god's tooth in its own right, sparking these heroes alive. Lu Junyi is a personal favorite, and her relationship with Lin Chong is a bond that binds not just two women together, but a whole revolution. If, like me, you grew up on the martial arts movies of the '80s, and are enamored by queer genderbent monks or rebels loud and quiet both—grab this book!"

—Suyi Davies Okungbowa, author of *Son of the Storm*

"S. L. Huang is a literary genius, and this book proves it. Breathtakingly researched, tightly plotted, and cunningly written, this book is full of delicious vengeance and sharp humor. I laughed, I raged, I was swept off my feet, and I loved every minute of it!"

—Jesse Q. Sutanto, *New York Times* bestselling author of *Dial A for Aunties*

"Spectacular. A whip-smart roller coaster of a book with action scenes that knocked the wind out of me."

—Sarah Gailey, bestselling author of *Just Like Home*

"An utter delight and rip-roaring treat for anyone who grew up on wuxia films and Shaw Brothers movies and loves fantasy. Clever, cunning, tightly plotted with brilliant martial arts fight scenes that had me grinning. S. L. Huang delivers all of what I enjoy about the genre: loads of action, no shyness of profanity, fantastic levels of research, and characters who leap off the page in their largeness. This reimagining of *Water Margin* is freaking awesome!"

—R.R. Virdi, author of *The First Binding*

"This queer fantasy novel inspired by the Chinese classic *Water Margin* by Shi Nai'an doesn't pull any of its anti-authority punches, and it's all the better for it. . . . Huang has delivered an exciting martial arts adventure!" —*Book Riot*

"Feminist, fantastical, and queer AF, this action-packed martial arts adventure will knock your socks off." —*Ms.*

"Reimagining the famed Chinese novel *Water Margin*, this epic wuxia fantasy will blow you away. . . . Huang's dynamic prose and animated action will keep you hooked 'til the very last page." —IGN

"Huang has written a gloriously cinematic novel, one that delights in martial arts tropes. . . . *The Water Outlaws* is a hell of a lot of fun." —*Locus*

"This queer epic fantasy retelling inspired by the story of the fourteenth-century Chinese classic *Water Margin* is perfect for everyone who loved Shelley Parker-Chan's *She Who Became the Sun*. A feminist, action-packed tale of bandits and found family that's bursting with martial arts tropes and rich mythology." —*Paste*

"A fantastic novel of resistance. It breathes new life into a classic saga with scintillating action. *The Water Outlaws* teaches us to refuse to be defined by people who don't care about us."

—John Wiswell, author of *Someone You Can Build a Nest In*

Also by S. L. HUANG

Burning Roses (novella)

CAS RUSSELL SERIES

Zero Sum Game

Null Set

Critical Point

S. L. HUANG

THE WATER OUTLAWS

TOR PUBLISHING GROUP
NEW YORK

This is a work of fiction. All of the characters, organizations, and events portrayed in this novel are either products of the author's imagination or are used fictitiously.

THE WATER OUTLAWS

Illustrations by Feifei Ruan.

A Tordotcom Book
Published by Tom Doherty Associates / Tor Publishing Group
120 Broadway
New York, NY 10271

www.torpublishinggroup.com

The Library of Congress has cataloged the hardcover edition as follows:

Names: Huang, S. L., author.
Title: The water outlaws / S. L. Huang.
Description: First edition. | New York : Tor Publishing Group, 2023.
Identifiers: LCCN 2023942742 (print) | ISBN 9781250180421 (hardcover) |
ISBN 9781250198761 (ebook)
LC record available at https://lccn.loc.gov/2023942742

ISBN 978-1-250-84798-0 (trade paperback)

First Tordotcom Paperback Edition: 2024

Printed in the United States of America

0 9 8 7 6 5 4 3 2 1

For my grandfather, who taught me crosswords, cryptograms, and cards . . . You always encouraged my inquisitiveness of mind; took me seriously from my first spoken thought. *Per te, un giorno entrerò nell'elenco dei bestseller del* New York Times.

Author's Note on Potentially Disturbing Content

This book is a genderspun retelling of the Chinese classic novel *Water Margin,* in which antiheroic bandits rise up against a tyrannical government on behalf of the people. I've reimagined it as a melding of epic fantasy and wuxia, an action-packed battle against patriarchy that's rife with indecorous women and fantastical sword fights.

In that context, this story is intentionally, gloriously violent—mostly in a cinematic style (based on the wuxia genre—think Chinese martial arts films). However, you'll also find a few scenes of torture, the occasional extremity such as cannibalism, and one attempted sexual assault. The background society, in its regression and misogyny, also holds a number of values as normal that may disturb a modern reader.

That said, I hope this is primarily a joyous, toothy escapist adventure, one in which a group made up almost entirely of women and queer folk—who are in equal parts devastating, powerful, righteous, and terrible—stand up as self-proclaimed heroes to tear the world asunder.

—S. L. Huang 黃士芬

DRAMATIS PERSONAE

CITIZENS OF BIANLIANG

LIN CHONG. Master Arms Instructor of the Imperial Guard.

LU JUNYI. Wealthy socialite and intellectual. Friend to Lin Chong.

LING ZHEN. A scholar and experimenter of materials. Husband to Fan Rui. Nickname: "Thunder God."

FAN RUI. A scholar and priestess of the Renxia. Wife to Ling Zhen. Nickname: "Chaos Demon."

JIA. House companion to Lu Junyi.

THE BANDITS OF LIANGSHAN

LU DA. Formerly a monk of the Fa. Nickname: "Flower Monk." Weapon of choice: iron staff.

CHAO GAI. Transcendentalist-trained ghost hunter, chief of the village of Dongxi. Nickname: "Heavenly King."

WANG LUN. Founder and chieftain of the bandits. Nickname: "The Scholar."

SUN ERNIANG. Former "black tavern" owner. A little too good a cook. Nickname: "The Witch."

SONG JIANG. Former celebrity poet. Nickname: "Spring Rain."

WU YONG. A very clever strategist; allied with Song Jiang. Nickname: "The Tactician." Weapon of choice: copper chain.

LI KUI. Foul-mouthed killer; allied with Song Jiang. Nickname: "Iron Whirlwind." Weapon of choice: double battleaxes.

AN DAOQUAN. A skilled doctor. Nickname: "Divine Physician."

HU SANNIANG. A talented and classically trained fighter. Nickname: "Steel Viridian." Weapons of choice: double sabers and lasso.

SECOND BROTHER RUAN, FIFTH BROTHER RUAN, and SEVENTH BROTHER RUAN. Fisherfolk who helped build Liangshan. Weapons of choice: cudgels.

ZHU GUI. An innkeeper and lookout for Liangshan. Nickname: "Crocodile."

NOBLEWOMAN CHAI. A wealthy aristocrat. Nickname: "Cyclone."

JIANG JING. An accountant and calculator. Nickname: "The Mathematic."

YANG XIONG, SHI XIU, SHI QIAN. A group sworn to each other and known as the Three Fleas.

DU QIAN, SONG WAN. Lieutenants of Wang Lun.

LI JUN, LI LI, WANG DINGLIU, THE ZHANG SIBLINGS, THE MU SISTERS, THE TONG SISTERS, THE XIE TWINS. Other bandits among the members of Liangshan.

IMPERIAL GOVERNMENT OFFICIALS

GAO QIU. An Imperial Grand Marshal and friend to the Emperor.

CAI JING. The Chancellor of the Secretariat. One of three men second only to the Emperor.

MINISTER DUAN. The Minister of War. Gao Qiu's superior; supervised by the Chancellor of the Ministry.

OTHER RESIDENTS OF THE EMPIRE

YANG ZHI. A former captain in the Imperial Guard; demoted to commander and exiled to Daleng. Nickname: "Blue Beast."

BAI SHENG. A wine merchant. Nickname: "Sunmouse."

HUANG WENBING. Husband to Bai Sheng.

PART I

LIN CHONG

CHAPTER 1

Every morning just after dawn, Lin Chong taught a fight class for women.

The class was always well attended, and Lin Chong welcomed any from the lowest beggar to the highest socialite. Women choosing to apply themselves so seriously to the arts of war and weaponry might have been seen as unusual, even in the highly modern Empire of Song, but Lin Chong was so well established in the prefecture, and so well respected, that men rationalized the participation of their wives and daughters. *It will help her excise any womanly hysteria*, they would think, or *She will be able to improve her grace and refinement.* Besides, they trusted Lin Chong not to be too rough, or to act inappropriately. She was, after all, a master arms instructor for the Imperial Guard, and besides which was also a woman herself.

If the men had ever come to watch their wives and daughters at work, they may have revised their concerns about the roughness.

Today, after a meditation and warmup, Lin Chong had divided her attendees into pairs to practice a new combination of techniques. A block and throw—very useful, especially for a weaker opponent against a stronger attacker. Lin Chong paced between the pairs, watching, adjusting, correcting. Occasionally she even added a short word of praise, which inevitably made its recipient glow.

In the front of the group, Lu Junyi swept her opponent to the ground and gave Lin Chong a devilish grin. Tall, slender, and with a face an artist would invent, Lu Junyi had the same self-possession here, shining with sweat, as she would overseeing one of her intellectual salons. She kept Lin Chong's eye and made a motion across the courtyard, as if to ask about the woman she had brought with her today.

Lin Chong only nodded her back to work. They might be old friends, training under Zhou Tong together back when they were both barely nineteen, but that was no excuse for inattention during class.

Lu Junyi gave a good-natured sigh and reached out a hand to help her opponent up.

Lin Chong did need to see how the new participant was faring, however. She'd heard some grunting and swearing from that corner that did not presage well. She turned and circled in that direction.

When Lu Junyi had introduced Lu Da before the class began, Lin Chong had not exactly been surprised—despite her social status, Lu Junyi somehow managed to meet a wide diversity of people. And Lu Da was an eclectic patchwork of the human condition all by herself. The sides of her head were shaved in the tradition of a monk of the Fa, but the ink characters of a criminal tattoo marched down her cheek, and her mannerisms were as far from a monk as could be imagined. When Lu Junyi had introduced her, Lu Da had spit on the flagstone ground and then nearly shouted her salute, smacking her hands together so hard the respectful gesture might as well have been crushing a melon. She was likely strong enough to crush melons, too—she towered over the other students, and her girth was easily twice Lin Chong and Lu Junyi put together. But she'd seemed an eager enough student, bounding over to leave her heavy two-handed sword and even heavier metal staff at the side of the practice yard at Lin Chong's direction.

When Lin Chong stepped back over to her, however, it was to find that Lu Da and her opponent had somehow devolved into a wrestling match.

Lu Da had her partner in a bear hug and was squeezing her so hard her feet had come off the ground. But the other woman had been training with Lin Chong for many months, and she managed to twist and break the hold. She dropped back to her feet and spun lightning fast.

"Why, you donkey!" Lu Da bellowed, and swung a massive fist, which her partner dodged.

Lu Da let out a roar that seemed to call earth and wind to her command. She thrust out a palm, striking the empty space between them, and from a full pace away blasted her opponent back. The woman flew into the air only to land on her back and roll until she hit one of the neighboring buildings.

"Stop," Lin Chong said.

She didn't speak loudly, but she never had to. The entire class halted and turned to attention from where they were. Several of them had already been distracted into watching Lu Da, their faces dazed and fascinated.

"Attention," Lin Chong said.

The class drew their feet together and stood straight, hands behind their backs. Lu Da looked around and then clumsily imitated them.

"You are uninjured?" Lin Chong asked the woman who had hit the ground.

She scrambled back to her feet. "Yes, Master Instructor."

Lin Chong turned to address Lu Da. "You have a god's tooth."

Lu Da had the grace to flush red across her broad face. "I do, Master Instructor."

"Show me."

Lu Da pawed at her loose collar. Beneath her tunic, a magnificent garden of tattooed ink peered out, far more wild and fantastical than the impersonal criminal brand on her face. She grabbed at a long leather cord around her neck and drew it forth to reveal a shining shard of stone or porcelain.

The piece hung from the leather, smooth with age and deceptively inert, and drawing every eye in the class.

Lin Chong raised her voice to the class again. "Who here considers themselves a philosopher?"

About a third of the class lifted a hand.

Lin Chong shook her head slightly. "I don't mean you tell your children to follow the tenets of Benevolence, or you make sacrifices to the gods for favors of luck or wealth. Who here dedicates themselves to the practice of one or more religions?"

Most of the hands went down.

Lin Chong nodded to a young woman in the front, a newer student she didn't know well yet. "Yes. Which do you practice?"

"I follow both Benevolence and the Fa, Master Instructor."

Perfect. "And what do your religions teach you about the gods?"

She looked confused. "They don't, Master Instructor."

"Quite correct." Lin Chong raised her voice, making sure the whole courtyard could hear. "The gods are irrelevant to the teachings of the Benevolent Order. The Fa teaches that gods differ from us only in an advancement of immortality and its power, and that all were once human—we could become the same by studying enough to attain enlightenment, and in fact, the early stages of enlightenment are what the Fa believe grant the abilities we know as 'scholar's skills.' The Followers of the Fa aspire to move past mere scholar's skills and attain that godhood, but otherwise do not look to the gods for help."

She'd been pacing the front of the yard as she talked, and slowly came back around to face Lu Da.

"Student Lu. You are a monk of the Fa."

"I was," Lu Da corrected genially. "They kicked me out."

Lin Chong could feel her eyebrows rise. "You were expelled from the monastery? Why?"

"I missed curfew," Lu Da answered.

"I see."

"A hundred and seventy-three times."

"That would—" started Lin Chong delicately.

"Because I was drunk!"

Lin Chong waited a moment to make sure nothing more was forthcoming. Then she said, "You still know the teachings, however."

"Sure, whichever stuck in my head. They do leak out my earholes."

"Then tell us, Student Lu. What is a god's tooth?"

Lu Da flushed a bit redder. "It's like you said. *You* know. They told me not to use it, because, well, it's the power the gods left behind, in artifacts and the like. Sort of cracks in the world, right? Wherever the gods went long ago, and the demons too, god's teeth are what let that bust through a bit. But the monks said it doesn't help me reach enlightenment, so I should put it away and never touch it. 'God's teeth never make a god,' as the saying is." She shrugged her massive shoulders sheepishly. "But they also always wanted me to be a better fighter, and my tooth makes me a better fighter!"

"The martial arts were to be your path to enlightenment?"

Again the sheepish shrug. "I'm good at them. Master Instructor."

"Ah, but it is not raw power at your art that brings enlightenment, according to the Fa. You attain that only through the journey."

"Right," Lu Da said, sounding uncertain.

"Let me put it another way," Lin Chong said. "After deep study, monastery training is known to grant scholar's skills in your art, yes? If you studied hard enough, and long enough, you would learn to bend a fight to your will in ways even someone such as I—who has made a study of decades, of all five forms and across all the eighteen weapons—even someone such as I could never hope to best you. Do you think your god's tooth does the same?"

"Well, yeah. That's what god's teeth are, right? Sort of a shortcut."

It was what most people thought.

Monastery training was a route of great dedication and sacrifice that not many pursued, despite any potential reward. Many dreamed of leaping a building, of living for two hundred years, of having dream encounters with queenly demons—or any other number of storied scholar's skills some monks and priests were said to develop depending on their study. If they stayed the path. If they excelled to the rights of legend. But the necessary years of strictness, of internal and external training, of mental and physical discipline . . .

A god's tooth bestowed that power without strings. Without sacrifice.

Supposedly.

Lin Chong had already caught half her class casting glances of grudging envy at Lu Da. The Empire and the aristocracy had done everything they could for generations to push a social attitude of scoffing at god's teeth, labeling them trinkets and fragments of a bygone age, ones outclassed by modern technology. But Lin Chong strongly suspected those most vocal in their dismissal were the ones who secretly coveted what they did not possess.

Certainly everyone here in her class was shaded in jealousy.

God's teeth were *power.* They made things easy.

They were also rare enough that she might never see one in her class again. Lin Chong decided a demonstration was in order.

She faced the class.

"I am not religious." She might remind herself of the tenets of Benevolence in daily life, as did most people, but she was no philosopher. More importantly, she was no monk. "I am not religious, and as I have said, I would never claim to be able to best the scholar's skills of a monastery-trained monk. Student Lu. That is your staff, correct?"

She gestured to the heavy metal bar Lu Da had set aside before class. Easily taller than Lu Da, it looked to weigh at least sixty jin.

"Yes, Master Instructor!" Lu Da said proudly.

"It is your weapon of choice?"

"It is!"

"Then take it up, and face me with your god's tooth."

Lu Da stared in confusion. The rest of the class shuffled in their places, a few murmurs going up even among the well-disciplined students.

"But I'll kill you," Lu Da blurted.

"I admire your confidence," Lin Chong said dryly.

"I wouldn't *try* to kill you, I just mean I could hurt you bad . . ." Lu Da glanced around at the rest of the students, clearly trying to check whether she was speaking as honorably as she thought she was. After all, it wasn't right to smash in the head of your teacher, was it?

"Take up your staff," Lin Chong instructed. "Unless you are too afraid to face me."

"I'm not afraid!" Lu Da shot back. She tucked her god's tooth back under her tunic with her forest of inked flowers, then shuffled over to pick up the staff. She lifted it as if it weighed no more than a toothpick and whirled it above her head, in one hand and then the other.

"Clear an area," Lin Chong said, and the other students hurried to gather up their reed mats and line the sides of the courtyard, whispering in anticipation.

Lin Chong took a moment to unwrap her heavy coat and lay it carefully to the side, along with the sword she'd untied and set apart before class. The robes underneath she tucked up in her belt, out of the way. Then she stepped to the middle of the courtyard, hands clasped behind her back, the hemp of her shoes quiet and sure against the flagstones.

"But Master Instructor! You won't use any weapon?" Lu Da cried.

"I have weapons in my hands and feet," Lin Chong answered. "I have weapons in my years, and in my training."

Lu Da ambled in to face her, doubts scrawled transparently across her face. "This doesn't seem all right. I don't want to injure you."

"You presume a lot, Student Lu," Lin Chong answered. "I instruct you to wield the full power of your god's tooth, and I shall wield my training, and we shall see if the monks of the Fa lied to you or not."

Lu Da spun her massive staff between her massive hands. "As you wish, Master Instructor. I guess."

"Begin."

Lu Da's face drew together in focus. She sidestepped, her staff at a slow spin, matching the same careful distance from Lin Chong.

Lin Chong stepped to pace her, evenly, calmly. Her hands stayed clasped behind her back. She breathed deep, inhaling the movement, the connections, the intricately fitted puzzle pieces of the universe.

The meditative state was as familiar as the moves of her muscles through forms, or the feel of a sword hilt or axe or halberd settling its weight against her hand. Familiar as worn cloth, calming as a childhood home. Like reposing to drink with old friends.

Lu Da reared back, and the movement rippled all through Lin Chong's senses. Leaning to the side was an easy dance move, as if Lu Da had asked a question and Lin Chong answered without thought.

The heavy metal staff whistled through the air. A tentative strike, without Lu Da's full weight behind it. Lin Chong could see the other woman's balance, the way the weight was in her arms instead of backed by the vigor of her body.

"You hold back," Lin Chong said.

Lu Da grunted and swung again. And again.

Lin Chong dodged once, twice, a third time. Always the smallest movement, always that fluid answer to Lu Da's question. Before long Lu Da had forgotten her trepidation and was bringing the staff down with all her might, blows that would have surely crushed Lin Chong's skull, had they landed.

"Your strength cannot bring you victory," Lin Chong said calmly, slipping to avoid a downward swing, then twisting to let a thrust by.

Lu Da overbalanced, her face going red with exertion all the way up the sides of her shaved head to her bobbing topknot.

Lin Chong saw the moment Lu Da's decision firmed, the instant her mind reached for the god's tooth. Her posture rolled in on itself, her muscles tensing, her eyes squinting at the corners. She shouted her intention to Lin Chong as surely as if she'd proclaimed it from her lips.

Lin Chong felt the god's tooth open.

Even the most minor god's tooth tapped into something primal. Untamed. The deep caverns of a secret essence, the bright joy of an unbridled desire. A lack of inhibition that was difficult for even a studied practitioner to harness and guide.

Lu Da's grasp on the power was tenuous at best. A whip streaking out that might snap against the intended target, or might smack a bystander—or might come rushing back to bloody the cheek of the one who wielded it.

She flung that power at Lin Chong.

It had been some time since Lin Chong had handled the power of the gods in a fight. But she remembered. She leapt, catching the edge of the wave and using it to climb an invisible staircase, foot to foot middair above Lu Da's attempt. Then she landed lightly back on the flagstones, on the soles of her hempen shoes.

All with her hands still behind her back.

Lu Da stared in disbelief. Then she let loose.

The depth of the god's tooth sucked free, thrashing against reality. Lin Chong lightly jumped one tendril of it, then let another wrap her leg just enough to snap it back with a kick of her foot. Lu Da roared, trying to wrest the power and aim it, but unsuccessfully. One curl of it slashed high on the next building, splintering a wooden screen over some of the windows. Another hit lower on the wall, causing some of the watching students to duck and cry out.

Lu Da was struggling to imbue the strength into her staff and ride it into a quick and crushing blow, but she was battling it as much as she was controlling it. As if she were attempting to raise a tiger by the nape of its neck and hurl its snarling and lashing claws in Lin Chong's direction.

Lin Chong decided the demonstration had gone far enough. She leapt again, this time inward, toward Lu Da. One foot dancing against the groping power of the god's tooth before it vanished in retreat or snatched her down; then the other diving closer. Lin Chong twisted like a snake to avoid the flailing of Lu Da's heavy staff, her spine curving and arching around it. Just when she reached Lu Da's side—a little way past—she dropped.

The sole of her foot arrowed down in the flesh behind Lu Da's knee.

Lu Da squawked in surprise. Her knee came down hard on the stone, and she fell forward all at once, like a mountain that had been axed at its base. Her metal staff clanged against the flagstones.

Lin Chong landed lightly on her other foot. Around her, the power of the god's tooth petered out. Like the last flickers of a dying flame, its effects fluttered out of the world, sucked back to the artifact that had granted them entrance.

Lin Chong's students straightened cautiously, stunned and silent.

"Student Lu," Lin Chong said.

Lu Da groaned a bit and rolled over. "You have beaten me, Master Instructor!" she roared dramatically from the ground. "I, the fearsome Flower Monk! I am yours to destroy!"

She flung her arms out to either side.

Lin Chong tried not to show reactions in front of her students, but it was so very difficult sometimes.

"Rise, Student Lu," she said. "You are uninjured?"

She was almost certain so. She'd been very gentle.

"My pride, Master Instructor," Lu Da said grievously, trying to scramble up. "The pride of the Flower Monk. Crushed under your feet."

Lin Chong took her hands from behind her back and raised them in front of her. "I did not even use every weapon in my arsenal. You are many times stronger than I, and you wield a god's tooth. Why did you fail to best me? What have you learned?"

"That you are very fearsome, Master Instructor!"

Lin Chong permitted herself a small smile. "Other than that."

Lu Da's forehead knitted up. "You . . . you train without the support of a god's tooth, as the monks told me to. And that's your weapon. One that can whale the piss out of me."

"Eloquently put," Lin Chong said. "If I had consistently leaned on a god's tooth, I would have limited my skill either with or without it. God's teeth may be power, but they are an artificial power—one you must still put in the years of work and training to control. They are no true shortcut. They are not the same as scholar's skills grown from self-discipline and rigor. And just as your god's tooth would have stymied you in your path to enlightenment with the Fa, Student Lu, it will stymie your training in the martial arts outside the monastery. You must have the finest control over yourself before you wield a power beyond yourself."

Lu Da did not look entirely happy about that, her mouth turned down in an extravagant sulk. "And how long did it take you, Master Instructor?" she asked after a moment.

"More than four decades," Lin Chong answered. "I have practiced my training for many watches of every day since I was a small child."

"I'd rather drink wine," Lu Da said. She scooped up her staff and shook herself out. "Four decades, aiya! I haven't even lived *three* . . ."

Lin Chong turned slightly to face her class. "If you take one lesson from today," she said, "let it be this. If you continue to train, with hard work and no shortcuts—no matter what beginnings you enter from—the control you have over yourself will equip you, unmatched, in any situation you encounter. Dismissed."

Calls of "Yes, Master Instructor" and "Thank you, Master Instructor" floated up as the students bowed in her direction and began a disorganized exodus back toward the gates to the outer city. The murmurs swelled as they clustered together to gather their things, untucking gowns and robes and untying headwraps. Furtive, awed glances found Lin Chong where she still stood in the center of the courtyard.

"You kicked me into the ground today, Master Instructor," Lu Da said jovially. "I did not enjoy it! But I'll think about what you said. I still think I might like the shortcut."

She saluted with a bow and ambled away across the flagstones, rubbing her various bruises.

"A fascinating person, isn't she?" Lu Junyi had come up next to Lin Chong.

"Fascinating. Where did you meet her? Not at one of your salons, I would wager."

"She was shouting on the street. Challenging some ruffians who would have abused a beggar girl. I helped defuse the situation and then bought Lu Da a bowl of wine—several bowls, strictly speaking. I told her about your fight class, and she insisted on coming to meet you. I think she is quite taken with you."

"I don't have high hopes she will have the discipline of continued study," Lin Chong said, with a small sigh, "but if she does, she is welcome here."

"She may surprise you. It would be good for her . . . She got that brand on her face for killing a man. Though for a reason you might be able to find approval for."

"A civilian?" Lin Chong asked. As far as she was concerned, war was the only defensible context for killing another. "You may overestimate me. I could never excuse that."

"Even a butcher who extorted and forced one of his concubines, only to throw her out on the street and insist she owed a debt to *him*? I hear tell he was a butcher in more ways than one. Nobody would miss a man like that."

"Then the law should address it."

Lu Junyi huffed out a breath. "I always forget how much more conservative you are than I. We women will have to take our power someday." She reached up to unwrap her hair, untucking her robes and shaking them out. A brief drumbeat reverberated across the courtyard, from Bianliang's towers where men struck out the watches of the day. "Aiya! Class ran long; I'm late. I have a meeting with Marshal Gao Qiu this morning, about my printing press. May I use your barracks to straighten myself?"

Lin Chong laughed lightly. Only Lu Junyi would play so fast and loose with her presentation before a grand marshal. "Of course. Come."

"Good, and we can continue this conversation. I am not letting you out of the cause so easily."

Lin Chong grunted. She did not share Lu Junyi's passion for pushing the boundaries of society. Women in the Empire of Song today had more advantage than at any other time in history—Lin Chong herself was proof of that, advancing to a scholar-official position directly under Grand Marshal Gao Qiu. She had the respect of the people—of any gender—and even without the aid and status of a husband she had managed to arrange creditable stations and marriages for both her grown children, which she considered proof of her accomplishments.

Pushing harder would only lead to those opportunities being destroyed. Lin Chong could never countenance it.

Lu Junyi's idealized visions betrayed her far more elevated place in society. Lin Chong might have an examination title, but Lu Junyi had been born to wealth and clan advantage. Without the gradual allowance for those of the female sex to burst from some measure of their historical strictures, Lu Junyi may not have owned her newly modern printing press, but she would have remained a charming socialite. Likely still high status, holding her salons, wealth and family name insulating her into being forgiven for the eccentricities of progressivism.

She could not understand. Small bites must be taken carefully, lest the whole meal be snatched away.

Lin Chong had much more to lose.

"You are the type of story men nod at as a successful example of the woman's cause," Lu Junyi pointed out, as they gathered their things and crossed the courtyard together. "But I do not think we can stop in the place where we still garner praise. I would like to see us have a trifle less approbation from men and a trifle more fear."

"Violence is not the way." Lin Chong thought of Lu Da, and her mouth folded into a frown. Violence was never the way. Anyone skilled enough in the fighting arts to be a master arms instructor knew that to her bones.

"Oh, not violence," Lu Junyi said. "Not in the general sense. I only mean that as yet, our advancement has not come at the expense of men. But it shall. It must. There is not sufficient room for us otherwise. Our true success will mean some of them lose power . . . and that will not come without anger and fear."

"Then we should slow its progress. A tidal wave spread over many generations becomes a gentle flow, and either one gets to the end."

"A flow! You mean a trickle."

"Even a trickle can wash away a mountain eventually."

They continued the mostly friendly argument out of the courtyard and onto a stone-paved street toward Lin Chong's rooms, which were adjoined to the barracks of the Imperial Guard. Bianliang's inner city towered up around them, multistoried pagodas of brick and wood climbing up among the less-grand houses and offices. The inner city of the capital was the seat of government and Empire, and was several li across and as large as a small city itself—even as it lay nestled within the teeming population of the rest of Bianliang.

This was the inner city's southern district, where the bureaucrats and soldiers of the central government lived and worked. A few people passed on the street, but not nearly as many as the bustle visible every time they came into view of one of the swooping, crimson-painted gates that led to the outer city. In the outer city streets, people and carts and carriages packed against donkeys and goats and hogs being driven to market, all hurrying and running and shouting in a steady stream.

Lin Chong's rooms were airy and pleasant, if not expansive, with carved beams climbing the walls and windows whose shutters opened onto a garden. Lu Junyi took up a comb from the side table and settled on a stool, unwinding her hair to shake it out and begin brushing it smooth.

"Do you have any powder?" she asked. "I should not have come at all this morning, but I do hate to miss one of your classes. You should have a much higher position than master arms instructor."

"I am perfectly satisfied with—"

"Oh, come now, we are alone here! You know what Marshal Gao Qiu is. He is a wet stocking. A trick of braggery and playing football with the Emperor. He toys with the city as if it is his playset—"

"Quiet!" Lin Chong hissed, glancing around. But they were alone in the small rooms. Outside the open windows, trees rustled over an empty garden.

"Ah, you know what I would say anyway," Lu Junyi said, unperturbed. She began winding her hair up and fastening it with combs and clasps. "Gao Qiu is seeing me today about printing paper banknotes, if you would believe it. He read my circular on the subject. But do I expect him to understand or listen to my recommendations? No, I do not."

Paper money. Lin Chong knew Lu Junyi's arguments, but the idea did not sit well with her. Strings of coin and taels of gold and silver were heavy in your hand, worth something when weighed. What was paper worth? Burned in a fire, it would become nothing at all.

Lin Chong set her powder case down in front of her friend with a click against the polished table. "I will leave the intellectual arguments to you. I am content to remain in my post until I die. Marshal Gao has been nothing but fair."

"To you," Lu Junyi murmured, but she did Lin Chong the favor of not continuing, focused on fixing her face instead. Lin Chong knew what would have followed anyway: an accounting of all the plum positions Gao Qiu had granted to friends, all the political enemies he'd had jailed or sent to work camps, the favors he gobbled from the Emperor or the taxes he spent on lavishness for himself and his cronies.

Lin Chong could be aware of all this, and not condone it, while still seeing the wider context. Gao Qiu was her direct superior and had great political influence—and that would not be changed. His dealings with Lin Chong had been lazy but not malicious; he was worse than many men but also better than some. She could keep working for him, and would, and keep her opinions on his greater conduct to herself.

She kept her mouth tightly closed against the *other* whispers of Gao Qiu's conduct, the ones that might anger Lu Junyi to the point of torching the entire inner city.

Lu Junyi finished retying her blouse, smoothed her skirts, and layered her long silk scarf into place across her shoulders. For a woman who had just spent the first watch of the day sweating in a courtyard, she had somehow assumed a refinement to her countenance that other society women lacked even after meticulous plucking and painting.

Lin Chong was old enough now not to envy it, and her position afforded her the ability to stay in her staid and functional robes, with no facepaint and her hair pulled back in a simple queue. It was a perk of her title she would be forever grateful for.

"I think I shall be just on time," Lu Junyi said. "Now, will you point me toward White Tiger Hall? I am not familiar with that building."

"White Tiger Hall? Marshal Gao is meeting you at White Tiger Hall?"

"Yes. What's the matter?"

Lin Chong frowned, foreboding stealing over her. White Tiger Hall . . .

The inner city—the Imperial City—had three districts. Commoners could enter from the sprawling outer city only into the southern one, where they were now—the district that housed the grinding bureaucracy of the city government as well as the garrisons of the Imperial Guard. Gao Qiu's yamen, with his rooms and offices, was here as well, and Lin Chong had never been called any other place for a meeting with him. Beyond the southern district, the central district existed for the Emperor to descend and meet with officials of far higher rank than Lin Chong. She'd only entered its gates a handful of times.

The central district was exceeded only by the north, which housed the Imperial Palace itself.

White Tiger Hall was in the central district.

It was where councils of war were decided on. Not the milieu for a simple discussion of economic policy in which the marshal was no doubt humoring his supplicant.

Gao Qiu has been nothing but fair . . . to you, Lu Junyi had said.

Lin Chong thought again of those other rumors. The ones she had been scrupulous about ignoring, never repeating, burying down in her consciousness with only a thread of wariness to protect herself, a thread that had, in her case, never been needed.

But Lu Junyi was a beautiful woman. A beautiful, unmarried, wealthy woman. Not as young as others, but it could not have been told from her energetic, unlined face. Unlike Lin Chong.

White Tiger Hall. Despite her defense of the marshal, apprehension gripped Lin Chong.

She did not share Lu Junyi's passion for challenging the Empire or society. But protecting a friend . . .

That mattered to her very much indeed.

Lu Junyi caught her sleeve. "Sister Lin. What disturbs you?"

Lin Chong did not know how she could answer. All she knew was the way the uneasiness simmered in the pit of her stomach. "Would you mind if I accompanied you to this meeting?" she asked.

Lu Junyi's eyes narrowed shrewdly. Then she said, "I would be honored. Please, lead the way."

CHAPTER 2

Lin Chong led Lu Junyi deeper into the Imperial City, all the way northward until they climbed wide stone steps to another set of guarded, elaborately carved gates. Dragons and phoenixes were caught mid-furl among lofty clouds in the woodwork, overlooking any who would pass.

Lin Chong found herself thinking of the gods again, gone from this world so many centuries. Rumor held that dragons, too, had faded from the earth at about the same time. To the same place? For the same reason? Perhaps it was their power and not that of the gods that remained connected somehow, locked in the fragmented god's teeth.

Unlike the gates to the outer city, which remained fully open as a matter of course, these gates were shut fast, with guards standing at attention on both sides. But many in the Imperial Guard knew Lin Chong by sight.

"Nuo!" cried the guards on either side, clasping their hands in salute.

"We enter by order of Marshal Gao Qiu," Lin Chong announced, and the guards saluted again and unbarred the heavy crimson gates to haul them open for the two women.

If the southern district had been sparse, the central district was a city of ghosts. Aside from the odd guard or servant crossing at a distance, nobody passed on the streets or between buildings. The architecture here was more colorful, more elaborate, more storied. Swooping, brightly tiled roofs pierced the sky. Columns and brackets blossomed into their eaves with intricate carvings.

Lu Junyi looked around curiously.

"Been here before?" Lin Chong asked.

"Never." Lu Junyi's voice had a hush to it, as if they were in a temple.

Lin Chong led the way up the empty boulevards, toward the massive central structure that was White Tiger Hall.

Why had Gao Qiu called her friend here?

Perhaps it was nothing more than convenience. Still, her stomach remained unsettled, a quivering in her gut.

She reminded herself, again, that she'd not personally witnessed Gao Qiu's rumored conduct with women. Not strictly speaking. Perhaps, once or twice, a girl fleeing in tears with disarrayed clothes; conclusions could be drawn, if one chose to draw them. Or a whisper from the odd visitor, to have a care, veiled words and knowing looks. Or sometimes a sense of how Gao Qiu acted in person—nothing to pin down, but a way he balanced his lean body, looming over people, asserting *ownership* over young women in his vicinity in a manner that always crawled under Lin Chong's skin.

Never enough for her to speak, of course. Never enough to say that he was wrong, that she was challenging him, even if it would have been possible for her to do so. He was her superior; he was a Grand Marshal and personal friend to the Emperor; attentions from someone like him might be considered as much flattery as threat.

And were, often.

The young women would have to learn to look after themselves, Lin Chong always thought. As she had, when she was young enough to attract such notice.

The steps of White Tiger Hall were as long and polished as the elegant grandeur of the building. As at the district gates, guards stood at either side of the entrance, spears upright in hand, the small rectangular scales of their layered armor gleaming dark in the sun. Their postures had an exacting straightness that Lin Chong noted with approval. She stopped halfway up the steps to untie her sword.

"Do you carry any weapons?" she asked Lu Junyi.

"No. Why?"

"None are allowed in White Tiger Hall, on pain of death. It is considered a potential assassination attempt against the Emperor."

Lu Junyi stared, her jaw gone a little slack. "I shudder to think if I did not have you accompanying me."

"The guards would have asked, if you did not know to disarm yourself," Lin Chong assured her. That was not what worried her.

She surrendered her sword to one of the guards—a man who had trained with her, as all the newer guards had. He and the others saluted her, and Lin Chong and Lu Junyi passed into the hall.

The inside of the hall spread wide and deep and luxurious, high-ceilinged and ornate. Carved wooden screens gave way to gilded and painted rails around the perimeter, and the most detailed of woodwork made monkeys and cranes, phoenixes and dragons, tortoises and qilin, all dancing in studied elegance up the walls and beams.

A long wooden table stretched the length of the hall, one Lin Chong could only imagine regularly seated the most powerful men in the Empire, with the Emperor at their head.

Right now, instead, at the head of the long table slouched Gao Qiu. Eating.

He lounged alone, his robes open down the front and fallen off his shoulders to pool at his elbows, baring his sinewy chest. Gao Qiu was a thin man, an athlete and footballer, with a thin mustache and beard in a thin beaky face that somehow matched his physique. In front of him, spread on silver platters of varying size, was a spread that would have sated five men: savory, delicately sliced duck, crab-stuffed oranges, bird's nest soup, scallops swimming in sauce, braised mutton and pork belly, a whole chicken on a bed of lotus leaves . . . aromatic plates of steamed vegetables, bowls of dried fruits, and raw fish in such fine thin sheets it was almost transparent. Gao Qiu picked among them with a set of silver chopsticks joined at the top with a fine silver chain.

The scene was so disconcerting Lin Chong wondered if she had invented it. Or had she invented her reverence for this hall, for the central district itself? If a man was best friends with the Emperor, did he simply avail himself of the right to feast wherever he pleased, because to him these things were nothing?

Lin Chong could not grasp having such a position. Such a view on the world.

Lu Junyi stepped just past the foot of the table and bowed. "Honorable Grand Marshal. I hope you do not mind that I have brought my friend, Honorable Master Arms Instructor Lin Chong. She has been invaluable in discussing these calculations with me, and I would lean on her counsel for our discussion."

If Gao Qiu was bothered by the request he gave no sign. "Of course, of course," he said, waving them in, and then called for a servant. "Boy! Table settings for our guests!"

The two women crossed the hall carefully. Lu Junyi led the way to place herself with cautious respect at Gao Qiu's right hand, at the long, empty wooden table. Lin Chong settled next to her.

"Will you have some wine?" asked Gao Qiu, sucking scallops off his chopsticks. "The finest yellow rice wine, aged to perfection—I'll wager you have never tasted its like."

Lu Junyi and Lin Chong both tried to demur. "I do not have the constitution—" started Lu Junyi, at the same time Lin Chong attempted to say, "You do me too great a compliment—"

Gao Qiu swatted down their protestations with a hand. "Boy! Two cups of wine for the women. Wine will be necessary. You're here to discuss such a boring lot."

"Marshal Gao," Lu Junyi began. "The availability of the modern printing press gives us such a fine opportunity. I believe it could be a great boon to the Empire if licensed presses could begin issuing official paper banknotes, guaranteed by the Imperial Throne. Merchants would thrive if not weighed down by coin or metals, and large purchases could happen with the most frictionless ease. If we printed an expiration date of three years, the economic—"

"Not yet, not yet," Gao Qiu cut her off. "Not until we've dined and supped. Here, partake of this duck, it is the tenderest in the region!" He stabbed at the dish with his chopsticks. Servants were placing matching silver plates and cups before Lin Chong and Lu Junyi, along with wine and fragrant white rice.

"You are most kind," Lu Junyi murmured. "I fear we intrude upon your hospitality too much."

"Nonsense," Gao Qiu said. "Now eat, and drink, and let us talk of something less stultifying than *money.* How gauche and tired a topic."

Lin Chong could not help running her eyes across the silver tableware and rich, exquisitely prepared food. When Lin Chong had been a very small child, her family had been lucky to have meat some days, instead of only rice and cabbage—or occasionally nothing but the last handful of grains boiled thin in water. It was a long ago memory, but the hungry ache of it was real.

Only those who had money could dismiss its concerns as *gauche.*

Lu Junyi made polite conversation with the marshal while Lin Chong nibbled at some slices of the duck. Its promised tenderness melted on her tongue, but she could not taste it. She did not share in the wine—except when Gao Qiu urged it and would accept no other answer; then Lin Chong only touched her lips to the liquid, nothing more.

"We ladies have such weaker constitutions," Lu Junyi put him off, laughing, when Gao Qiu tried to protest their temperance. "I am confident you could drink barrels full, Marshal Gao! But you must forgive our more fragile state, especially so early in the day."

Lu Junyi might desire a greater social latitude for women, but she was not afraid to use her femininity to advantage, Lin Chong noted.

"My master arms instructor has no weak constitution, eh?" Gao Qiu slapped a hand upon his thigh. "Master Instructor Lin! You have the constitution of a man, surely."

"Forgive me, Marshal. I must retain my wits for my duties today," Lin Chong said.

"So serious, this one," Gao Qiu said to Lu Junyi, conspiratorially. "She puts my other officers to shame. Never any fun. Never a bit naughty."

Lin Chong knew too well what would happen if she ever zigzagged off an arrow-straight path. She had no margin for raucous missteps, not the way her male colleagues did.

Lin Chong did not resent the fact. But it was still a fact.

"I strive to serve you well," Lin Chong said to Gao Qiu. "And to serve His Imperial Majesty the Emperor."

Gao Qiu guffawed at her solemn answer, but allowed the conversation to turn.

Lu Junyi managed to engage him in small talk until he permitted, with great, put-upon groaning, for a modest discussion of economics. By that time, Lin Chong's hips were beginning to ache from sitting for so long. How long would this stifling meeting go on? Her usual duties were far more active. Most days, at this time she'd be wrapping up her own private exercise time and returning to her quarters to prepare for leading the morning drills.

She had been too hasty in her apprehension about this meeting. Clearly Gao Qiu only wanted to bask in his status; that was why he had called for the appointment in this room. Lin Chong began to feel exceedingly foolish.

Next time she would not let such flights of fancy take hold.

Gao Qiu finished hearing Lu Junyi's proposal—at least, as much as he was willing to hear. Though Lu Junyi gave little sign of it, Lin Chong had known her old friend for enough years to note the slight stiffness of annoyance as Gao Qiu effusively dismissed her.

"I thank you for this audience, Marshal," Lu Junyi said. She stood and bowed very properly. "I await your wise decision on the matter."

"I'll take it to my advisors," Gao Qiu said, with a casualness that suggested anything but. "And to the Emperor, it will ultimately be his decision. I daresay he would feel more positively toward such a daring proposal if he heard it from so graceful a woman!"

He laughed. Lu Junyi and Lin Chong smiled politely.

"I would be glad to come repeat it for His Imperial Majesty," Lu Junyi said.

Gao Qiu laughed harder, as if she had told a joke. "That would be something to see! Now go, go. I can't say this was interesting, but you have an engaging manner, at least. Wait, Master Arms Instructor—I would speak with you a moment longer."

Lin Chong had risen to leave with Lu Junyi. At Gao Qiu's words, she paused and nodded to her friend. "I shall see you later, Lady Lu."

"Good day, Master Instructor Lin," Lu Junyi replied, equally formally, and retreated out of the hall.

"Sit with me," Gao Qiu said, patting the space Lu Junyi had left. "I desire a report on the state of my men. How do they fare?"

Considering that Lin Chong reported this to Gao Qiu weekly in the more mundane setting of his yamen, this extra request was puzzling. Sensing Gao Qiu did not wish her usual level of detail, Lin Chong answered in summary. "I have no complaints about the improvement of their technique, but I continue to be concerned with their discipline. Their carelessness with the military hierarchy troubles me."

"Yes, yes, so you've told me," Gao Qiu said. "Better for them to be a bit undisciplined, no? Then they can't rebel against the state!"

He laughed like it was another joke, but Lin Chong wondered if it was. She'd grown frustrated to the point of stating her concerns baldly, and still neither Gao Qiu nor the Emperor would take such matters seriously. Lin Chong could not be the only person who had heard the whispers of border skirmishes to the north—an undisciplined army would break against determined invaders like a wave upon stone.

If the Emperor thought he could prevent a coup against his throne by weakening his own men, Lin Chong feared the whole Empire would pay a price for it in blood.

Lin Chong herself was not technically a soldier—arms instructors were purely civilian positions, scholar-officials with a specialized skill set, bureaucrats who happened to handle weapons. But even in this time of relative peace she'd been adjunct to a number of minor conflicts as part of her duties, and the battlefield rarely respected a lack of official military designation once weapons had begun to fly. Even beyond her experience, she had taught, broken bread with, or drunk wine and spirits with enough officers over the years to fear her own knowledge of army readiness might exceed the marshal's.

Or at least, exceed *this* marshal's. Gao Qiu's high military rank notwithstanding, Lin Chong had private doubts about how many times he'd ridden with his troops.

Such a thing was never to be voiced, of course. Nor was it for her to make any broader change regarding the Guard's discipline. She could only enforce it within her own drills, as she trained the men in sword and truncheon, battle axe and spear, lance and crossbow and rake and every other weapon they might be called upon to handle.

Gao Qiu held a chicken leg with two fingers, slurping the soft flesh off the bone. "The men say you are a most extraordinary instructor, you know."

Lin Chong blinked. Her ruminations on tactics and military preparation fled.

She did not know how to respond. It was a shocking thing for Gao Qiu to have been told by any in the Guard, and even more shocking for him to relay it to her. The men respected her, she knew—she had no doubt of that. She ensured it. But no praise had ever been rained upon her for correctly doing her job, nor should it have been. Her reward for excellent conduct was that she was granted the chance to *continue* doing her job.

Gao Qiu's praise made every small hair on her neck and back prickle.

He was singling her out. Lin Chong strove with every moment of every day to avoid being singled out.

"The men speak too plainly," she settled on after a beat. "I serve at the pleasure of His Imperial Majesty the Emperor."

"Don't we all."

Gao Qiu's words were slurred slightly, sotted with wine. He tossed the chicken bone to his plate and leaned forward, letting his hand fall across Lin Chong's wrist.

Lin Chong froze.

In the first instant she wanted to believe it was an accident. Or that she imagined it. The contact jolted her with its wrongness, the violation of every social boundary.

Her mind kicked—*it's only a drunken mistake, he means nothing by it, nothing*—even as every instinct inside her screamed.

Even as she knew.

The thought welled up: *But I am too old—I was past this—*

How could she respond without causing any slight? Without embarrassing the marshal, or provoking his ire?

None of the occasional complicated navigations of her youth had entailed rejecting a Grand Marshal and bosom friend of the Emperor . . .

The unreality of the central district, of White Tiger Hall, rang eerily through her, so far from anything known or familiar.

Carefully, she went to move her hand away, as if to reach for her wine. Casually. As if no other hand pressed hers and made her throat close like she wanted to be ill. Marshal Gao would let it drop. She would give him the space for a dignified fiction, a polite deniability; this never happened.

Instead, the moment she moved, his hand lashed over like the strike of a viper. His fingers tightened around her wrist, the force so savage it was as if his bones clamped against hers.

Lin Chong could have broken away, but at the same time she could not move.

"Why so hasty, my master arms instructor?" Gao Qiu asked.

"Your pardon, Marshal." Lin Chong's voice did not feel like her own, tinny and strange. "Please excuse me. I must go to lead the morning's drills."

"They can wait. Come, sit closer to me."

Lin Chong did not obey. Her limbs were leaden.

She could not understand what was happening, or why, why *now*. Had she foiled some base intentions against Lu Junyi only to bring them upon herself? Had this been in Gao Qiu's mind all along? But he would not have expected her here today, how could he have expected her . . . *why were they in White Tiger Hall . . .*

The question kept circling, echoing in her ears, as if it were of any importance at all.

Gao Qiu tightened his grip, forcing Lin Chong toward him. She resisted without moving, her arm a tug-of-war between them for a long and terrible moment of space. She didn't know what else to do.

"Come *here*," Gao Qiu barked, and reached his other hand as if to yank at the front of her coat.

Lin Chong's reflexes reacted for her before she could decide. She wrenched away, breaking his hold against her wrist, and scrambled up from her seat.

"How dare you." Gao Qiu lurched to his feet, his skin reddening across his chest and face. "You are in my employ! You will do as I say."

"Marshal, I beg you—" Lin Chong was backing up. The trap was on all sides. She could not run. She could not fight him. Her shoulders hit the lacquered wall. "You do me too great an honor. I am old and tough. You deserve a woman younger, more beautiful—"

"I deserve whatever I want." He heaved into her space, hands against the wood on either side of her, his breath hot on her skin and stinking of wine. "You work for me."

Lin Chong flashed back almost brutally to merely earlier that morning, when she had told her students: *The control you have over yourself will equip you, unmatched, in any situation you encounter.* The lie twisted hard in her chest, like the blade of a knife.

If she fought Gao Qiu, she would win. The imaginary future splayed before her. She would win. She could bloody him here, in White Tiger Hall—if she wished, she could kill him. She would win while burning her position, her own life, her future; flames that consumed every path or chance or ending for her . . . The consequences would spiral, each collapsing into the next until they poured into an avalanche. Not only her place torn away from her, but then the Emperor, His Imperial Majesty, the Lord of Heaven, the embodiment of the Empire, who was boyhood friends with Gao Qiu—

The imagined future in Lin Chong's mind swirled into a maelstrom, choking her. It could not be thought of.

Gao Qiu fisted a clumsy hand against the front of her coat. The hand crawled over, groping to shove against the bottom of her breast through the layers of cloth.

She felt dizzy.

Her inhales moved her chest against his grip, and sick crawled up her throat. She tried to stop breathing, stuttering to shallowness, to the stillness of a corpse.

"Better," Gao Qiu huffed against her face. "You'll see. I can be a benevolent man."

Lin Chong's mind had vibrated apart from her body. She could withstand this. She had withstood worse. It would not last very long. Less than one watch of the morning, surely. Half that, or a quarter. That was no time at all. No time at all.

And then she would be free to leave. She told herself she was transported to that time already, only moments hence. Walking freely from the hall, returning to the southern district and resuming her duties, unencumbered on the streets. Away from here.

It would not be long at all.

Gao Qiu's hand squeezed rough against her, disarraying her coat and bruising her flesh beneath. The pain was there, but small. She could bear pain.

His breath snarled warm and lustful against her ear, and he took her by the shoulder to shove and turn her, the wall crushing against her chest. The scents of cedar and dried lacquer filled her nostrils. Gao Qiu pawed inexpertly at the back of her coat, her robes, shoving the cloth up and aside.

It would be over quickly. She could withstand . . . not long at all . . .

His hand came up and grabbed her wrist from behind, slamming it to the wood, pinning her arm.

Thought and feeling surged back into Lin Chong's body like two ships colliding at full sail. Instinct rebelled and reacted before her sense could override it.

She twisted, sharp and hard, breaking his hold while her arm followed to sweep his grasping hands aside. He squawked angrily and lunged to pin her body. Her foot came out, upsetting his balance, his face falling straight into the hard strike of her palm.

Gao Qiu staggered back, his hands coming up and muffling him as he yelled, "*Whore!*"

It was only then that Lin Chong's mind caught up with what she had done.

The hall closed in on her, suffocating. This was worse—so much worse—she should have—she should have shut her eyes, she should have let him, the discomfort would have lasted only moments, *what had she been thinking*?

Warring impulses battled within her, paralyzing her. Should she run? To *where?* Could she salvage this? Soothe his ego? Perhaps once he was sober—

"Strumpet! Whore! You belong to the Emperor. You belong to *me!*" Crimson had begun to dribble below Gao Qiu's nose, pooling against his upper lip. He railed through it, bloody spittle flecking across the space between them to pebble against Lin Chong's face. "I gave you this position. I gave it to you! People warned me about you, they said it was only trouble, hiring a woman, but I *made* you!"

His history was so wrong she could not even have found the words to argue it—she had been working up as an arms instructor before he was ever a Grand Marshal; he had never taken more than cursory notice of her career or her as a human being under his command—he took her reports and stared past her, through her, until today, until today . . .

"I made you, and I can unmake you. *Guards!*" Gao Qiu roared.

It was the last moment Lin Chong could have fled. Even in that moment, she did not believe, could not believe; she had envisioned the reality but could somehow not conceive that it would come to pass.

Two of the guards sprinted in from the entrance, the dark layered plates of their armor rattling, their spears lowered and searching for the danger. Imperial Guards responding to a threat were the one, the only exception to the ancient prohibition against weaponry here, a permissible violation of the deep taboos when some terrible boundary had already been crossed.

The guards stopped a short distance from Lin Chong and Gao Qiu, looking between their two superiors in confusion.

"Where is the master arms instructor's sword?" Gao Qiu barked at them.

"I have it, Marshal," one of the guards answered, gesturing to his side, where Lin Chong's sword hung next to his own.

"Give it to her!" ordered Gao Qiu.

The guard hesitated, mired in confusion, and Lin Chong had the howling, incongruous thought that the lack of instant discipline she had so complained of was giving her one moment more of reprieve.

"This is White Tiger Hall," the guard said doubtfully, with a timid look to Lin Chong.

She knew him. A man called Shu. Decent in drills, good-natured, though little intelligence that he did not borrow from others.

"I said *give it to her!*" Gao Qiu screamed.

The guard could not disobey the Grand Marshal. He hastily twisted to remove the sword and stepped forward to offer it to Lin Chong.

She did not reach to take it. Of course she didn't. She was still a master arms instructor of the Imperial Guard, and she knew the laws here—especially the marrow-deep ones, the ones etched into the bones of anyone who lived and worked in these districts of the Imperial City. This was White Tiger Hall, and Gao Qiu expected her to . . . to do what? Become traitor? Turn into a criminal on his behalf, so he could feel justified in whatever he did next?

She would not do it. He had every advantage, but she would not give him the excuse.

Gao Qiu lumbered forward, took Lin Chong's scabbarded two-edged sword, and flung it at her chest. Lin Chong jerked back, forcing herself to raise her hands and avoid catching it. The sword clattered to the floor against her feet.

Lin Chong winced with the incongruous reflex of someone who did not treat her weapons that way.

"You see Master Arms Instructor Lin Chong," Gao Qiu proclaimed to the guards. "She possesses a weapon in White Tiger Hall—you see it with your own eyes. I order her arrested for attempted assassination against the Emperor!"

Lin Chong's only thought, dulled as if it occurred to her from a great distance away, was that she should have known. She should have seen ahead.

It did not matter whether she had caught the sword or not. It did not matter that she provided no excuse. It did not matter that everything she had done, her whole life, was intended to live within the strictness and narrowness of the most upright member of society, to serve the Empire without straying.

Numbness overtook her. The guards hesitated again—especially approaching their master arms instructor, especially after the farce they had witnessed and everything they knew to be true. But they could not disobey the Grand Marshal.

Lin Chong would not have expected them to.

Hands clasped over her arms, dragging her wrists behind her, and the guards marched her out of White Tiger Hall. The last she saw of Gao Qiu, he lounged against the polished table, blood dribbling down onto his bare chest, his gaze pinned on her with all the knowledge that he had won.

CHAPTER 3

Lu Junyi pushed through the crowds at the Bianliang prefectural yamen. Unlike those that did the work of the central government of Empire in the inner Imperial City, this yamen was in the far larger, more crowded outer city streets of Bianliang, overseen by the prefect of the entire region. Lu Junyi had to sheathe her impatience to keep from plowing people aside.

Some of Lin Chong's techniques would have served her very well in doing so.

Lin Chong, in jail! Arrested! What lies, what shattering injustices. Lin Chong barely drank or swore, would not say a bad word of criticism against government officials even when deserved—and they said *she* was a traitor. Lu Junyi tasted sourness in her mouth and concentrated on not driving elbows into the jabbering, plodding bodies in her path. Why did they refuse to move fast enough!

Lin Chong wasn't even the first friend Lu Junyi had come to a yamen or court for, armed with gold and silver, throwing her own slight weight against a justice system of back-scratching magistrates and rusted, failing processes. So many, too many people, acquaintances or friends or friends of acquaintances who came begging to Lu Junyi behind closed doors because there was nobody else, nobody to care. She'd beseeched, bribed, filled palms with silver and promises for more, weathered Jia's disapproval and gotten partial amnesties granted and exiles reduced to soft penal assignments as far as she was able. Among all Lu Junyi's other friends, many of whom she'd worried for late into the night, she had never thought she would have to fear for *Lin Chong*.

It was too much. She felt like her skin would split with it, the injustice of it, the knowledge that Lin Chong could have followed all the rules, every rule, and still die for it, and Lu Junyi might be powerless to stop it.

She'd never tried to fight the pull of an Imperial Grand Marshal. She wasn't even sure it was possible.

But she'd be damned if she wasn't willing to give every last piece of herself in trying.

She managed to shove her way through the public front area of the yamen in a less than genteel way, though she did refrain from causing any bruises. Once past, she wound through a back hallway, took a breath, and rapped on a paneled wooden door.

She tapped her fingers against each other, waiting, the nervous energy bleeding everywhere, demanding urgency. The prefecture liked quick executions of traitors and assassins, especially when urged on by a Grand Marshal . . .

Traitor and assassin. How could anyone even think of those words and Lin Chong's name in the same breath?

The door pulled open, revealing a man with a gentle, lined face. An ink stain smudged his cheek, and his thinning hair stuck up in places in an absently lopsided manner.

"Lady Lu Junyi!" he proclaimed with a smile that crinkled up to his eyes. "Come in, come in. To what do I owe the pleasure?"

"Secretary Sun Ding," Lu Junyi greeted him in return. "I have urgent need of your aid." She swept into the office—as with every other time she had been here, not a surface was without stacks of paper, loose sheets of densely inked characters along with some pasted and wrapped folios balancing among the chaos. Today, however, she had no eyes for any of it.

Sun Ding's position as a secretary to the prefect wasn't why she'd pursued his friendship, after he'd started dropping in at some of her intellectual salons. Her salons attracted all sorts, from eager-eyed students to even occasionally celebrities . . . the polymath Ling Zhen, for instance, or the poet Song Jiang, who had both been intermittent guests until recently. On one memorable occasion General Han Shizhong had come—those present had been awed to watch him speak animatedly to Ling Zhen on inventions of war and to Song Jiang on poetic literature, as if Lu Junyi's salon brushed a domain of the gods. Of course, that was before Ling Zhen had been arrested, and before Song Jiang had so famously and mysteriously disappeared from society . . . likely also thrown into a dark hole of a prison someplace, Lu Junyi thought bitterly. Though she hadn't become close with everyone who came by, she did have a genuine passion for building relationships of intellect regardless of status, and Sun Ding's friendship had not been attached to some ulterior motive.

But she'd be lying if she said she hadn't known his position might serve necessary to her someday.

She'd never thought she would call on him so soon, in a matter of such desperation. Life and death of one of her closest friends. A sisterhood of decades.

She wasn't even sure how much influence he had. Her other successful interventions had been with district magistrates—if those were puddles, the prefectural court was an ocean. Deep with politics, ready to swallow human lives without a ripple.

"What can I do for you?" Sun Ding asked, returning to sit behind his desk and motioning Lu Junyi to take the stool across from him.

She paused a moment to gather her thoughts. "Are you familiar with the case of Master Arms Instructor Lin Chong? It went before the prefect yesterday."

Her mind still buzzed with the urgency of getting here in time. She herself had not heard until this morning, when she had arrived for Lin Chong's daily fight class to find students wandering in disarray. When Lin Chong had made no appearance, Lu Junyi's aggressive questioning—with some eager volunteer help from the intimidating Lu Da—had eventually yielded answers.

Lu Junyi had not been allowed in to see Lin Chong, even with liberally applied silver. But she'd armed herself with the particulars of the case. The prefect had heard Lin Chong's statement and, in an unusual move, not yet decided on a judgment. Lu Junyi had met the prefect before, but only once and in passing—she'd known her first, best, and maybe only option would be Sun Ding.

If he would help. If he *could* help. He would at least hear her out; he had an open mind, he had to hear her out . . .

More importantly, he was an honest man. A good man. She had to believe that.

"I did hear of the case," he said now, his expression going troubled. "The prefect is gray with making a decision on it. Marshal Gao Qiu has stated plainly that he wishes a quick execution."

Even though she'd known, Lu Junyi's stomach folded over at such a bald confirmation. "Lin Chong is innocent. You must see that. Gao Qiu set her up. Attempted assassination? I know her—it's not possible. I spoke to people in the Imperial City—they say the guards only arrested her at the orders of Gao Qiu, not because she attempted any treachery. Gao Qiu, you know what he is!"

Sun Ding sighed, his face betraying pained agreement. She hadn't spoken too intemperately, then, thank the heavens.

She pushed on. "If the prefect interviews the guards, Lin Chong's innocence will become clear—"

Sun Ding held up a hand. "That's not the problem, Sister Lu. Prefect Teng has delayed because the case is already very weak. Gao Qiu changed his story with every report—first it was an assassination attempt against the Emperor, then against himself; the guards rescued him in one version but then in another he arrested Lin Chong on his own . . . it's clear to the prefect where the truth lies. Unfortunately, as you know, truth is not the only consideration that carries the day."

"You mean Gao Qiu's demands of a guilty verdict." Lu Junyi swallowed. "And his demand for her death."

"I'm afraid so."

"Brother Sun, please. You know this is wrong. Take me to the prefect. Help me argue the case. Lin Chong is one of my dearest friends—we have known each other since we were barely more than children. She's the most upright of citizens. You would not find a more moral, upstanding servant of the Empire in all of Bianliang. Please."

Sun Ding's face drew into a frown, but, finally, he nodded. "I had a great deal of discomfort with this case as it was. Now hearing she is *your* friend . . . we will do our utmost. I can't promise, but—come with me. The prefect should be retired in his chambers for a midday rest; it's a good time."

Sun Ding ushered Lu Junyi with him out of his office and led the way through a warren of corridors among the rear buildings of the yamen. The prefect's private retirement chambers were out and across a courtyard, separated from the bustle of the offices.

Prefect Teng was a stout man with a round face, and he welcomed them in when they begged his pardon for intruding.

"I always have time for Secretary Sun Ding," he said jovially. "And Lady Lu, I believe we've met before. Such a privilege to see you again."

Lu Junyi forced herself to nod and murmur the pleasantries back in restrained politeness.

"You may revise your opinion of us in a moment, Prefect," Sun Ding said. "We come to plead with you on the case of Master Arms Instructor Lin Chong."

"Ah!" Prefect Teng lowered himself heavily to a couch, gesturing for them to seat themselves and join him. "In fact, if you give me an answer on it I shall be much in your debt. I see no solution but to follow the directives of Marshal Gao Qiu, but I would like a better way out. It is not seemly, executing a woman."

Lu Junyi bridled at such a thing being his main objection, but with some effort kept her calm in hand. "Prefect, I have known Lin Chong for a great many years. Her character is unimpeachable. This case is a fabrication to injure her—I beg you to show mercy."

"She's accused of a great offense," Prefect Teng answered, even as he nodded. "Marshal Gao Qiu has demanded I wring from her why she entered White Tiger Hall with a sword in hand, if not to assassinate him, and what treachery she harbors against the Empire. Either of these are capital crimes."

"That's what he claims?" Lu Junyi could not quite keep her voice from climbing. "Prefect Teng, I was with Lin Chong directly before this incident. She instructed me very clearly not to enter White Tiger Hall with any weapon, and she left her sword with the guards outside. I will swear to it!"

"Prefect, let us speak plainly," Sun Ding said, quiet and urgent. "You and I know, we all know how Marshal Gao Qiu uses his power and influence. He has sent more than one rival to this court for judgment—not only rivals, but anyone who displeases him. He uses us to dispose of his political enemies for him, and we have turned our eyes from it . . . he would send a child to prison for pestering him, and demand them locked away or beheaded. Is this yamen to be the private tool of Marshal Gao's petty grievances?"

"Of course not," the prefect said. He seemed taken aback, but not angry. "Marshal Gao Qiu has no authority over us, Secretary Sun! You know that. Our mandate is from the Imperial Court."

"Then let us prove we are not his possession. If you order Lin Chong's execution, we will have sealed our own servility to him."

Gratitude welled up in Lu Junyi at his words, along with an exhausting, fearful hope. She had known Sun Ding was a good man—she believed she had known—but to see him so sincere, so blunt, saying things she would have spoken in private but never aired here . . . she had been right that he was the ally she'd needed. She never could have declared such a speech without consequence, especially not to a prefect. But Sun Ding was known to him; Sun Ding was trusted; Sun Ding could, apparently, gently challenge the very legitimacy of the yamen and its judicial oversight without provoking the prefect's wrath or endangering their cause.

Prefect Teng kneaded his hands together. "You speak uncomfortable truths, Secretary Sun. I want to agree. But the fact remains . . . we cannot simply ignore the demands of a man like Gao Qiu. So tell me, how can we settle this matter? Give me a solution,

I beg you. I will take any excuse not to execute a woman, particularly one of such good character and innocence, as you have sworn to—frankly, even before that, I believed her statements were the truth of it."

Sun Ding and Lu Junyi exchanged a glance. "Perhaps some intermediate punishment," Sun Ding suggested. "A guilty verdict, but a softened sentence. Allow Lin Chong to plead to a lesser crime and live, and show Gao Qiu we do not bow to him, while also not flouting him entirely. He knows his case is lacking. He will have to accept your authority, as long as you do not challenge him outright."

A guilty verdict was still a grave injustice. But Lu Junyi had moved about the edges of politics enough to know when her position was weak . . . and right now, every other consideration must pale against preserving Lin Chong's life.

"I think such a thing could be arranged," Prefect Teng said thoughtfully. "If, for example, Lin Chong admits to having entered White Tiger Hall with a weapon unintentionally, owing to ignorance of the law . . . there would have to be lashes, and a branding, but then—a far-off work camp, perhaps, far from the sight of Gao Qiu. Satisfactory to everybody."

It was not satisfactory to Lu Junyi. Not at all. But she clamped her lips against each other. This was already more than she'd dared hope for.

"Yes, it will take some doing, but I think this can be managed," the prefect continued, nodding to himself. He turned to Lu Junyi. "There will be expenses to such an arrangement, levied against your friend. Can her family pay them?"

"I will pay." She would have to give Lin Chong several ingots of silver directly, too, for bribing the guards at the work camp. Otherwise she might not even survive this lesser sentence.

As for Lin Chong's family . . . her only family was her two children. Lu Junyi wondered if her friend would want them to know, or if the disgrace would be something she preferred to keep locked away.

Lu Junyi would ask her, once they were permitted to speak. A courier could be sent if so.

If one of Lu Junyi's loved ones were convicted of a false crime and imprisoned, she would have wanted to be told everything. But Lin Chong was not like her, and neither were her children—raised with a strictness that Lin Chong had always seemed convinced would defy their lack of a father, the siblings were dutiful and hardworking, but each lived far away now. Lu Junyi did not think either had ever returned to Bianliang to visit. In her observation, Lin Chong had always seemed to love them, but rarely smiled on them.

Lin Chong had always been too concerned about the future to take enjoyment in the present.

And this was where it had brought her.

Lin Chong hunched against the cell wall, trying to take any pressure from the wounds on her back and face, and attempting with every fragment of training she possessed to force her mind to blankness.

She could not manage it. Bitterness welled up in her, like bile concentrating itself in her skin and flesh.

She had done nothing. Nothing. Gao Qiu had . . .

He was power. She was nothing more than a mouse, one to be batted about and then discarded.

She had not truly understood that before now. More fool her.

She'd thought she would be beheaded on the spot, the same day. The jolt of living longer had been only one more burst in the chaos, part of a reality she no longer comprehended. A reality that had turned against her with no warning or remedy.

The prefect's offer of clemency would have been a shock, if she could still feel shock. She'd almost rejected it, the wild urge filling her to proclaim loudly that she was *innocent,* that she would not admit to doing something she had not, even if it was a lesser crime. Even if it would stop her from being executed.

She was guilty of one crime, though, one she did not, *would* not regret. Gao Qiu could have pressed for a charge against her for her assault of him. She did not know why he hadn't. Embarrassment, that his desired conquest had bloodied him? Perhaps he only thought an assassination attempt more dramatic, and far more likely of gaining him the result he wanted.

Her death.

It was the thought of that—Gao Qiu's manipulation, his screaming power, his designs on her fate—that convinced Lin Chong to give in and say the words. She would not grant Gao Qiu the satisfaction of her dying. Even if she had no life left. Even if it meant she had to make a false admission, to lie, to act as if she possessed a level of criminal stupidity that had allowed her to accidentally walk into White Tiger Hall armed when she had perfect knowledge of the law.

The confession tasted of ash and sand, but she forced her mouth around the words.

After that had come the lashes, twenty strikes with bamboo that set her back aflame. Blood still trickled down her legs now, half a day later—under her clothes, collecting against the creases at the backs of her knees. Every twitch seemed to wrench the wounds open in the wrong way. The lashes had been followed by her branding: a fast and rough tattoo down her cheek by a rushed, impersonal inker, who'd slashed the characters into her flesh and then sent her back to her cell. It still burned.

She would be forever known as a criminal now. Marked for life.

They'd fastened the cangue around her neck before locking her back in the cell. The wide square of wood and metal yoked her and weighed her weakened body down, multiplying the ache in her shredded back and shoulders. It made relief impossible in any position. As was no doubt its purpose.

None of that was the core of the blackness inside Lin Chong's souls, however. Pain she could endure. Pain was nothing.

Pain, you should have endured. A quarter of a watch, and it would have been done . . .

But somehow, the echoing voice of rationality had ceased its power over her. No. No, she should not have endured. She should not have been *forced* to. Gao Qiu was the villain here—the only one. She would not blame herself alongside him.

She would grant herself that.

Besides, the pain was nothing, not next to her slithering *anger*. It had reached so deep inside, fetched into corners of her she had not known existed. It dazed her. Never had she known herself capable of such unsteady emotion. The sick rage pulsed through her in an unending tide, swelling and ebbing before swelling up yet again until her skin seemed ready to split with it.

She thought she understood, now, why people were moved to kill.

It was a dangerous thought.

"Sister Lin?"

Lin Chong tried to raise her head. The cangue prevented it. But she got her eyes up enough to see Lu Junyi.

Lu Junyi, her friend, as lovely as ever . . . now with a face creased in worry. Grief for Lin Chong.

Lu Junyi nodded to the guards who accompanied her. A knowing nod. They stepped back in deference. Lu Junyi hurried to the gridded bars of the cell and knelt in front of them.

"Dear Sister Lin. I cannot bear what they have done to you—it's not fair . . ."

Lin Chong had not wept at the lashes, nor at the branding, but somehow tears sprang up behind her eyes at such a blunt statement of fact.

It *wasn't* fair.

She managed to shift forward until she could reach through the bars, clumsily turning so the cangue would not block her. Lu Junyi grasped her fingers tightly.

"My dear friend, I've brought you some food—and more importantly, gold and silver, for when you reach the camp. The constables who are to take you to Canghu have already been paid. I will send more silver after you—give some to the guards but most to the supervisor, and they will treat you gently."

Lin Chong's eyes crept to the guards outside *this* cell, the ones who had treated Lu Junyi so deferentially. She wondered how much silver Lu Junyi had given *them*. "This is the way of things, then," she murmured, in a voice that did not sound like her own.

"I will do anything in my power, pay anything, to see you suffer less," Lu Junyi said, low and passionate. "Now is not the time for debate. It is a time for survival."

"I cannot pay you back," Lin Chong said. It seemed important, somehow.

Lu Junyi was weeping, silently, without sobs or wails of any kind. Only tears, flooding down her face one after another, chasing each other's tracks in a waterfall Lin Chong was not sure she deserved.

"Oh, my friend," Lu Junyi said. "Survive this, and it will be payment enough. Now tell me—is there anything else you need? Is there anything I can do?"

"My rooms," Lin Chong managed. "I don't have many things there, but if you would take them for me and keep them, before the barracks clear the space . . ."

"Done," Lu Junyi said. "Is there anyone I should tell? I can send word to your children, if you wish it."

Her children.

One of the things in Lin Chong's room was a box, and inside the box were two items she had kept close for many years now. The first was a toy—a long feather attached to a stick that her son had played with for days on end as a young boy. The other was a poem, a child's piece, written by her daughter at about age ten.

Lin Chong did not consider herself a sentimental person. These two items were what she kept, and what she used to spark her memory. She would open the box and remind herself that she had raised her son with the skills to gain an examination title and that she'd then secured him a civil service post in the city of Xijing, and that she had found her daughter a marriage to a wealthy landowner some distance to the south.

There had been times neither had seemed possible. She had

worked hard, and feared much, in doubt she would be able to make such security come to pass, for two children without a father.

She could close the lid on the box and remember her children as something good, something she had accomplished well. A success in her life that would remain unsullied by the way their parent's fortune had turned.

Tomorrow, she'd been told, she would depart for the prison camp at Canghu.

"I do not wish to tell them," she rasped to Lu Junyi. "Let it lie."

CHAPTER 4

The abbot at the monastery had given Lu Da the name "Zhishen," meaning "Deep and Profound." He had told Lu Da he hoped it was aspirational, with a little bit of pleading in his eyes as he said it. It was the same look of despairing patience he got when he happened upon Lu Da when she was drunk and cheerful with song, or when he caught her with a side of pork or a handful of duck legs tucked in the front of her robes.

(How did vegetarianism help with enlightenment? Lu Da wished to eat her way deliciously toward becoming an immortal, and she couldn't fathom any problem with that. The other immortals would tear their hair in jealousy when they saw her in their ranks chowing down on pork belly!)

Lu Da did not let it bother her overmuch that nobody had achieved immortality in hundreds of years, not even the ascetic Fa masters. She also did not hold with her erstwhile abbot's sad aspirational sighs. Deep and Profound? She was plenty deep and profound already, thank you very much. The haojie out at Mount Liang certainly seemed to think so, and Lu Da was coming to believe she was far more suited to their ways of thinking than the monks' anyway. What a boon that this new fellowship had opened their ranks to her and welcomed her among them! How they would all change the world together!

Lu Da did believe in the way of the Fa—well, except for the vegetarianism, and the temperance, and the celibacy, and also how was it possible one needed *that* much practice at one's art to reach enlightenment? But as little actual philosophizing as she might do, her heart was the heart of a philosopher, and she would live according to the Fa (with her own adjustments) until the day she died. Or preferably didn't die and became an immortal forever.

But the way of the Fa didn't have to be the way of the *monks,* did it? What a revelation—there, was that thought not the peak of deep and profound? She had not been with the Liangshan group long, still some distance shy of a year, but she was already coming to believe they were her own type of monks . . . sort of, if she tilted her head and squinted. They were heroic and chivalrous, after all, with the most strict codes of belief. What was more monk-like than that? Chao Gai even had religious training in a monastery, though as a Transcendentalist rather than with the Fa, and for the practice of ghost hunting, which fascinated Lu Da. Ghosts! She very much wanted to meet a ghost. She thought it must be wild, like wrestling a boar or running naked with panthers. In fact, Lu Da thought she might want nothing more than to be like Chao Gai—such a powerful official and ghost hunter, with so many connections and such genius in plans and tactics—and who chose to break from those dastardly societal hierarchies to crusade for true justice.

What a magnificent haojie, a genuine hero. And such a pure example of Lu Da's new family at Liangshan!

Such were Lu Da's convictions that she did not have to wonder for even an instant what Chao Gai or her other fellows at Liangshan would think of the situation with Lin Chong. A loyal patriot of the Empire, locked away on a pretense, on the whim of one of the region's most putrid and gutless bureaucrats? A man whose innards were so rotten with corruption that even maggots would gag at them? Unacceptable! Chao Gai would say so; their leader Wang Lun would say so; and Lu Da *certainly* said so.

She would have even before meeting the other haojie. After all, had she not brought pulverizing justice to the skull of that predatory butcher? And had the brand to prove it, thank you very much!

Her righteous rage did not keep her from devouring a plate of steamed pork buns, however. Or two sacks of salted duck egg yolks. Or several platters of fried tofu. Or five bowls of wine. Lu Junyi had left her with a generous meal stipend while she waited . . . how rude it would be, Lu Da reasoned, if she did not make fullest use of it? Lu Junyi had seemed to think she could make headway at the prefectural yamen with words rather than fists, and she'd declined Lu Da's offer of accompaniment.

Lu Da didn't mind, especially when Lu Junyi asked if she would wait at a very well-stocked inn.

With exuberant cynicism, Lu Da privately did not expect the foray to have any effect. Everyone knew the ways of the bureaucratic courts these days. She kept her staff leaning up against the table, determined to stay fully prepared. As capable and fancy as Lu Junyi seemed, Lu Da thought it very unlikely she could *talk* the master arms instructor's execution out of happening. It would be as easy to convince a fish to marry a dog. And when the effort crashed in failure, then it would be down to trusty staff and sword to make things right.

At least Lu Junyi could also fight—skillfully, too. Her martial talent was only a little surprising. After all, many of these rich folk learned the martial arts alongside music and calligraphy from the time they were pushed out from between their mothers' bloody legs. Learned from private tutors, too, not scraping to find a master like Lu Da . . . only a little jealousy gnawed at that thought.

A little more unusual that Lu Junyi had kept on with her study, though. Lu Da was willing to bet most society women retained only the most basic forms and then went on to pop out well-educated broods of their own—at least, she didn't *think* most rich people practiced eye gouges for amusement, though to be fair she'd never known enough rich people to be sure, so maybe they did. Maybe they gouged out the eyes of all their servants on the regular! Though in that case, Lu Da probably would have met a few more eyeless people than she had, so probably not. The point was, Lu Junyi's skill was satisfactory enough to have a person's back, which made for better odds when busting up a prison together.

Hypothetically.

Lu Da was just finishing a plate of pork-fried noodles and a twelfth bowl of wine when the curtain at the door pushed aside and Lu Junyi slipped inside the inn. The setting sun slanted in briefly behind her before the curtain fell closed again. She came over to Lu Da's table to join her, sinking to the bench and raising exhausted hands to her face.

"How did it go? Does Master Instructor Lin still live? Are we burning down the jail to get her out?" Lu Da slurped the grease from her fingers and tightened a hand around her staff. It sure would be glorious to break apart the jail. Likely even she and Lu Junyi together did not stand a quarter of a chance, but if they failed it would be an excellent death.

"She's alive." Lu Junyi inhaled sharply and tried to straighten the fatigue out of her posture, without success. "Prefect Teng agreed to keep her from the headsman's sword. Oh!"

She appeared gripped with such emotion that Lu Da felt profound sympathy. Lu Da did not have any similarly lifelong friend, but already she knew she would die for her Liangshan martial fellows, and if one of them fell to such injustice . . . well, she would rend limbs from bodies to make it right, until the ground was knee-deep with arms and legs and heads. All of them would.

When she'd met Lu Junyi only days ago, Lu Da had been quietly and a little huffily intimidated—what with Lu Junyi's rich clothes and delicate table manners and porcelain-white hands. Even the fact that her fingers were streaked with ink pointed to a far more erudite life than Lu Da had ever known. Not to mention that the skin beneath the streaks was the kind of pale that wealthy women lusted after and Lu Da privately thought looked sickly, as if some creature had sucked the blood from the woman's body. Lu Da's own skin was the bronze of her hometown to the south, darkened and cracked further by the sun and thickened into calluses by swords and fistfights and a day-to-day life that had never known servants . . . but seeing Lu Junyi's despair over her friend somehow made her feel much more like a sister. Even more than discovering a mutual interest in the fighting arts.

I will make sure she does not have to suffer the loss of this friendship, Lu Da swore to herself. *It's only right.*

Lu Junyi managed to compose herself. "She's to be taken to the work camp at Canghu. It's at least ten days' hard journey. I need . . . she asked me to go to her rooms, her things . . ."

"How can I help?" Lu Da had to admit she felt a prick of disappointment that they were not to break Lin Chong out of prison. Maybe she could take this to Liangshan once Lin Chong was in Canghu, though. The haojie would never tolerate hearing such a story, standing for justice above all as they did. Chao Gai would come up with a plan to bust Lin Chong from the work camp in three whisks of a rat's tail. Lin Chong was an honorable woman, so it should be done whether or not her own friend thought it was the right move, shouldn't it?

Lu Da knew her grasp of politics was tenuous and often taken over by more hotheaded goals, but she could consult with Chao Gai and the others. They would know what to do.

"If I can ask . . ." Lu Junyi pressed her hands to the table. "You have no obligation to us, but as a charitable monk, perhaps you would be willing . . . ? The guards are to take her tomorrow. The journey will be treacherous; she is already very weak, and I—I do not think I would have the endurance to follow. But I think you are stronger than I—if you are willing, I would give you gold and silver for the journey, of course . . ."

"Say no more," Lu Da declared. "I will see that they deliver her safely to the prison camp. Such a contradiction, though, isn't it? A prison camp isn't very safe."

"No. It isn't. But I have sent a courier to the supervisor, and I've given Lin Chong gold for him—I've done this for others before; enough gold will see her a soft assignment. Sweeping out one of the temples, or keeping watch . . ."

Hrrmph, Lu Da thought. Lu Junyi's way of solutions was to fling ingots of gold and silver at the matter, like flinging meat to quiet a yapping cur. Not an option that had ever been available to Lu Da, and less noble in her eyes than bashing a few heads together, freeing Lin Chong, and taking her to Liangshan. But she could also see how Lu Junyi's hands knitted against each other, how worry and grief bit over the skin of her face. *I will dance your dance for now.*

It would do no harm to watch over Lin Chong. Make sure she was protected on the road.

"I've paid the guards already also," Lu Junyi continued. "With a promise of more upon their return, so they will be motivated not to mistreat her. But I hear increasing reports of bandits roving to the northeast of here, and I fear the abuse of her punishment will make her take ill on the journey. If you would—forgive me; it is all so much to ask."

Bandits, thought Lu Da, with a private chuckle. *Yes indeed, that's what they call us!* But she did not mention the Liangshan haojie. She'd decided she liked Lu Junyi, but a woman who could walk into a yamen and demand an audience with the prefect—and obtain it!—was one she would wait to trust with the truth about the honorable "bandits" of Mount Liang.

Less honorable bandits also roamed the roads to the northeast, of course, ones who would slash innocent travelers in the back rather than carefully target those they stole from. Lu Da had full confidence she could protect Lin Chong from *them.* And if she ran into any of her Liangshan family, so much the better. Too bad she didn't have time to get back and speak to them now.

"You have no need for more worry about Master Instructor Lin," she told Lu Junyi. "I'll see her to Canghu alive and intact—I swear on my life."

Lu Junyi bowed her head. "I don't know how I can thank you. I will owe you a great debt."

"No debt," Lu Da replied carelessly. "As you said, I am a monk of the Fa! Protecting those in need is what we do." *And I am a bandit of Liangshan, and protecting those in need is also what* we *do.*

The people of Bianliang would know the name of the Liangshan bandits soon enough. And Lu Da would help carve out those stories on the lawless roads, beginning with the protection of one Honorable Master Arms Instructor Lin Chong.

By the second day on the road, Lin Chong's feet were bleeding.

The heat beat down from a naked sun above, and the cangue weighed heavy on her shoulders. They'd resecured the wide square of wood and metal to be locked fast around her neck, and its dimensions extended for nearly a pace on each side. Its weight crushed down her spine, reigniting stripes of fire where the bamboo lashes had struck. In the shadow of the cangue, the manacles dragged at her wrists as if she hauled her own corpse alongside her.

She did not know the reason, but her shoes had been confiscated back at the jail, and the guards had presented her with a much thinner pair of straw sandals that were woefully inadequate to a hike. The two constables prodded her along with cudgels and showed no patience when she stumbled. They were not men she had trained—likely recent transplants to the capital, from their accents, rather than having advanced into the Guard at Bianliang.

No doubt such a choice of escorts had been intentional.

"Get a move on. We have three hundred li to Canghu," one of them complained—she'd caught his name as Dong Chao.

"We were told you were a master arms instructor before you were a traitor," added the other mockingly, the one called Xue Ba. "What lies. Can't even keep up."

He bent and whipped his cudgel down hard, not at her body—but against the top of her left foot. Sotted with exhaustion, Lin Chong was too slow to move in time. The full brunt of the hit was like a stone urn dropped to crush every small bone.

She gasped, listing to the side.

"Weakling! Walk faster. Faster!" Xue Ba yelled. He let loose with the damn cudgel again, buffeting her about her knees and feet. Lin Chong managed a clumsy slip from some of the blows, but then the other guard grabbed her cangue and shoved her back to the first with a chuckle. He held her in place while Xue Ba wound up for one more smack against the side of her left ankle.

The cudgel landed so hard that the pain jolted up her whole spine and back down in a black flash.

He hadn't splintered the joint. She knew what that felt like. This wasn't that bad; she could shake it off, she would shake it off. She'd suffered worse . . .

"Now go. Run!" cackled Xue Ba, giving her a shove. "Sprint, or you'll get a proper beating!"

Lin Chong wobbled into a staggering jog, every step another thumping stab. One of the straw sandals came loose and a rock sliced against the bottom of her foot. The cangue overbalanced her and her knee came down hard on the road.

Behind her, she could hear the guards laughing.

She stayed on one knee, trying to breathe. Her feet throbbed, knots of pain.

"What a lazy old fart," Xue Ba said, the guards ambling up abreast of her. "Get up, you floppy prick of a traitor." He smacked her with the cudgel again, against her elbow this time, in a starburst that shot up to her shoulder.

Lin Chong reached for some level of inner stamina, but she felt her body collapsing in on itself. More than she ever had in her life, she wanted to kneel before them and beg.

For decency. For mercy.

Not even the most grueling of her training, nor the ruthlessness of the combat field, compared with this slow erosion of her strength. Her instincts warred with each other. If she asked for leniency—it was humane—it was deserved . . .

But she had never in her life gained results by showing herself weak. Even against guards such as these, someone else might have succeeded in elegant pleas or humble charm . . . someone gentler, or more pitiable. But Lin Chong had never been the type of person others gave leeway or compassion. Her vulnerabilities only became targets for their resentments.

So how have you succeeded, then?

Hard work. Persistence . . . and seizing for respect instead, when she couldn't gain pity.

"Constable Dong," she said, as she pressed herself back to her feet by what felt like force of will alone. Her tongue was swollen in a cracked mouth, but she forged on—she'd wondered, when she'd first heard him speak . . . *Ask. You have nothing to lose.* "Your accent is of Yu Province. Might you have fought at the pilgrims' revolt two years ago?"

The older constable hesitated, and his eyes slid toward her suspiciously. "I was there. What of it?"

"I rode with the Imperial Guard. Perhaps we were allies on the field."

A slow recognition stole over Dong Chao's countenance. "You . . . a Master Arms Instructor Lin Chong led the left flank when Captain Xia fell to the rebels' arrows. You're that Lin Chong?"

Some type of crusted hope lit in Lin Chong's aching joints. She had only been trying for some connection—but if he had truly heard her name—"I merely did my duty. It was the stalwart holding of the line by yourselves in the Yu regiment that won the day."

Dong Chao's eyes had gone from lazy scorn to a dazed shock, and he moved his hands unconsciously toward each other as if he wanted to salute. "We would have perished had the Guard not arrived when it did. We owed you all so much that day."

"Think nothing of it," Lin Chong said hoarsely. "We were all serving the Empire to the best of our ability."

"Until you turned treasonous," Xue Ba cut in loudly, jostling back uncomfortably close to her. "Come on, get going."

Lin Chong knew she must grab this opportunity with both hands, and she ignored his jibe even as she began limping down the pitted road again. She didn't dare ask yet to fix her shoe, but instead threw the very highest gamble she could. "Constables, it's nearing midday, and it is so hot. I see an inn up ahead—it would flatter me if you would allow me to buy you both a rich meal. As gratitude. For your kind protection of me."

The guards looked at each other.

"Well, we must eat," Dong Chao reasoned aloud.

"We can eat while walking," Xue Ba objected.

But Dong Chao was the senior of the two, and the starry reverence when his eyes caught on Lin Chong had stuck. At least for now. Overruling Xue Ba's grumbles, he led them to the inn.

Blessed, blessed shade, and coolness, and water for her parched throat. Lin Chong invited the constables to order whatever meat and wine they liked, with as much grandness as she could muster, and then managed to rest the edge of the cangue against the wall and tilt her feet up so her burning soles could get some slight relief. She also clumsily managed to retie the loose sandal, though she could feel the blood sticking between straw and skin, gluing the strands against her toes.

Not only on the foot that had hit the rock, either. *How can they expect me to walk three hundred li this way?*

She had to focus on this day only. Make it to sundown. Then worry about the next. She had Dong Chao on her side now, or at least the edge of it. It was something. And they'd allowed her to buy them a meal.

Lin Chong had worried about revealing to the constables how much money she carried, the ingots from Lu Junyi. She'd also hesitated to spend more than travel coins on meals because Lu Junyi had directed her to use the heavier riches for the guards at Canghu—but if she did not gain the better graces of these constables, she would never make it to Canghu.

I must survive. Each day separately, I must survive.

Beneath all the immediate obstacles, her anger from the prison still simmered, a caustic pit threatening to suck her into self-destruction. It kept rising to grasp and choke her at unaware moments, like the strike of a snake. She tried to press it down, bind it into a swollen bundle to be dealt with later, reminding herself over and over: *Before anything else, you must live. You must live . . .*

She had to live, or her poison confession, the lashes and branding, all she endured even now—it would be worth nothing.

The wine and rest loosened the constables' tongues more. Xue Ba was still reticent, but Lin Chong roused herself to engage Dong Chao in a patter of conversation and found it did not take much effort. She learned he had a wife and daughter, and that they had moved all the way from Yu Province to the capital so they could be nearer the wife's sister and brother-in-law, the latter of whom was a clerk in the outer city. A glow came to Dong Chao's face when he described his daughter—"Perfect as a plum blossom, and can't stop asking every question she can think of. Four years old last Spring Festival! She's now begging me to find her a dragon egg so she can raise one as a pet. I tried to explain that dragon eggs take three thousand years to mature and that no dragon would consent to being a child's pet—and besides which no one has any idea where the dragons have got off to these last hundreds of years anyway. She sniffs and says I'm just not looking hard enough!"

He guffawed. Lin Chong managed to smile slightly and speak all the appropriate flattery of the child, making the father light up with pride.

At Xue Ba's grumbling urging, they took to the road again as the sun trailed past noon. The men's bellies were full and they seemed in good spirits, and Dong Chao continued to speak to Lin Chong now as a fellow soldier. Xue Ba only sniffed and threw the occasional snide taunt her way, but at least his abuse had left off for the moment, perhaps in deference to his superior.

As the day crept on, and Lin Chong's feet again threatened to curdle and give out beneath her, she risked enjoining upon Dong Chao to take another rest under a copse of trees. He allowed it with only a slight hesitation, and she sank into the shade and closed her eyes.

Though her feet swelled and burned and every muscle and joint was jagged metal, she began to think she had found a way through.

If I can continue this cordiality, surely I have the strength to reach Canghu. And then . . . then she would figure out what came next.

"Give me some of that flask of water." Xue Ba's voice drifted from a few paces away, where the guards stood watch over her in the shade. A pause. Then Xue Ba again: "I hope you aren't softening on what we've got to do."

Dong Chao made a frustrated grunt. "I wish now we had never taken the money."

"Take the money, don't take the money, it's all the same," hissed Xue Ba. "We discussed this! We have no choice but to obey a grand marshal. Be more afraid that after we return to the city we'll be arrested by Marshal Gao for murder, even with all his promises. But it'll be far, far worse for us if we fail at killing her—both for us and for *our families*."

Lin Chong's breath stopped in her chest. She stayed very still, not reacting.

Gao Qiu had paid her guards to kill her.

Survive. How could such a thing feel increasingly impossible? How was Gao Qiu not *satisfied*, after everything he had done, everything he had stripped from her?

The anger slithered up her throat again, filled her to the hollows of her fingertips, like ink soaking into paper until it was stained so black it could take no more. And this time, it stayed.

He will not be content until I'm dead. That is what his pettiness demands.

She could not allow him this final satisfaction. But how? *How?*

"We're due to turn off the road and cut through Yezhu Forest by midafternoon." Dong Chao's voice was toneless and resigned. "We'll do it there."

Yezhu . . . why did that name ring dull familiarity in Lin Chong's mind? Ah, yes, the butt of jokes, of sideways euphemisms—travelers getting "lost" in the shortcut through Yezhu Forest and never returning. Always, somehow, travelers who suffered some grudge against them—exiles or debtors or prisoners or runaways.

She had never connected that this was a real practice, that the sly jokes were out of fear because those in power—they *did this*—they truly did it, like it was normal, like it was nothing, without compunction or regret. Yezhu Forest, the place where escorts were bribed into murder.

Cracks in civilization. How much blood soaked that forest floor?

Now Lin Chong's blood too would mingle with those loamy layers of ghosts. Unless she did something. Unless she found a way to act. Here on this lonely road would be the most important contest of her life.

She tried to enter a meditative state and gather her strength. But despite her desperation, she only had fitful success before the end of Xue Ba's cudgel poked up under her ribs. Not gently.

"Wake up!" he barked. "Time to walk again. Quickly this time!"

Lin Chong made a show of obeying while quietly dragging herself to slowness as much as possible. Maybe if she delayed them past dusk—would they enter the forest in the dark? Surely not; they would have to find an inn for the night. She could keep forging a bridge with Dong Chao, and maybe he would have compassion for her, or at the very least hesitate . . .

But Dong Chao would no longer meet her eyes, and gave one-word answers when she tried to engage him. After a few more tries he snapped, "You're a prisoner! Stop trying to talk to me like we're fellows in arms."

After that, she stopped.

She surreptitiously tested her freedom of movement. Abysmal. Even those parts of her body that were not weighed down by cangue or manacles, not bruised or bleeding—all the restraints had acted to harden her body's fluidity into stone. As if the dragging weights and festering injuries had all worked together to warp and fossilize her.

I must be able to defend myself somehow. They only have cudgels. If I can leap, take them by surprise—a knee, a groin—will it be enough? She could not outrun them, not in this state. She would have to incapacitate them, and then . . . ?

Survive first.

Xue Ba's cudgel again, this time against her damaged back. Pushing her up off the road. Trees loomed above, rising into a sloping hillside with blackness beneath their canopy. Lin Chong glanced back—should she try now, her last chance while they were still on the road? Even with no other travelers in sight, she might be better off here than lost in the woods . . . but Dong Chao was too far ahead of her for her to have a hope of striking them both in quick succession. If she failed at surprise, she would fail.

She stumbled across the ditch at the side of the road, undergrowth snagging at her feet and ankles, then climbed to follow Dong Chao into the trees.

Yezhu Forest closed over them.

The trees were like a warren of caves. The undergrowth alternated between walls of denseness and tracts of empty, spongy ground where the canopy closed off all light above them.

How many skeletons were hidden in the brush? How many people had this forest tightened its fist on until they disappeared?

The road winked out behind them as if it had been extinguished.

"Aiya," Xue Ba moaned, stretching his arms in a clearly theatric performance. "I've gotta rest a moment. Let's stop here."

This is it, Lin Chong thought. *No more time.* She tried to roll to the balls of her damaged feet in preparation and almost fell, the cangue taking her dizzily to the side.

"Go ahead, sit down and rest," Xue Ba urged her. He and Dong Chao had taken up tense positions to either side, both just out of range from easy attack.

"Thank you for your kindness." Lin Chong did not think her brittle statement any more believable than theirs. "I shall . . . rest by that tree."

She moved toward Xue Ba.

He whipped back his cudgel and swung downward at her head like he would drive her into the ground.

Lin Chong was expecting it. Her training tried to respond. She moved, clumsily, dropping in a duck and slide in, but not fast enough. The cudgel made a glancing blow with her head and then bounced off the cangue, a loud *crack* in the quiet forest. But she managed to use the half-dodged move to get in close, and as much as her slide was turning into a stumble, she brought her leg around with all the energy she could dredge from every reserve.

Her shin smashed into the side of Xue Ba's knee.

His unearthly scream echoed to the treetops, and he fell away from her. Dong Chao was coming up from the side. Lin Chong only had to regain her balance this one time—if she could make this single attack, just this one, he would soon be in range—

But Dong Chao did not wait to get into her range at all. Instead, he swung the cudgel when he was still too distant to hit her.

Because he wasn't aiming at her. His cudgel slammed into the edge of the cangue.

It was as if someone had taken an iron bar to Lin Chong's throat. Her windpipe crushed in and the world shredded inside out with the edge of death, vibrating into every limb as if all control to her body had been cut. The momentum of the hit took the cangue in a wheeling arc to the ground, and Lin Chong's head with it.

She had no way to break the fall. Sky and brush and trees yanked past her vision in one sickening instant before the cangue hit the dirt so hard the corner dug straight into the loam, and Lin Chong's head snapped back against it with so much force that for one delirious moment she was certain her neck had been severed.

She couldn't move. The forest alternately went dark and bright, the shapes of branch and leaf becoming nonsense abstracts.

Two shadows moved among the jumble. One lopsided, limping. Both with cudgels.

Lin Chong reached for her discipline, her control. A finger twitched against the ground.

"You finish it," keened one voice, high with pain. "I'm not getting within striking distance again."

"You shouldn't have let her get that close in the first place. You heard me talking about her military skill. We would've been in trouble if she wasn't weakened."

"Avoid her face. Remember, Marshal Gao wants us to cut the face off to bring in the tattoo as proof. Hit her in the back of the head."

Hesitation. They were still wary of getting close to her.

"Should we tie her legs first? Just in case."

"Break them, if you think she's so much of a threat. I think you've near killed her already."

Lin Chong tried to move again, but her last wandering thoughts had divorced from her body. She didn't even feel pain.

This is where I will die, then. In a corrupted wilderness, folded into its deadly fissures as if she had never been.

When the shapes in her fading eyesight exploded in an echoing howl of rage, Lin Chong could only assume it was a vision of every one of her souls screaming at the injustice of it all.

CHAPTER 5

Lu Da bellowed again, so loud it shook the canopy of the forest above, and she roared straight into the guards who stood over Lin Chong.

She didn't try to arrest her momentum in the least, but instead rammed into the first of them with her full weight, her staff ahead of the rest of her, and mowed him to the ground. She felt his bones break into at least fifteen pieces as his life snuffed out.

The second one tried to fight, but too slowly, as if he was frozen between knowing whether to charge her or run.

He should have chosen running. Even with his knee twisted backward. Lu Da's staff whirled in her grip, and the wet smack of it colliding with his temple was extremely satisfying.

The woods fell quiet.

Lu Da huffed over to Lin Chong. "Sister Lin! I mean, Master Instructor! Speak, I beg you, or I shall impale myself on my sword in failure."

Lu Da was feeling massively grievous with herself. She'd refused Lu Junyi's offer to pay for the rental of a horse, reasoning that a horse would overtake and catch a person, but to shadow people on foot, walking both attracted less attention and didn't need feeding or bridling before a hasty departure. But she'd been obliged to keep far back enough not to be noticed, and in staying just out of sight she'd missed the guards' quick turn into Yezhu Forest.

She should have known right away! Lu Da knew these parts like her own hometown; she knew very well that Yezhu was often used as a shortcut. She also knew the penchant it had for eating people who entered it for that shortcut, never to be seen again if they were so unlucky as to step inside with someone who had malintent.

Realization of her dreadful mistake had just risen up to smack her, and she'd turned back in panic, when Xue Ba's scream of pain had brought her racing to the right spot.

"Lu Zhishen! Deep and Profound Lu, how could you let this happen?" she moaned at herself. "You don't use your head, that's how. You're a clay-eating donkey's anus all the way through. Now Sister Lin is monstrously injured—you should have fallen on those evil constables from the beginning, that's what you should've done. Run them both through and left their bodies in a ditch where they belong!"

Declaring this monologue at lusty volume, she crouched down next to Lin Chong. The master arms instructor's lower body lay sprawled against the ground, her upper body sagging and supported only by her neck in the cangue. Heavy manacles weighed down her wrists, blood and bruising caking the skin beneath.

Well, that part was easily fixed. Lu Da cast about and found the keys on the belt of the older man, the one with the fully pulverized head. She freed Lin Chong's hands and rubbed them vigorously.

"Sister Lin! Please speak. I've removed the manacles but I see no key for unlocking this awful cangue. I could tear it apart with my hands, surely I could, but the fragments would explode into your face and shred it bloody like cleavers. I could throw you over my shoulder and carry you to Liangshan without breaking it off, but the demon thing has nearly taken your head off already, so that would surely cause some ghastly injury, wouldn't it? My god's tooth would blast it to bits, but it's the same problem, I'd crush up your tiny skull along with it and then where would we be. Oh! I should have learned better. Just as you told me, and as the monks said . . . Abbot Zhi was always telling me, 'Lu Zhishen, you have great potential, if only you changed the way you do nearly everything.' He was right, wasn't he—'Deep and Profound,' my eye, better call me 'Head Full of Mud' . . ."

What to do? There was no doubt in Lu Da's mind that she must get Lin Chong to Liangshan. Not only would she be safe from more assassination attempts behind the mountain's natural barriers and not-so-natural entrapments, but Liangshan had medicines, and beds, and people who knew much more about treating dreadful wounds than Lu Da, who was much more likely to cause them.

Besides, they were already more than halfway to Liangshan. Even carrying Lin Chong, Lu Da reckoned she could reach the edge of the marsh in a day or less. She was a very fast runner. But what to do about the cangue?

A soft groan sounded behind them.

Lu Da released Lin Chong's hands and leapt straight up. One of the guards was not dead! She marched up to him, staff raised, and drew her sword with the other hand for good measure. It was the second guard, the one she had hit in the side of the head only. But Lu Da was very aware of how hard she could hit.

"You dog! How can you still be alive? You must have an iron skull!" she ranted. "Well, it's easily fixed. I'll smash out your brains until they mix with your eyeballs, and then I'll chop through your neck and kick your head into a pine tree, just to be sure."

"No . . ."

Lu Da looked around in surprise. It was not the guard who had spoken, but Lin Chong.

Energized, Lu Da sprang back to her side. "You speak, Sister Lin! Are you alive? I beg you, forgive me for being so late in beating these murderous curs off you. If they've maimed you I'll never be able to redeem myself."

"You . . . saved my life . . ." Lin Chong coughed. Her voice was thready, weak, like an old woman who had long been sick. But she seemed to be getting stronger. "Let these men live."

"They were extremely intent on killing you."

"Not they . . . Gao Qiu. He uses people . . . let them live."

"One's dead," Lu Da said. She felt no remorse for that, not one sliver. "But since you ask it, I'll spare the other."

She marched back toward where the living guard still lay, his cudgel some distance away from him. He cowered away from her, shivering.

"Sister Lin Chong says to forgive you," she declared. "I don't agree.

I was determined to mash you up like meat between my teeth. It's Lin Chong you have to thank for sparing your life. Now go!"

The man was in no shape to move quickly, but holding his head he began to stumble away on bad legs as fast as he could, leaving his cudgel in the dirt.

"Wait," Lu Da called.

The man turned, but only a little, not meeting Lu Da's eyes.

Lu Da sheathed her sword and took her staff in both hands, then whirled it about and rammed it into a nearby tree trunk that was four times the thickness of one of her wrists. With a tremendous noise, the staff buried itself more than halfway through the trunk. The top half of the tree creaked ponderously and then, with a very slow cracking noise, fell away from Lu Da against its fellows in the forest.

The guard squeaked.

"And that's without even my god's tooth!" Lu Da cried with satisfaction. "You're very lucky, I must have struck you a glancing blow before. Do you think you could withstand *this*?"

"No . . . Reverend Monk?" The words turned into a frightened question as his eyes took in her top knot.

"That's right. And I'll do to you what I did to this tree if you ever bother Lin Chong again. Get away!"

The guard hurried off into the trees, as well as he was able.

Lu Da checked the other man just to be sure, but as she had thought, he was quite dead.

"Daughter," Lin Chong whispered. Lu Da hurried closer in order to hear. "He spoke about . . . his daughter . . ."

"If he hadn't tried to kill you, I wouldn't have mashed him to bits," Lu Da said crossly. "It's very simple. The girl is better for it without a murderous father teaching her. I had no parents at all, and I am nothing but excellent."

Lin Chong sighed a little, but apparently she didn't have the strength to counter this, which Lu Da took to mean she had won the argument.

"Now, we need to remove that cangue from you," Lu Da continued. "If you have any ideas . . . oh! I've thought of something." She knelt down by Lin Chong very solemnly. "*You* must use my god's tooth."

Lin Chong recoiled. Not a lot—she didn't have strength nor space to move very much—but the way her eyes dipped away with taboo and revulsion, Lu Da could tell.

"Not right . . ." she whispered. "Yours."

Lu Da couldn't say she disagreed. The prohibition against touching and using the god's tooth of another was so strong, it was akin to the most intimate violation. Legend had it that attempting to leverage a god's tooth that was not one's own would also lead to a warping of its powers until it corrupted and perverted the user. The only ways a person could acquire their own artifact free and clear were to be gifted one through family—either family of blood or family sworn; to find a new one—a very rare feat, not accomplished in a thousand years; or to kill someone in fair combat and take rightful possession of theirs.

God's teeth might be rare, but the legends that "everyone knew" of them were not.

And they must hold true, surely, because never had there been a story of a thief who stole or swindled one gaining its power. That didn't stop it from ever happening, but all the tales warned that the god's teeth knew somehow. Even if they did not become corrupted, any artifact would dwindle accordingly if not passed on with perfect intent, with neither underhandedness nor coercion.

Thus, the vast majority of god's teeth were passed on as heirlooms or through fair and fatal conquest.

Or so everyone knew.

Lu Da didn't want Lin Chong touching her god's tooth any more than Lin Chong wanted to do it. But she saw no other way.

"Here," Lu Da said. "Let's do this. I'll gift you something—this dagger; it's a damnably fine blade." She drew the sheathed dagger from her belt and tucked it into Lin Chong's robes. "You don't have much to your name, do you. But if it isn't too much to gift me a lock of your hair, we can be sealed as sworn sisters. If we're family, it's not so strange for you to use it, yeah?"

"Still wrong," murmured Lin Chong. But after a moment she added, "I would be . . . nothing but flattered . . . to be your sister. Use the dagger, that would be right . . ."

Lu Da took back the dagger for a moment and very solemnly lifted Lin Chong's braided queue from the dirt. Her heart beat faster, the solemnity of the ritual taking over, the vulnerability of being bound to another.

She carefully pressed the blade against a small piece at the end of Lin Chong's queue. The blade was so sharp that a few fingers' width of hair fell immediately into her hand.

This is more intimate than a lover, Lu Da thought, and with great care tucked the lock of hair away in her pouch before returning the dagger to Lin Chong's belt.

"Now we are sworn sisters," she said. The words felt like very importantly shaped things, even though they were all individual words she had said before in other sequences. "You are not just Sister Lin who I hope to make my martial sister, but my sister in truth. It's done. Now please, Sister Lin, you must."

And before she could think more of it, Lu Da swept the god's tooth from around her neck and pressed it to Lin Chong's palm.

She felt naked. No. More naked than naked. Being naked was fine, and Lu Da had on occasion gotten in severe trouble for being naked—not always on purpose; sometimes it had been because she was drunk or on a bet or had run out of her bed in the middle of the night to defend some righteous cause only to see it was a cat wailing at a bat. But her god's tooth . . . even though it usually lay dormant beneath her robes, it had a constant hum to it that had become a part of her. Removing it was like sloughing off her own skin.

Lin Chong sighed slightly, and Lu Da, who still had her hand atop her new sister's, felt the god's tooth open.

Distantly, though. Without its touch against her skin, she could not reach for its strength herself, and even the sense of it rang like an echo of an echo. Was this the kind of thing that Lin Chong had trained to be able to see, when they fought?

She could well imagine what Sister Lin felt now—it wasn't so much power, although that too, but *wonder.* The feeling of standing at every point in every universe, past or present, real or imagined, and seeing and breathing them all at once.

Would Sister Lin be overwhelmed? Her training was what the monks had always driven Lu Da to aspire to, but if she had never practiced with a god's tooth—should Lu Da worry?

"Be careful," she couldn't help saying. "Remember, you want to break the cangue from you, but carefully!"

She expected the wood and metal to shatter and fly in all directions. That certainly was what would have happened if she had attempted it. Instead, something . . . popped. And then another pop, soft but definite.

The cangue cracked, very smoothly, along sixteen lines that crossed it exactly in the pattern of a star. Then, all at once, the pieces slipped from Lin Chong's neck, clattering into a neat pile below.

Fortunately, Lu Da was ready, cradling Lin Chong's body so she wouldn't fall with the wood and metal. Lin Chong gave another slight sigh and released the god's tooth, letting it tumble from her hand.

Lu Da held her god's tooth for a moment and stared at it, then at the neatly fissured stack of what had been the cangue, and not a little jealousy of her new sister rioted inside her. But as usual for Lu Da, it was a cheerful sort.

"You will have to teach me that, Elder Sister," she murmured, swinging the god's tooth back around her neck, where it settled into place against her tattoos.

Lin Chong seemed to have lost consciousness, and didn't make any reply back.

Well, they had no reason to wait any longer. Lu Da didn't fancy trying to crash through Yezhu Forest after dark. As gently as she could, she heaved Lin Chong up across her broad shoulders and set off at a steady jog through the woods.

Lin Chong was not certain she could distinguish between waking and dreaming.

She was aware of being carried over Lu Da's back. She was aware of steady movement, of pauses to rest, of a jug of water being pressed against her lips.

But she was also aware of drifting among the stars. Of seeing every living thing in all the known and unknown world, outlined in its own vibrating energy. Of being connected somehow in a giant, infinite web—but not trapped, no, only aware that every small movement twanged and echoed along innumerable links to every other breathing creature, through history and into the future.

Such was the window the god's tooth opened. And somehow . . . it hadn't gone away.

Or was that her delirium?

It was some time before she realized she was no longer lying across Lu Da's shoulders, but on the softness of a mattress.

"She is hot with fever," someone said. Wet cloths pressed against the skin of her forehead. Lin Chong tried to form words, but her throat felt swollen with tumors. She pried her eyes open.

Even in Lin Chong's wobbly vision, the woman who had spoken seemed far finer in dress and bearing than might be expected, with maroon silk drifting from her elbows. Her accent fell into place as the diction of the upper classes of the northern Ji Province—but what would a landed noblewoman be doing at the side of Lin Chong's sickbed?

The strangeness intensified with the sound of water wringing into a basin, as the noblewoman pressed another cloth against Lin Chong's skin next to the first.

"I think Sister Lin has very hot humors." Lu Da's voice, distinctive and recognizable from somewhere off to the left. "So a fever is only natural. She'll recover, won't she?"

"You are taking her to the Divine Physician?" asked the noblewoman.

"Of course! Sister An will know what to do."

"I'll send a signal right away," said a third speaker, moving at the edge of Lin Chong's blurred view. A rougher-sounding woman, in clothes of coarse and mended cloth, who glanced back only for their eyes to meet. "Ho! She sees us!"

"Sister Lin!" Lu Da bounded forward and grasped her hand. "Are you aware? Do not strain yourself to speak. This is Noblewoman Chai—we call her Cyclone—and Sister Zhu, who owns this inn. We call her the Crocodile. We're right on the edge of the marsh here; you'll soon be safe."

Lin Chong did not understand half the words spoken. What marsh? Where were they going? Who was this Divine Physician? Lin Chong wondered, muddled, if she had died and somehow reached the Heavenly Plane. *I did try . . . I lived according to Benevolence, however I could . . .*

Nonsense rattled through her mind.

"I'll go call for the boat," said the woman called Crocodile, when Lin Chong had not managed to respond. "And then I'll make some broth and tea with chrysanthemum and peppermint to draw out the fever while we wait. Not as good as the Divine Physician, but it worked on all five of my children, eh!"

A cheerful rustle of footsteps and she was gone.

"It's very nice to meet you, Sister Lin," said the noblewoman. Her features were sharp and sculpted as a dragon's. "Our Flower Monk tells me you were a master arms instructor."

Lin Chong had a moment's disorientation before she realized Noblewoman Chai must mean Lu Da. The Flower Monk—she'd called herself that.

A drawn-out whistling sounded through the air, fading into the distance and only adding to Lin Chong's confusion. She knew the sound before she'd put words to it—but they were not on the battlefield, were they? Or were they? A signal arrow, one with the head carved to let out a long whistle as it arced through the air . . .

"I don't think she's sensible," Lu Da said, dragging Lin Chong's wandering mind back to her surroundings. "Or her throat is so bruised she can't puke out any words. It looks bad . . ."

"Sister An will help." Noblewoman Chai put a comforting hand on Lu Da's shoulder. Then she glanced back at Lin Chong and added thoughtfully, "Will she want to stay and join us? A master arms instructor would be a great boon, and much needed."

"Of course she will!" Lu Da answered, and then added, more doubtfully, "Won't she?"

"I can't imagine she has many other places to go, having escaped Imperial custody," Noblewoman Chai said. "I must return home—here's what you must do. Talk to Wang Lun. Impress upon her how beneficial it will be to invite in a master arms instructor of the Imperial Guard. You can get Chao Gai to help you, I am sure. If Lin Chong is open to staying, we must convince Wang Lun to welcome her."

"Of course she will!" Lu Da said again. "Why wouldn't she?"

Noblewoman Chai smiled. "You are a very good-hearted sister, Flower Monk. Do this: tell Wang Lun that I have personally given our arms instructor my highest recommendation, and my friendship."

A grin blossomed on Lu Da's broad face. "Oh, yes! I loved Sister Lin the moment I met her, too—she's so impressive, isn't she? If it turned out her farts stank of perfume I wouldn't even blink once."

The "Cyclone" noblewoman gave her another smile but didn't respond, and even in her bewildered, half-conscious state, Lin Chong could tell that Noblewoman Chai understood something here that Lu Da did not.

Lin Chong's strongest suit had never been politics. But nor could she have advanced to the rank of master arms instructor without a basic understanding in navigating political winds. Lu Da, it was clear, entirely lacked such an understanding, with her hot head and her equally passionate optimism about anyone she saw as a good person. Noblewoman Chai, on the other hand, saw the currents and dangers lurking beneath . . .

Perhaps it was the fever and injuries, or the residual awareness of the god's tooth. But even before the woman called Crocodile came back into the room with a strong, sharp-smelling tea, Lin Chong had begun to sense crocodiles all around her, lurking beneath the water, waiting in the marsh outside this inn. Crocodiles with the faces of people.

But Lu Da patted her hand and smiled, and the rich Cyclone and the innkeeper tended to her gently, and Lin Chong did not grasp all that was happening but she did know she was still alive.

Survive. Survive in this strange new reality of noblewomen and crocodiles sending a whistling arrow over a marsh. Survive, and then see what came next.

CHAPTER 6

"*Escaped?* What do you mean, *escaped!*"

Chancellor Cai Jing let the screeching wash past him like river water around a rock. Grand Marshal Gao Qiu was such a detestable sort, and an unfathomably far two ranks below Cai Jing on top of it—Cai Jing, who was Grand Chancellor of the Secretariat and one of only three men sitting second to the Emperor himself. But Gao Qiu was also a childhood friend of the Emperor—the Lord of Heaven, may he reign forever—and such relationships had to be coddled.

Besides, he could use Gao Qiu. The insipid man was so very easily manipulated.

Cai Jing let his writing brush bend against the paper with a pressure that did not vary, the same weight, the same angle, brush straight in his hand, back straight where he sat, feet flat against the floor with the evenness of meditation stones. His calligraphy was the most famous in the Empire, and with reason. Cai Jing prided himself on his very smooth temper.

Meanwhile, Gao Qiu rained blows and verbal abuse on the soldier who had tentatively interrupted their conference. Grabbed the messenger's own cudgel and whacked him with it, then kicked him in the shins. He had no restraint at all.

Cai Jing had people beaten because he enjoyed it. Gao Qiu did it because he lost control. This, Cai Jing felt, was a salient example of their differences.

Cai Jing's brush lifted in a perfect hook stroke before slowly and rhythmically falling to meet the silkiness of the paper again. The gold and pearls of his rings glittered as the sun slanted across his work and kissed the perfection of his movement. *The calligraphist is himself a poem,* he mused.

"Forget this woman," he interjected, when Gao Qiu had paused for a moist and heaving breath. "We have loftier concerns. To go back to these border skirmishes in the north . . ."

They were more than skirmishes. Cai Jing had some small talent at augury, and what he saw in the bones had begun a deep vein of worry within him. The darkness of the omens, the echoes of smoke and fire and blood screaming endlessly into the wind . . . the depth of the possible horror yawned nearly unfathomable. The idea that civilization could fall—it seemed too massive a threat, and yet it had begun haunting his sleep.

The Empire. The Empire's very existence could tumble into such an abyss.

It must be put right.

"The skirmishes are nothing," Gao Qiu spat. "Exaggerated reports so we'll send them money and men. The northern outposts are *spoiled*."

Unfortunately His Imperial Majesty agreed, and so did the Chancellor of the Ministry and the Minister of War—or at least, they did not dare to voice an opinion distinct from their Emperor. Cai Jing was not a man given to despair, but he had begun to feel the very alien sensation of *frustration*. He had tried to convince His Imperial Majesty to consent to a better-disciplined military, to no avail; to further deployments to the north, to no avail; to drafting more able-bodied young men from the outlying provinces to serve in their Empire's divine army . . . all to no avail. The rural provinces had more children than they had purpose for, useless mouths that were only a strain on the Empire and could be put to good use here . . . Cai Jing had argued further conscription would only be to those families' benefit—as members of the Guard, the young men would have a chance at advancement and status they never would back in their home counties. But such a policy would be unpopular in the southwest, and His Imperial Majesty, Lord of Heaven, long may he reign—he wished to be loved.

A sentiment that did not bother Cai Jing.

Failing at improving their traditional defenses, Cai Jing had changed tactics. An army did not have to be large or well-supplied if it towered over its foes technologically. The Empire of Song was in the midst of an explosion of science and invention, and Cai Jing had applied himself to a hunt for all manner of sorcerers, machinists, alchemists, architects, ghost hunters, chemists, and scholars of immortality. He'd also pored over scrolls and records for lost discoveries that might revolutionize a war effort, and he'd sought any who had made a study of such things. So far, however, his quest had been stymied at every turn. He had already beheaded a fair few monks who had claimed such knowledge only to come up short, and he'd assembled only a fraction of the expertise he strove for.

He thought he'd had all the luck of a magnificent breakthrough after the recent incident at Anfeng Monastery and its results, but even that had, for some unfathomable reason, failed to whet the Emperor's interest.

The Emperor. Lord of All, protector of the realm. Unquestionably correct in all he did and yet Cai Jing could not help but fear he led them toward an uncertain doom. He'd dismissed all of Cai Jing's efforts as frivolous and had refused more than a pittance of resources and support.

Even after Anfeng.

Cai Jing had tried to explain what it might mean . . . for the Empire, for the power of the Emperor himself, and his throne . . .

He had begun debating whether he ought to leak the reports of the incident at Anfeng Monastery among the Court, records he'd so carefully destroyed. Letting that secret dangle would be a dangerous move, yes, but surely it would force the Emperor's hand . . .

Not that Cai Jing thought himself above the Lord of Heaven. Of course not.

Gao Qiu had turned his rants back on the unfortunate messenger. "Find her family—parents, brothers, uncles and aunts! Issue arrest warrants for them all. They will pay for this. And that sniveling guard who ran—he must have helped her. I'll cut the truth from him and have him hacked to death in the public square!"

"Yes, Grand Marshal—yes, it shall be done—"

"And what's-her-name, who was with her? Lu. The Lady Lu, drag her in here by the hair!"

"Yes, Grand Marshal—is that Lady Lu the wife of the district magistrate?"

"No, you dolt! The ridiculous one, the rich unmarried dilettante who writes all the circulars. Why are you still in my sight?"

The soldier bowed his way backward as rapidly as possible and shuffled out.

Gao Qiu's face had flushed red, and spittle flecked his lips. "Lin Chong defied me," he informed Cai Jing, as if to justify himself.

"And she'll receive her reward, I am certain," Cai Jing answered calmly. Lady Lu, with the circulars . . . hmm. He had read something of this woman's, he thought . . .

"Ignore this trouble to the north," Gao Qiu said, swinging himself carelessly to lounge on a settee as if there had been no intrusion to their meeting. "The Empire's army is larger than the whole Jin population. Something gets out of hand, we'll throw our military at the northern border and have it be done."

"And the reports of strange new tactics and sorceries of the Jin?" Cai Jing asked. "If such a move would lose us half the Imperial Army, when we have other borders to defend—what then?"

"That's what an army's *for.* Besides, half of ours would mean we scour them from existence, and then that's one less border."

Cai Jing did not sigh, and his hand did not grip more tightly, and the brush kept moving slowly and steadily, but it was all a closer thing than he might have liked.

Cai Jing had decades of experience at maneuvering a court, however. As many as the white hairs of his beard, so were the governmental victories he'd engineered without their initiators being any the wiser. Many times he did it to secure his own preferred policies, but this . . . this was far more important. Far greater than himself.

This was the future of the Empire. The future of everything.

It would *not* be the first thing he failed at.

"This woman," he mused. "This arms instructor who so irritated you."

"Made an attempt on my life, you mean. She was out to assassinate His Majesty the Emperor!"

Of course she was. Cai Jing kept that thought to himself. "Perhaps some unnatural talent is what you need here," he said aloud, as if the idea was just coming to him. "You could be right that advancing our military as a whole is not necessary. In fact, I am sure you are right—after all, your position is one of military matters, and I am merely our Empire's legislator." Gao Qiu smirked, well-pleased—exactly the reaction Cai Jing had aimed for. "But forget the north for a moment. This woman has weaseled away from your grip not once now, but twice. Think what power you would have to correct her offense if you only had other tools at your disposal."

Gao Qiu's expression went thoughtful. "What other tools?"

"I know His Imperial Majesty does not wish the army to have unlimited strength, to ensure their proper subservience to the Empire. But one or two people could be directly controlled by you. Or, even better, an artifact under your own power—which could then be put to your own worthy uses, as judged by you alone."

Gao Qiu grunted. "Those clumsy sons of whores in the army I sent for scholar's stone, they lost the lot of it."

And Cai Jing's heart leapt, even though he gave no sign of it. *Gao Qiu had been hunting down scholar's stone.*

What a thing to let slip! It had become so fashionable in these modern days to scorn god's teeth as mere cheap tricks, not useful for anything beyond a boxing match—but Gao Qiu coveted even some adjacency to their power, enough to send men on a deadly fool's errand. Cai Jing berated himself for not having ferreted this secret out earlier. This useless, odious little man was about to become exactly the game piece he had been searching for.

He carefully kept his face schooled to quiescence.

"You would be a most deserving possessor of a god's tooth," he murmured. "I can think of no one better fit."

Gao Qiu snorted lightly, but it was all for show. He wanted this. He wanted it past all current propriety.

Cai Jing strongly suspected that the reason for the vocal dismissal of god's teeth was not their lack of power, but the fact that those in power could not control them. They could be stripped from their rightful family lines—and were, sometimes, if one were so foolhardy as to risk conflict with the custodian of a god's tooth—but all that did was reduce the number of artifacts with any strength in them. Somehow, a god's tooth always knew how it had transferred ownership. Knew, and rendered its own judgment.

The Emperor himself could not dictate different. Even he, the Lord of Heaven—may he live forever—had fully more than a dozen god's teeth in his noble possession, but all mostly minor, ineffectual ones. Likely given as tribute over the years and thenceforth sucked of their vitality, though no one dared make mention of it.

The sole member of high government with a true heirloom god's tooth was the Minister of War, Gao Qiu's direct superior. In fact, Cai Jing strongly suspected that Minister Duan had only attained his position because of the possession, no matter how people scorned god's teeth as meaningless relics in this forward-thinking era. The Minister did have some small worth as a general, but military prowess had not been the deciding factor in such posts in a long time . . . and as for political savvy, Minister Duan had so laughably little that he had never even attempted to curry favor with Cai Jing the way he should have, which was mildly shocking and more than a little irritating.

If Gao Qiu obtained a god's tooth . . . if Gao Qiu obtained one far more powerful than the Minister's . . .

Not that Cai Jing would particularly appreciate Gao Qiu as Minister of War either, but at least he was malleable. And for Cai Jing that would be but a first stroke of the brush.

"I have been applying myself to much research on the subject of late," Cai Jing went on in a meditative tone. As if this meant nothing. An academic fancy rather than the potential fate of all. "I meant it militarily, for the service of Empire, but if that is truly unneeded I shall cede such knowledge to you. You see, I have become convinced that finding a god's tooth or having one pass between custodians are not the only ways to acquire one." He paused, subtly building the drama. "I believe that a god's tooth could be *made*."

Gao Qiu sat up straight, like a hound with a scent.

"It would be a vast scientific undertaking, and possibly involve the use of scholar's stone, as you yourself so adroitly suspected," Cai Jing flattered, carefully not mentioning Anfeng and all its implications. "But think of it. If we could create a god's tooth more powerful than any seen on this earth, one that would make its possessor unto a god himself . . . a god's tooth which has never been found or possessed by anyone before. If you convince His Imperial Majesty that we should apply resources to producing such an object . . . allow me to help you attain this, Marshal Gao. And then you will also have assuaged the silly fears of an old man, in that if you attain great power for the Empire, no one will dare bring us harm."

If Cai Jing could at last gain the Emperor's blessing, this would be the largest stride forward he'd yet been able to make. With the resources of the Imperial Treasury and the right manpower—and Gao Qiu would act as his tool.

The future of the Empire must be safeguarded.

Cai Jing neglected to mention exactly how foolish bonding with such an experiment might prove to be. The men from Anfeng had succumbed to devoured minds and souls within mere moments of their attempts to draw on any otherworldly power. Of course Cai Jing meant to fix that, but it was not his fault Gao Qiu was too seduced by the potential potency of a god's tooth to ask the obvious questions. Too swept away—and too arrogant—to wonder why Cai Jing did not prefer to preserve this power for himself.

Gao Qiu's fist closed against itself, as if he could reach out and strangle the woman he held his silly grudge against. "I'll crush everyone who dares defy me. I'll drink to *that*. Let's call a servant for some wine."

"Tea for me." Cai Jing's brush slipped up off the page, the final stroke. The characters of the old adage glowed in balanced perfection: *Inner tranquility enables great accomplishment.*

Time to pretend to be grateful to Gao Qiu for humoring an old uncle.

Happily, the wooing and flatteries were cut short after not too lengthy a time when a servant announced the same soldier as before. The hapless man entered Cai Jing's sanctum and stopped just barely close enough to satisfy etiquette—and still out of Marshal Gao's petty striking range. Then he bowed deeply to both of them.

"Grand Chancellor Cai Jing, Grand Marshal Gao Qiu. The constables have brought the Lady Lu Junyi, if it pleases you. Shall she be placed under arrest?"

"No," Cai Jing said quickly, as if the answer were so obvious he could assume it. He thought he remembered, now, what he had read by this woman . . . "The marshal merely wishes to ask her some questions. Send her in."

Two constables accompanied Lady Lu into the room. They had not bound her, and they did not abuse her—according to her station, no doubt—but her posture radiated displeasure. She might comport herself properly, as a woman of wealth and status, but her face and movement gave away how close her heart lived to defiance.

She thought herself better than the law of the Empire.

Arrogance. Cai Jing could use that. She should be grateful to be treated so kindly.

"You," growled Gao Qiu. "You're friends with Lin Chong. Where is she?"

Lu Junyi bowed very deeply, but she stopped short of taking herself to the floor, Cai Jing noted. "I swear to you, Grand Marshal, I have no knowledge. The last I knew she was embarking to Canghu, on your orders. I understood she intended to serve her sentence as a loyal citizen of the Empire."

"Well, she didn't!" Gao Qiu got right up in her face. So unbecoming, to allow this inferior person such power over him, but he never understood such things.

Gao Qiu reached out a hand with snakelike speed and grasped Lu Junyi's hair, yanking her head back to face the carved ceiling. "What do you know? You helped her escape, or you know who did. Tell me!"

Lady Lu's breath came fast but steady. "I promise you—if Arms Instructor Lin had shared any plans of escape with me, I would have counseled her against it. I would have told her to serve the sentence for which she was convicted—"

"Counseled her? Surely you mean you would have reported her to the magistrate," Cai Jing said amiably.

The woman's eyes darted to him, sideways from where Gao Qiu still held her, and in that moment he was certain. She did know something about her friend's escape, something she was refusing to say. Or, at least, she suspected.

Fascinating. Cai Jing didn't care in the least about Gao Qiu's obsession with some woman who had scorned him—but secrets, he thrived on secrets. And knowing Lady Lu's secret just might bring a perfect end to this afternoon.

"Perhaps the Lady Lu could formally disown her friend," he suggested. "As witnessed by us now. Questioning of her household would prove whether she has remained in the city, and presumably show she had no direct hand in this vile treachery, but a denunciation would preclude any indirect involvement with no doubt."

Gao Qiu scowled and shoved at Lu Junyi with his hand, finally releasing her. She stumbled and almost fell, but caught herself on one knee, head bowed. Her disarrayed hair fell across her face.

"Well, Lady Lu?" Cai Jing said. "We await your words. Surely it is the easiest thing on earth to denounce a traitor to the Empire."

The woman wet her lips, her fingers clutching white-knuckled against the skirts of her outer robes. "I disown former Arms Instructor Lin Chong as ever having the smallest breath of friendship with me. She is a traitor to His Imperial Majesty the Emperor, and she can live or die according to his will. I renounce any interest in her fate."

"Very pretty," Cai Jing said.

Lady Lu's eyes came up—just a little, suspiciously. She must worry whether he spoke in jest. Precisely as he intended.

"Grand Marshal Gao," he continued, "surely such a well-crafted word from such a respected lady is all you need. You can freely pursue other avenues in this matter. I will bring texts to your chambers later to explore our other discussion."

"Arrest her," Gao Qiu spat to his constables, as he turned heel to leave Cai Jing's chambers.

"A moment, gentlemen," Cai Jing interrupted. "Grand Marshal, I can only presume that your need of investigating this woman is at an end, as she knows nothing. I would be much indebted if you let her remain here with me."

His beady eyes narrowed. "Why?"

"Come now, Marshal. Do I ask you why you have a woman brought to your chambers? You understand the delicacy. Consider the matter closed, and I shall come join you later."

It was not the type of dismissal Gao Qiu could question. With one last glare at Lu Junyi, he gestured the constables sharply behind him and left.

Lady Lu lifted her eyes again to Cai Jing. Apprehensive. Sometimes sparing a person was a more powerful move than punishment—they could never escape the awareness of how he held their life in his fingers.

Cai Jing indicated the seat Gao Qiu had vacated. "Join me, Lady Lu. I shall call for more tea."

She rose, slowly, and settled herself on the settee, just at the edge.

"You need not fear me," Cai Jing said. "I have no intention of telling Marshal Gao you know about that convict woman's escape."

The quicksilver flick of her eyes again. Startlement and fear. She was a good liar, but not good enough. "I swear to you, Grand Chancellor, I know nothing—"

"Save your words." He waved her silent. "I wish to discuss

something else. When Marshal Gao had you brought here, I had a memory of seeing one of your circulars. 'Incendiary composites in the modern field of war,' I believe was the title."

"Yes, I . . ." She sat up straighter, gathering herself. "Monks of the Fa and priests of the Renxia have utilized incendiary mixtures for quite some time for religious and celebratory purposes, but only recently has control of such tinctures begun to outstrip their inherent instability. However, I believe it is only a matter of time before this power is harnessed for destruction, and it would greatly benefit the Empire to be prepared against such weapons, either in rebellions or in incursions by our foes."

"Tell me," Cai Jing said. "What do you know about the alchemy of such mixtures?"

"They are not strictly alchemy, though alchemists discovered them. But even the untrained could compose the ingredients. A mix of sulfur, saltpeter, and birthwort in the proper proportions, with realgar and honey . . ." She had gained animation as she talked, but now she trailed off, her eyes catching on her interlocutor. "Forgive me, Chancellor. I write on many passing fancies; I had not conceived of someone of your stature seeing my nonsense. I would hardly be equipped to provide the Imperial Army with incendiary mixtures for use in war. Even among those who know its use, the instability is still far too great for focused offensive purposes, and any experimentation without expertise would likely result in loss of limb or lives."

Cai Jing said nothing, simply pinned her with his eyes.

Her head dropped. "My apologies, Grand Chancellor. I am guessing at your questions before you pose them."

With acuity, though. This Lady Lu was a sharp woman.

He could definitely use her.

"If you believe they cannot be harnessed, why do you write warning of their use in weapons?" Cai Jing asked.

Lu Junyi hesitated, seeing the trap. "I only meant—if others, if our enemies, had made discoveries we have not yet stumbled upon . . ."

She swallowed.

"If it's only a matter of time, as you say, then it is obvious we must act on experimentation in order to reach such discoveries ourselves before anyone else, is it not? Now, the monks use these compounds in purifications and rocketry. You are the first I have seen suggest their use in war."

"Not the first, Chancellor. It is said the Rebellion of the Three Sects used a similar mixture to create their flaming arrows, though they were destroyed before we could know. Others have also written such cautions, such as—such as Scholar Ling Zhen. Or Scholar Zeng Gongliang. I am merely the conduit of the conversation, and hardly an expert."

Ling Zhen was in prison for suspected sedition, and Zeng Gongliang was dead. Cai Jing should know; he'd had the man executed for inciting disaffection against the state. Pity. If he'd known Scholar Zeng had such mastery locked away inside, he mightn't have been so hasty.

Cai Jing's fingers stroked against the stones of his rings. "Tell me. What would happen if you combined this science with the properties of scholar's stone?"

That startled her. Her eyes widened, and she shifted on the edge of her seat. "I—I have no knowledge of that. Forgive me. I—I would conjecture that the instability would be multiplied by many times . . ."

She wasn't wrong. Cai Jing kept that information to himself for now.

"I am assembling a group for the development of scholarship in this area," he said instead. "You will have access to any resources you require. You and the others I designate will be responsible for using these materials in the creation of new weapons for defending the holy borders of His Majesty's Empire, according to my specifications. Your usefulness will be rewarded, your failure punished, and if you speak of any of this to another person, you will be executed."

Gao Qiu would have his god's tooth. Whether he lived through the experience was yet to be seen, but either way, great strides would be made in the Empire's security.

The conclusion was all but wrought.

This time Lu Junyi did go to her knees. She slid elegantly from the settee to bow with hands flat against the polished floor. "Honorable Grand Chancellor, you flatter me too much. I fear my abilities are too feeble for such an important duty—"

"If you refuse, I can always tell Marshal Gao that you gave him false testimony."

"I—I swear to you, Honorable Grand Chancellor—"

"Swear all you want. It hardly matters whether I'm correct, only that I choose to say so. But I am. Correct."

She stayed bent to the ground, but it seemed he had shocked her to silence. Good. It would never do for a subordinate of the Empire to think too much of herself.

Still. As the Renxia would say, hard and soft practices were sharper blades than each alone: Cai Jing knew it was best to offer punishment on one side while dangling a plum reward on the other. Even if that reward might never be made truth.

"You are being drafted into service of the Empire," he soothed the woman. "It is a great honor. If you perform ably, the Emperor himself may take notice of you. He enjoys intelligent and dutiful women, and if you do your job well he may even be moved to credit you with a place among his concubines. I have seen such advancements before; it is not out of the question. This is a magnificent chance for you to draw the eyes of the Lord of Heaven."

Lu Junyi still did not rise, but the fight seemed to seep out of her, turning her supplicant position more truth than lie. And Cai Jing knew he had tied the knot correctly.

"It is my privilege to serve the Empire," she murmured to the floor.

As it should be.

PART II

LIANGSHAN

CHAPTER 7

Lin Chong woke to firm fingers on the pressure points at the base of her head.

Her vision came into focus. A woman with snow-white hair bent over her, face a study in concentration. Despite the white tresses, she didn't look old at all, surely not much older than Lin Chong.

Her eyes met Lin Chong's, and she smiled. Her hands drew up, fluttering like butterflies, and she turned to gesture to someone on the other side of the room.

Lin Chong turned her head slightly, and was surprised to discover she could do so without pain. She reached up a hand—bandaging and poultices wrapped her throat and plastered her cheek over the brand. But her head was clear.

The person whom the doctor—was she a doctor?—had beckoned came closer, backlit by the brightness of a window. Lin Chong had subconsciously expected Lu Da, but this woman was far shorter and slighter, with the fully shaven head and small geometric forehead tattoo of a Transcendentalist monk.

"Welcome," she said, sweeping up her robes to seat herself at Lin Chong's bedside. "How are you feeling?"

"Much improved," Lin Chong said, and though her throat felt swollen still and her voice scratched, it wasn't difficult to talk. "Where am I?"

"You're on Mount Liang, in the middle of Liangshan Marsh. You're safe here. The waters are too dangerous for anyone who doesn't know the safe paths, and even if someone did risk all to come through, we keep good watch." She gestured to the white-haired woman. "Your doctor is Sister An Daoquan, the Divine Physician. My name is Chao Gai."

An Daoquan smiled at Chao Gai with a bit of impishness and touched her own forehead.

Chao Gai's mouth quirked. "Yes, they call me Heavenly King. It wasn't my own invention, I promise."

"You've saved my life," Lin Chong said to them both. "I'm in your debt."

An Daoquan acknowledged her with a reverent bow of her head, then reached for Lin Chong's wrist and motioned her to open her mouth for an examination.

"Sister An does not speak," Chao Gai explained. "But she hears and understands, and you will soon be used to her ways of communicating. You're in capable hands. Her medicinal skill has not been seen since the days of Hua Tuo."

Lin Chong obeyed the Divine Physician in her examination, and An Daoquan concluded by grasping her hands, another smile wreathing her face. She nodded to Chao Gai and then stood, extending a hand back to Lin Chong.

"That means she's pleased with your progress," Chao Gai said, with a warm smile of her own. "Do you feel you can rise?"

In answer, Lin Chong pushed herself to one elbow, then to sitting. She took the Divine Physician's offered hand and pressed herself up to her feet.

More bandaging shifted against her back, and her soles were still tender, but she did not feel as if she was likely to fall.

An Daoquan gave her hand a pat and then released her. She bowed to both Lin Chong and Chao Gai, then retreated out of the room.

Lin Chong turned to Chao Gai. "I beg your pardon," she said. "But I still don't understand. What is this place? How did you all come to be here?"

"Perhaps it would mean more to explain who we are." Chao Gai offered Lin Chong a supportive arm. "Shall I show you our home?"

In truth, Lin Chong felt strong enough to walk on her own, but she took the proffered elbow anyway in case her strength was only temporary. It was not the first time she'd recovered from wounds.

"This is, in many ways, a refuge," Chao Gai began, slowly leading them to duck out of the structure Lin Chong had woken in. It was solidly built, but rustic, constructed of unfinished logs and beams with tight caulking between them. "You already know Lu Da. Many others here have a brand or a warrant on their person, as you and she do. Sister An, for example, who cured you, is wanted in Jianye Prefecture for the murder of her entire family."

A jolting revelation, even more so for the casualness with which Chao Gai said it. "Did she do it?" Lin Chong asked in a low voice.

Chao Gai made a noncommittal motion with her free hand. "Who knows the truth of it, other than Sister An? I don't think she did. But officials found her in a house soaked in blood, surrounded by untold carnage—parents, siblings, nephews and nieces, and with 'I, An Daoquan, committed this crime' scrawled across the walls in blood."

Lin Chong felt a chill.

"But it's very easy to frame or blame the woman who cannot speak for herself, at least not in any way magistrates have patience to understand. Fortunately, she had saved one of our number from a terrible illness a few months before, and we were able to spirit her here."

You can't render judgment, Lin Chong reminded herself. *You yourself have been tried and convicted, and you confessed in the official court. You've seen now how the law works.*

She'd known before this, if she let the sharp needles of honesty prick at her. Known but had refused to know. She hadn't wanted to admit that injustice was anything more than a rarity, the sad result only when a thousand turns of luck all landed wrong. How could it be the usual way of things? How could civilization be rotten to its core and still function?

"Don't misunderstand," Chao Gai continued, ushering them down onto a wooded path. "Many of us here will freely admit to past criminal guilt. The founders of this place were women who had fallen off the edges of society, and they created their own clan in defiance, to fight for what was theirs. But they welcomed others in dire positions, and many of those have been the truest of haojie—heroes who have run afoul of the courts because they insisted on defending the poor or weak, or challenged the rights of the powerful. Or, sometimes, people who have been abused merely because of their sex. Eventually, many of us who found our way here have espoused a higher calling. We continue to violate laws, yes—by harboring fugitives, by theft or violence—and we are labeled as bandits for it, but our purpose is to aid and protect."

Lin Chong wanted to offer polite support of such ideals, but her throat twisted closed. This was not a type of thinking she had ever condoned. Could ever condone. But where was she to go, if not here? She was a fugitive. If they offered safe harbor here, could she spit on it?

And the person telling her all this—a *monk*—

"How did you come to be here, then?" she asked, hoping the stiffness did not sound like an accusation. After all, Lu Da was a monk too, and had committed murder. But Lu Da had also saved her life, and was now her sworn family—Lin Chong could never condemn her—

Confusion swirled through her.

"Oh, I committed no crimes before joining Liangshan," Chao Gai said. "In fact, I don't make my home here—I split my time between the mountain and my role as chief of the village of Dongxi."

Lin Chong stopped walking. "You're a village chief?"

Chao Gai laughed gently. "It's not as surprising as you're thinking. I am one who 'rides the sixteen winds'—I'm a man as chief of Dongxi, though my people know my eccentricities now and are unbothered that I become a woman elsewhere. I saved Dongxi from an infestation of evil spirits, you see, and they begged me to stay. But I believe I have found my calling, because by also being a part of Liangshan I can ensure great generosity to the people of my village, and my heart is full seeing them prosper. I love my people, every one of them."

"You're a ghost hunter, then? Not a monk?" Lin Chong asked in some amazement. And she had never met anyone of the sixteen winds before—people who changed the gender they lived as, either for a time or permanently. "Perhaps it would have made my life easier, to live as a man," she wondered aloud.

Though if she imagined hiding herself away, the idea was stifling.

"Only if it feels like freedom. If not, it becomes just another kind of cage," Chao Gai said, intuiting the line of Lin Chong's thoughts. "But for me, and for others here, it's the most freeing thing in the world. Yes, others—this place attracts wind riders just as it attracts women, and we welcome all. Now come and see."

Chao Gai tugged Lin Chong to start walking again. The building they had exited was one of a cluster of similar cabins, all built among the fragrant woods of a mountainous slope. Now the path curved up suddenly onto a high crest, overlooking a wide vale of green space.

One that had been turned into a fighting ground.

Lin Chong recognized Lu Da right away, spinning her staff in both hands and huffing as she tried to land a blow on her much tinier opponent, who kept dancing out of the way while twirling double sabers.

"That's Hu Sanniang," Chao Gai said. "Also known as Steel Viridian. Don't be deceived by her size. She could use those swords to take down a dozen men, and she came to us already an expert in the lasso—ah, see there."

Lin Chong had already noted the small woman's skill as she somersaulted away from Lu Da to land in a crouch, the lasso whipping out from her waist with no warning. The throw was expert; it caught Lu Da's staff and tore it from her hands, flinging it aside. Hu Sanniang retrieved her sabers and advanced, but Lu Da wasn't surrendering so easily—she drew her own great two-handed blade and faced off against the spinning steel.

Lin Chong found herself silently rooting for her newly sworn sister. *Don't fall for the spins; that's intimidation only . . . don't let her distract you . . .*

Hu Sanniang's martial arts were lightfooted and fancy, clearly the result of a privileged upbringing. "What crime did she commit?" Lin Chong asked Chao Gai as they watched.

What a strange reality, to wonder that about everyone she met here.

"None," Chao Gai answered. "She's the daughter of wealthy landowners, and when they arranged for her to become a nobleman's concubine she ran away to become an adventurer instead. You can see how spirited she is."

"She came here just to escape a marriage?" And one to a nobleman—most women would be grateful for such luck, even if they were not the first wife. "Did he abuse her?"

"Not to my knowledge," Chao Gai answered. "Some people wish for more choices. I'd think that would seem natural to you, Master Arms Instructor."

She leaned very slightly on Lin Chong's title, sounding amused.

But Lin Chong had found her own way in life because she'd had to. By the time she was an adult, she'd had no one to arrange a marriage or a future for her—and the more she made her own way, the less anyone of status had found her desirable as the head of a household.

She'd always assumed she was already living everyone's second choice. But if given the option between her life and a husband—

It was such an odd question.

"You remind me of a friend of mine," she said wryly, thinking of Lu Junyi. "Who are the other fighters?"

Lu Da and Hu Sanniang still feinted and stabbed, whereas the other three combatants on the field had deteriorated into a brawling free-for-all. Their technique made Lin Chong wince even as she appreciated their enthusiasm. *I could teach them,* she caught herself thinking. *Such natural skill, but they've had no training . . .*

Noblewoman Chai's words floated back to her, muddled through Lin Chong's delirium at the time: the benefits of having a master arms instructor as one of their group. Noblewoman Chai, who was evidently some sort of—of ally, or sympathizer? Or maybe even a part-time bandit also, the same way Chao Gai was simultaneously a literal *village chief.* These successful, privileged people put their lives and positions at risk for—what? The ideals Chao Gai had spoken of, becoming heroes who could defend and protect, steal from the corrupt and gift to the needy?

But could Lin Chong really train a group of—of bandits? *Would* she?

"Those three are the Brothers Ruan," Chao Gai said, her reply breaking up Lin Chong's ruminations. "Second Brother, Fifth Brother, and Seventh Brother. They're not criminals either, but fisherfolk from the other side of the marsh who were taxed to poverty by the local prefect. They were invaluable guides in the building of this sanctuary."

"They're brothers?" Lin Chong asked. They were a distance away, but she could have sworn two of the three wore women's clothes.

"Ah yes, their eldest is a sister, but she proclaims they are the Brothers Ruan regardless," Chao Gai said easily.

"Sixteen winds?" Lin Chong confirmed.

"Sixteen winds, indeed."

That would take some getting used to, but perhaps it made sense in this place that drew in people of such unlikely skills and histories. Lin Chong thought of An Daoquan's extraordinary physician's education, Lu Da's remarkable size and strength—but of course, Chao Gai's point was well taken that Lin Chong herself had an unusual training and history, and she had never lived as a man. She supposed one could never know, unless a person was as open about it as Chao Gai.

"Ah, and here come Wang Lun and Sun Erniang," Chao Gai said, shading her eyes to gaze toward a path that wound down to the other side of the fighting ground. "Wang Lun is the group's founder. She'll want to meet you."

A tall, thin woman hiked down the path next to someone dressed in a mishmash of the brightest colors Lin Chong had ever seen, so garish and clashing they hurt her eyes. But Lin Chong hadn't missed Chao Gai's studied neutrality, or the fact that she'd referred to Wang Lun as a *founder* and not their *leader.*

As the two newcomers arrived at the green, the tall woman's gaze caught on where they stood, and she thrust out an arm to stop her flamboyant companion. Black eyes riveted on them, unblinking.

Wang Lun. Lin Chong fought the urge to shift back a step.

"We'd better go down and greet her," Chao Gai said, unruffled.

Some instinct warned Lin Chong not to take Chao Gai's arm again as they made their way down. It might make no difference to Chao Gai whether a person showed physical weakness, but to Wang Lun . . .

Lin Chong was certain Wang Lun would take notice. Take notice, and use it.

The four of them reached the training ground at about the same time—Wang Lun and her companion on one side, Chao Gai and Lin Chong on the other. As soon as they drew close enough to give perfunctory bows of greeting, Wang Lun assumed charge in a tone that was not *quite* hostile.

"I'm the leader here. They call me the Scholar," she said, and despite the nickname, her accent belied any formal education or extended training. "This one here's the Witch, Sun Erniang. I'm told you were some sort of drill instructor."

"I was a master arms instructor of the Imperial Guard," Lin Chong said cautiously.

"Ha!" Wang Lun said, though it was unclear what was funny. "Show us something, then. Show us *all* how it's done!"

Her words dragged in sarcasm, the edge of her lip turning up in a sneer. Lin Chong wasn't sure what she was supposed to have done to challenge this woman, other than existing here as a successful combat teacher. But she recognized the attitude, having seen it in more than one military officer before she trounced them in demonstration.

Wang Lun considered her a threat. Not a literal threat, but a threat to her own dominance.

Chao Gai laid a hand on Lin Chong's arm. "Sister Lin is still healing," she said. "Let's save the demonstrations for another day, shall we?"

"It's all right." Lin Chong stepped forward, apart from Chao Gai's protection. "What would you like to see?"

If she was to stay here, she'd have to do the same thing she'd always done: Show no weakness. Prove that she would not be trampled beneath anyone's boots. And do it while maintaining perfect respectfulness.

In a way, this all felt so familiar.

Though her stirring of resentment—that was new. Here they stood, so far outside the bounds of normal society, the society that had defined her for so long. Surely that meant something. Shouldn't she have some broader freedom now, to decide her own rules? To reject these sorts of games?

"You think you're so much better than us, eh?" Wang Lun said. She turned to the training ground and barked, "Five on one! Let's see what this 'master arms instructor' really has to offer!"

The two groups left off their tussling and came to disorderly attention. Lu Da and Hu Sanniang had at some point lost their weapons and fallen into hand combat as well, and they took a few chaotic moments to relocate swords and staff and lasso.

When Lu Da saw Lin Chong, an enormous grin split her face. "Sister Lin! You're awake! And you've met Sister Wang. Sister Wang, Master Instructor Lin Chong is amazing, isn't she? She's like a fighting *god*!"

Please stop helping me, Lin Chong begged silently. A blood vessel had begun to pulse at Wang Lun's temple.

"I'm no god," Lin Chong assured everyone. "I have some small skills borne of training; that's all." She turned to Wang Lun. "Five on one, you said? What weapons?"

Wang Lun shrugged as if she didn't care. "Weapons of choice, for all."

Despite making outwardly calm responses, Lin Chong's energy had begun to fade, her back and throat pulsing slightly in something that wasn't pain—but might become pain if she left it long enough. This wasn't the time to show off as she had in that first fight with Lu Da . . . had it been days or weeks or thousands of years ago?

It was possible this wasn't a time she should be fighting at all . . .

"Should the swords be felted?" Chao Gai asked her quietly.

"Unnecessary," Lin Chong said.

She wasn't entirely sure that was the case. If she fainted in the midst of the sparring match and someone inadvertently stabbed her with an unwrapped weapon, she would deserve whatever humiliating epitaph mocked her recklessness. But under ordinary circumstances, she had more than sufficient skill to avoid bloodying another, or to keep from getting bloodied herself. She hadn't sparred with felted weapons in years, save for the occasional more matched bout against some of the highly skilled military ranks.

She was not about to underrate herself now. Not today—when for the first time since that damnable day in White Tiger Hall, she could stand for herself with her own feet and hands.

A muscle in her right calf twitched, almost upsetting her balance.

"Bring me a halberd," she said. A halberd would extend her reach without overtaxing her movement—and she could use the blunted end as a staff, if she ceased to trust her control with the blade.

The haft was pressed into her hands. "You need not do this," Chao Gai said in her ear. "Wang Lun does not have unchecked power here."

"I need the exercise," Lin Chong answered, at a normal volume. She moved away.

But her thoughts beat at her in a growing chorus. *Why push this? Why take the bait? This is ill-considered. Turn away . . .*

No. I've made my decision clear. I can't change my path now.

That wasn't true. It wasn't even the real reason.

The real reason wasn't even deep below the surface, nor complicated. She hadn't been able to fight back against Gao Qiu. She hadn't been able to fight back against the guards. For all her training . . . she had been helpless.

She wasn't going to be helpless again. Ever. Even in a ridiculous test set by a woman who wanted to see her fail.

She paced onto the fighting ground. The grass was soft against her bandaged and wrapped feet. A breeze stirred the light fabric of her robes—when she'd woken she hadn't been wearing her heavier outer robes or coat.

She bowed to the five bandits.

They all bowed back. The Ruan brothers had retrieved cudgels, Lu Da had her staff and sword back, and Hu Sanniang brought one foot behind her into a graceful guard position with her double sabers.

Five against one should not be so bad. To be sure, Lin Chong would have hesitated to face five highly ranked military officers even in her best health, but for all their enthusiasm, these fighters should not issue that level of challenge. She could do this.

Sister Lu is powerful but depends too much on her brute strength. Hu Sanniang—well-trained, but impetuous. The Ruan brothers are the weak side; take them out fast and first.

Lin Chong slid her feet into a fighting stance.

The Ruan brothers yelled lustily and ran at her at once. Perfect. Lin Chong moved to glide in.

But the moment she lifted her foot, something slithered around it and she slammed into the ground on her side. All the breath gusted out of her at once.

That damnable lasso! Lin Chong had not thought Hu Sanniang was close or precise enough.

She spun the halberd and brought it down hard at the same time as she rolled, trusting the blade to bite into the ground and through the line next to where it wrapped her ankle. The slender rope gave way, and Lin Chong came up into a crouch just in time to block inexpert swings by the Ruan brothers' cudgels. She kept low and rolled again, taking herself past them.

Aiya. She should have seen Hu Sanniang move before the throw. Her focus was not what it should be . . .

She changed tactics. The Ruan brothers might have seemed the easier first targets, but they would also get in each other's way—and in the way of Lu Da and Hu Sanniang. Lin Chong knocked aside a strike of Lu Da's staff and took one of Hu Sanniang's sabers on her halberd while spinning past them, putting them between her and the siblings. The Ruan brothers scrambled in confusion, trying to get back close to her without bumping into their two allies, and Lin Chong slipped in a circle, intentionally making it hard for them.

Her breath was beginning to flag. No; she could not tire, not so soon . . .

Hu Sanniang was grinning at the challenge. Up close, she had a pointed, pretty face, her hair swept back under a head wrap. She twirled her sabers in a steady silver whirlwind, enjoying the dance. In contrast, Lu Da's face had gone red and pinched with concentration.

Breathe, Lin Chong ordered herself. *You will not win by stamina, only by timing.*

Her long years of training buttressed her and held her up, embracing her and allowing her to find that meditative concentration.

Although . . . something was different this time. Some other energy twanged through her, something she didn't recognize . . .

She had no time to contemplate it.

Lu Da lunged. Lin Chong dipped to the side, avoiding the heavy staff at the exact instant she needed to dart in the blade of her halberd and tag one of Hu Sanniang's sabers.

The sword tore out of the woman's hand and pinwheeled away. Hu Sanniang scrambled back, looking startled.

The Ruan brothers tried to tumble forward again, but Lin Chong let her footwork lead, and they couldn't reorient fast enough to get her within the reach of their cudgels.

Hu Sanniang leapt and spun with the grace of a gymnast. Lin Chong made the unanticipated reply, sweeping in close and levering the halberd around and down. It came down on top of Hu Sanniang's remaining saber, burying the blade in the dirt.

"Ai!" the small woman cried, letting go and falling out of the way.

Lin Chong twisted to meet Lu Da coming in from the other side. At that moment, two things happened at once.

First, one of Lin Chong's legs gave way.

She knew it was happening only an instant before it did, her borrowed energy finally draining dry. She tried to turn into it, to catch herself in a crouch rather than a fall, but black lights had begun dancing in her vision, and her still-swollen throat seemed to be clogging her entire chest.

Almost at the same time, she felt Lu Da's god's tooth open. And Lin Chong knew she was finished.

Only . . .

Something was different.

She didn't only feel the god's tooth. The energy rushed past her—*through* her—as if she was in the midst of it, as if she were part of it. Somehow as close and real and tangible as the smooth haft of the halberd against her palms.

What in heaven . . .

Time seemed to slow. Lu Da roared forward, swirling the power of the god's tooth up in her staff, and Lin Chong, strangely detached, thought, *Good, that's more control than you showed before.*

And she thrust out a hand.

Even at her full strength, she could not have arrested Lu Da's charge head on, nor grabbed the sixty-jin metal staff to stop her cold.

But that was, somehow, what she did.

Without her hand ever touching the metal—it didn't touch, she *knew* it didn't touch—Lin Chong caught the staff and wrenched it to the side. It spun out of a shocked Lu Da's hands and into Hu Sanniang, smacking her across the shoulder and head. Lin Chong sprang from her crouch—and somehow her legs obeyed her again, somehow she flew up with all the speed of a falcon—and she brought the haft of the halberd hard against Lu Da's chest.

With a squawk, Lu Da tumbled straight into the still-jockeying Ruan brothers, taking all four of them flat to the ground. The Ruan family weren't particularly small, but Lu Da was a sizable woman.

Particularly when Lin Chong had just—had just *flung her like a weapon, what is happening, what did I—*

Lin Chong landed lightly back in a crouch, one knee against the ground. The world seemed to vibrate around her, every object gaining an extra dimension in a dizzying mosaic.

What is happening . . . ?

Usually her years of training would have prevented her from

using her weapon as a support staff, but she found herself driving the butt of the halberd into the grass, hard, to keep herself from keeling to the side. The Ruan brothers were still struggling to push Lu Da off them, and Lu Da was groaning and rubbing her chest. Hu Sanniang stirred from where she had fallen and tried to rise, then slumped back down.

I won.

I won?

Lin Chong's senses buzzed, cutting into her like a thousand small knives. Sensation bounced against memory, recalling the woods, Lu Da's god's tooth smooth in her hand—but she hadn't wielded it this time, so how could . . . ? Besides which, the god's tooth had closed now, and this still wasn't stopping, why wasn't it stopping . . .

She didn't dare to look around behind her. What had the watchers seen? Fights happened fast; had any of them discerned how her hand had not even made contact with Lu Da's staff? Had *Lu Da* registered it? Lu Da already revered Lin Chong's fighting skill; maybe she only thought the move had happened with too much speed for her to see. They had been so close together. She might not have realized.

Chao Gai would have seen. Lin Chong felt certain of that.

A horse whinnied up and to her left.

Lin Chong roused to look up. Riders—people she didn't know or recognize—more women, more bandits, new arrivals who had doubtless seen the end of the fight. The leader at the front of the riders was dark-skinned and statuesque, her coloring and features that of the southwest tribes, with rougher, curling hair that was more brown than black. She radiated a presence, a charisma, that drew the eye—even the way she sat a horse was regal. As if she forced events to bend around her without trying.

She nodded to someone outside Lin Chong's field of view, then wheeled her horse around to take it up the path, the other riders following.

"Impressive," someone brayed.

Wang Lun.

Lin Chong managed to stand, with the taboo help of her halberd pushing her up. Her strangely fractured senses were finally receding, leaving her a drained shell of fatigue. She needed to sit down—or lie down.

Wang Lun strode across the fighting ground toward Lin Chong and the beaten, heaped opponents, her brightly garbed lieutenant scurrying to one side. Chao Gai followed on the other, a little apart from them.

"Most impressive," Wang Lun continued when they neared. "I guess I see why they call you an 'arms instructor.' It's so unfortunate, *most* unfortunate—we're so short on food and supplies here. This place can only support so many people living on the mountain, you know."

"You don't have room for me?" Lin Chong forced her failing lungs to speak. She was fairly certain Wang Lun was flat lying.

"Oh, we're just going to be in such trouble if we keep taking in more mouths," Wang Lun said, gesturing as if that explained everything. "We've got past three dozen folks now, coming in and out. I wish we had a place for someone of your fighting talent, I surely do. Of course, we'll set you up and supply you before you go, and show you all *possible* hospitality."

It wasn't a test to see if I was worthy to stay, Lin Chong realized. *It was a test to see how much of a threat to her I was. And I failed it by winning.*

She can't have me here now.

"Surely our last two supply runs are more than ample to take in someone who is such a good friend of Noblewoman Chai," Chao Gai interjected, in the most reasonable tone of voice in the world. "Remember, Sister Wang? Noblewoman Chai sent her highest recommendation and asked us to welcome Master Instructor Lin as one of our own."

"Oh, and we'd *better* not flout Noblewoman Chai, eh!"

As derisive as Wang Lun sounded, Lin Chong sensed some truth in the words. The "Cyclone" noblewoman had influence here. And she wanted Lin Chong's skills, and had known Wang Lun would feel too challenged . . .

"I wouldn't dream of partaking in your hospitality if I'm not wanted," Lin Chong said, then added impulsively, "If you would give me the grace of a short time to recover my strength, I'll leave and return to Noblewoman Chai. Perhaps she can give me sanctuary."

She hadn't planned to say such a thing. She hadn't even been sure she wanted to stay here at all. But she wasn't about to let this worm of a woman think she had all the power.

She would never let anyone have that position again.

"Aiya," hissed Wang Lun under her breath. "All right, all right, only because you come so highly recommended. But! You must pass our application first, of course."

"Of course," echoed Lin Chong. "What do you require?"

"A head," Wang Lun said. Then she cackled. "Bring me a head. Any one will do! You can go down to the roads—once you're healed, of course—and find a passing traveler. We need to know you're truly with us, you see, and I don't know you."

"I'm not going to murder someone to satisfy your fancy," Lin Chong answered, very quietly. "There; now you know me a little better."

"Ah—if I may," Chao Gai cut in. "I have an alternate proposal. The good Noblewoman Chai has passed us a very valuable tidbit of information, about a shipment of birthday gifts to Grand Chancellor Cai Jing from his son-in-law. A bit more than one turn of the moon from now, all that gold and silver, jewels and pearls—more than a few carts full—will be traveling from Daleng all the way to the capital, and along such dangerous and bandit-infested roads! Our clever colleague Wu Yong has an excellent plan to relieve the couriers of their burden, and I thought I might lead a small number of us to acquire these presents and make our own gifts of them instead. I think Cai Jing would be delighted to know his birthday treasures are going to the very people his policies beat so much taxation from."

Wang Lun crossed her arms. "Very well. Do it. What do you need this arms instructor for?"

"I think Master Instructor Lin would serve admirably as one of this team, and it would be a prime opportunity to bring you such an 'application'—only we'll be targeting those who work in compliance with Cai Jing's whims, rather than any innocent traveler. I daresay it is this that bothers Lin Chong's mind so."

Wang Lun looked between them both, and then, apparently unable to think of any objection, she spat on the ground. It was aimed off to the side—not at Lin Chong's feet, exactly—but the sentiment was clear.

"Run your little operation," she said to Chao Gai. "I expect results. When you're done I'd better be swimming in gold and pearls."

Chao Gai inclined her head slightly. Wang Lun turned on her heel and walked away, sweeping her lieutenant along with her.

As soon as they were out of sight, Lin Chong let herself collapse against the halberd's haft. She wasn't sure she could have prevented it from happening if she'd tried. Chao Gai moved hastily to take her arm.

"Cai Jing?" Lin Chong said to her weakly. "You're going after the Grand Chancellor's gold? And you want me to help you." She'd only met Chancellor Cai in passing, and been glad that was the extent of it. Cai Jing was . . . powerful, untouchable, nearly on the level of the Emperor himself. Like a god or demon beast from legend.

"Who better to steal from?" Chao Gai asked brightly.

Lin Chong did not know how to answer that. Except for one singular certainty. "I'm not going to murder someone."

"Oh, don't be too concerned. Either one of us will kill someone in the midst of things and we'll give you the head to toss at Wang Lun's feet, or, more likely, the plan will go off without a hitch, there'll be no heads at all, and she'll be flush with so much gold she won't notice."

Lin Chong had no idea how to respond to that, either. Any of it. Perhaps it was just talk. If not . . .

If not, she had no room in her head for it now anyway. The enormity of it would keep, for later, in private, when she could think.

On the ground, Lu Da rolled over with a groan, and the youngest Ruan brother finally got his leg free and leapt to his feet. "That was a good fight, Sister Lin. You're a tiger! Eh, I think I should get the Divine Physician down here, shouldn't I?"

"I don't need—" started Lin Chong.

"He means for us," moaned Lu Da. "Heartless fighting god sister of mine! You've quite bruised me, again. If you weren't my sister I would thrash you."

Despite everything, Lin Chong couldn't help a small smile. "You've tried. Twice."

Though the second time . . . the second time should have worked.

She wanted to ask Chao Gai about it. A Transcendentalist-trained ghost hunter, surely she might know something . . . The afterimage of it all still danced through Lin Chong's senses, like an echo that bounced off every surface over and over, forever intensifying.

But she didn't want to speak of this in front of the others, even Lu Da. Best to let them think they hadn't seen anything strange.

Besides, she needed to lie down.

"I'll take you back up to your room," Chao Gai said, as if she could read minds—although holding up half of Lin Chong's weight probably gave it away.

"Thank you," Lin Chong murmured.

"However . . . if you have a little strength left, Song Jiang wants to see you."

Lin Chong blinked.

And blinked again.

The world stayed the same: fuzzy and increasingly bizarre but tactile and real. She wasn't dreaming.

The woman on horseback . . .

"Song Jiang the *poet*?" she croaked. "Song Jiang the famous poet is . . . here?"

CHAPTER 8

Chao Gai took Lin Chong up a different path to a building that was structured like a low meeting hall. Outside the door stood a broad and compact woman who looked like she could punch her head through stone, in both musculature and expression.

She had been another one of the riders, Lin Chong remembered. She had the shoulders of a blacksmith and skin even darker than the leader she'd been riding with, her complexion verging on an unusual reddish black and her eyes fierce and suspicious. Thrust in her belt were double battleaxes more than half as tall as she was, thick and heavy and so well-honed their edges winked in the sun.

The woman scowled at them. "What business do you have with Sister Song?"

"This is Master Arms Instructor Lin Chong," Chao Gai said, with the same social grace she might have used over tea. "Sister Lin, this is Li Kui, otherwise known as the Iron Whirlwind. The origin of that nickname will become clear the moment you see her with those axes."

Li Kui only scowled more deeply. "I asked what you cunt-eaters want here. Are you going to answer or not?"

"Sister Li is very protective," Chao Gai said to Lin Chong with a smile. She turned back to Li Kui. "Sister Song wished Lin Chong to come for a meeting as soon as her recovering health allowed."

Li Kui acted as if she were holding back vomit, but she stepped aside.

Inside the building, a small group sat in conference, though they'd left the seat of highest status empty—the one facing the entrance. A short moment of confusion followed; Chao Gai tried to usher Lin Chong to sit at the head of the meeting but Lin Chong kept trying to refuse until she realized that if she did not sit she was likely to fall where she stood.

She did get up again to bow to Song Jiang and the others. She recognized An Daoquan the physician, as well as two other people she didn't know, and, of course, the brown-skinned woman who'd led the arriving riders, the one who *must* be Song Jiang. Between her southwestern features and that shocking magnetism—Lin Chong had heard of how the poet Song Jiang riveted audiences, had heard it called a phenomenon, a force of nature, the talent of fifty generations. And as if such a reputation needed anything added to it, nobody could speak of Song Jiang without mentioning her generosity, her philanthropy, the way she had led networks to aid poor women or those used ill by their husbands; the way she bought out the contracts of prostitutes and found them positions as domestics or hired them as her own stewards . . . the way she followed Benevolence to such an enlightened degree that people swore she had grown the head of a phoenix and could cure illness or poverty with one touch.

Lin Chong rather doubted that last bit.

But when Song Jiang had disappeared some months ago, the people of the capital had gossiped on little else. Murdered, some said; others claimed she was guilty of great crimes and the Empire had made her disappear to spare her fame the indignity of a trial. Still others declared with certainty that she had ascended to immortality and was living as a god. Each guess more outlandish than the last.

But now seeing the woman up close—in person—Song Jiang was seated next to a window, the square of light limning her hair and clothes as if it could not help but highlight her, and she was somehow hard to look away from in a way that barely felt real. People's reactions and exaggerations began to seem as if they had understated the case.

Lin Chong also caught herself thinking, with a suddenness that socked her in the chest, about her own mother, who also had the coloring of a birth among the southwest tribes. There the resemblance ended, and Lin Chong's memory of her mother was so long ago now as to be faded and washed out like a painting left in the rain, but it was a treasured one. Lin Chong herself had been born with her father's features and family name, and thus it fell out that she most often thought of her mother now with a painful jolt when unknowing residents of the capital took jabs at the southwest in her presence. How many times had she heard it proclaimed—falsely, so falsely!—that the southwest provinces were not truly loyal citizens of the Empire, or that all who came from there were unsophisticated dullards. It was somehow . . . beautiful . . . to think of her mother now, when seeing *Song Jiang.*

She bowed to the poet first and last and deepest.

"You must be Song Jiang, famed across the forty-five prefectures. The one they call the Empire's Dark Daughter—the stories of your talents are innumerable."

"I am," Song Jiang said, and even the cadence of her voice was music. "Though I ask you not to use that nickname. I don't prefer it."

Lin Chong bowed her head. "My apologies. They also call you Spring Rain, I've heard? For the way you're called upon to settle conflicts and are known to give away all your fortune to those in need—I beg your pardon, I've heard so much of your reputation . . ."

Perhaps it was her fatigue, but her tongue was rambling on far more than it usually would. She forced herself to silence.

Song Jiang laughed lightly. "I'm nothing but a poet. A woman of low talents. Let me introduce Wu Yong, our Tactician, and Jiang Jing, whom we call the Mathematic for her wizardry with any sort of numbers or accounting. And of course you have met Chao Gai and our physician An Daoquan."

Lin Chong's mind was becoming rather full of her new acquaintances' names and persons, but she nodded to them all and did her best to fix them in her memory. As an arms instructor, she could remember vast numbers of students, but only as long as she had seen them fight—already she was automatically tagging these Liangshan rebels with their weapons and martial styles. Hu Sanniang, of the double sabers and lasso; Li Kui, with her heavy battleaxes; the Ruan brothers, at home with fists and cudgels . . .

An Daoquan made a motion to Song Jiang. Lin Chong almost missed it—the white-haired physician's hands always seemed to be moving, spinning against each other. But the intentionality of this gesture became clear when the others in the room shifted to her, reacting as if she had spoken aloud.

"Yes, thank you," Song Jiang said, and turned back to Lin Chong. "Sister An is reminding me that you still need much rest to convalesce properly, so I shall keep this conference short. I saw that you met Wang Lun on the training ground."

The question sent up a note of caution in Lin Chong, shaking her from her strange enchantment. "Yes," she answered.

"Wang Lun founded this group here at Liangshan," Song Jiang said. "The initial band was of some female rogues wanted by the law. Most of them were killed in earlier skirmishes—we have much more effective methods now, with the clever talents of people like our Tactician." She nodded toward the one called Wu Yong. "Now we fight, but we fight astutely. As time went on, and those of us you see here became drawn to this idea of a group of brigands who were a different sort from scurrilous highwaymen . . . whether we came here by circumstance or purpose, we have also brought a different sort of ambition."

"And what ambition is that?" Lin Chong asked.

"Justice."

When Song Jiang said it, the word was the clarion call of transcendence.

"Chao Gai mentioned as much," Lin Chong managed.

"I shall be open with you, Master Instructor Lin. You could be quite helpful to us."

"My talents as a teacher are only moderate . . ." Lin Chong began automatically.

"You misunderstand. Your talents at instruction are prodigious, I'm told, and I'm sure your wits are sharp enough to understand already how someone of your skills could help us do great good in the Empire. But you could also be of help to us as a woman of class and discipline, as a role model for the more . . . unrefined of our number."

An ugly feeling crawled up Lin Chong's spine. Especially having had her mother come so recently to mind . . .

Her mother who was poor. Her father who was clanless, and had no station.

"I'm afraid you mistake me," she said. The words echoed stiffly in her ears. "I'm merely a scholar-official. I have no claim to either nobility or prestige."

Song Jiang waved a hand. "You've passed the Imperial exams. That's enough. Let's be candid, Sister Lin. Our fighting strength here is great and growing, but some of that strength requires a firm hand to guide it. One Wang Lun does not provide."

Lin Chong thought of Lu Da. Despite the failed monk's impulsiveness, she had the best heart of anyone Lin Chong had met in a long time.

Even if she killed someone?

Even if she killed someone again, with no remorse, in front of you? And how many more, as one of these strange brigands? Even knowing that?

The answer was yes. This smaller group with upper-class postures and scholarly accents, with the education of ghost hunter and poet, mathematician and physician—they claimed moral superiority, but all they had was high station. Lin Chong might share their opinion of Wang Lun—though her mouth soured at them so readily blackening their leader's name to a newcomer—but if they were serious about their stance as bringers of justice, then members like Lu Da should have been in this room too. Whether or not those members cussed or slurped their food or could read or write or play the lute.

"You're speaking of people like your loyal sister at the door," Lin Chong said, keeping her voice mild. The vulgar Iron Whirlwind and her battleaxes must have been told to remain outside, not truly welcome in this group she was so clearly aligned with. "They're not children to be molded."

Song Jiang's eyes narrowed. "You talk of Li Kui. I understand your suspicions of us, that we judge too harshly or too quickly considering we're in this same place ourselves. Let me lay it out for you:

Li Kui is *exactly* who I mean. Sister Li enjoys killing. She kills for fun, because it gives her joy and pleasure—or simply because she hasn't killed anyone in longer than she prefers. She would murder old uncles, young children; it makes no difference. But in pledging her loyalty to *me*—it makes her a weapon aimed only at the villainous. It makes her *better.* Haojie, it makes her a hero."

Lin Chong had no answer for that, nor for Song Jiang addressing her in a manner both uncomfortably lionizing and uncomfortably familiar. Beads of cold sweat had begun collecting beneath her bandages.

"Sun Erniang, whom you met today—Wang Lun's lieutenant, known as the Witch? She was worse. She and her husband—who joined us as well, until his death—they owned a black tavern."

No. Lin Chong had heard of such places . . . but they were only rumors . . .

"Yes," Song Jiang continued. "They murdered travelers to cook the flesh into their soups and steamed buns, which they sold to the next people who happened along. Not everybody here is a chivalrous crusader . . . but everyone here *can* be. With the right guidance. And we want to continue shaping ourselves into a place that wholly provides it."

Lin Chong unstuck her tongue in a mouth that had gone dry. "What do you want from me, then?"

Song Jiang smiled. "Only your support. Act with us to make Liangshan unimpeachable, in your role as an arms instructor. We will help so very many lives, the Empire willing."

The Empire willing . . . the strangeness of that common expression struck Lin Chong—for Song Jiang to be using it here, about *this* . . . when the Empire would in all literal sense be doing everything it could to arrest and condemn them all . . .

Is this who I am now? Lin Chong wondered. *A traitor? A traitor who trains killers and cannibals?*

As if Song Jiang knew her thoughts, the other woman said, "We are all loyal to the Empire here, and the Emperor. All of us. We fight to improve the Empire *because of our love for it.*"

That sounded like a rationalization to Lin Chong.

But a beautiful one. One she wanted to let herself believe: that she could stand up and fight, and still call herself loyal.

An Daoquan made another gesture at the rest, presumably reminding them again of Lin Chong's physical condition, because Song Jiang nodded at her and stood to bow. "I've taken you from your rest too long, Master Instructor. Please think on what I've said here. I think we can do great good together."

Lin Chong allowed Chao Gai to come help her up, and had enough wits to murmur polite, rote farewell exchanges. But before they reached the door, she paused and turned back to Song Jiang.

"If I may ask," she said, "how did *you* come to be here?"

"I killed my husband," Song Jiang answered, very calmly.

Scattered thoughts collided in Lin Chong's head—then how could Song Jiang think she was *better*; weren't they all one and the same, all criminals here—but that was also all mixed in with shocked disbelief because this woman was still *Song Jiang* and she had done *what*?

"It is not impolite to ask me why," Song Jiang said, when Lin Chong had hesitated for more than a moment.

"Why, then?"

"For all the reasons husbands so frequently need killing. But the law does not recognize a wife's rights here, alas." Song Jiang smiled slightly, as if they shared a private joke. "Fortunately, I had many friends, and was an ally to the Liangshan heroes already. We are growing in members across the Empire all the time, beyond even what you see here."

Like the noblewoman and the innkeeper, the Cyclone and the Crocodile. The nicknames seemed to take on new significance, the secret monikers of heroes in the night. Song Jiang—Spring Rain—had doubtless been with the Liangshan bandits for years, and nobody had known. Her audiences and fans had only seen how she'd helped people.

Lin Chong was not sure her shaky lightheadedness was only from her physical ailments.

CHAPTER 9

"This is to be where you conduct your research."

In a wide, low building, deep in the central district of the inner city of Bianliang, Lu Junyi looked around cautiously. The space was large enough to be almost cavernous, with long counters and shelves that some quiet, cowed servants were in the midst of stocking with paper, ink, equipment, and countless packets of chemicals. Lu Junyi's heart did a funny little flip—she had no doubt that every mineral formula she'd ever want to reach for was represented on these shelves.

And on some of the counters—large, rough-cut tonnage of what was unmistakably scholar's stone. Even its rough-hewn state could not produce smooth blocks of it. Instead, the holes and whorls and fantastical twists, the lace-like porous veils as if the stone had frozen in barely connected droplets, all combined to make the ore seem to writhe from the chunks as if alive.

Lu Junyi could not help but feel herself bend both toward and away from it. Scholar's stone. A material with untold potential locked beneath its volatility. Some even opined that god's teeth were not truly left by the gods, but merely scholar's stone refined by some lost art. As found in nature, however, it was inert, and could be mined, cut, or chiseled, such that sculptures showcasing its wild and gravity-defying form dotted many a garden of the rich. The fantastic shapes could be coaxed by artists to curve into benches and gates so the wealthy could lounge safely adjacent to power.

Safely . . . or so they thought. Even untouched, scholar's stone was the accused cause of many an otherworldly occurrence. Lu Junyi herself had always scoffed at such tales as merely the fears of the superstitious masses. Scholar's stone only became perilous when altered by more than a tool—burnt, or exposed to an apothecary's caustic acids, or touched by the material-bending scholar's skills of a high-level monk . . . to fear otherwise was ignorance; everyone knew this.

Until Cai Jing had begun sharing his collection of scrolls on the matter. In the two weeks since he'd recruited her—conscripted her—Lu Junyi had swiftly fallen into a massive quicksand of study, so extensive and absorbing that it often kept her up until near dawn. Far more research had been done on scholar's stone than Lu Junyi had ever known, mostly by monks in obscure monasteries over the years, and most of it far more chilling than the common knowledge.

Though most of the scrolls exploring the stone's deeper properties cut off with no completion. That told its own tale of what had befallen their authors.

Even the quests rich nobles sent out for, to retrieve chunks of it for garden decoration . . . it turned out those journeys had ended in unexplained calamity as often as they had succeeded. Such aesthetics were not only a wealthy whim, then—but a potential death sentence for whatever servants were unlucky enough to be charged with the pursuit. Lu Junyi hadn't known. She had always avoided the type of people likely to insist on such reckless vanity.

What perilous power of scholar's stone did Cai Jing seek?

She had wondered, at first, why the Chancellor hadn't assigned this task to one of the academies, the Imperial shuyuan that housed the Empire's finest scholars outside of monasteries. The shuyuan were the beating hearts of innovation within the Empire, scholars head-deep in ink and scrolls, building astrolabes and water clocks and great chain-driven windlasses, every one of their advancements helping to march the Empire into the future. Instead, however, Cai Jing had drafted prestigious scholars and monks *out* of their positions at the academies and monasteries, grouping them with lone eccentrics—like her—all ordered to dedicate themselves to this research toward some future yet-unrevealed goal.

The mystery itself drew her in, almost as much as the rigor of the scrolls she'd been ordered to study. Whatever the Chancellor wished of them, he considered it to be of the highest secrecy. This very building was proof of that, abandoned of any other use, repurposed for their needs alone with thick lines of Imperial Guardsmen standing watch outside. A place like this would have been chosen precisely because it was not one of the busy and frequented Imperial academies. The far distance from any possible prying eyes reinforced just how furtive the Chancellor meant this to be.

Not that it needed reinforcing, after Cai Jing's frequent and casual reminders that execution would be the immediate consequence if anyone divulged a hint of what he passed to them to study.

Scholar's stone—and high-energy materials. Either one an area fraught with danger on its own, let alone combining them.

On the other hand, Lu Junyi had never in her life had such an opportunity to explore this level of curiosity. She stood on the very edge of discovery, terrain no one had yet dared tread . . .

For good reason! Jia's voice echoed in the back of her head, along with a hot needle of guilt. Lu Junyi's determination to make the best of her precarious situation—to treat it as opportunity—had crashed back to earth after only a short stint of poring over information day and night locked in her home study. For the first few precious days she'd pushed aside any of her own anxiety, her own anger, the helplessness of being drafted this way—and for a time she'd managed to shove it behind a wall, mostly, and see the delicate blossoms of wonder among the spikes. This work invigorated every part of her mind, energized her, expanded every possibility.

Besides, despite his initial recruitment tactics, spending more time with the Chancellor had revealed he was not the specter of mercilessness she'd expected. Instead he was practical, and polite, and listened to her when she spoke. This didn't have to feel like feeble forced labor, she told herself. This research might prove high in peril—but potentially also high in reward . . .

Maybe even something she would have chosen to pursue, had she been offered the choice.

She'd been shoved off that precious knife's edge of optimism by Jia's constant fretting.

Jia's disapproval.

Jia's resentment.

Jia's *fear.*

Jia did not even know the danger of *what* Lu Junyi studied. The screaming jeopardy of the precipitous political position she'd been thrown into was enough.

"What other answer do you think I had?" Lu Junyi had finally demanded. "Would you have me go to the Chancellor and refuse? I'll buy you a gilded box to put my head in."

"Don't make jokes!" Jia had sounded close to a sob. "You can at least stop being happy about it—"

"Oh, so you agree I daren't refuse but you'd have me live in dread and panic."

"I want you to live in *caution*! And I want you to *live*. How, how can you act like this should be nothing to me?"

She did start crying then. Lu Junyi had never been able to maintain an argument when Jia was in tears. She took the other woman in her arms, stroked her liquid silk hair, the flushed skin of her cheek and neck. Pressed their foreheads together, their bodies one against the other, inhaling the peach blossom scent of her, until Jia's tears slowed.

"I thought you'd be proud," Lu Junyi murmured. "You and your great love for the Emperor and all his officials—"

She'd meant it to be a tease; their political differences a longstanding point of departure. But Jia made a noise and pushed away. "You ought to sew your mouth shut, the things you say about the Empire. Of course I love the Emperor, may he live forever. With my whole heart, and always will, as you should too—"

"Then serving him isn't a bad thing," Lu Junyi said. This time she kept her tone serious. Gentle. "Even—even if I should die for it, being conscripted by the Empire—you know who I am and it would never be my first choice, but with your love for the Emperor, can you see it as that? Please? That if I should die in service, it will be—it can be something proud?" She clenched her jaw on more words. She needed—heaven and earth, she *needed* Jia to stop worrying at her. She could not maintain strength for them both.

Not while she lived under an axe that hung upon a single silk thread of Cai Jing's whim. Not when she so strongly suspected that this experimentation itself, once they started, might very well be her last act, a grasp at hubristic progress.

Jia wiped at her eyes and turned her face away. "And the best result is that you join the Imperial Court," she whispered. "We promised . . . we *promised* we would never marry."

Aiya. Of course. How could Lu Junyi not have realized.

She could do nothing then but take Jia in her arms again. She was not naive enough to think the dangled offer of Emperor's concubine was at all likely, or that she would be allowed to decline if the offer ever *was* put before her. But nor could she ignore the power of such a possibility.

The power to be elevated to the Court. To wield political influence beyond her wildest imaginings. The chance to push for reformations she'd only dreamed about, bring progress and change to the Empire from *within*.

She could not pretend she would want to refuse such a thing.

She shouldn't have mentioned it to Jia. She'd been thinking of it as one of the brighter spots of this demon's choice she'd been forced into. But to Jia . . .

It wasn't uncommon for a wealthy unmarried person to take a house companion of the same sex, though it *was* uncommon for such an arrangement to last more than a short time, and even less common for that house companion to be of a similar social class—as Jia was—instead of someone far unequal in wealth and power. More usually a house companion might be a well-bred but economically struggling young person who needed a start in life, and would be given a generous gift when their more monied partner did what everyone did and moved on to join in a proper marriage contract. House companions weren't entirely unheard of in married households, but their existence in such a structured unit was somewhat frowned upon, the same way a man might be frowned upon for taking too many concubines.

Jia was not a rebel the way Lu Junyi was, in either action or opinion. She was proper, and traditional, and beautiful, and had been destined for a wealthy husband and a household of her own to run. Her family had not gone so far as to drag her into a marriage contract by force, as they could have. Instead they'd merely disowned her. In one stroke she had lost parents, kindred, wealth, and family name.

No one *chose* to remain unmarried as another wealthy woman's house companion when a contract with a proper husband was available instead.

It was the only time Jia had ever turned aside society's expectations for her. But what a turn.

Lu Junyi never should have mentioned Cai Jing's implied offer. It was more unlikely than a blood moon anyway. And while Jia must know she would be well taken care of if their arrangement ever ended, that was not the reason they'd whispered mutual promises never to take a husband.

Lu Junyi could not pretend such a break wouldn't destroy parts of her own souls either, deep within her where she wasn't as strong as she liked to believe.

So Lu Junyi tried, after that, to be more sensitive to Jia's feelings. Not showing any delight at the vast stores of knowledge and resources that had suddenly been made available to her, the scholarly scrolls she might have only dreamed of gaining access to, the charts of numerical analysis that seemed to be working out with breathtaking possibility under her brush strokes.

But she'd also stopped sharing the fears. The ones she was only able to ignore when she could wall them away in her heart. Because when she saw them reflected in Jia's eyes—when Jia spiraled to such high anxiety and panic that it was Lu Junyi who had to comfort her . . .

The tension between them had begun to feel like ill-fitting roof tiles, never meeting, always fractured.

Some part of Lu Junyi was secretly relieved that she was about to have an official research space to escape to rather than her home study.

As for Chancellor Cai Jing . . . she could not forget how he could extinguish her life with no more than a turn of his palm. But he'd also treated her with nothing but kindness: the airs of a gentleman, and the wit of a scholar. He could grasp most of what she explained, and during several of their conversations the time had flown quickly, long into the night as he encouraged her detailed discussions of the possible theory.

Strangely easy to forget how frequently he threatened her with execution.

"If you see any changes that would speed you in your work, you need only ask," Cai Jing said, trailing beringed fingers down one of the countertops as they walked slowly through the new research space. He reminded Lu Junyi of an amicable old uncle. "The courtyards to the rear are being fitted with furnaces and you will have access to penal workers trained in their use, for any annealing steps you would like to perform. The courtyards also have ample space for the manufacture and testing of incendiary materials. Do try not to maim anyone important."

Unsettling, that the Chancellor seemed to be addressing her as if she had unbridled power here. She had twice now met Shen Kuo, the scholar who was to oversee them all—a bit aloof, but he'd begun listening to her more once she began speaking numbers instead of words. She weighed her response, trying to determine the most politic one.

"The space here is more than suitable," she said sincerely. "I doubt we are missing any needed materials, but if we are, I shall make sure you are informed. I'll defer to Scholar Shen in any large change, of course, but I feel sure he will be just as pleased and thankful."

"Oh, I had him killed this morning," Cai Jing said, leaning over a servant's shoulder to read herb and mineral labels.

Lu Junyi's step stuttered. Her skin tightened all over her body, as if she'd suddenly had all the liquid sucked out of her.

"I—I didn't know, Grand Chancellor."

"Yes, it turns out he'd already begun falsifying numbers in his briefings to me. He'd taken it upon himself to decide no one should be meddling in these areas of research, not even the Empire, long may it prosper. Pure treason."

Lu Junyi could not have said that such thoughts hadn't crossed her own mind, once or twice. She struggled to keep any expression off her face.

Cai Jing's beetle-black eyes swung to fasten on her. "*You* didn't know anything about his traitorous mathematics, did you?"

"No, Grand Chancellor. He had only taken summaries from me so far, to assess my understandings of the base knowledge . . ." She'd thought the man biased against her input, as a woman. The accusation felt uncharitable now. "He'd spoken to me very little as yet."

"Good."

"May I ask—" Lu Junyi couldn't help it; her breath hitched. "Ah—may I ask, who will be overseeing our work going forward?"

"Yes. That's a problem." Cai Jing considered her. "For one who claims to be nothing more than curious literati, your understanding of the specialized knowledge in this study appears to be quickly outstripping the other men I have recruited. By some large measure."

Lu Junyi was suddenly dizzy, as if she had drunk too much fragrant wine.

"Your service to the Empire just increased," Cai Jing said. "Be warned. I shall now consider the success or failure of this project to be on your head alone."

"Grand Chancellor. It is a great—but I'm not—" Lu Junyi was having trouble speaking. "I do not have—"

"It's done," Cai Jing said. "Now. What do you think of your new research space? Does it need any changes?"

This is a dream, Lu Junyi thought dazedly. Only she wasn't sure whether or not it was a nightmare.

"It's—it's excellent," she managed. "No changes needed . . ."

"I'll want your detailed assessments of the rest of the men," Cai Jing went on. "If Scholar Shen had his hooks in any of them, you will be able to tell from their calculations, correct? If so you are to report it to me immediately. I also expect to be notified if any of them are not up to the necessary standards for our work. Have no qualms of speaking to me freely about any adjustments that must be made."

"And if any of them are, ah, not up to standard?" Lu Junyi asked faintly. "What will happen?"

"They'll be sent home, with the Empire's thanks and a warning never to speak of what they studied here. Only traitors are executed, Lady Lu."

She wasn't certain whether she felt relief at that. No—definitely not relief.

"What *will* merit immediate execution of your team and their families and households is if any whisper of our true purpose becomes known." Cai Jing's tone could have been one used to discuss flowers in a garden. "I have read more than your academic circulars, Lady Lu. You have an unfortunate propensity for challenging your betters."

Jia's face flashed through Lu Junyi's mind, threatened here so casually—"I promise, Honorable Grand Chancellor, I have kept the strictest confidentiality—"

"Do not interrupt me."

Lu Junyi stopped speaking. Nearly stopped breathing. She felt herself swaying slightly where she stood.

"I wish you to continue in this propensity of yours, but channeled only toward myself. If you need information or materials, I expect you to request them. If you need more workers, I expect you to make it known. If you believe a different path is necessary for success, I expect you to make that case. To me, and only to me. With the attendant respect, of course. I have no patience for obeisance eclipsing truth. However, if your head wanders toward opining on these subjects outside of what we do here, I will know, and it will be your ruin. Do you understand?"

Lu Junyi wet her lips. Her voice was faint, a whiff of wind struggling to rustle against reeds. "Yes, Grand Chancellor. I understand."

"Good. In that case, it is time to apprise you of our true purpose here."

Lu Junyi swallowed. The dizziness had only increased.

Cai Jing led her out of the room and to an inner sanctum with Guardsmen three deep at the door, even beyond the lines of officers outside. They made no motion as Cai Jing and Lu Junyi stepped through.

"I have handpicked the guards," Cai Jing informed her, once they had passed into the room. "Though they do not know what they protect, only its importance. You alone will have access to this room. I had this brought here earlier today."

His hand had come down on an ornate chest, carved wood and gold with a heavy lock. A bronze key fell to dangle from within his sleeve.

"Earlier this year, the monks at Anfeng Monastery were experimenting with incendiary powders in rocketry. There was a mishap. The monastery was leveled, and forty-seven monks killed."

Lu Junyi stifled a gasp. *Oh, Benevolence . . .*

"They did not realize, you see, that part of their blast had caught some undiscovered scholar's stone."

Lu Junyi tried to steady herself, to absorb this information.

The consequences must have been unfathomable. Incendiary powders already tripped so far past any safe understanding—some thought they tore cracks in reality the same way the god's teeth did, to release that amount of energy. Opinions varied as to whether this meant they merited further examination or were a demon's tool that no man should attempt to grasp, lest humans tempt their own destruction.

Such a release of energies in proximity to scholar's stone . . .

Part of Lu Junyi was surprised only forty-seven people had died.

"It's likely that most of the scholar's stone was destroyed in the blast," Cai Jing continued calmly. "However, among the debris were found thirteen small pieces still intact. Unusually, they seemed to have been . . . changed." The key dangling from his sleeve fell into his hand, and he slid it into the lock on the ornate chest. "Nine of those pieces still exist, and three have been brought here."

He raised the lid.

Inside, on a bed of plush, rich fabric, lay three chips of polished stone.

Lu Junyi raised a hand toward them, but only partway. Was she imagining it, or did the air vibrate above them?

"They put me in the mind of . . ." The thought felt too foolish to finish.

"God's teeth?" Cai Jing said. "Yes, more than you know. It was shortly discovered that whatever transmutation had occurred, they function very like god's teeth."

This time Lu Junyi could not help the sharp intake of breath. "That would mean—"

If new god's teeth could be created—

"Precisely," Cai Jing said. "You see the import here. Unfortunately, gaining this knowledge is what lost us four of the pieces, along with the minds and souls of four people."

"The bonding between the god's tooth and person—it didn't work as it should?" Lu Junyi guessed. The possible outcomes of such a failure were beyond imagining. Aiya, those poor people.

"It worked exactly as it should," Cai Jing answered, his voice silk. "Until the shards devoured them from the inside. It seems there is still a problem with . . . stability."

"That's what you wish of us." It was the only conclusion. "To find some way of controlling and neutralizing the instability . . ." The task towered in her head. Could it even be done?

"That, and to replicate the feat." The Chancellor dropped the lid of the chest, closing away its staggering secret. "Carefully."

Cai Jing wanted to be able to manufacture god's teeth out of scholar's stone at will.

How that would change the Empire. How that would change everything. Lu Junyi could not even imagine . . .

What a discovery it would be. For the ages.

"Save the Emperor himself, no one outside of this room knows the details of what I have just divulged to you," Cai Jing warned softly. "No one alive, that is. I had all the records of Anfeng destroyed. You can imagine what violence such a temptation could bring, before its use has been properly organized."

She very well could.

In the back of her mind, Lu Junyi was aware that her own opinions about how such an invention should be handled would likely not match the Chancellor's. But . . . that could not block a technological step that was ripe to so fundamentally change the world. Even Cai Jing had no way of predicting if his carefully laid plans would hold up to the reality, and Lu Junyi could not know either. This would be too large, too uncontrollable a change . . .

If it worked.

If it worked, Lu Junyi herself would carry the secrets of how within her head.

Even more dangerous. Even more worth the chase.

Cai Jing turned to sweep back out of the room, and Lu Junyi followed, her mind a scramble, her skin numb.

"Now that you know, you understand the study I have required of you," Cai Jing said. "Sadly, I have been disappointed in my other recruited scholars thus far. The Empire faces a great threat from beyond its borders. We must have the most learned minds in the Empire on this task—if you know of anyone else like yourself, who may have been passed over, tell me their names and they will be yours."

Lu Junyi hesitated.

"You have something on your mind," Cai Jing said. "Speak."

Damn the man and his otherworldly perceptions. Lu Junyi did not wear her heart on her face, she knew she didn't. Somehow he always seemed to know too much.

In truth, Lu Junyi had taken note of how many of the buried

treatises provided by Cai Jing bore the name of Ling Zhen. Ling Zhen, the merry old scholar who had shown up at her salons a half-dozen times or more, sometimes with his wife Fan Rui. Ling Zhen, with his gleeful, infectious delight at anything that would produce a spark or a noise, despite its dangers.

Ling Zhen, who'd been arrested months ago—on charges of suspected sedition, Lu Junyi had heard, a report she could not square with the old man's grinning mischievousness. She'd read some of his work before—found it fascinating—but until now, she'd had no idea of the depths of his discoveries.

She'd also begun to notice just how often his wife was mentioned in his notes. Fan Rui was an unlikely person herself, a Renxia priestess of some accomplishment, though in front of Lu Junyi she'd never shown any of the ruder tendencies people liked to ascribe to the Renxia. Except perhaps a more biting if rarely deployed wit.

Reading between the lines of Ling Zhen's notes, it had struck Lu Junyi that he spoke of his wife as an intellectual equal. A research partner. Many a mention was made about her particular scholar's skills in alchemy, for which she had apparently gained some renown, and he would regularly consult with her on his materials research.

The rumors said that Fan Rui, too, had been imprisoned by the Empire, along with her husband.

Lu Junyi chose her approach carefully. "Grand Chancellor, an idea caught at me while studying the materials as you ordered. I could not help but notice that many were by a man—and his wife, I believe—whom I knew in passing. I have been impressed with their acuity of scholarship in the past. However . . ."

Cai Jing waited, letting her words hang, his drooping white eyebrows drawing together fiercely. "You speak of the scholar Ling Zhen. And his wife, I presume."

Lu Junyi hesitated. "I do, Grand Chancellor. I am aware that they are . . . not in the good graces of the Empire. Forgive me, I only mention their names because I know how much they could help with this process, how deep their knowledge . . ."

She stuttered to silence under the Chancellor's ferocious stare.

But he said—he said to tell him—thrice he asked me . . .

Fool. That did not mean you ought to suggest someone the Empire has deemed a traitor.

She'd assumed, still assumed, that Ling Zhen's arrest had been unjust, the charges of his sedition manufactured because he had been so audacious as to experiment with incendiary power outside the Empire's control. With perhaps Fan Rui caught up by association, as so often happened. It had never occurred to Lu Junyi to imagine they might be guilty. Somewhere in her mind she had been righteously hoping that by raising their names here, she might justly save them from execution, and thus win on all fronts—but Cai Jing—Cai Jing—

To him, *of course* they were guilty.

Still he did not speak. Fear began to buzz against Lu Junyi's skin. She dropped to her knees, bowing low against the floor.

She had miscalculated, miscalculated everything.

"I beg your pardon, Grand Chancellor . . . it was a most foolish suggestion . . ."

"I am well-versed in these areas of research," Cai Jing said. "I know of all the obvious scholars, seditious or no. You are ill-advised to think I do not."

How could she have thought—? He had never truly wanted her to challenge him, of course he hadn't; she had never been anything but the mouse in the tiger's loose jaws . . .

"However," Cai Jing said. "You have answered me honestly, and shown acceptable regret for your mistake. It is your opinion that they could advance this process significantly?"

The floor of the room was stone, cold and flat against Lu Junyi's hands, its chill seeping into her bones. "Yes, Grand Chancellor," she said softly.

"Rise and follow me."

Cai Jing was a swift walker. Lu Junyi hurried to keep pace, staying a proper number of steps behind him, his personal Guardsmen jogging in their wake as they left the building.

They strode through the lines of guards, through a wide, walled courtyard and back into the central district. Cai Jing did not call for sedan chairs, but that was usual for him—he was prone to walking much farther distances than most people of his status. Exercise, he claimed, promoted the mind.

Lu Junyi had to gather up the hems of her skirts to match his pace.

Cai Jing led them along the entire front wall of the Palace on their left, its crenellations and silhouetted guards on high looking out over their passage. Once they were past the Palace, they turned through several twists of street that Lu Junyi had never seen before—not that she was terribly familiar yet with the central district, or anywhere else in the inner city. Lacquered and carved roofs towered over them on one side, with the other becoming more prone to gardens and wild areas that crept toward the mountain slopes, the same mountains that haloed the Palace and pushed up as Bianliang's northern wall.

Lu Junyi knew better than to ask where they were going.

Eventually, the buildings to their right dropped off as well. They might still be well within the city walls here, but for all the congestion of the outer city, this place was almost country-like in its green sparsity. Cai Jing turned on his heel down a path between arching trees that led toward the mountains.

Nursing a stitch in her side, Lu Junyi followed. They must have gone three li already. Her slippers had not been made for such a walk.

The trees darkened the day above them until it felt as if they entered a twilit forest. Eventually, the path ended at a heavy, shuttered gate, one embedded in a slumped wall that was beginning to be overgrown on this side. As hushed and mysterious as these woods were, however, the wall reached imposingly to twice Lu Junyi's height, and was straddled by extremely well-kept watchtowers. The angle was wrong for Lu Junyi to see up into the towers properly, but a crawling sensation up the back of her neck suspected very well-trained watchers, in well-polished armor, wielding vigilantly loaded crossbows.

What was this place?

"Open it up," Cai Jing ordered. He didn't speak loudly, and Lu Junyi wondered how the watchers would hear before the Guardsmen that shadowed them ran forward and called up the orders, declaring the Chancellor's arrival.

Heavy clangs sounded, followed by the ponderous gates beginning to creak outward. Instead of being made of wood, the gates themselves appeared to be wrought entirely of iron . . . although lumpy, somehow, with veins of silver-gray snaking through them . . .

"Welcome to the Pit, Lady Lu," Cai Jing said silkily.

Lu Junyi's mouth had gone dry, her fingers cold. The Pit—the Empire's deepest prison, a place no one ever returned from. So shrouded in mysticism and rumor that half the Empire's citizens might have wondered if it was more legend than fact. Not the type of Imperial prison she'd visited Lin Chong or too many others in, no block of cells in a building where the accused were shuffled in and out of cages filled with dirty straw to meet judgment and then punishment. The Pit was instead a place for the permanent. The dangerous. Those whose fate was eyed by the Emperor himself.

Lu Junyi did not think many of them left here alive.

The gates completed their lumbering journey.

If the outside of the gates gave off an air of hidden mystique, the inside was a stark and fierce military ground. Within the lumpy, misshapen wall, a vast circle had been scooped out of the earth, giving the impression of some great arena open to the sky. Concentric tiers of stone paved the ground and led downward to a central pinprick at the bottom, where an ugly geometric mound pimpled up—a building that must be the prison itself, far below. Instead of civilian jailors, Imperial Guardsmen paced each ring of the massive tiered ground, hands on the hilts of the gleaming scabbards holding single-edged swords at their sides.

No structure had ever been so clearly designed to keep people in.

Lu Junyi glanced back up at the walls as they passed through. On this side, without the forest shadows and the patina of ivy and mosses, the walls did not seem to be formed of stone blocks, but some sort of rounded, sculpted barrier of a matte black that sucked in the bright daylight to swallow it. Except where hints of silver-gray clawed its way across the surface of those walls—the same silver-gray that threaded the misshapen gates.

Lu Junyi turned away and hurried after the Chancellor.

The journey down the stepped grounds drew out like raw noodles pulled too far. Even invited, Lu Junyi could feel the crossbows painting stars on her back, as if one stumble would bring death. The soldiers who marched past them expressionlessly showed an eerily smart alertness despite the monotony of their march, with a hardness to their faces that shouted how little they would think of drawing a blade and opening a man's throat in a single move. These were not raucous constables, but some of the Empire's hardest-forged troops.

Sweat slipped down Lu Junyi's back under her light gown and mantle.

They hiked down tier after tier, descending lower and lower until they reached the flat circular ground at the bottom. It was broader than it had looked from above, the epicenter of this whole dizzying endeavor. More rows of soldiers stood at attention here, all facing the single lump of a structure at the prison's heart.

The only man facing outward wore the single tassel of a detachment commander. As they approached, he came to attention, hands coming together in salute. "Nuo! Welcome, Grand Chancellor."

Notably, the other soldiers didn't move. Lu Junyi hadn't realized how accustomed she had become to everybody always snapping to attentive deference in the Chancellor's presence until among those who had clearly been ordered not to.

The soldiers here had a higher purpose.

Cai Jing stepped up and addressed the commander. "Bring me the prisoners Ling Zhen and Fan Rui."

"At once, Grand Chancellor," the man answered, and barked a few commands at his men. A small group hurried forward; the others spread back to the border of the flat ground, still at attention but leaving a space before them.

Lu Junyi conjured a memory of the couple from one of the handful of times she'd met them. For all his obsession with explosive minerals, Ling Zhen was as threatening as a stuffed child's toy, with a rolling chuckle and his long hair and beard going wispy with age. Fan Rui, by his side, had been a quiet woman with an occasional sudden humor, the lines of her face telling a lifetime of both joy and sorrow. Her husband had unfailingly been able to startle a laugh from her, though. They'd both been comfortably soft and gray with their advanced years, but Lu Junyi remembered a childlike curiosity nonetheless.

When Ling Zhen had disappeared from her salons—he had not been a regular, but still, she should have investigated. Ferreted out more information. She'd known him so little, comparatively, and she'd had other cases to press her weight against, cases like Lin Chong's . . .

What could you have done for him anyway, if he and his wife landed here?

The men the commander had called forward entered a dark tunnel that could only be an entrance to this terrible building, a prison with walls so thick it could not sustain a normal door. Cai Jing and Lu Junyi stood at the entrance to the tunnel and waited, the Chancellor serene, Lu Junyi breathing carefully to strangle her apprehension.

Cai Jing had killed her superior only this morning. What had she done, asking for this . . .

She'd staked herself on Ling Zhen and Fan Rui without even thinking it through, her own safety, her own life . . . What if they refused? *What if they were guilty?*

She tried to take her mind off it by turning to gaze up at the dread structure, this prison that buried people forever. Part of her wished she had never seen the reality of it. The building—if it could be called that—had the same lumpy, misshapen texture as the walls high above them; it appeared *shaped* rather than built, slumped into a vaguely pyramidal mound. This close, she suddenly saw that the inky stone must not be stone at all, but mortar—a grainy black mortar flecked with shiny debris glittering from its depths.

Lu Junyi had read of such a thing. Black rice mortar. Made from a slurry of lime, sticky black rice, and crushed stone or ceramic, it would withstand an earthquake or fire, or war, or the ravages of wind and time. The Empire used the material in its most formidable fortifications: vast city walls and watchtowers and great impenetrable garrisons.

And here, in a prison buried deep in the core of the inner city of Bianliang, nestled in close proximity to the Imperial Palace itself.

Lu Junyi reached out a surreptitious hand to touch the uneven roughness of the wall. This close, the silver veins disrupting its surface in undulating waves were much . . . stranger. Smooth where the mortar was rough, silver against a deep black, snaking with its own texture and plan in twisted designs . . . it was almost as if the mortar had merely been poured around it . . .

Lu Junyi jumped back, as if the wall had burned her.

"Yes. The walls are laced with scholar's stone, left in its natural state before being integrated with the mortar," Cai Jing said at her shoulder, close enough that she felt his breath against her neck. "A sensible precaution for a prison such as this, don't you think?"

A prison such as this. One used to lock in people like . . . like Fan Rui . . .

Fan Rui, a Renxia priestess with scholar's skills.

Of course. Those with advanced scholar's skills—if judged a danger to the Empire, how else might they be contained before their doubtless foreordained execution, but in a Pit like this?

She'd never asked the question before. How had she not thought to wonder? A sufficiently advanced monk—no ordinary prison could contain such a person. She supposed she'd never envisioned such an advanced personage in the role of a criminal at all. The image of those so near enlightenment was of ascetic masters living on cloud-soaked mountaintops, far from the concerns of ordinary humans.

Yet she had met monks like Lu Da. Fan Rui had to be far more advanced, with a true array of scholar's skills . . . yet, like Lu Da, the Empire had deemed her a threat, no matter her discipline and history of philosophic study. Reality did not hew neatly to imagined archetypes.

"What happens if a . . ." Lu Junyi drew together her scattered thoughts. She'd been doing nothing but read up on these esoteric materials for weeks, not to mention Cai Jing's story of the forty-seven dead at Anfeng Monastery. If any attempt was made to disturb these walls with more than the strength of a chisel, whether it be flame or alchemy or one of Ling Zhen's explosive rockets, the effect would be . . .

Wildly unpredictable. Beyond a nightmare for the person who tried.

This prison might hold even that archetypal centuries-trained monk, the learned scholar who could commune with all secrets of the universe.

"You surmise correctly," Cai Jing murmured, and moved away.

Iron clanked—a door somewhere deep at the hidden end of the tunnel. The soldiers that had been sent inside filed back out, and in their midst, held at bay by at least five sword points—

Lu Junyi would not have recognized them. Wasted to thinness, filthy, stinking of their own mess . . . each had an iron bar across their shoulders and between their feet, wrists and ankles chained heavily so their steps were a hobbled shuffle and their necks forced forward. Hair crusted with mud fell across their faces, flies buzzing in thirsty attendance. One of Ling Zhen's eyes was swollen to the size of an orange and caked black with blood.

Horror blanked Lu Junyi's mind to nothing. *Even if they are guilty, what merits this . . . how do we call ourselves a civilized land . . .*

A gag cut tight across Fan Rui's mouth. The wardens were not taking any chances with an accomplished priestess of the Renxia.

The two prisoners squinted and blinked, hunching against the bright daylight sun. How long since they had seen anything outside the Pit they had been thrown in? With even greater horror, Lu Junyi realized the scholar's-stone-laced structure had no windows. No vents to the outside.

Ling Zhen's watering gaze found Lu Junyi. He stared at her, uncomprehending. Fan Rui seemed slower to adapt to the light, her eyes roving like she saw everything and nothing—until they found Cai Jing and pierced him.

The soldiers brought them to the center of the open space and forced both prisoners to their knees, the chains clanking. Ling Zhen nearly pitched forward onto the stone, but one of the guards yanked him upright. Once their charges had been presented, the soldiers moved back—but only a sword length away, their blades unwavering.

Cai Jing stepped around them, surveying the two. Ling Zhen kept his eyes lowered, out of either respect or fear or both. Fan Rui's attitude was much more unmistakable.

Lu Junyi's heart beat faster. *Please let the Chancellor not see it,* she begged silently. However justified, angry defiance would only earn them all punishment. *Perhaps if she cannot speak, she cannot destroy us . . .*

The thought felt unconscionably cruel.

Cai Jing stopped in front of them and stared downward. The yard seemed to hold its breath.

"I am told you know my companion, the Lady Lu," he said finally, calmly.

Ling Zhen's mouth worked for a moment as if he could not recall how to speak. His eyes went from Cai Jing to Lu Junyi and back again.

"Yes, Grand Chancellor," he murmured, the words cracked and barely audible.

"She suggests to me that you and your wife should be given a second chance, to serve the Empire ably and loyally. Tell me, Scholar Ling. Is her request . . . merited? If called upon, would you dedicate every breath of your skills to Emperor and country?"

Again, that quicksilver flash of Ling Zhen's eyes between Cai

Jing and Lu Junyi herself, this time veiled with confusion. *Please,* Lu Junyi begged silently. If Ling Zhen spat on this—how could he, but if he did—it had not weighed on her how much she had risked herself, raising their names to the Chancellor—

"It is our humblest honor to serve, Grand Chancellor," Ling Zhen said.

Lu Junyi exhaled slowly.

Cai Jing would not be satisfied so easily, however. Of course not. He began pacing before the two prisoners, his hands clasped behind his back.

"A scholar specializing in incendiary minerals, and an alchemical priestess of the Renxia," he mused. "Experimentation with both fire powders and scholar's stone. Lady Lu had some sense to her when she suggested you. So very good, except that you performed those experiments in defiance of your lord and Emperor."

"We meant no . . . disrespect . . ." Ling Zhen managed. "Grand Chancellor, our knowledge is yours. Anything."

"I'm not sure your wife agrees. Even you may be only tickling my ears with the sweetness they wish to hear." Cai Jing smiled. "You are the matched pair, aren't you? Such a perfect balance of alchemical skill. Fortunately, it also means there are two of you." He nodded to the soldiers. "Unchain the husband and clean him up."

Ling Zhen's face hovered between terror and disbelief as the manacles dropped off his wrists and clattered to the stone, as the guards caught him before he collapsed and dragged him, wobbling, to his feet.

But he still mustered up the energy to speak, to beg, once more. "Grand Chancellor, please—my wife, she is guilty of nothing. Her great skill, the work we can do for you together—"

"Is work you will have to do separately," Cai Jing said. "You see, as long as I have one of you in these cells, the other will understand they are on a leash. Especially important for that wife of yours. She can come out next week, when you're back in your chains, and when she knows that a word out of line from her will be the end of your life. So no bringing on a plague of toads and centipedes,

Renxia priestess," he added to Fan Rui, wagging his head at her genially. "Imperial alchemical science only. Lady Lu will report to me on you both, and she will also be responsible for your good behavior."

He gathered his robes and made as if to turn away, but then he stepped back.

"Oh. It might do well to remind you that death isn't the only possible punishment. Scholar Ling, I expect perfect behavior—any misstep from you, and I have many ways to discipline you using your . . . lovely wife."

With that, he slipped a dagger out of his robes, glided over to Fan Rui, and grasped her ear through her filthy curtain of hair.

In one motion, he sliced the blade through.

Fan Rui bucked in pain, arching against her chains, and Ling Zhen screamed, a great long cry of anguish that seemed to echo across the whole cursed arena of death.

Cai Jing tossed the ear to the ground with the clump of hair that had come along with it. Then he took out a hand cloth, wiped his fingers and the dagger, and tossed the cloth after. "I trust the lesson is learned. You have your personnel," he added to Lu Junyi, and strode calmly away, beginning the long journey back up toward the monstrous gates.

CHAPTER 10

Lu Da squatted to the side of the training ground, sweating in the sun and watching Sister Lin train Steel Viridian and the Iron Whirlwind. Metal against metal, Lu Da thought, with a snicker at the apt nicknames.

But the two had martial styles that couldn't be more different. Lu Da didn't think it evil of her to take a wee bit of private enjoyment at seeing both of them out of their gourd in frustration with each other—she liked Steel Viridian well enough, despite her coming from everything perky and rich, and Iron Whirlwind was all right though a bully sometimes, but Lu Da wasn't going to feel guilty about watching either of them get taken down a smidge.

Li Kui kept whaling after Hu Sanniang with those double axes like a cyclone made of razors. Hu Sanniang had ducked away, time after time after time, until Li Kui had gone swollen and profane with rage. But Hu Sanniang wasn't getting the better end of it either—she'd started out grinning and spinning and throwing that lasso of hers, but Li Kui swatted away every attempt like it was a gnat. Sister Lin had Steel Viridian training in only the lasso today, no swords, and she wasn't getting hit but she wasn't doing much hitting herself either.

The worst kind of fight, Lu Da thought. *Give me a good pummeling any day, as long as I can punch 'em back.* The two of them should know by now that if they'd listen to Sister Lin's calls of advice they'd do better, but neither one was much in a listening mood anymore.

Poor Sister Lin. Starting in the first week she'd been here, she'd tried to institute routines and drills for her training regimens, but even in the month since, she'd only succeeded halfway. What could you expect? The heroes of Liangshan weren't all used to having a martial arts master. Lu Da was pretty sure Li Kui, at least, had learned to fight by beating up everyone in her hometown and stealing all their money. They'd sparred together two bouts previous while Sister Hu sat out, and Lu Da had been all set to pummel her until the match ended in disqualification when Li Kui had tried to grab Lu Da's god's tooth off her. Sister Lin had been *very* angry, much more than Lu Da, who had tried to point out that it was good, wasn't it, for her to be prepared for an opponent being so low-down and dirty as to try such a thing. After which Li Kui had thrown a clod of earth in her face and Lin Chong had made Li Kui sit down while Lu Da sparred Hu Sanniang.

Sister Lin was very accomplished, but she'd have to get more used to people breaking the rules.

Lu Da reached under her clothing and fingered where the smooth edges of the god's tooth lay against the most magnificent of her tattoos, chrysanthemums and lotus flowers and peonies cradling it in their bristly inked wilderness. Of course, right now both she and the god's tooth were slick with sweat—the perspiration dripped off her nose and chin and stuck her tunic against her in floppy wetness. The breeze off the marshlands kept Liangshan uncharacteristically cool, but not when you were a very large monk fighting in the sun all day, Lu Da reflected genially. Especially after Sister Hu had beat her so soundly in their match. Lu Da wasn't *too* fussed—Sister Hu was very good, and Lu Da had only been using her staff. She did hope Sister Hu also beat Li Kui, though. Then she'd feel fine about it all.

Maybe today Sister Lin would agree to give her a lesson in fighting with her god's tooth. Lu Da had been so good, doing as she'd been told and not using it in sparring at all, because Sister Lin said it would make her better, even if in the short term it made her *worse*. But she'd been *perfect,* she hadn't cheated at all. Or at least not more than once or twice. And she'd told Sister Lin, she also had to learn *to* use it, though maybe in separate lessons or something and that was fine, but when they fought Guardsmen and villains and other brigands—well, those guys weren't going to wait forty years for her to master her art without the tooth, were they? She couldn't do much mastering if she was dead.

The sparring match came to an abrupt end when Sister Hu got Li Kui around the neck with her lasso. Li Kui ended plowed into the dirt and banging the ground with one fist in violent submission. Lin Chong called a halt and helped free the Iron Whirlwind, who swatted aside an offered hand and bounded back to her feet with only a slight wobble.

"I don't see how this makes me a better fighter," Li Kui complained. "If I met someone all trained and balls-out like Sister Hu, I'd punch them when their back's turned. Then I'd hit them with an axe. Then I'd hit them with my other axe. Then they'd be dead."

"Engaging in honorable combat—" Lin Chong began, in a teaching voice.

"Honorable combat, ha! I like dishonorable combat, because it means I'm the one who lives and they die," Li Kui proclaimed.

"Sister Lin will make us better fighters no matter what," Lu Da retorted loyally, despite having had a not dissimilar thought only moments before. "Someday you'll meet someone you can't axe in the back, and if you're not ready, you're the one who'll get gutted."

"You rat-tailed donkey!" Li Kui swore. "Come finish our bout. I dare you!"

Lu Da jumped up, her blood going hot enough she didn't hear whatever calm teacher-like thing Sister Lin tried to interject. But at that moment, they were interrupted—by probably the only thing that *could* have stopped Li Kui and Lu Da.

Sun Erniang with a tray of steamed buns.

"Hey! Food," she called, wending down to the field. Today she was in gold-embroidered pink so shiny it was like a baby's cheek, and her face was rouged to match. Lu Da quite liked Sun Erniang's getups.

Her food wasn't bad either. As long as it was only proper meat inside.

"I'm not gonna find pubic hairs in this, am I?" Lu Da asked, grabbing three of the buns in one massive handful.

Sister Sun shot her a baleful look. "Where am I going to get man meat out here on the mountain? You'd have to bring travelers back for me to get it, and no one provides me with anything but mutton and pork."

"You're all so prissy about man meat," Li Kui said, through the bun she'd immediately stuffed in her teeth. "I'm with the Witch here. It's meat like any other. Why let it go to waste? When I kill someone, they smell just as good roasted as a pig does."

"You're disgusting," Hu Sanniang said to Li Kui, though she joined them and reached for one of the buns with two delicate fingers.

Sun Erniang yanked the platter backward. "What did you call my food?"

"Pardon me, Sister Sun, I didn't mean—"

"Yeah, you're the one who's disgusting!" Li Kui bellowed, and smacked the tray right at Hu Sanniang's face. Sister Hu dodged, and the tray glanced off her shoulder, scattering hot fluffy buns in all directions.

Sister Hu gave a yell of anger, and in the same instant, she and Li Kui launched themselves at each other as if they really *would* kill the other. Sun Erniang fell back out of the way with a squeak, and Lu Da lunged to hold back one or both of her sisters-in-arms, reaching hard for her god's tooth for help and letting its welcome energy roar through her.

They'd all forgotten, momentarily, that the only fighting they'd seen Lin Chong do these past weeks had been in gentle demonstration.

With a rush of wind, Sister Lin flew into the air—literally *flew.* One hemp sole flashed against Hu Sanniang's sternum, propelling her a full three paces back before she hit the ground and rolled against the grass. Lin Chong spun off the kick and her hands and feet flashed from the air, one two three four five six, attacking Li Kui at her pressure points before somehow swinging behind the other woman with an elbow squeezed about her neck. In a blink, Li Kui had slumped to the ground, submissive.

"You can brawl in your own time," Lin Chong declared. "Not during my classes. I expect discipline and respect while you're training here."

Lu Da stumbled to a stop, all geared up for an entire lack of anything to do. With a regretful sigh, she let her god's tooth energy seep back out of her.

Lin Chong looked up sharply.

Yes, I opened my tooth, Lu Da thought snippily. *I've done what you said in training, but this looked to be a real fight with my sisters doing something they'd regret. I was just trying to do the right thing.*

If Lin Chong hadn't stopped it so damn quickly.

How was she that good at sensing Lu Da's god's tooth anyway?

How was she able to do such god's tooth–like things herself, without holding one of her own? It wasn't *fair.* Sister Lin might train for scads of time every blasted day, but she still shouldn't have been able to do *that* when even Lu Da couldn't. It was almost like Sister Lin had some sort of scholar's skills—but nobody except monks and masters got those. Sister Lin might be a fighting god, but she was still only an arms instructor.

Lu Da stewed a little, while Lin Chong forced the other two to make stiff apologies—to each other and to Sun Erniang—and then dismissed them back up the mountain. Sun Erniang followed with her empty tray, the delicious buns now scattered in the mud, and if that wasn't a tragedy Lu Da didn't know what was. Maybe some of them had landed on grass and she could rescue them for her stomach.

Sister Lin touched Lu Da's elbow. "Are you all right?"

"I'm no whiner," Lu Da answered brusquely. "That Sister Hu gave me a bruising, but I'll get her next time."

Sister Lin nodded. "You're improving every day."

"I'd improve more if I could train with my tooth."

Sister Lin hesitated, and for a heartbeat Lu Da thought she would say something else, but then she only repeated the same thing she had this whole month: "In time. It's better for you now to leave it dormant."

Lu Da jerked away.

"Little Sister, I promise, we'll get there—"

Lu Da didn't hear how that sentence ended, because she stomped away. She loved her older sister, really she did, but by the light of the Fa could she be irritating. Holding the training Lu Da wanted more than anything like a tempting treat, but refusing any approach! It wasn't fair. Lu Da might have been tempted to think Lin Chong couldn't train her in this anyway, given Sister Lin didn't have a tooth herself—but she already knew how false that was. Lin Chong was so accomplished she somehow understood how the whole cursed world fit together. In the first instant of opening Lu Da's tooth she'd done more with it, more precisely, than Lu Da had ever managed in four years. Ever since she'd killed that butcher.

She strode up to the common area outside the cabins, where rough-hewn tables stretched outside for group meals when the weather was good. Maybe she could seek out some food that hadn't met its end in the mud, and fill her gut with meat instead of feelings.

Despite Sun Erniang's prior profession—or because of it—she oversaw the lion's share of provisions, and Lu Da found her stirring up a stew over an open fire. She allowed Lu Da some of the leftover buns, on account of Lu Da not having been one of the people who either insulted or smashed them, and Lu Da took the plate over to one of the tables to eat. Wu Yong, their Tactician, was seated there alone, sipping on a bowl of clear broth. A copper chain—Wu Yong's weapon of choice—lay draped across the bench. Must be going down to train next.

"Professor," Lu Da said in greeting, throwing a leg over the bench to start tucking in.

"Sister Lu," Wu Yong acknowledged. Their Tactician was a funny-looking person, but in a way Lu Da rather liked. Lean and bony where Lu Da was large, Wu Yong had the look of an extremely handsome and intelligent skeleton that had dressed up in a human suit, with deep eyes and high cheekbones and knobby elbows. A lack of headwrap at the moment showed off spiky hair chopped close to the scalp. Lu Da had never known a person to chop their hair off on purpose, except for monks who shaved bits or all of theirs, but there was no religious discipline for short spikes. The fiercely strange hair was made more so by being a wild streaky brown-yellow color—Lu Da had never asked if it grew that way or if Wu Yong rubbed in herbs and vinegar to make it so.

"What ails you, Flower Monk?" Wu Yong asked, squinting.

Oh, and the Professor was *way* too good at people. Lu Da just grunted.

"Come now." Wu Yong leaned forward, hands dropped flat on the table. "You can talk to me. Is it the friction between Sister Wang and our new Sister Lin? I know you and she are close."

Lu Da blinked. She hadn't noticed any friction between their leader and Sister Lin. But if Wu Yong said there was, then it must be true . . .

"There's no shame in supporting Sister Lin," Wu Yong went on, low and almost conspiratorial. "Sister Wang needs to be nudged into lessons sometimes, just like all of us. Sister Lin sees most clearly, doesn't she? Whatever tactic she chooses in teaching Sister Wang, it's doubtless for everyone's own good."

That was true, Lu Da thought.

"Tell her she has your support. It'll make you feel better," Wu Yong encouraged her.

"It's Sister Lin I'm mad at right now," Lu Da blurted.

"Oh?" Wu Yong's eyebrows jumped. "Why is that?"

"She keeps putting off training me in my god's tooth. I can't ever get better if she won't train me! People think I'm useless. I'm not useless. I can bash all kinds of heads in!" Lu Da smacked her staff into the edge of the table, gouging the wood.

Wu Yong didn't twitch in response, only smiled. "You're very wrong. No one would dare think you're useless. How could we?"

"Then why aren't you taking me on the heist next week to steal Chancellor Cai's birthday presents?" Lu Da demanded. "Sister

Song didn't take me on her last few raiding parties either. And right now the Zhang siblings and the Tong sisters are out smuggling with Li Jun and Wang Dingliu and nobody wanted old Lu Da with them—"

"Come now. This should be obvious," Wu Yong said.

"What? Why?"

"I'm the one who came up with the scheme to steal the birthday presents, and we're all going to go dressed as helpless women merchants—yes, even myself and Seventh Brother Ruan. It's all down to cunning; I hope there will be no fighting at all. You are amazing, Sister Lu, but even dressed as a merchant you would intimidate people, and we'll need them off their guard. And of course our boat folk didn't take you on their smuggling operation, as it's all water and you don't swim. We know the strengths of our family here, Sister Lu, I promise! When it comes to making war on officials and burning down towns, you'll be the one we want in front, a thousand times."

Lu Da sat up with a thrill. "We're starting a war?"

Wu Yong laughed. "Not yet! But if we do, it'll be on behalf of the people. Now go find Sister Lin and tell her how you feel."

"Hmmph." Lu Da wrinkled her nose suspiciously. "Everyone says you've got a slick silver tongue in that mouth of yours. You're not using it on me now, are you? To make me think I want to make nice with Sister Lin."

Wu Yong sat back and continued sipping at the bowl of broth. "If I were, it would all be in good cause. You love Sister Lin. Go talk to her."

Lu Da grumbled, but she gave the last crumbs on her plate a broad lick and then got up to do as Wu Yong said.

Sister Lin, however, wasn't in her quarters. Nor was she in any of the common areas, nor back on the fighting ground—only Wu Yong doing solo exercises with that copper chain, plus a trio of bandits practicing Sister Lin's drills in half-hearted disorder. Upon a second look, Lu Da could see it was the damn Three Fleas. *Harrumph,* she thought. *Can't believe they're even practicing at all.* Yang

Xiong, Shi Xiu, and Shi Qian had come to Liangshan after an infamous streak of burglary, arson, and murders—ever lumping one crime upon the other to cover up whatever Shi Qian's sticky fingers wiggled into. All the while they'd proclaimed themselves setting off to join "the great hero bitches of Liangshan" until the whole countryside from Xijing to Hengqing had been cursing Liangshan's good name. And until Liangshan was the only place left the three could escape to.

Lu Da had not been impressed. Shitting on the name of Liangshan by stealing livestock and burning down inns! What an affront. That was *not* what it meant to be a hero. Lu Da had been in favor of tossing them out on their ears for the magistrates to descend on and peck to death like a bunch of crows, but no one ever listened to her. Chao Gai had gone further, though, shocking everybody when she made a case for displaying the three bandits' heads on pikes as an extreme warning for sullying Liangshan's reputation. "Our good standing is gold," she'd proclaimed. "Our good standing is all."

Lu Da was still not sure if Chao Gai had been serious. But Song Jiang and some of the others had stepped in, arguing for amnesty and that the three only needed to be given a chance among a righteous group to direct their energies more correctly.

A chance? Lu Da was pretty sure Shi Xiu had stabbed Yang Xiong's husband's mistress seven times and then cut off the head of the mistress's maid, and then tried to point all ten fingers at a hapless porridge seller who happened upon the bodies.

And that was before they fled and oath-bonded with Shi Qian and did all the thieving and burning together.

Still, Sister Song was right, wasn't she? They gave second chances here at Liangshan. That was what they did, and if they lost that, then where would people like Lu Da be, branded criminals no matter how virtuous their motives? The Three Fleas had groveled and begged forgiveness, and sworn every oath imaginable that they would never more thieve or stab for any untoward purpose, but only under the greater mission of Liangshan. And here they were practicing their martial forms without being told, so Sister Song had probably been right all along.

The mountain could be everyone's second chance. Even Sister Lin seemed to treat everyone with painful equality in training.

Which wasn't equal at all! Lu Da was her sworn sister, and Lu Da had not murdered *nearly* as many people as the Three Fleas had. Or as many as Li Kui, or the Zhang siblings whose ferry toll used to be throwing people out of their boats, or Sun Erniang or Li Li who *ate people*, or, well, at the very least Lu Da had killed people for *very good reasons.*

Wu Yong was right. She had to talk to Sister Lin. But where *was* she? Lu Da turned from the training ground and stumped back up the slope, swatting grumpily at the tiny biting flies that liked to land on her sweat-crusted skin. Where on this blasted mountain was Lin Chong?

It wasn't until Lu Da hiked up near Chao Gai's quarters that she heard Sister Lin's voice.

"It happened again," she was saying. "But I don't . . . I think I was wrong."

What happened? Lu Da slowed down to listen.

"Tell me," Chao Gai's voice answered gently.

"I said it didn't happen when I was just demonstrating—when I was not, ah, not in a meditative fighting state. Not truly trying to win. But I think I've been wrong. I think I've been feeling it this whole time, I just—I told myself I could ignore it. And I became used to it. Like an insect hum, always in my ears. When Sister Lu opened her god's tooth . . . I realized it had never gone away."

"What happened when you felt the god's tooth open?" Sister Chao asked.

"It was everywhere. In my skin, in my head, and I couldn't ignore it—but then when she closed it—I knew. It hadn't gone away. It had never gone away."

"This power is not evil, nor wrong," Chao Gai said. "Does it bother you?"

Lu Da crept up to the corner of the cabin and peeped around the edge. Sister Lin and Sister Chao stood on a rocky outcrop behind Chao Gai's cabin, a vista of clear blue sky backdropping them. The mountain breeze plucked at Lin Chong's braid and Chao Gai's loose monk-style robes.

Sister Lin gazed out from the precipice into the sky. Chao Gai watched her, letting the silence rest.

"I don't know," Sister Lin said finally. "What does it all mean? You told me what the Transcendentalists think, but . . . what do *you* think?"

"You're connected," Chao Gai answered. "If we consider the Transcendentalist view that the god's teeth are not, themselves, powerful, and merely open such a connection . . . I don't think that's far from truth, or at least *a* truth. Our understanding of the natural world is only disconnected tips, as the occasional reed poking up from below the ice. If we instead held a deep knowledge of all the earth's mysteries—how a sapling bursts from its seed, how dreams come upon us, how the sun hangs in the sky or spirits speak from beyond the grave—or how scholar's skills develop among the very learned—I think we would find it is all part of the same weave. A universal understanding, as a puzzle that fits along every seam."

Lu Da frowned. She had not come to eavesdrop. But this—a discussion of god's teeth—how could they be keeping this from her? Her, the only bandit with a tooth! And Sister Chao talking like it meant *nothing*? Like it had no power at all?

Something twisted hard inside Lu Da, like a hand had squeezed down on her liver and kidneys and stomach.

"You spin my head," Lin Chong was saying out on the outcropping. "I'm no philosopher. And I certainly don't have scholar's skills."

"I think you ascribe too much to that label. You see them as incompatible with your own life—"

"They are," Lin Chong said. "I'm a drill instructor. I don't ride in the clouds. I've made no spiritual study."

"Your training itself is a spiritual study. Why do you think the Fa require dedication to a particular art? But that's not exactly what I meant. What people call scholar's skills . . . they're not a discrete achievement that you either attain or do not. Like the fighting arts. There is a vast distance between throwing a badly formed punch and your level of expertise—a martial ability is not something black and white, but gradations of learning."

"You're saying I should see myself as a beginner. At—whatever this is."

"No. I'm saying you have been a beginner for a long time."

The breeze rustled over the outcropping, filling the silence.

"I've told you that while training at the monastery, I also studied my forms there," Chao Gai said into it. "This awareness you speak of, I think of it not as a sudden unlocking, but a building of the muscles. The senses sharpening. More inner strength delivered into blows from a centered body . . . this is all familiar to you, yes? It is not separate from some greater skill, but the same spectrum. Interacting with Sister Lu's god's tooth may have accelerated it, or your awareness of it, but your body and mind were primed for those connections. If you were training with a master I believe you would find it the most natural glide from one skill to the next, and not even question whether they differed in kind."

Lin Chong scraped a hand across her face. "This is all so new. I've spent my life—I thought—I thought I was at the point where—it's been a long time since I've stepped into a fight or held a weapon and it didn't feel like a part of me. When I didn't feel in control. I don't know how . . . This is new."

Chao Gai nodded. "It scares you."

Lin Chong gave a hoarse laugh. "I would not like to say so. But . . . perhaps."

Chao Gai shifted one foot back and raised her hands, one above her head and one out in front, a knifehand guard. "Come. Dance with me, then. Try to embrace it. I'll tell you what I see."

Lu Da was not angry, she was *not* angry, she was not—but Sister Chao had always been so kind to her, and so *marvelous,* but—*why did she never offer to teach me?*

Lu Da had never even seen Chao Gai fight, only doing slow solo forms in the early dawn glow, and of course Sister Chao had martial arts skills because she was a monk and a ghost hunter and had *all* the skills but why had she never asked Lu Da to dance? To open her god's tooth and say *I'll tell you what I see?*

It had never occurred to Lu Da to ask, but how could it! And here was Sister Lin, here only a month and already banded together like filthy thieves talking god's teeth and connections and leaving Lu Da out in the cold.

She wanted to storm off, but had one more moment of being torn. Because she'd never seen Chao Gai fight. Because Chao Gai was about to fight *Lin Chong.*

Lin Chong saluted and also took a guard stance, and Chao Gai whipped in—like a rainbow, a riotous river, a flock of eagles, all thunder and lightning and pure beauty. Lin Chong blocked and leapt and her body spun in midair as if she were a creature of spider silk, defying the earth, beholden only to the sky.

Lu Da's rage roared up, and she was *definitely* angry, and she turned around and stomped away.

She stomped all the way to Loyalty Hall. Wang Lun was in the high seat wrapping up a conference with a few of her chieftains, Du Qian and Song Wan and a few others, and Lu Da didn't even care, she just grunted "Get out" at them and flopped down in one of the vacated seats.

"And what do you want, Sister Lu?" Sister Wang demanded, steepling her fingers against her chin. "By the way, that's the last time I'm going to excuse your rudeness. If you've come to campaign for your vaunted Sister Lin, I've already been more than generous. Those who want to are training with her, and I'm allowing it, at least until she passes or fails in applying to join us. But we believe in freedom here, and I'm not going to force anyone to—"

"And I support you!" Lu Da cried. She hardly knew what she was saying. She'd come here to—to—she wasn't even sure, but her mouth was going on faster than she could plan it. "She's not such a great teacher. She wouldn't even teach me, and I *asked*. I don't think it's right that she wants to try to teach *you* a lesson when you didn't ask, when she won't even teach me!"

Wang Lun leaned forward, elbows on her knees, and her voice went all silky smooth in a way that should have sounded nice but somehow made all the little hairs on Lu Da's body stand up.

"You are an excellent, loyal sister, Reverend Lu," she said. "Please, start at the beginning. What's this about Lin Chong wanting to teach me a lesson?"

Lu Da stopped talking, her mouth open like a carp, Lin Chong and Chao Gai's beautiful, beautiful fight replaying over and over in her mind. And Wu Yong's words bouncing through it, confusing her even more.

Lin Chong was her sworn *sister.* Chao Gai was the most amazing person in the world.

How could they have betrayed her like this?

Wu Yong considered the field of battle with great care. When making sacrifices, one should always be very sure—and once done, never look back.

Decisive fingers plucked up the Fifth Guardian to place it squarely in Song Jiang's vanguard.

"Are you certain?" Sister Song asked in surprise. Then she held up a hand. "Of course you are. Let me see if I can discover what nefarious trap you've laid." She gazed down at their gameboard for a long stretch, then sighed. "I don't see it. And if I don't take you, you'll devour my entire vanguard. All right. Show me."

She jumped to Wu Yong's position and lifted the sacrificial piece off the board. Twelve rapid moves later, Song Jiang's army had been decimated and Wu Yong had full domination of the game.

Song Jiang leaned back and flicked a finger at her defeated side. "I've figured it out. I know how you do it."

"Oh?"

"Clearly you've become an expert augur without telling anyone. That's the only possible explanation. An augur with skills far beyond any the world has ever seen, no less . . . precise enough to see my every move on the General's Gambit board . . ."

Wu Yong chuckled. "I'm afraid it's only a knack. Low tricks, but they do come in handy sometimes."

"All of tomorrow's contingencies are accounted for, then?"

"If you see any remaining flaws, I will happily accept criticism." Wu Yong's predatory smile betrayed the humble words. Tomorrow would go off beautifully, no matter how events branched. It was all accounted for.

"I have no doubts in your plan," Song Jiang said. "Never in one of *your* plans. But you didn't choose the people; it's the only part that gives me any pause. You trust Chao Gai's outsider?"

"Chao Gai does," Wu Yong answered. "I admit it's the weakest point, but her reasoning is sound. Much superior to using one of our own for the role. Besides, I may be no augur, but you heard Sister Chao's dream yourself—best to follow the omens when we can."

The night had shown Chao Gai the great dipper in the stars while she slept, seven brilliant points that had no other interpretation than matching seven of their own glorious number. Wu Yong had ignored the omens before in life, to great peril. Even with no higher skill at interpretation, common wisdom was enough to know signs this clear were not to be trifled with. Especially when Sister Chao's Transcendentalist training confirmed it.

The heist would be performed by seven of them, no more and no less. They would need all seven to transport the treasure, which meant an outside recruitment for their wine merchant. And it was fortuitous anyway; Chao Gai's friend was a wine merchant in truth, so would be naturally unsuspicious.

The tips of Wu Yong's fingers tingled. This was always the best part: the anticipation, when outsmarting the other party was all but assured, the prize dangling just within reach but not yet in one's palm . . . whether that prize was a victory in General's Gambit or barrel upon barrel of jewels and ingots to be cleverly lifted from one of the Empire's most powerful figures.

Wu Yong ran through the plan mentally once more, each possible complication splitting into probable paths until every one had been thoroughly accounted for. *This* branch would be taken care of by the addition of Lin Chong, *that* one by the extra packets of specially prepared dates . . . every eventuality considered and its defense planned. Very much like a game of General's Gambit.

Truly, this was better than a nighttime pleasure roll. Wu Yong had never been able to understand why others could forego such a delicious high.

Before finding the higher-stakes glory at Liangshan, Wu Yong had long fed this addiction with riddles or games of strategy. Or rhetorical study, or, often, convincing anyone convenient to follow an odd whim if only to see what was possible. Always moving pieces on a board closer and closer to the win.

"I do trust you both," Song Jiang said now. "One more question, though, indulge me. Talk to me about Lin Chong."

Wu Yong knew what Song Jiang asked. No one doubted Lin Chong's skill. Her loyalties, however . . .

There could be no question of the woman's larger heroism. But strict moralities sometimes did not fold well into Liangshan's shadowed abstractions.

No matter. Wu Yong merely regarded that as one more challenge. They could benefit so greatly from Lin Chong's presence here—and Wu Yong had plans, so many plans, that could be brought more suddenly to fruition with her on the board—but the arms instructor would have to see herself as fully one of their own, and with no divided loyalties to someone like Wang Lun.

It could be done. Luckily, Wu Yong greatly enjoyed challenges.

Two long fingers reached out to turn over the General tile on Song Jiang's side, so the black obverse gleamed in defeat. "Don't worry. Every contingency is prepared for."

CHAPTER 11

"It is done," Fan Rui said, and cackled, lifting her hands from above the bowl. "Done! Like a man's souls trapped in ice forever, never to be reborn." Her tiny, wrinkled grin jumped in an expression her chaperoning guards couldn't see, and above the guards' heads, the minerals on one of the shelves spontaneously combusted in a flash and a thunderclap.

The guards leapt to attention and shouted, their spears pointing everywhere at once.

Lu Junyi held up a hand to calm them. Smoke drifted from the blackened shelf, turning the air rancid. Fan Rui covered her face, giggling at disturbing length.

"Those materials are—very flammable." Lu Junyi tried to cover for her, flashing on nightmares of what would be done to Ling Zhen if Fan Rui were blamed for her prank. It was hard to speak clearly enough to be heard over the priestess's unsettling glee. "The minerals combust by themselves sometimes . . ."

Thank Benevolence, the soldiers nodded warily and straightened.

Lu Junyi stepped away from her own alchemical measurements to gaze at Fan Rui's work. The shard of scholar's stone, the would-be god's tooth—the *god's fang,* as they'd somehow, ludicrously, taken to calling it . . . it drifted against the bottom of a solution of carefully mixed salts and minerals, chunks of heavy dark metal surrounding it like a mountainous prison.

The god's fang itself had now taken on a dull sheen reminiscent of the metals.

Astounding, even knowing Fan Rui's priestess skills, even watching her stand over this basin of materials for so many watches of the day, concentrating on the power of the minerals within. Outside, clouds had drawn in from every direction, thunder rolling in roiling darkness above where she worked. Rain had begun to slash at the outer courtyards before she was done.

The scholars and monks who worked walled away in the other side of this building must have wondered. Some of the monks, at least, would recognize the effect of powerful scholar's skills being leveraged nearby . . .

Lu Junyi would have to be vigilant as to whether any of the scholars' work revealed they knew what was at stake here. In her apprehension she'd begun manufacturing some irrelevant calculations and experiments in addition to the needed ones, all to muddy the trail and protect her men from inadvertently stumbling over a conclusion that would tempt Cai Jing's hand. She must not fail in her duty to protect them.

The Chancellor had continued to be fearsome in his orders that only those deemed absolutely necessary would be told the truth of their project. Lu Junyi had to defend the decision rigorously before even Fan Rui could be told. She was still the only one.

Not even Ling Zhen had been permitted to know.

Despite the veil over exactly what the end purpose was, the little old incendiary expert had worked to repeat the phenomenon from Anfeng at much smaller proportions—but to no avail. With the aid of the team of scholars and alchemists provided to them by Cai Jing, Scholar Ling had carefully analyzed crumbs of ashen dust gathered by Lu Junyi from the existing god's fangs, then tested that dust to ferret out its constituent parts. He and Lu Junyi had together built the tiniest of delivery systems: a rocket the size of a pea. A few grains of explosive powder mixed with gravel, then wrapped in a tiny twist of lantern paper—which would snap with a loud crack when thrown against a hard surface. Sweating nervously, Lu Junyi had shaved a fine sprinkling of scholar's stone into splinters and spread it across a flat rock in the middle of one of the vast empty courtyards, after which they had propelled the tiny incendiaries from a blow gun many paces away.

No matter how consistent the formula, the results always differed. Once the scholar's stone burst into a column of purple flame. Once the flat stone table melted through, bubbling up as though dissolved by acid. Once tiny stabs of lightning cracked out across the courtyard with a bang that took their hearing for an instant. Ling Zhen yanked Lu Junyi down only just fast enough to avoid being punctured by its searing fire.

They varied the proportions of materials time and again, all with equally unusable results.

"It's the nature of scholar's stone," Ling Zhen had said helplessly. "If there is an exactness that makes it repeat itself in a predictable fashion, we humans cannot achieve it. Whatever results the Chancellor wishes to guarantee, it's not possible."

He'd begged her not to tell Cai Jing, fearing some punishment to his wife.

Instead, she'd reported their failure fully. She had to. If the Chancellor ever discovered them hiding the smallest piece of what they researched—it wouldn't only be her head, but Ling Zhen's and Fan Rui's and the life of every scholar she gave directive to, whether they knew the secrets here or not. The idea that either Ling Zhen or Fan Rui might suffer fallout from the discovery that nature's reality did not bend to their project's needs—it anguished her, but it could not turn her decision.

Any punishment would be far worse for hiding their lack of progress.

Ling Zhen had been correct in his fears, however. Cai Jing had not been well-pleased. He'd thrown the little old scholar back into his hole of a prison and had Fan Rui brought up instead. Cleaned, bathed and dressed, Fan Rui put Lu Junyi in mind of a saucy grandmother.

Except where her gray-white hair dangled lank over the healing stump of her left ear. Or the way her skin hung off her bones now like too-loose clothing.

Cai Jing had not had much choice in whether Fan Rui knew the truth of everything. Not if he wanted her to be able to advance their goals. Somehow, Lu Junyi felt sure the priestess would have guessed anyway, the way she breathed deep and closed her eyes when in the presence of the god's fangs for the first time.

"Wobbling, wobbling," she'd murmured. "The energy isn't settled, it tips like a sinking boat . . ."

"You can feel that?" Lu Junyi had asked.

"Steady it, he says, is that all. Steady like a steersman, steady like an Empire. Steady like a corpse."

She laughed.

That was when Lu Junyi realized what the Pit had done to her mind.

The few times they had met before, Fan Rui had been a quiet, primarily playful presence at her husband's side, but when she'd spoken, it had made sense. Lu Junyi remembered a shy but cutting cleverness, her rare comments landing in conversation in the manner of a subversive surprise, like biting down on a whole clove. Often unexpected, but Lu Junyi had never doubted Fan Rui's cleverness, nor her capacity for reason.

Now she spoke in scattered metaphor and senseless rambles.

Lu Junyi had feared, briefly, that it meant the alchemical priestess would no longer be able to understand the work. Fortunately, her scholar's skills were still intact, and she appeared to comprehend Lu Junyi's explanations, if in a nerve-rackingly sideways manner. "A metal cloak," she'd said abstractly. "Heavy, dark metals to weigh it down, make it slow and lumbering. Or a cooling elixir to draw out the negative energy . . . Lodestone may cause it to dampen, if my Thunder God can alter me some—oh, let it go, overflow, let it go to somewhere else, the power must leak somewhere . . ."

The Thunder God, it seemed, was Ling Zhen's all-too-fitting nickname. Fan Rui had revealed in one of her rambles that in her youth she'd been called Chaos Demon.

As omens went, it wasn't the most auspicious.

It had taken some discussion to determine the meaning behind all those words. Or the methodology behind the processes Fan Rui spun out of her vast alchemical knowledge. In the end, the priestess was exactly what Cai Jing had desired: someone with plenty of ideas of how to temper power within minerals, and with the alchemical scholar's skills to enact them. Lu Junyi was but a student at her knee—able to follow and understand, but barely. She had read much on the theory of alchemy out of interest's sake, as many scholars did, but knew only the broad basics of how to practice.

She'd had Fan Rui begin teaching her. While the priestess worked at the far more advanced metallic plating, Lu Junyi toiled to master the foundational tenets of alchemy, then to apply their exactitude to constructing various cooling and healing elixirs Fan Rui named as having a chance of calming the god's fangs. Elixirs Fan Rui claimed needed little proficiency or finesse to accomplish. Lu Junyi privately differed, perspiration turning her hair to wet strings as she attempted to cram the principles into her head while bending over hot crucibles or grinding insect legs to the finest powder.

Feel the pieces of it in your mind! Fan Rui kept telling her, before laughing about it.

So far Lu Junyi's potions had shown no effect at all on scholar's stone. Either the wrong avenue, or she lacked the proper skill.

Happily, the dark metals did seem to shield some of the volatile effects—enough times in enough ways to apply one to a singular precious god's fang. Today, under Cai Jing's orders, would be their first true test.

Lu Junyi had failed to eat even a single morsel of food that morning.

The Chancellor had so far been pleased with the advancement they had wrought since Fan Rui had begun work. It would all fall to nothing if they did not see at least marginal success today.

In her reports to Cai Jing, Lu Junyi had tried to emphasize and credit Fan Rui's usefulness, eager to provide a reason for leniency toward her. Instead, the Chancellor's response had been a pleased resolve to search for other skilled alchemists to draft.

"Scholar's skills in materials . . . unfortunately such a rare talent," he'd groused. "You say she's instructing you?"

"I am barely at the level of an apprentice," Lu Junyi tried to explain. "I have studied much of the theory, but working in tune with the various materials is another matter entirely . . . in only weeks I could never hope to come close to a Renxia priestess. It is not only her skills, Grand Chancellor, but her instincts. I can follow her reasoning, but I would never think of the avenues her experience guides us toward."

"It seems the husband's reputation had the wife's Renxia sorcery behind it, then. That's good to know, Lady Lu; I thank you."

Lu Junyi breathed deep to prevent herself from now panicking on behalf of Ling Zhen. Could nothing bring these two redemption in Cai Jing's eyes? "Begging your pardon, Chancellor. Scholar Ling is extremely adept as well. I do not think anyone could equal his skill at these new incendiary powders. In fact, Priestess Fan has stated that she will need him to construct certain elements for her tests."

"I see. Very well." Cai Jing tapped his rings against the table he sat at to take her report. "I shall survey the Empire for more alchemists. In the meantime, you'll need test subjects. I have selected a handful of military volunteers. Prisoners would be better, considering the expendable nature of these experiments, but if you succeed we cannot risk a traitor gaining that level of power."

Cold beads of sweat broke out across Lu Junyi's skin. She hadn't thought ahead . . . of *course* they would come to a point of testing their work.

Military volunteers. How athwart was it for her to wonder just how voluntary this duty, one that could hollow out and ravage these men, body and mind?

Once again, however, she had no other path . . . this tightrope led in only one direction. Besides, how many soldiers might such a weapon save, if these same Guardsmen were sent to defend the Empire's borders against those who would mean its people harm?

If they truly were volunteers . . . good soldiers who considered their own self synonymous with the needs of Empire . . . such an attitude prevailed commonly among the Guard. Jia would even go so far as to say any other way of thinking bordered on improper. Disloyal.

The values of the Empire have long diverged from your own. This is no different. They may take true satisfaction from serving here.

Succeed, and you yourself may achieve the power to change everything.

Succeed, and Ling Zhen and Fan Rui might be saved from a fate of execution. Succeed, and she might gain the Imperial Court. Succeed, and she'd help protect the Empire from invaders who would destroy it before it *could* be changed—Cai Jing had not been shy in impressing upon her the threat to the north.

Succeed, and they would unlock a door to power that could be democratized across all, and reshape the face of the land in ways no one could imagine.

Lu Junyi had always believed in progress.

Her abstract elocutions on the value of innovation had never considered that she might stand in a vast, cleared courtyard in the heart of the inner city, about to test an untried weapon on bonding with a living person.

She held the altered god's fang on a tray, carefully, so she would be in no danger of touching it. Fan Rui stood beside her, the chaperoning guards hovering behind.

"Are you sure it feels correct?" Lu Junyi had asked the question a dozen times in a dozen variations.

"It bobbles instead of wobbles," Fan Rui answered, bobbing her head herself. "Oh, yes, very close. Metals temper the energy, tamping down the heat . . ."

"Does it feel as a regular god's tooth does?" Lu Junyi pressed. While speaking to Fan Rui, she eyed the man who stood a ways away in the center of the courtyard, a man sent to them by Cai Jing. Two tassels marked him as a garrison commander. "How certain are you?"

"Life is uncertainty," Fan Rui provided helpfully. "Let him burn!" She began to laugh again.

Lu Junyi had not detailed this type of behavior in the reports to Cai Jing.

She would have liked to have more assurances, but could think of no other precautions to take. She'd required Fan Rui to show her this method on raw scholar's stone first, which had allowed Lu Junyi to painstakingly—and with some jumpiness—record the decrease in reactivity when the stone was plated through with various weights of heavy metals. Odd, how only certain metals had such an effect. Odd and admittedly fascinating. Fan Rui had demonstrated the same method with kohl instead, and when she had, stone, liquid, and basin had frozen solid halfway through the process, then dissolved into dust at a touch.

Lu Junyi had run as many observations as she dared and passed the charts to the other scholars to calculate patterns and write out tables. Every exploration of understanding had been attempted before she'd presented the data to the Chancellor.

She'd known when she did that he would declare it ready. That they must wait no longer before performing this first test.

She had expected he might be here today. She could not help a nervous relief at his absence.

Likely he chose not to risk himself near a potentially building-leveling experiment.

Her relief was nonsensical anyway. If they failed—provided Lu Junyi lived through the failure—the Chancellor's absence only meant any consequences would be delayed, not mitigated. If they failed . . . Lu Junyi shied away from imagining how she might deliver that report. Absurdly, her tangled apprehension balled up with as much eagerness as fear. As much as she wished to avoid Cai Jing's wrath, she equally wanted the satisfaction of proclaiming her own success to him.

Ridiculous. Such flights of fancy would only bring her to ruin. She must be tempered by caution, modesty—and never forget the lives that hung in the balance, the lives that were not her own, starting with the man in the middle of this courtyard.

Standing here in silence, however, would hardly improve the matter.

Lu Junyi moved toward the stalwart commander before her. As

she drew closer, he straightened and saluted her with a sharp shout of respect.

"What is your name, Officer?" she asked him.

"My family name is Wen, madam. I am here to serve."

"Have they informed you what the dangers are today?" She had to know.

"I am to take possession of a god's tooth that has been deemed unstable. If I can I am to wield it for the Empire. If fate determines otherwise, I will die."

Lu Junyi lingered, unsure what else to ask, to say, what might selfishly soothe the prickling of her ethical doubts. "If I told you we might find reason to delay or defer . . ."

A look of appalled shock fell over his stoic expression, and he dropped to one knee. "I beg you, madam, tell me how I have offended. I will scrape my hands to the bone to rectify it."

"You have caused no offense," Lu Junyi said automatically. "Why would you think so?"

Commander Wen hesitated. "It is always my honor to serve the Empire, but I was granted this chance as a reward, in recognition of my deeds in service at the northern border . . . Any Guardsman would yearn for it, madam. To wield a god's tooth for the army is to advance in the footprints of Minister Duan, General Han, or General Gao."

Minister of War Duan, who wielded a god's tooth. General Han—known as the Undefeated, and one of the few other military leaders who possessed one. And General Gao, a cousin to Marshal Gao Qiu, and one of the only high-ranking men in the Guard who could deploy scholar's skills on the field of battle. Famous names, all. Names that had written their deeds in legend, names of wealth, of favor from the Emperor.

This man would gamble his own existence to become one of their number. He would beg her not to deny him that chance.

"This is the artifact in question," she explained slowly. Every word felt fragile, as fragile as a human life. "When you touch it with your bare skin, you will feel its power. Enter a state of meditation if you can, and only draw the smallest breath of energy from it. If you feel a wrongness, do not drop it, but attempt to deepen your relaxation and separate yourself from its pull. That may give us some time. Do you understand?"

"Yes, madam."

"Even if we have succeeded in our efforts at stabilization—all god's teeth are dangerous by their nature, and from what we can tell, this artifact is even more powerful. If it works as we intend, you will still need time and training to achieve skillful wielding of it. God's teeth escape control easily, and this is no ordinary one—drawing on it too broadly *will* cause great energy to release in destructive or deadly ways. Be cautious. Take only small sips."

"I understand, madam," Commander Wen said gravely.

Lu Junyi had never held a god's tooth, but after reading every scrap in existence on the subject, she felt world-heavy with knowledge of them. Of god's teeth, and of the tragedy at Anfeng Monastery, and of the four men who had died in its aftermath discovering the initial properties of the god's fangs.

"Wait until I reach the edge of the courtyard," she said to the commander. "We shall give you a signal."

She placed the tray on the ground and retreated, all the way back against the building. Several stone plinths stood empty near this end of the space, doubtless left over from when this garden had housed statued lions or even its own sculptures carved of scholar's stone. Recalling the lightning-soaked experiment with Ling Zhen, Lu Junyi beckoned Fan Rui partially behind one of the heavy stone weights, and ordered the priestess's guards to arrange themselves behind other barriers.

"If it starts to go wrong . . ." she reminded Fan Rui.

"Then we learn." Fan Rui said the words as if she swooned in the arms of a lover. "Failures spawn greatness."

"No. Or, that may be true, but—" Lu Junyi turned Fan Rui to face her, speaking seriously and severely. "We discussed this, Priestess. If it starts to go wrong, you will do everything in your power to hold him safe, to unbind him if possible, and keep the god's tooth stable. Can you do that?"

"People who ask the impossible should not be so disturbed by uncertain answers," Fan Rui sniped.

"You said you would do all you can. Swear to it. I don't want anyone to die today."

"Everyone dies. Odd that we make so much of it." She pushed away from Lu Junyi. "I swear your swears, even though they give me bad breath."

It was the most Lu Junyi could hope for. One way or another, this had to happen today. The Chancellor would expect her results this evening.

"Commander," she called. "You may begin. Remember—slowly."

Commander Wen leaned down, and after the barest hitch, he closed his fingers around the god's fang. Straightened. Beside Lu Junyi, Fan Rui's eyes had closed.

A whisper in the air. Did Lu Junyi imagine it? That tickle on the edge of hearing, like a light wind through new growth . . .

The rustling increased. Commander Wen's eyes had closed too, and he reached out his other hand straight in front of him. Dry leaves danced across the stone, pattering to swirl under his outstretched palm.

Lu Junyi tried to keep hope from somersaulting through her. The unaltered god's fangs had functioned for only moments before corrupting their hosts from inside . . .

"Oh." Fan Rui made the sound very softly.

Lu Junyi gripped her arm. "Is something wrong?"

Fan Rui didn't answer. Across the courtyard, the lines of Commander Wen's face had begun to harden, struggling into a grimace. His hands shook as if he clung to something too tight.

"Priestess!" Lu Junyi cried. "What's happening?"

"He cries," Fan Rui whispered.

Lu Junyi gazed across at the commander. She wanted to run to him, but dared not.

Tears. As Fan Rui had said.

Thick tears. Tears of some shining dark gray that welled from his eyes. Slid down his cheeks.

Not tears—more like blood—blood of molten metal. Creeping drops at first, then rapidly multiplying, becoming a flood. More molten gray leaked from his ears, his nose and mouth, squeezed out from his hand where he gripped the god's fang . . .

"Commander!" Lu Junyi shouted. "Back away from it. Release its power!"

He either couldn't or wouldn't. Dark metal streamed down his neck and chest now, hardening on the folds of his clothes. All over his body, it welled from every pore, flowing against itself to drown skin and hair and eyes . . .

"Do something—" Lu Junyi begged Fan Rui. "Do something, stop it—"

Fan Rui had begun to hum. Very lightly, but for a long and terrible moment, the tune carried in harmony with the still-rustling breeze.

Then everything died to abrupt stillness.

Lu Junyi slipped out from behind the plinth. Her hands were trembling. She felt as if she should not be able to stand upright.

In the center of the courtyard, Commander Wen stood, encased in a shell of dull metal. The hardened material outlined his eyes, the tendons of his neck, his teeth in a mouth that had partially opened as if to scream silently forever. The last slow drips had frozen in time to create a metal man caught in the moment of melting to nothing.

It had all been so quiet.

Fan Rui spoke by her ear. "Ah. You feared death. He lives still."

Lu Junyi had thought her horror total. Now it eclipsed her whole mind, made it hard to speak. She caught the plinth with her hand, its roughness anchoring her.

Such a state of living death—surely it could not last long, not without breath and air. Surely Commander Wen's peace was near.

The moments stretched. Behind Lu Junyi and Fan Rui, a disturbed shuffle came from the priestess's guards, the consternation a break from their usual discipline.

"Priestess." Lu Junyi's voice was brittle, barely a whisper. "Please. Surely he can't . . ."

Hear them, see them, sense this world he'd been walled away from . . . still be living . . .

"His life force draws on the god's fang," Fan Rui murmured. "Hmm. I wonder if the Fa monks ever tried this version of immortality."

Immortality.

Immortality.

To live forever, sustained by the energy of an unstable god's fang, every sense screaming to nothing.

Commander Wen had been willing to die for his Emperor.

No one had ever warned him of this.

CHAPTER 12

Upon reflection, Lin Chong realized she had not known exactly what went into banditry. Although—she supposed it was possible the Liangshan bandits followed methods different from the other brigand groups who plagued the rural hills outside the Empire's cities.

For instance, she suspected that among other bandits, making ready for a complicated robbery would not take on a tone similar to that of a bridal celebration. Lin Chong hadn't been invited to many such events, not having come from either a very wealthy family nor a large one filled with sisters and cousins, but the occasional higher-class friend had honored her with inclusion in the most traditional three-day ceremonial preparation. The cheerful bonding during those rituals as the women carefully attended to each other's cleansing and dressing, to hairstyles and face makeup, reminded her of . . . well, now.

At least in a slight, more abbreviated sense, as Fifth Brother Ruan helped Seventh Brother tie his women's clothing correctly, Hu Sanniang expertly wrapped Chao Gai's bare pate and hid her Transcendentalist tattoo, and Seventh Brother chuckled with Wu Yong about checking everybody's faces for unplucked hair.

"I'm going to be the prettiest woman out of any of you," Seventh Brother bragged, peacocking in his new getup.

"Speak for yourself!" Fifth Brother shot back with a laugh. Lin Chong had learned he switched back and forth between men's and women's clothes on normal days according to his whim, which here at Liangshan went entirely uncommented on.

Not that they were trying to be dressed up in their finest today. More . . . unremarkable. Female merchants traveling in a group for safety, blending into all the other weary denizens of the road in worn garments and unthreatening demeanors. Certainly no one who would be remembered out of the crowd. Wu Yong had laid out functional merchant smocks for all of them, though accompanied by short swords and a few other choices of weapon that would lie flat beneath the clothes just in case, and was taking turns with Chao Gai to have head wraps wound and minutely adjusted to hide every bit of both of their unusual hair—or lack thereof. Lastly, unlike for a wedding, face painting was no requirement for a role like this . . . except for Lin Chong.

"Here," Hu Sanniang said, marching up to Lin Chong where she sat and reaching out to grasp her chin and tilt her face up. "I'll do you up. My ama taught me all sorts of tricks to hide skin flaws. 'Wipe it away till the wedding day,' was her saying."

Lin Chong could feel her color rising. She'd never been ashamed of her face.

She'd never had *cause* to be ashamed of her face. But then, her face had never been something that could lead to instant arrest.

Hu Sanniang ran a clinical finger down the convict's tattoo on Lin Chong's left cheek. Now that it was healed, Lin Chong found it easy to forget—too easy. After all, she wasn't seeing her own face. But when others looked at her . . .

It would always scream her history before anything she was, anything she did. Cleaved into her forever.

Hu Sanniang's hands, so deft with her double sabers and lasso, were equally deft with a makeup brush—although just as lacking in delicacy. She painted Lin Chong's skin with both skill and a disinterested firmness.

Lin Chong closed her eyes and tried not to flinch away. Now that she'd remembered, the skin beneath the brand felt raw, tender, as if Hu Sanniang's ministrations were pressing the cuts in further.

She had to be imagining that. It must be healed by now.

"Saddle the horses," Wu Yong directed Second Brother, who was monkeying around with her crossdressed younger siblings while the rest of them finished. "I want to be across the water before full morning. We have to be in Haozhou by midday or we'll miss the window on Huangni Ridge."

Lin Chong still wasn't sure what to think of Wu Yong. Tall, spindly, and always ready with a listening ear—and then, alternately, with prying questions and the exact words to set people at ease—Wu Yong had an almost aggressive skill at social grease. Lin Chong envied and harbored suspicion against it in equal measure. But that wasn't even why people seemed to speak about Wu Yong so favorably in the camp.

Instead, it seemed impossible for anyone to speak a breath about Wu Yong without extolling their Tactician's cleverness. Wu Yong the clever, Wu Yong the resourceful, Wu Yong the brilliant—and yes, Wu Yong the Tactician, as the nickname went.

Perhaps it was not the uniqueness of the Liangshan bandits, but Wu Yong alone that made this plan feel so different than Lin Chong expected. After all, the Zhang and Tong families had come back yesterday rowdy and mud-covered, dried blood still spattering the side of Tong Wei's face from an incident she laughingly refused to disclose, only telling taller and taller tales. First she claimed a brawl with a dozen drunken monks, then a wrestling match with a tiger, then an attack by a vengeful bull demon, as the wine flowed long into the night and the feasting with it . . . the bandits did love a good feast here, celebrating with slow-cooked pork and fat salted carp and cherries cooked over rice until they burst in sweetness. The returning victors had been on some type of smuggling operation, Lin Chong had surmised—salt or silver or maybe porcelain, she hadn't figured out the straight answer. She did know they had brought back with them load upon load of provisions, gold and silver but also rice and mung beans and leather and tools, plus five great butchered hogs stretched across their horses.

Lin Chong was likewise not clear on whether these provisions came from the smuggling operation itself, had been bought with those proceeds, or had been pillaged in an entirely separate endeavor. She'd nibbled at some fish, declined the wine, and tried not to think too hard about it.

Does living here, eating this food, sleeping under these roofs—does it already mean I am partaking in this? Does it already mean I am guilty?

Worse, she knew the question barely mattered, considering that she was expected to go on this heist with Chao Gai come morn to reappropriate jin upon jin of jewels and precious metals, all being sent to Cai Jing from Daleng.

Astonishing, how such an unreal thing had become part of her reality. Chao Gai's directed preparations week after week, training councils with Wu Yong and the others, a carefully devised plan that they had talked of with such unbelievable normalcy, over and over, until Lin Chong looked around bewildered and realized just how far she had traveled past any reasonable moment to be appalled.

Now here they were, on a day she had not quite believed would come to be, and she had not even once tried to refuse. Every time her thoughts edged in that direction, they were balanced by how precarious her position was here, how little she understood, how few her options were if she were to leave. She'd made excuses to herself, and hesitated . . . until here she was about to rob the Grand Chancellor of the Empire.

Maybe the fact that it *didn't* seem real made it easier.

She tried to tell herself that at least she was not being asked to burn a village or steal from those who would starve. This was a Wu Yong plan, and Wu Yong's plans, Lin Chong had come to understand, tended to be . . . different. Sneakier. Tricks and schemes to get around putting anyone in direct danger. Some of the bandits seemed to prefer the danger—Lin Chong was already getting an idea of which; the edge of violence she sometimes witnessed in her lessons here engendered a wariness she had rarely felt when teaching in Bianliang—but Wu Yong did not seem to relish danger for its own sake.

Wu Yong, Lin Chong strongly suspected, instead liked to *win*.

Seeing how closely aligned with Song Jiang's contingent the Tactician seemed to be, Lin Chong wasn't sure if all that made the group gentler or more dangerous.

In her innermost uncharitable misgivings, Lin Chong wondered if the relative moral palatability of this plan was why Chao Gai had suggested she join on this robbery in particular. After all, Lin Chong was not best-suited to its guises of playacting. But Wu Yong had assured her that was fine, that her job was only to keep her martial skills ready in reserve, in case they encountered an unexpected hitch. If all went according to design, this was a mission that would involve no killing of innocents or destruction of property at all—Lin Chong was only along in case something went wrong.

Even if she came and watched and did nothing but help ferry the spoils back, however, that would still forever solidify her position with them. Stealing from Cai Jing . . .

Every time Lin Chong let herself remember the depth of it, her souls seemed to drop from her as if she had stepped off a cliff, falling and falling forever.

Grand Chancellor Cai Jing. So close to the Emperor that the aura of the Lord of Heaven might as well envelop him too. Stealing his wealth had the audacity of stealing from the sun.

How could they not get burned?

They would succeed because of Wu Yong's plan, the others would say. Because nobody ever outsmarted Wu Yong. Because Wu Yong had plans within plans, first unthreatening disguises and drugged wine, exactly at the right time and place, and then for every twist, every unexpected obstacle, another contingency—or so everyone seemed to believe. With Lin Chong herself as one of those contingencies.

Lin Chong had seen Wu Yong and Chao Gai with their heads together too often to truly doubt the depths of their preparedness.

Second Brother Ruan brought the horses. Lin Chong's was to be a spirited gray-white beast who danced in anticipation when she took hold of the harness. She was no expert in horseflesh, but it seemed to be a fine animal—maybe too fine. Like everything else at Liangshan, she tried not to think about where the steed might have come from.

She checked the girth and adjusted the stirrups, then swung up astride, to more prancing by the horse. The short sword and long knife she wore bumped against her thigh under the skirts of her borrowed merchant's clothes.

"Calm," she murmured, reaching out to pat the horse's neck. "We've a long ride. You'll get your chance to move."

"We call that one Little Wujing," Seventh Brother said, sidling his mount up alongside hers. "She likes turnips. Will devour them by the barrelful. Ai! Here we go!"

Ahead of them, Chao Gai called a whoop out into the morning and waved for them to follow. In the headwrap and without her monk's robes, she was barely recognizable but for her arrow-straight posture in the saddle. A long staff was thrust upright through the straps of her horse's tack—a very unsuspicious but effective weapon.

"Have you been back down the mountain yet?" Seventh Brother asked Lin Chong as they fell in behind. "If not, I'll give you the proper tour. I think you'll like the setup, Drill Instructor!"

His excitement was infectious. Lin Chong found herself murmuring gracious approval as he pointed out the watchtowers, the defensive positions, the way the terrain of the dense mountainside and the twisty marsh below constricted any substantial force to a single approach. A deep natural fissure folded the mountain vertically to one side of the trail they rode down, and Seventh Brother bragged of the further defenses they had set up far in advance upslope, for the day any large army came: logs and boulders and floods that could be released to roar down the fissure and bury anyone making a landing on the mountain.

Lin Chong nodded along while conflicting emotions bit into her heart like bee stings. Listening to the violence this bandit stronghold was prepared to bring, it was like seeing two sides of the same coin—on one hand instant horror; she could *see* exactly how many military officers would die in any doomed assault on this outlaw place. And yet—here was Seventh Brother, young, decent, someone she liked, swelling with pride at the way they kept everyone safe . . . people like Lu Da and An Daoquan who had saved her life, and others she had been coming to know through training, plus her own self and life and future—all hidden behind these armaments that were so primed to kill the very Guard she'd so recently held loyalty to.

The horses picked their way down the trail, the dawn sun stabbing through the leaves and the delicate dewy scent of early morning rising around them. Insects buzzed among the lush greenery, birds calling above and the rustling of small animals through the undergrowth as they took advantage of this pleasant time before the heat of the day. Not that it ever got too warm out here in the middle of the marsh.

As they neared the base of the mountain, the trail became narrower, with soft boggy spots soaking through in deceptively spongy pitfalls between the rocks and dirt. Reeds and marsh grass spiked up in tall clumps, with fat dragonflies zipping among them.

The horses spread out into a precise single file, Hu Sanniang ahead of Lin Chong and Seventh Brother Ruan behind. Chao Gai whistled at them from up ahead, and Hu Sanniang turned in her saddle to call, "Make sure you follow exactly!"

The warning was unneeded. Lin Chong knew the dangers of terrain like this. Her spritely horse seemed equally adept, not showing any further inclination to dance out from beneath her, and staying carefully to the firm, winding bit of earth Chao Gai led them along.

Truly there could be no more defensible place for a hideout.

The watery stretches eventually took over more and more of the ground. The early sun flashed through to glance off an algae-soaked pool to one side or a swamp of logs and squat gnarly trees on the other, with roots trying to claw above the wet and never quite succeeding. Even on the path, Little Wujing's hooves began sucking against the ground, the mud churning up in the riders' wake and spattering up above their mounts' fetlocks. Perhaps half a watch of the morning after they'd set off from the bandits' settlement, they came out onto a peninsula that was buttressed against the encroaching marsh by heavy stacks of logs slugged horizontally against the muddy earth.

Ahead of them, the mud submerged into a glassy lake, islands of more mud or reeds rising up here and there among the water. Two large ferry boats had been moored against the peninsula, a cheerful clatter rising from them as the Tong and Zhang siblings prepped the boats for launch.

"Ho!" the elder Tong sister called, as lustily as if she hadn't been awake all night drinking and feasting. "Ready to set off? Bring us back some treasures, eh? You won't be beat by us lowly salt smugglers, will you!"

"We're only simple merchants," Wu Yong bantered back. "How could we ever compare to your magnificent hauls?"

"Kings of the marsh, we are!" crowed Zhang Heng, the aptly nicknamed Boatman. "Not just Liangshan Marsh neither. We're the captains of the bog, brigands of the riverways, with our stronghold on the mountain that rules every plain of the Four Great River Deltas—"

"And Heroes of the Empire!" Seventh Brother finished, hopping out of his saddle to land in the mud with a great smack.

"You'll ruin your disguise!" Fifth Brother chastised, dismounting with significantly more grace. "Quick, rinse the mud off in the water."

Seventh Brother rolled his eyes but did as he was told, dipping his muddy hems in the marsh water, which wasn't entirely clean itself but at least saved him from looking like he'd walked out of a swamp. Meanwhile, Lin Chong followed the others one by one in carefully coaxing their horses onto the two ferries. Little Wujing tossed her head and whinnied a bit, pulling against the bridle when her hooves clattered against the rocking boards of the deck. But at last both people and horses were aboard, and their jovial ferry captains called to each other and pushed off, shoving long poles deep into the marsh to guide the flat-bottomed craft through.

"They know Liangshan Marsh better than anybody," Seventh Brother piped up to Lin Chong, having apparently taken it upon himself to be the bringer of all information Liangshan. "Except for me and Second Brother and Fifth Brother, of course! The waters here are real tricky; even when it seems smooth there might be mud piles lurking underneath, so you gotta know where you can slip a boat through. Easy to dead-end and not be able to find your way out ever, or get run up aground and stranded. But the fishing's dang good in some of the deep bits, if you know where they are."

"You and your siblings are fisherfolk, I've heard?" Lin Chong replied politely. "I was told you came from not far from here."

"We're from Shijie—little village about ten li thataway." Seventh Brother flung his hand roughly toward the northwest. "Made a good living on the carp in the marsh, until we didn't. The county magistrate kept sending his snakey men to take everything we owned and said it was our duty to the Empire. Ha! I'll serve the Empire all day long, but if our fat golden carp went anywhere other than into the mouths of the magistrate and his cronies, I'll eat my sword."

"And that's when you joined the bandits?"

"Not right away. We hated the Liangshan bandits at first—when they first set up on the mountain, we couldn't use any of our old hunting grounds on this side of the marsh, which was all the deepest ones with the fattest fish. They'd put out the word, you see, that this was Liangshan territory now, and no one dared cross 'em—with good reason. So squeezed from both sides, we were, and Fifth Brother tried to win us back on top in the gambling parlors and lost his shirt and shoes. Came barefoot back home, he did. It was a fine trap. But the Professor had lived in Shijie back fifteen years ago or so, and liked the look of us then, even though we couldn't read or write for nothing, and we were nobody next to someone working as an official tutor and stuff. But I guess we've got valor and we fight well and we know this marsh like our own hands and feet, and when the Professor came and said Liangshan could use us, we jumped that instant. Scrape a living that gets stolen from us by the rich bums in their yamen, or live a good life as heroes? Easy choice!"

"The Professor—that's Wu Yong?"

"Yup, cleverest person in the Empire! And life's so good here.

We eat well and live well and we can act as true haojie. And we can fish and fight and build up a home. Hey, do you know how long I can swim underwater?"

Lin Chong cleared a queer feeling out of her throat. "How long?"

"See that island out that way? The one that looks like a qilin head? I could get all the way, not one breath!"

Lin Chong gazed out across the marsh. She found it harder to judge distances out here on the water, but that little horned isle had to be at least a quarter to half a li . . . she wondered if Seventh Brother was exaggerating. If not, it was an impressive feat.

He and his older siblings were clearly flourishing at Liangshan, after too long in a poverty Lin Chong felt achingly familiar with. Now here he stood on the boards of an illegal ferry, proudly showing her his home, shoulders thrust back and head high—with Mount Liang rising up behind him, far enough in their wake to become a majestic peak above the water. Seventh Brother was a handsome, lithe young man, with skin mottled dark or gold in places across his neck and fine-featured face, and here catching the early sun he struck Lin Chong as being uncannily in the mold of a carved bronze statue. A hero of the Empire, as he'd proclaimed.

What choice would she have expected him to make?

Even scraping her body raw with hard work for years upon years, Lin Chong had only clawed out of poverty with the luck of the gods. If her life had taken a few different turns . . . or if she'd been raised illiterate, as the Ruan brothers, with not even a chance at the Imperial exams . . .

She was under no illusions about how close it had been. A knife's edge separated the life she'd fought for from being dead, or forced to brothel work, or begging on the street corners.

And what had she done once that life had been torn away? She, too, was here, landing in the same place as Seventh Brother Ruan.

The two ferries glided through the water under the certainty of their crews, twisting first one way and then the next, with the mountain behind them and then to the left and then behind them again, until a more solid-looking shoreline finally came into view.

A handful of buildings clung to the edge of the marsh, their back ends on stilts that drove deep into the wet, and beyond them, a low flood wall showed the presence of a proper road that snaked out of the hills and followed the boundary of the swamplands.

The ferries seemed to hone in on the far end of the buildings, gaining speed until they bumped up against the shore next to what appeared to be a good-sized inn. "Ho, Crocodile!" someone called out.

Crocodile, Lin Chong suddenly remembered. An inn Lu Da had brought her to when she was hot with fever, where a woman called Crocodile had fed her strong-smelling tea and sent a whistling arrow across a marsh. Lin Chong had not been sensible enough to see any of this the first time.

"Ho!" The innkeeper herself came out—Lin Chong could not recall her proper name—and helped the ferriers lash themselves in among some pilings up against the back of the inn. Lin Chong's horse now seemed to be wary of the notion of dry land, and Lin Chong had to coax her back out onto the dock.

"I've got some hot bean curd to see you on your way," the Crocodile told them with a grin. "Aiya, Master Instructor Lin! So good to see you on your feet again. And you've got that awful convict's mark hidden nicely, I see."

"It was all Sister Hu's doing," Lin Chong answered, her hand halfway coming up before drawing back to avoid smearing the work. The makeup had started to itch slightly.

"Ah, Steel Viridian! She has too many talents. Here, have a hot cup."

Lin Chong took the offered snack gratefully. "Thank you. And thank you for all you did for me last month when I arrived."

"It was nothing. Only what little humble comforts I could offer here. Glad the Divine Physician was able to fix you up proper." The innkeeper flashed another smile and turned to bustle among the rest of them. "Ai, Tactician, it's been ages since you've been down the mountain! You're the picture of health!"

Despite the warm welcome and the even warmer food heating

their hands and bellies, Chao Gai and Wu Yong were not people who allowed the efficiency of the day to meander away. In only a little more time than it had taken to lead all the horses off the ferries, the two of them had everyone mounted again, with the cups returned to the Crocodile—Sister Zhu Gui, Lin Chong had caught her name at last—and both the innkeeper and the ferry crews lustily waved them off on their way.

They rode westward all morning, only taking time every so often to rest and water the horses. The landscape in these rural counties was wild and beautiful, with few travelers and long stretches of dense forest or fields green with new growth. As they moved west, more and more chains of hill and mountain began poking up through the wetlands, until the ground grew rockier and the beating sun began to make Lin Chong sweat beneath her borrowed clothes. Every so often the vista opened up to show a stretch of valley or farmland, the villages clustering where the roads crossed or along the banks of the rivers. Other travelers passed—sometimes even packs of Imperial soldiers; Lin Chong turned her face away—but nobody took any notice of them.

Eventually, Chao Gai led them off the road and up an overgrown track that wound into one of the small towns dotting the landscape, identical to all the others they'd passed. They pulled up the horses at a cottage tucked back against a mountain slope.

A pleasantly round woman hurried out, face wreathed in a smile beneath graying hair. "Chief Chao! Welcome, welcome. Welcome to all of you. Come in. We can take the horses back around that way—here, here, I'll help you."

This must be Chao Gai's friend, the staging house they'd been told to expect, and wine merchant Bai Sheng, the Sunmouse. She and Chao Gai began an animated catchup—"How is Dongxi? We miss living there very much" and "The village misses you as well; how old is your niece now" and "This is her eighth summer already, and oh you must see what we've done with the garden."

Lin Chong took Little Wujing behind the small house where directed and relieved the sweaty horse of saddle and provisions.

Bai Sheng had a trough of water and bundles of hay and leafy vegetables prepared for the beasts to have a repast in the shade, while their riders headed inside the cottage. A general hubbub followed as everyone took the opportunity to rest or take some dried meat and water.

"You have the wheelbarrows ready?" Chao Gai was asking Bai Sheng.

"Of course," she answered brightly. "Everything exactly as you said. I wouldn't—"

A noise sounded at the door.

A flurry of nervousness rippled through the group. Wu Yong raised a quiet hand at the rest of them and began shepherding everyone out the back of the house into the garden. Lin Chong moved along with the rest. She caught Bai Sheng's panicked whisper—"It's my husband—he wasn't supposed to be back this afternoon—"

The back door shut behind them.

Lin Chong's pulse thudded through her veins, a nervousness unlike any she'd experienced before actual combat. *You're already a convict, how can your standing become any worse, even if you're caught?* But it mattered to her, somehow—because this time she *was* acting illegally; this time she deserved it if they were seized, dragged before the magistrate, to her shame across this life and any lives that followed, forever—

Getting branded as a convict once—she suddenly felt sure she had survived it only on the strength of the knowledge of her own innocence.

Chao Gai lifted her hands and lowered them, quietly, following the motion herself by crouching in the tangled honeysuckle that twined up the back of the cottage walls. The rest of them followed her example, hunkering down in the shadow of the stone, out of sight of the window.

Bai Sheng had apparently not told her husband that she planned to play a key role today in robbing one of the richest and most powerful men in the Empire.

Lin Chong glanced at Wu Yong, who was grinning wide enough

to reveal teeth and gums from ear to ear. Like a corpse. This was *fun*? A sudden sharp weakness appearing in Wu Yong's own plan?

Doubtless the Tactician was already figuring a way around it. Jumping ahead, laying the traps.

Or maybe, for Wu Yong, this was what gave the game its rousing high. That even with the closest careful planning, no one could predict everything.

Lin Chong slid a hand beneath her merchant's smock and gripped the hilt of her short sword. Not that she thought she would kill an innocent man, if Bai Sheng's husband were to happen out here and rightfully proclaim an intention to run straight to the magistrate . . . if that were to happen, she didn't know what she would do. What she could do.

What if one of her new kindred-in-arms tried to kill him instead? Would Lin Chong betray *them,* in defending an innocent life?

The time slid by as if she could feel each droplet slipping down the edge of a garden water clock, slow and tremulous. Lin Chong rebalanced herself in the shrubbery, rolling her weight to guard against cramping.

Finally, the back door to the little house burst open. All seven were on their feet in an instant—the reflexes of birds of prey all honed on a sudden target, hands beneath clothing gripping short swords and chain and lasso—

Bai Sheng tumbled outside, and only Bai Sheng, bowing deeply and apologizing again and again.

"Forgive me! Oh, we had it all arranged, Chief, you know we did. He was to be at the markets all day today while I was to sell wine, we had it set up; he's never returned home like this before! I'm worthless, I've let you all down . . ."

"Shush now," Chao Gai said, placing a hand on her shoulder. "It may be that no harm was done. Did he notice anything?"

"He heard voices," Bai Sheng said, head lowered. "I told him it was a friend of mine from my old village, and that she'd just gone out to get some fruit and wine . . . he seemed to believe it."

Chao Gai looked across the rest of them. "We all know what

reward today can bring us. And we all know the risks. The decision to go ahead must be unanimous. Including you, my dear Sunmouse."

"I would never—this was my mistake; I could never back out," Bai Sheng answered, wringing her hands against her apron.

Chao Gai raised her eyebrows at the rest of them.

With a clink of what must be that favored copper chain, Wu Yong's hands came out from reaching beneath the merchant's smock, body straightening from a ready stance into a more familiar careless languor. "Stakes make the game, Heavenly King. We can still achieve the win."

"We're in too," Second Brother Ruan said, with a nod to her siblings, and Fifth Brother added, "A gamble is good for the blood! I'd never forgive myself for not going after such a reward."

Hu Sanniang had drawn a short, sharp knife and was casually trimming down her nails with it. "Heavenly King, you know you don't even have to ask."

Chao Gai turned to Lin Chong. "And you, Arms Instructor?"

Lin Chong hesitated. Should she be the voice of reason who stopped them all? Was this quest worth the high risk, the bottomless, endless punishment they would fall into if they got caught?

But then, had it ever been worth it?

You still have much to prove to them, a whisper in her mind reminded her. *If you want this life.*

So this was it, then. Two paths before her. If she declined, she did not have to read the stars to know Wang Lun would bid her a mocking farewell from Liangshan upon their return.

And if she did this, she was swearing her loyalty to these bandits—both proving herself to them in their eyes, and bonding in blood. Past any point of return.

These bandits who had welcomed her. Sheltered her. Healed her . . . after the system she'd sworn loyalty to before this had allowed a man to try to violate her and murder her, after it had given him no repercussion and he retained the highest of positions, while tearing every shred of her life to nothing.

What was she hanging on to?

She took a deep breath. Almost laughed. A dizzying freedom rippled through her.

Lu Da had been right, in her blunt, brash way. Perhaps these were the true haojie.

Perhaps it was time for the Empire's officials—officials like Gao Qiu, like Cai Jing—to see a consequence to their actions at last.

"Let's go," she said to the rest, with the keen sensation that somewhere behind her, a door had already closed.

CHAPTER 13

The sun beat down like it wanted to fill their bones with heat. Lin Chong's clothes sopped with sweat under her arms and down the front of her chest. She'd donned a headwrap as well as they hiked up the ridge, which kept her eyes clear, but the greasepaint on her face felt as if it were melting, and every second li or so she felt compelled to check with one of the others that it remained in place. But so far Sister Hu's work held.

The hike would not have been so taxing if she hadn't been shoving along a wheelbarrow piled high with dates, a cloth tacked over them to keep the fruits from spilling onto the road. It was no ruse; nothing lighter had been stuffed underneath to spare them on the journey. It was genuine mounds of cheap dates, prearranged as part of the preparatory investment by Chao Gai and Wu Yong, and stashed at their staging area at Bai Sheng's house.

Lin Chong found she did not envy real merchants their backbreaking daily journeys to sell their wares.

". . . Lu Da to encourage it," Wu Yong's voice drifted down from up ahead.

Lin Chong exerted herself with a grunt, shoving her cart so the wooden wheel bounced against the pitted road and jarred up her arms, but she managed to push up abreast of Wu Yong and Chao Gai. Fast enough to catch Wu Yong saying, "She went in the opposite direction I predicted, but a boon to us nonetheless. Better, even. It will be soon."

"What was that about Sister Lu?" Lin Chong asked.

Wu Yong twisted around, in surprise and—did Lin Chong imagine it?—a slight and quickly smothered irritation.

"Nothing important," the Tactician soothed her. "Simply a personal matter I was advising her on. We love Sister Lu greatly at Liangshan."

"No doubt," Lin Chong replied automatically. She wasn't paranoid, exactly, but . . . she felt an elder sort of protectiveness about her new sister. One she had no shame about.

It wasn't that she thought she ought to distrust Wu Yong—after all, the Tactician's loyalty to Liangshan seemed fierce and absolute, with that intense conniving directed purely outside their ranks. But perhaps it was not Wu Yong as a person, but that silver-tongued cleverness that Lin Chong couldn't quite trust. That, plus the continuing undercurrents of politics between Song Jiang and Wang Lun, and Wu Yong's place in that tangle . . . whatever that was.

No one had approached Lin Chong about it since that first day, and in everyday life no fault lines in the group were obvious. Even so, she'd made a wary effort not to be seen as aligning with any faction or person. Her enforced neutrality had required more struggle than anticipated, however, because she'd reluctantly begun to understand Song Jiang's reasoning.

Particularly regarding Wang Lun.

Every interaction with Wang Lun had developed into dodging invisible arrows, as Liangshan's nominal leader seemed to take even the most innocuous words from Lin Chong as the beginning of a fight. An overture to talk about the training schedule became instantly perceived as a challenge to Wang Lun's leadership. A question about the quartermastering of supplies, a smear on Liangshan's luxuries. Even Lin Chong's most pleasant and polite morning greeting when passing each other on one of the compound's paths was met with a suspicious sneer and a demand of what she meant by it.

Needless to say, Wang Lun had never subjected herself to Lin Chong's tutelage by coming to a training session herself. Supposedly, she had been an outlaw long enough to claim no need. Lin Chong could not say she minded.

But she felt no ease about Song Jiang's methods, either. Sister

Song's ways were more genteel, certainly . . . but that gentility would only serve to make the pitfalls more insidious.

Lin Chong would rest easier when the settlement of all this became clear. Especially as she looked toward a future of being one of this group—a member of Liangshan, its politics shaping her life and reality . . .

Chao Gai paused and scanned the road behind, waiting for the rest of the group to draw level with their barrows. They were the only travelers in sight at the moment, with the road empty all the way from the pitted valley they'd emerged from through its winding curve up into the rocks.

"We're almost to the top of the ridge," Chao Gai announced quietly, when everyone had caught up. "They will have found it impossible not to rest along this stretch when ascending from the other side, and now will be the time. Remember, from here no names—Elder Sister and Little Sister only to address each other. We are longtime friends who have made this journey for many years."

The others murmured their understanding. Lin Chong was not privy to how Wu Yong had managed to plan such exact timing here, what whispers of information had led to this careful calculation, but it had been impressed upon all of them that the heist was as finely tuned as a set of delicate pulleys. Lin Chong strongly suspected some network of eyes and ears, one that leaned heavily on Chao Gai's many, many friends.

"Luck to us all," Chao Gai said softly, and led them up the last stretch toward the top of Huangni Ridge.

Lin Chong's pulse had increased its steady thump again. But not, she thought, from fear. Not this time.

This time, for the first step into a future she was choosing.

Their wheelbarrows came over the last hump to make the peak. The road at the top of the ridge unspooled onward for several li here, its edges alternately butting up against further slopes with bits of woodland clinging to them or dropping away to spectacular views of the plains below. The sun glanced off the dirt and stone and even the far-off rivers snaking through the region, flashing against their vision and flattening the whole landscape as if into one long sheet of bronze metal.

Lin Chong kept her gaze on her wheelbarrow and on the road and on her trudging feet, not glancing off to either side. Her other senses stayed wide, but Chao Gai and Wu Yong would tell them when to rest.

When to pretend to rest.

She swiped a hand across her eyes, the headwrap no longer keeping them clear of sweat out here in the bright. Made sure not to catch her cheek with her sleeve and rub her criminal status clear for all to see.

They rounded a bend in the road. A few travelers passed in the opposite direction, merchants bowed under bamboo shoulder poles, trudging with the same weary gait as they were. The ridge rose up a bit on one side, widening into groves of trees deep enough to hide the dropoff. The shadows beneath them were liquid, calling through the heat.

Up ahead, Chao Gai slowed. Very subtly, she nodded to Wu Yong. They stopped.

"Let's rest here, sisters," Chao Gai called back to them.

Lin Chong forced herself to continue keeping her eyes down, only just ahead. It wouldn't do to seem too alert.

They heaved the wheelbarrows off the road, over the hump at its edge and bumping over roots and grass and brush. The shadows under the trees were so intense it was as if the world had been cut off. Light and dark. Past and future.

Lin Chong was not sure how Chao Gai had spotted the eleven men who already lounged under the trees. But somehow, she had. The rest of them followed her meandering lead to somewhere close by the other group, but not *quite* adjacent. In these times, with the threat of being accosted on the road so great, very few travelers would choose to rest neighboring one another—but Chao Gai was not moving near enough to break those unspoken boundaries.

Yet.

Still, the leader of the men unfolded fluidly to his feet, hand on a broadsword at his side. Military. Lin Chong could tell immediately, somehow, even though he, like them, was disguised in the tunic of a merchant, or perhaps a merchant's guard. But her eye could see the training—well-balanced, disciplined, alert to the changes around him. This was a role of such importance, marching these costly presents down to Bianliang. And banking only on subterfuge—they all must have been so aware that even ten companies of the Imperial Guard would not have been able to keep them from the rampant robberies along these roads, not with the value they carried, and hence landed on this more minimal plan. The porters, too, must be soldiers in disguise, Imperial Guardsmen conscripted to play pack mule in this covert detachment. Relying on obscurity to make sure they succeeded in what otherwise would have been pure folly.

Lin Chong spotted the bundles . . . disguised in lumpy wrappings and hanging from poles that the exhausted soldiers had shrugged from their shoulders for this moment of rest.

Unfathomable to imagine what riches lay hidden here. Chao Gai had explained to them her intelligence on the treasure, however she had gotten such facts; it still seemed unreal.

"Ho, we're resting here," the leader called. "What's your business?"

Chao Gai stopped cold, as if she had only just noticed the others taking up space beneath the trees. "What's yours? We want no trouble. We don't have anything of value."

"We're not bandits," the soldier said. He ran an eye over them, took in their number, their appearance—seven women merchants with carts of some product for market. "Show me what you carry, if you want to rest here."

Some part of Lin Chong approved of this officer's scrupulousness.

"Only dates," Chao Gai said, tugging back an edge of cloth to show the fruit beneath. "My sisters and I are fatigued. We won't disturb you."

The officer relaxed and waved his acquiescence.

Chao Gai slid her staff out from where she'd stowed it on the side of her wheelbarrow, as if she wished to lean on it while moving about the grove. Then she shifted the dates to a spot that would both be visible from the road and help block them from any passing eyes—even as it would signal to others of their presence here and keep honest passersby away, skittish of an occupied place.

The dishonest ones they weren't so worried about. Any other dishonest travelers they encountered could be dealt with.

The others followed her example, then settled down in the shade as if resting. Lin Chong was careful to keep changing position, never letting her muscles grow lax. It wouldn't be long now.

She had her back to the disguised soldiers, mostly—though she kept half an eye on their leader, who was some paces away across a clearing in the grove. He looked to be a bit older than Lin Chong, as might be expected for someone in charge of such a commission. A long scar marked his face with the history of hard experience, the puckering of skin at opposite angles from a dark blue birthmark that covered his cheek and one eye. He seemed to have relaxed toward the presence of the merchant women, instead returning his alertness more toward the road.

The other soldiers had no such unwavering attentiveness, taking advantage of their break to rest and chatter in low voices. Two of the closest, though out of Lin Chong's view, were near enough for their voices to carry, and she let their crude jests and complaints about the heat wash over her. It reminded her of being back in Bianliang.

Until two very different syllables caught her ear.

Gao Qiu.

"I heard it was Gao Qiu," one was saying to the other.

Hot anger flooded up in Lin Chong, nausea pooling in her gut. Once again she was back in White Tiger Hall, while with a handful of words he ripped her life away—

She furiously flipped back through the overheard conversation. They had been gossiping about their commander, someone surnamed Yang. One had asked how such a skilled officer as Commander Yang had ended up at *Daleng,* his voice dripping scorn for their shared, shameful position in life. Daleng was a far northern penal colony—much like the one Lin Chong herself had been intended for.

Intended for, and never arrived, because Imperial Marshal Gao Qiu had done his best to make sure she didn't.

"I heard it was all because of some scholar's stone, if you can believe it," the one with the gossip continued. "Commander Yang was in charge of getting it to the marshal. It was the typhoons last year, the ones that flooded all the Four Great River Deltas and drowned half of Qing Province. The commander and his men were transporting the stone down the river on barges when the storms hit. He barely got his men off the water, and the stone had been chiseled out in blocks of a thousand jin each—it all sank, every pebble of it. Commander Yang said his men were faultless, took full responsibility before the marshal."

"Of course he did," the man's companion replied, in the hushed tones of someone who already reveres his commander, and cannot fathom why the man would have been sent to such a piteous place of punishment with the rest of them.

"Marshal Gao stripped him three ranks and banished him to the deployment at Daleng. But then of course the commander saved Governor Liang's wife and the governor granted him a new commission—you heard all about that, yeah? He's a hero. That's why he was handpicked for this. Who knows, if it goes off smooth maybe he ends up getting called back to Bianliang by the Chancellor. And takes us with him, eh?"

The other soldier chuckled. "What I wouldn't give to be down in the capital. Warm sun, willing women . . ."

"The commander'll get us there. It's his big chance to prove himself again. Last chance, probably, and he won't get it wrong. Did you see the tournament when Governor Liang first added him to his personal guard? The major and the general both got the piss beat out of them. Thought there was no way they wouldn't trounce a woman, and one who'd been demoted to Daleng besides, and then have all the cred of beating a Guard officer out of the capital.

Word is the commander went easy on them or else they would've ended the day in pieces. Commander Yang will get us to Bianliang, no matter how many bandits run these roads—we're already more'n halfway."

Lin Chong had to stifle a quick intake of breath. *A woman—*

The soldiers had made no reference to their superior as a man; the assumption had only seemed obvious. Obvious, but wrong. Detachment Commander Yang Zhi—formerly Captain Yang Zhi—was one of the few female military officers serving in the Empire.

Lin Chong knew her name, remembered her name. High-ranking women in the Guard could be counted on the fingers of both hands.

Yang Zhi's training had predated Lin Chong's tenure as an arms instructor—it must have; to attain the rank of captain without favors or connections took decades of dedicated service—so they'd never met face to face. But Lin Chong had a vague recollection of hearing tales of the former captain coming in and out of Bianliang on detachments. A well-respected officer, trusted with a string of far-ranging commands. Nicknamed the Blue Beast, for the indigo birthmark crossing her face and her brutal endurance as a fighter.

Apparently, Commander Yang had been stripped of those hard-earned captain's knots, demoted, and banished by a sniveling, insecure Gao Qiu.

Under her clothes, Lin Chong's hand had tightened on the hilt of her short sword until her knuckles ached. She consciously tried to relax it. *How dare he . . .* those storms had flattened the lands; no one could have rescued thousands of jin of stone from a swelling river. To ask such a thing was absurdity. Yang Zhi had wisely saved her men when all else was lost—and Gao Qiu had gutted her career with the same petty malevolence as he had Lin Chong's.

And now that Commander Yang had the stunning luck of a distant governor again recognizing her worth—now that she had the slimmest chance to prove herself again with an errand of highest importance and claw back some of the life that had been stolen from her—it was Lin Chong and the others who were about to snatch that chance from her.

That wasn't justice. Wasn't the heroism Liangshan was supposed to stand for.

It's not us at fault, though—not us, and not her. It's everything. The whole hierarchy. The marshals and the nepotism and the magistrates, the bribes, pettiness, favoritism . . . we're not to blame for Commander Yang being here. That was Gao Qiu—again—again—he put her in this place, disgraced her and banished her to this mountain where we now meet . . .

Gao Qiu had done this. He and the Chancellor. What had Wu Yong scoffed about during their planning sessions? "What kind of man would risk human lives to demand tribute to himself, and in the form of such superfluous treasures transported across such dangerous terrain? Treasures doubtless siphoned from the northern peasants in the first place! Only one of the greatest villains of the people."

Still . . .

Lin Chong glanced toward the road. No sign yet of Bai Sheng. She pushed herself to her feet and stepped over to crouch next to Chao Gai.

"What is it, Sister?" Chao Gai's eyes were closed, and she had settled on the ground with her back against a tree. But Lin Chong knew she saw all that went on, somehow.

"The leader of the soldiers," Lin Chong replied in as hushed a whisper as she could manage. "She's an honorable officer. A woman banished by Gao Qiu."

She spat the name without meaning to.

Chao Gai was a moment in answering. "What of it?"

"How can we—" Lin Chong's hands clenched tighter, her jaw gritting against itself. She tried again. "You said we were about justice. Commander Yang is not corrupt. I heard the men talking—"

"All those who serve such injustice are corrupt in their complicity. In some way," Chao Gai said, her eyes still closed.

"Even the Emperor?" She'd spoken the words before their meaning penetrated. Such blasphemy, even to consider, even to *question*—

"The Emperor is lied to by those around him. He does not know the rot they carry out in his name," Chao Gai answered. "Remember, Commander Yang, as you call her, transports ill-gotten gains from one thief and tyrant to another. She is no hero."

Lin Chong's gut had gone heavy.

She'd known, though, hadn't she? She'd known what aligning herself with Liangshan would mean.

Perhaps, when this was over—leaving everyone unharmed, as planned—perhaps Yang Zhi would run. She didn't have to return to her superiors, as she had after losing the scholar's stone; didn't have to take responsibility again only to be torn apart for something that had been beyond her control. The folly of sending that much wealth across a lawless expanse, only to stroke an old man's ego on his birthday—it had been a decision made far above her.

Lin Chong hoped Commander Yang would run.

She didn't think it likely.

Chao Gai's eyes came open. "It begins," she murmured.

Lin Chong squinted out at the road without being obvious about it. Her senses must not be as acute as Chao Gai's.

But in their conversations about Lin Chong's . . . newer abilities . . . Chao Gai had also told her she need not fear these sharpened sensations. That she should not hesitate to sink into their touch, that she could easily pull back . . . in meditations, it had been easy, but dare she try now? Even for a moment?

She took a slow breath and let herself open up to the tendrils that had continued tickling her mind, ever since that moment in the woods with Lu Da.

The surrounding trees—beetles burrowing against the bark. Branches that had grown knobbly around hardened knots of fungus. The grass folding beneath the thick soles of her hemp boots. The leaves rustling above, and a small tree squirrel bounding from branch to branch far over their heads.

Her bandit partners, crouched in their varying states of readiness. The soldiers, exhausted, slumped against their bundles, tiny grass flies buzzing about the dried salt on their skin. And trundling down from the street, crashing a little in the brush, another person . . .

Lin Chong inhaled quickly. She'd *felt* Bai Sheng approaching a moment before she'd heard and seen her.

It was so very strange.

Connections, Chao Gai had said. The earth, the elements, all living beings . . .

Bai Sheng was bent under a yoke carrying two large, covered buckets. They swung wildly as she stumbled through the brush from the road; she stopped and bent her knees to lower them to the ground with obvious relief. She shrugged the yoke from her shoulders and sank down on the lid of one of the buckets, fanning her face with her hands.

Commander Yang had stood up straight at her approach, ever vigilant, hand on her sword. She relaxed slightly when she saw Bai Sheng was a lone traveler, just a woman with her wine buckets, seeking a reprieve from the sun. It had become crowded under the trees, but Bai Sheng hadn't come close enough to any of the rest of them to arouse suspicion.

Just as Chao Gai had instructed.

Commander Yang's mind might have been more focused on the potential threat, but her men perked up for a different reason.

"Woman," called one of them—the gossipy soldier Lin Chong had been listening in on. "Woman, is that wine you have in those buckets?"

"It sure is," confirmed another one of the soldiers. "I saw her in the market when we passed through town yesterday, plying her trade. Say, how much to quench our thirst instead?"

Bai Sheng affected some thought. "In town each bucket goes for five taels of silver. You match that, and I'll sell one to you—but not one coin less."

The men eagerly put their heads together, muttering among

themselves. "We can do five taels—" "If we pool our coin, it's only two strings each—" "It's so hot, my throat is dry as a used whore—"

"Hold," Yang Zhi said. She had not moved, appraising Bai Sheng with a contemplative eye. "You all know the tales along these routes. Her wine could be drugged, with bandits waiting in the trees to slit our throats. No deal, madam."

"But Commander—" whined one of the soldiers, and Yang Zhi shot him a glare. The men likely weren't supposed to break cover with military titles.

"My wine? Drugged?" cried Bai Sheng, crossing her arms in great affront. "How dare you! I don't think I want to sell to you anyway."

"And we don't wanna buy." Yang Zhi had a strong Bing accent. It was just as at odds with the rank she'd achieved as her gender—people from Bing Province rarely made higher than lieutenant. Part of it was simple bigotry—Lin Chong was more keenly aware of such currents, given her own maternal line—but the youth from that far north and west were rarely literate or had any prior education in martial arts, tactics, military history, or geography.

Such a deficit was extraordinarily hard to overcome.

"Platters of meat 'n wine when we hit Haozhou," Yang Zhi said to her men. "As much as anyone can drink. My word on't."

The soldiers mumbled dour assents.

Wu Yong had told them all there was a good chance of this, if the commanding officer had any sense. The dangers of bandits on this road were well-known, along with all the accompanying commonsense cautions: Don't sleep outside an inn. Don't show any wealth on your person. If you travel at night, do it armed and in groups. Always keep a weapon near at hand . . .

And, among these oft-repeated warnings: Don't accept food or drink outside an establishment. Even when limiting to inns, tales abounded of travelers being drugged and robbed, or worse.

Like what Sun Erniang had done in her past life, and others who ran the black taverns. Lin Chong was still getting used to the fact that such things were not merely a legend manufactured to inspire fear . . .

Like Yezhu Forest. Or courts with no justice in their walls.

Nothing in this world was as it seemed. Nothing in this world had the order it pretended for itself.

"Five taels, you say?" Hu Sanniang called, pushing herself to her feet and stretching. "Sisters, what do you think? We have so long to go . . . I want some wine!"

Hu Sanniang had been a good choice to play this part. Lin Chong would have believed every word—the pretty young woman had even dropped the cultured edge of wealth that usually colored her articulation. She laughed and began to pull purse strings as the Ruan brothers got up to gather round in enthusiastic agreement.

Lin Chong stood mechanically to follow. Her face felt stiff, as if she didn't know what expression to make. She kept her back to Commander Yang's people. She need not accomplish the same playacting—she only needed not to contradict them.

Her own role would only come into play if the ruse failed. The hope was that her presence would be wholly superfluous.

Hu Sanniang thrust a triumphant fist in the air, clutching a small silver ingot. "What do you say, wine seller? We'll buy a bucket off you. Five taels!"

Bai Sheng harrumphed, wiping sweat from her eyes and not moving from her seat on the bucket lid. "I'll not sell to those who insult me. The town is only a few more li. No trouble to sell it all there, and they treat me right."

"Oh, come on, give a little," Hu Sanniang wheedled. "We weren't the ones doing insults! Why not sell to us? We didn't accuse you of drugging a drop of it."

"Yeah," put in Seventh Brother. "We're thirsty. We're coming up from the south, so we've been hiking the ridge all day, no food since Haozhou. And our goods are so heavy. Look, we'll throw in some dates."

Bai Sheng looked down her nose to where they were gathered

below her in the sloping grove. "Do you have your own ladle to drink with? I have none."

"We do!" crowed Wu Yong. "I have one in the baggage—wait a moment—"

A brief and cheerful scramble ensued, in which silver was exchanged, a ladle produced, and handfuls of dates pressed on the supposedly reluctant wine seller. Bai Sheng pried off the lid of one of her buckets and stood back to let them at it.

Lin Chong had not thought it smart to imbibe too much of the wine. But apparently bandits were like military officers, and saw no danger in becoming flush with drink right before a fight might be required. It was not what Lin Chong would have preferred, but nor was she in charge of this operation, and the others riotously gulped and chattered, passing around the ladle.

Lin Chong might not need to act at the same level of gregariousness, but she did take her turn. She stayed facing away from the soldiers and let most of the wine dribble down the front of her merchant's clothes. The rest were spilling enough anyway—as they drank and roughhoused and passed the ladle around over each other's heads.

After pretending participation, Lin Chong fell back slightly. Wu Yong's plan was working—she caught the rustlings of the discontent soldiers growing behind her. "Look, they're having the wine. It's not drugged at all!" "Can't we buy the other bucket? It's so pissing hot!"

The Ruan brothers had broken out more handfuls of dates and were sharing them around in a seemingly impromptu picnic. Wu Yong and Chao Gai, as befitted their slightly elder mien, were nibbling and laughing as they chatted. Fifth Brother began chasing Hu Sanniang around with the ladle as they reached the bottom of the wine bucket; she shrieked and covered her head.

"Ho, we'll buy the rest of that from you!" shouted one of the soldiers. Commander Yang shut him down again, but the soldiers did not sound as accepting of it as before.

"I won't sell to you anyway!" Bai Sheng retorted, then tried to swat away Hu Sanniang and Seventh Brother, who had used the distraction to pull at the lid to the second bucket. "Hey, you didn't pay for that!" She whacked at them with a kerchief, chasing them off.

"Our silver's just as good as theirs," one of the soldiers tried to argue with Bai Sheng. "And if you sell both buckets, you won't have to walk the rest of the way into town at all. Don't you want to go home and be lazy in the shade?"

"Your boss says no!" Bai Sheng lobbed back, but, distracted by the back-and-forth, she failed to stop the rabble-rousing younger bandits from pulling off the lid of the second bucket and scooping a ladleful off the top.

Bai Sheng yelled and picked up a stick from the ground to shake at them. Everyone regrouped back near Wu Yong and Chao Gai. The Ruan brothers and Hu Sanniang were giggling among themselves.

Lin Chong had to marvel in watching. Had they done this before? Had they trained for it? Or had Chao Gai chosen these four especially for their ability to play the part? She must have.

Just as Wu Yong had predicted, the continuing escalation eventually did its job.

"See! None of it's poisoned. Smell that fragrance!" clamored the soldiers. "It's so hot here. We can go the rest of the day if we can only wet our throats . . ."

Commander Yang, seeing that it was impossible for either bucket to be drugged—or so she thought—finally relented.

The soldiers cheered. They swarmed Bai Sheng, begging her to sell to them, apologizing wholeheartedly for any insult to her wares. She grumpily agreed once they swore their willingness to pay the full five taels despite the ladleful that had been stolen.

An agreeable rapprochement followed. The soldiers passed over the silver, and Bai Sheng ushered them to her wine. They weren't carrying a ladle or bowl with them, so Second Brother graciously piped up and offered theirs. "Would you like a handful of dates, too, neighbor? To make up for that drink of yours we took. Nothing like wine and dates under these trees!"

Her offer was gratefully accepted, the ladle and dates were shared around, and Lin Chong *tried* not to watch for it, tried not to seem as though she was doing anything but standing with her merchant sisters, but she knew it was coming and had the sharp eyes of combat training—so she was surprised when she didn't see a hint of the sleight of hand depositing the moonflower and angelica. An Daoquan had provided them a strong powder of the herbs, strong enough to take the soldiers' consciousness and steal their memories after.

What if they catch us at it? Second Brother Ruan had asked. *Can't we come in with one bucket drugged already?*

And Wu Yong had said no, that there was a very good chance they'd need to do more *convincing,* and that sleight of hand was the way.

Lin Chong was starting to see why all believed Wu Yong's plans could go so far as to bring back the dragons, if one of them claimed to.

The soldiers were chugging the wine and devouring dates, along with the still-grinning bandits. Bai Sheng appeared to be wholly satisfied with her ten taels of silver. Everyone had relaxed now.

Everyone, that is, except Yang Zhi.

She stood watching the proceedings, one hand on her sword hilt. Not participating.

And more importantly, not *drinking.*

Lin Chong caught Wu Yong's nudge of Hu Sanniang. The coquettish Steel Viridian retrieved the ladle, scooped up some of the wine, and sidled over to the commander. "Aren't you uptight! Here, join us."

"Miss, not for me. Gotta stay alert."

"Alert for bandits, right?" Hu Sanniang giggled. "It's only us here. By the time you get started again, the wine will wear off. Be nice to yourself."

"No need. The men can partake. Trust me, I'll drink my fill tonight." She grinned at Hu Sanniang. Good. Her guard was down at least a little.

"Here then," Hu Sanniang said. "At least have some dates from us. They're the *sweetest.*"

"Miss, you're too kind, I don't need—"

"For letting us join you under the trees here." She pressed a handful into Commander Yang's palm. "I'm telling you, they're the sweetest we've gotten all year. You tell me whether I'm a liar."

"You could wear down a rock, miss. Thank you, I sure will enjoy them." And the commander tucked the dates in the purse at her waist.

Aiya. Not good. Within a turn or less, her men were going to start dropping like overripe nuts—Yang Zhi had to be drugged by then, too. The dosed dates weren't as potent as the wine, but if they could get her to eat at least one . . .

Wu Yong sashayed over as if they had all the time in the world. "You're insulting my sister, Uncle. Why won't you at least have a date? They really are delicious."

"And I thank you. I'll have them on the road. It's a kind thing for you all to share with us."

Hu Sanniang had begun hanging on the commander's arm, and her face screwed up into a pout.

"Look, you're going to make her cry," Wu Yong cajoled. "Don't ruin my little sister's day! She gave you a present; she only wants to see you enjoy it. You ought to be ashamed of yourself, bringing everyone else down when we're having a little feast."

As always—as always—Wu Yong's words were the right ones.

Yang Zhi reached obligingly back into her purse, and she gave Hu Sanniang's hand an awkward pat. "Look miss, don't cry. I'll have a bit with you, yeah? Hey hey hey, stop. I'll have a bit."

Hu Sanniang cheered up and made a delighted noise at this.

Yang Zhi took out one of the doctored dates. Nibbled at it. Bit the top off the pit.

"See, aren't they sweet?" waxed Wu Yong. "Here, we'll give you some more. You're so glad you met us, I bet—"

At that moment, one of the soldiers walked face-first into a tree.

Yang Zhi's move to action was immediate. Dates flew and pattered against the ground and trees. Her sword leapt to hand, and she spun hard, taking Hu Sanniang by surprise and flinging her off against Wu Yong. Wu Yong danced aside, and Hu Sanniang landed in a quick somersault to her feet—and that gave the game away entirely.

Yang Zhi shouted an order to her men. They tried to obey, struggling with their sword hilts only to get the blades half out before they stumbled over their own boots. One managed to swing drunkenly only to be subdued by Second Brother Ruan. Another gave up on drawing his weapon and barreled himself bodily at Chao Gai, who sidestepped and swept his legs out from beneath him.

If Yang Zhi had eaten enough of the poisoned date to hinder her, it wasn't evident. Hu Sanniang came up from her somersault with a sharp throw of her lasso, but the commander's sword flashed and the thin rope fell in pieces. Wu Yong pounced at her back and got in one good lash of that copper whip-chain before Commander Yang caught the chain on her sword, yanked it toward herself rather than away, and kicked Wu Yong in the chest so hard the Tactician tumbled against a tree.

Wu Yong's body hit the ground and didn't move.

Lin Chong had sparred Wu Yong back at Liangshan. The Tactician was one of the bandits' sharpest fighters . . . and had just been shredded by Commander Yang like the thinnest lantern paper. No wonder she'd held the rank of Captain.

But this, now, was why Lin Chong was here.

In the mere instants it took for Hu Sanniang and Wu Yong to fail, Lin Chong had pulled the short sword from beneath her clothes and dived straight for Commander Yang.

Steel met steel. Lin Chong's weapon was only half the length of Yang Zhi's splendid broadsword, a sword so fine and sharp the dappled sun gleamed off its edge. Yang Zhi used the greater reach expertly, thrusting past what Lin Chong's guard could block while maintaining her own perfect balance. Lin Chong was forced to dodge, then dodge again, low and in retreat.

Hu Sanniang began to race in from the side to help, but behind them, Chao Gai whistled sharply and called her back away. Lin Chong was grateful. It was all she could do to hold off the commander; she could not protect another of the group at the same time. Commander Yang's skills were such that, yes—she would have to protect them.

Out of the corner of her eye, Lin Chong was aware that Wu Yong had still not moved from that too-still slump on the ground.

But she had no time or focus to consider it. She managed to meet or parry or dodge for the first bout, until she and Yang Zhi burst apart, both breathing a little faster, both circling warily. *I've held her off,* Lin Chong thought. *She hasn't gained a clear advantage, despite her reach . . .*

Lin Chong had sparred others at the rank of captain or higher before. Some, those who had attained the position through flattery or nepotism, she had beaten easily. Some, however, had earned their knots, and in those bouts, Lin Chong would not have bet on herself.

The former Captain Yang was clearly one of the ones who had earned.

But then—Yang Zhi blinked. Squeezing her eyes together with a slight shake of her head, as if her vision wavered . . . the poison. She had ingested some of it, only a touch, but perhaps enough to dampen her wits.

Without realizing what she did, Lin Chong's meditative fight state had begun to sink toward that new and frightening skill, the one she did not understand. Just the edge of it, just enough to know—Yang Zhi *did* hesitate; she could feel it. The commander's balance was not what it could be, her senses scratching at their limits.

Behind Lin Chong, her extended awareness laid out the positions of Chao Gai and the others. Binding the soldiers with thick twine, dumping the worthless dates to pack the treasure onto the wheelbarrows. Chao Gai directing Seventh Brother and Hu Sanniang to help up Wu Yong between them. The Tactician's body was moving in all the wrong ways, but moving . . .

Lin Chong now had a single task, and Yang Zhi was it.

Chao Gai appeared abreast of her for one breath. "Sister Lin! You are all right?"

"Go," Lin Chong answered, not taking her eyes from the commander.

Chao Gai gave a sharp nod, lifted her walking staff, and tossed it. Lin Chong caught the staff in her off hand without moving her gaze.

Now our reaches are equal.

With her eyes still on Yang Zhi, her feet moving slowly against the uneven ground, Lin Chong switched the weapons so her dominant hand held the staff, her other bringing back the short sword in a dual wield.

Yang Zhi gave a throaty yell, raised her pristine sword, and lunged.

The staff kept her back this time. Whirl and block the body not the sword—take the weapon on the flat—dart in with the short sword when an opening has been made. None connected; Yang Zhi was always too ready with a parry of her own or a twist away or the hooks of her forearm guards becoming steel spikes against staff or blade.

Lin Chong never dwelled on uncompleted blows. That way lay death. Look ahead to the next move, always, discard what came before as if it never was. Start from each moment as if it were the first.

Commander Yang's fighting style was brutal and efficient. No extraneous moves. No showiness. Her strength blended into skill, the training of countless years written in how precisely she leveraged her own body, her balance and economy paired elegantly with vicious force. Somewhere in Lin Chong's awareness she knew, *knew,* that if her foot stepped wrong, if her hand slipped, if she left even the smallest window, Yang Zhi's exquisitely honed blade would slide in like a law of the universe. Its kiss would land lightly in her ribs or throat or groin, and in one delicate moment her career as a bandit would end before it began.

They broke apart again. Both breathing still harder. Yang Zhi's expression had gone warier now.

"You fight well," she said. "Iron Crane form. Not many people know it."

The twisting sequence was one Zhou Tong had taught, so long ago. Lin Chong had used it in sliding past one of Yang Zhi's thrusts, spinning with a reversed strike to entangle their positions and break the commander's stance. It hadn't worked—clearly because Yang Zhi had recognized it.

Surprising, for its rarity. Lin Chong had passed it on to some of those who'd trained with her, but most couldn't master even the footwork for it. Except for—

"Captain Sun Shimin taught it to me. Back on the Western Reaches. After he beat me with it," Yang Zhi said, her brow furrowing.

Emotion spiked in Lin Chong. She had been the one to teach Iron Crane to a new and rising officer named Sun Shimin, years ago, when he was a fresh young hothead and before his skill shot him straight to a captainship. It had been back when she was only an Assistant Drill Instructor, and long before Captain Sun had perished on the sword of a rebel tribesman while keeping order over the Empire's far western reach. He had been one of the Guard's brightest flames, for a time.

Out on the far western reach . . . where Yang Zhi had served as well, side by side with one of the Empire's heroes, one taught by Lin Chong. Before fortune conspired to make the two of them fight to kill each other on this lawless ridge.

Yang Zhi's eyes flickered to the side. The treasure had been fully gathered onto the wheelbarrows now, the dates dumped in the dirt, with the bandits shoving the heavy loads back up out of the brush and onto the road. Winging away from here, soon to be lost, a speck in a vast Empire that could never again be found.

With her men trussed up and snoring on the ground, Yang Zhi could not pursue without going through Lin Chong. Lin Chong who stood here immobile in her path. All Lin Chong had to do was delay her—delay, just enough for the road to swallow bandits, treasure, and every chance of Yang Zhi's redemption to her place in the Guard.

Yang Zhi's expression rippled, and Lin Chong could understand the anguish of it deep in her souls, because for a soldier like Commander Yang, her mission was paramount, greater than her own life by far. No matter that it was the frivolous pushing about of ill-gotten gold by a powerful family—she would die for the pride of her job in defending it. Now it was slipping away like sand through a net, just like the scholar's stone that had sunk in the waves, and all because she had not been able to kill one troublesome woman quickly enough.

Lin Chong didn't have any doubt that if they'd met on equal footing, without Yang Zhi having been fed drugged food—she *was* the better fighter. Even now, if they fought for long enough, the outcome was likely assured. Lin Chong had trained for too many years not to know.

Unless . . . perhaps if she opened her mind fully . . .

She knew it was foolishness before she tried. Meditation practice or a light sparring dance with Chao Gai were no measure of a real fight. Even in the safety of Liangshan, Lin Chong's control of this new mental state had proved wobbly, flickering in and out of balance as if she learned to control new muscles.

But in thinking about it she reached out—unintentionally, incompletely, but for one precious instant her mind was caught between worlds, in the web of other.

Yang Zhi's blade came at her face. Lin Chong simultaneously tried to lean on the new power and tear apart from it, and her parry was off-kilter, barely raised and at the wrong angle. But she'd gotten her sword up in time—if she could duck aside, regroup—

Until Yang Zhi's sword hit, edge on edge, and sliced clean through.

The short sword fell in pieces. Lin Chong toppled out of the way, but not quickly enough. The momentum of Yang Zhi's sword had barely paused, and in it flashed, skimming across shoulder and neck before Lin Chong's clumsy dive took her out of range.

She dropped the useless hilt, her hand coming up to the wound—shallow, only a shallow cut, she had to rise, had to defend herself. She swung the staff around and up before she had oriented. The attack had to be coming to finish her off, here on the ground disadvantaged and injured—this would not last for many more moves, it was done, but she would fight till the end—

The staff found only air. Yang Zhi was not attacking.

Instead, she had spun away. Spun to where the rustle of trees had closed behind Chao Gai and the rest with their precious wheelbarrows, and Yang Zhi launched herself after.

Lin Chong was nothing—not compared to the mission. The moments it would take to dispatch her were more precious, moments Commander Yang needed to catch up and retrieve her vital cargo.

She'd kill the rest when she did. Chao Gai was the only one with any chance of besting her. Yang Zhi would rescue her own future, and wipe out the one Lin Chong had sworn to.

Lin Chong's mind rocked, the sting of blood and the heat of battle and the pull of that raw power that couldn't help her, all tumbling into the certainty of near-sealed failure. But then her realization from only a few moments before dropped through the chaos with the purest, wildest clarity.

She did not have to defeat Yang Zhi to save her new family of bandits.

She needed only to *delay her.*

The world seemed to freeze in place, stuttering to intense slow motion as if an echo of an echo of an echo. And through it all, piercing like the peal of a bell, the series of moves that would fall one after another into place, and this fight would be over.

It didn't mean Lin Chong would survive. She almost certainly would not. But this would do what was necessary.

Lin Chong let her mind fall into that uncomfortably open state, the power of the god's teeth, the web of all the world. For an instant she felt she would lose herself—but she only needed an instant.

This would take no finesse. No fine control or technique.

As Yang Zhi's attention dove toward her disintegrating commission and she dashed to sprint in its wake, Lin Chong wrapped herself in every tendril of power she could grasp, and she vaulted up from the ground.

At Commander Yang.

Fast, brutal, messy, and impossible. She *flew*.

The launch was violent and hard and terrifying, both to herself and—surely—to Yang Zhi, as a human-sized bat came at her face, staff whirling. Yang Zhi's parry attempt was a good one, ducking and getting her own blade up fast, but Lin Chong was not aiming to avoid it.

Her body fused against Yang Zhi's, all the wind and frenzy of a typhoon in that one focused tackle. The commander's parry not only turned the staff but Lin Chong felt that screamingly sharp sword slice straight through the wood this time, an unpleasant jolt as it twisted in and Lin Chong's own body trapped the edge between them, so sharp and so fast that she barely felt it cut her. The top half of the staff made glancing contact as it blew through, but none of it made any difference, because all Lin Chong had needed was to make her own self into a small and focused avalanche.

Together they spun through the air, each struggling against the other, Lin Chong gluing herself to her opponent with everything she had left and Yang Zhi pushing to pry her off. The collision took them back and back, breaking through twig and branch and rushing past rocks that tore at their clothes.

Back and back and back. All the way to the edge of the ridge behind the grove.

Then off the edge, into nothing.

CHAPTER 14

They tumbled together, clawing at each other. The drop was only free fall for an instant before they hit the slope—an unforgiving mass of boulder and root. Even falling, Yang Zhi's elbow came at Lin Chong's face, her sword flexing between them, and it was more than Lin Chong could do to turn from it or dodge away. Her mind was in free fall too, plummeting out of control, spinning her in all directions as she tried to cling and control and arrest their headlong dive.

Their plunge smacked into a plateau, rolling them each out apart from each other on a harsh ledge of stone and gnarled brush somewhere between earth and sky.

Lin Chong lay on her back and tried to breathe. Her side burned, wetness soaking her tunic. She couldn't tell how bad. She didn't taste blood, not yet.

The pieces of the staff had fallen separate from her. She groped for where she thought they might lay, hoping for an aid to push herself up, for at least the pretense of a weapon, but could find nothing.

A shadow fell across her, blocking the vast blue of the sky that walled their world. Yang Zhi. That magnificent sword in hand, the one that had sliced both sword and staff as cleanly as paper. She raised it to point at Lin Chong's throat, and when she spoke her voice was anguished.

"Why? You fight like some damned hero. And yet you drug and thieve for your living? Those skills, someone must've taught it—it's not just the Empire you betray here; it's your *master*."

Lin Chong did not know what her masters would have thought. Whether they would prefer she die here, rather than become one of Liangshan. Perhaps it would be best after all, if her life ended now.

"Kill me," she croaked. "It is your right."

Yang Zhi's arm jerked back as if she would deliver the blow, but then she stopped and her face contorted. "Then what? I kill you, who can do the Iron Crane and has the inner strength of a damned monk, and then what?"

She glanced up at the long tumble of rocks that was the cliff they'd fallen from, her eyes squinting against the bright. Too steep to have any hope of catching the bandits who had outwitted her. A cut on her forehead dribbled red across the scarred blue birthmark that covered her face. Her breath heaved, and she transferred her eyes to her sword, staring in revulsion, as if the sharpened steel were a viper.

"This here blade has been passed down generations. To me. My family's only inheritance, but such a fine one. Cuts through steel and copper like they're not more than a cooked noodle. If you blow a *hair* against it, 'twill slice right through. An' it can kill one like you so fast, so sharp, it comes away with no blood on it. *None at all.*"

Perhaps it was a trick of the light, but Yang Zhi's blade did seem as keen and unstained as it had when they started.

"It's a damn honor to die by this sword," Yang Zhi continued. She gave Lin Chong a look of pure loathing, and threw the weapon to the ground, flat on a dirt patch where it thumped up a puff of dust. "Use it better than I did."

Lin Chong was beginning to get some movement back. With difficulty, she rolled to the side, clutching one arm against her ribs to try to stop the blood. Her other hand reached, touched, automatically closed on the sword hilt, grasping for this advantage before it was removed. But why? Why? Why would Yang Zhi—oh.

No. *No.*

Commander Yang was not moving very fast either, limping thanks to their mutual bruising on the rocks. She turned away from the climb that would lead back toward civilization and stumped out across the ledge, out toward where its edge met sky.

"Stop . . ." Lin Chong gasped. She tried to push herself up. Failed, tried again, her hand that gripped the precious sword hilt fisting against the hard ground. "Stop!"

Yang Zhi did not stop. Did not even seem to hear. Simply continued walking, out toward where she could release her failure and her shame and the end of her career in the long-traditional way for a person to retain any scraps of dignity she had left.

And Lin Chong was *angry.*

None of this was Commander Yang's fault; it didn't merit suicide—Yang Zhi who had been given an impossible charge, and who had done as well as any person conceivably could have. It was the bandits who had taken it from her, Wu Yong's plan which had been designed to twine through every human vulnerability; the officials who insisted on such a dangerous and pointless and *frivolous* flattery, one that was damn well asking to get its handlers killed; and Gao Qiu in the first place, for knocking the legs out of Yang Zhi's esteemed career for a situation *no one* could have won, for banishing her to a penal colony where she had to prove herself anew with such ludicrous and wasteful tasks . . . Yang Zhi had done nothing but perform loyally for the Empire she served and the men she commanded, and every level of government and society had chewed her up and spit her out onto this mountain ledge like a piece of offal, the same way they had Lin Chong.

"Wait!" Lin Chong cried. She struggled to rise, first one foot under her and pressing against the ground, then the other. "Commander Yang! I heard your men talking. I know what Gao Qiu did to you!"

Yang Zhi's step hesitated this time, but only for a moment. She didn't turn, didn't stop.

"Wait and listen, please. My name is Lin Chong. I was Master Arms Instructor of the Imperial Guard. *I* taught the Iron Crane to Captain Sun, just as my master Zhou Tong taught it to me. Gao Qiu did the same to me as he did to you!"

This time Yang Zhi's step did pause, less than a pace from the edge. Lin Chong staggered forward, laboring to make the short trek. She was dizzy enough that she was afraid if she got too near the precipice she would go over by accident, so once she came even with the other woman she sank down on a boulder, resting Yang Zhi's sword beside her.

"Look," she said. "Look at me." And she reached up a sleeve to wipe the smeared makeup from her face.

Yang Zhi looked. She was listening.

"Gao Qiu did this to me." Lin Chong tried to speak plainly, but her voice shook, from somewhere deep inside her that wasn't yet healed. "He banished me for nothing. He sent his men afterward to kill me. If it hadn't been for the bandits of Liangshan . . ."

"Liangshan?" Yang Zhi stared, then threw back her head and let out a mirthless laugh. "Of course it was Liangshan that beat me. I know your ilk."

"Then you know what they fight for," Lin Chong said. "What *we* fight for. Can you honestly tell me this mission was anything but folly? Presents for Chancellor Cai Jing? He has enough personal treasure to fill a snakepit."

"Not my place . . ." The words sounded rote. They were words Lin Chong might have said, once upon a time only weeks ago.

"Cai Jing demands this theater, and the governor wants favors from his father-in-law, so he sends it," Lin Chong said. "There was no *reason* for this. You know that as well as I."

Commander Yang had tilted her head back, the sun against her face, and she stared into its brightness as if it would cleanse her. "I told 'em," she murmured, to the sky. "I tried. Not my place but I did. I said there's no way to do this, not right now. I said it'll lose good men, it'll only fail. They said they'd send all the pomp of fifty platoons and I said, then they'll really know we have stuff to steal, won't they? With some o' these bandit strongholds having full armies, it was no right risk."

"It was your idea to go small," Lin Chong realized. "It almost worked. I think if we hadn't gotten wind of the whole plan . . ."

Yang Zhi made a noncommittal gesture. "Not surprised. Too many knew. I'd only just dared to hope—that we'd made it far enough, that we'd make it all the way in. Two weeks ago I was sure it would be my death sentence. Never should've let myself hope different."

"It doesn't have to be," Lin Chong said softly. "You could walk away. Come back with me to Liangshan."

"And do what? Go bandit? Better to die here."

I might have thought that too, Lin Chong knew. If things had fallen out differently for her. "Sisters at Liangshan saved me from Gao Qiu's assassins," she said. "They healed me. They're not perfect, but many of them want to be . . . better. To be haojie."

Commander Yang didn't respond, but she didn't jump, either.

"It's not . . . easy, for me." Hard words to get out, as if Lin Chong spoke someone else's convictions. "But your souls don't have to end here. You could find heroism at Liangshan. You could live in the edges of the world and still fight for the Empire. It could be . . . it could be what you make of it."

And if it was true for Yang Zhi, it was true for Lin Chong too. She could remake this lawlessness into her own mold, one that didn't stray from being on the side of what she had always fought for.

Yang Zhi's feet shifted, wavering. Then she stumbled back a step and let her legs give out beneath her to sink down on a boulder opposite Lin Chong. A twin to each other. "Gao Qiu shit on your head too, did he?" she said.

The details still felt too raw to give. "I heard your men talking," Lin Chong answered instead. "You did right by your platoon. Any soldier who knew the field would say the same."

Yang Zhi looked down at her hands, flexing them against each other. "Master Instructor Lin Chong, eh? Yeah, I heard of you before. Got me some good people off your training a few times."

"I only passed on what I've learned," Lin Chong said. "People like Sun Shimin worked diligently every day to master what they did. I was merely the conduit."

"As are we all," Yang Zhi said with a grunt.

Lin Chong couldn't tell if it was sarcastic or not.

"Come back with me," Lin Chong said quietly. "Make Liangshan better. Make the Empire better. Do what you would have wanted to do in the Guard, but on the roads and in the hills, and live well while you do it."

She was uncomfortably aware she was echoing something too close to Song Jiang's justifications—that they were righteous because they fought for the Empire out of love and loyalty, even on the side of lawlessness. None of it had seemed entirely right then and it didn't now, but somehow it didn't seem entirely wrong anymore.

Either way, Yang Zhi should not die for Liangshan's crimes.

Or for Gao Qiu's petty cruelty, or Cai Jing's callous greed.

Lin Chong lifted Commander Yang's heirloom sword, blade tucked back under her arm so she could offer it hilt first.

The commander's mouth quirked. "Not afraid I'll cut you through?"

"You had the chance already." It had not even occurred to Lin Chong to doubt.

Yang Zhi nodded, and she reached out to close her hand around the hilt of her weapon.

It was a chaotic but giddy group who regrouped at Bai Sheng's cottage.

The little round wine vendor took her share of the treasure and secreted it in her shed. "I'll find a way to bring it out to my husband slow," she said with a laugh. "He'll think the town is drunk on my wine!"

She and Chao Gai bantered and joked as they taped the smaller cut across Lin Chong's collarbone and the wider laceration on her ribs, which had begun a white-hot burn all up and down her side. Yang Zhi's sword was so sharp that the edges of the wound did not tear, only gaped smoothly all the way down its length. It was luck that the angle had made it only a glancing slice, or she would be dead.

"The Divine Physician will sew it up when we return," Chao Gai assured her. "I am no match for her ministrations, but this will get you through to the mountain."

Bai Sheng also offered compresses for Lin Chong and Yang Zhi's various purpling bruises from their roll down the rocks, but Chao Gai refused on their behalf, saying they had to be on the road before evening dropped. The other bandits had assiduously divided the treasure among bags for the horses, and they mounted up considerably more weighed down than when they had arrived.

Wu Yong was still too woozy to sit a horse properly, so rode double with Hu Sanniang, the lightest of them. Sister Hu was also, happily, one of the best riders among them—fancier even than Lin Chong's cavalry training—and she seemed to take it as a fierce personal duty to keep her fellow bandit ensconced securely against her.

It left Wu Yong's horse for Commander Yang.

None of the bandits had seemed surprised when Lin Chong had shown up at the cottage of Bai Sheng the Sunmouse—long after the rest of them had arrived and begun repacking their new haul for travel—with Yang Zhi a respectful step behind, waiting to be introduced. Lin Chong had been girding herself for fear and argument; she had expected to have to convince them that the former commander no longer meant them harm and had sworn herself to join them. But no one even questioned her on the recruitment. Instead, they all acted as if it was a matter of course, with several polite compliments of how impressive Yang Zhi's fighting skills were and what a welcome addition she would be to the mountain.

It made Lin Chong feel somewhat as if she had gathered her strength to leap only to stumble when the gap was an illusion.

It also disturbed her. Something tugged at her mind, that conversation with Chao Gai in the grove, when Lin Chong had brought her the information on Commander Yang—telling Chao Gai that she was upright, honorable . . .

As they wound back down the road into the darkening sky, back toward Liangshan with their weighted packs, Lin Chong goosed her gray-white horse up next to Chao Gai's.

"You knew," she said.

Chao Gai did not pretend. "We knew Commander Yang was in charge of the convoy, yes."

"You knew, and you set us up to bring ruin to her life."

"I would say an Imperial Marshal, a Grand Chancellor, and a governor had more of a hand in that. We merely opened up . . . another path for her."

Lin Chong spurred Little Wujing in closer, so suddenly the horse tossed her head and whinnied. "Opened up a path? Only after we burned the last one. You set me up to undo her and then recruit her."

"Not so much 'set up' as 'hoped,'" Chao Gai said serenely, with no apparent shame. "The Professor called it fateful perfection, how well Commander Yang would fit with our number. And why should she be abused by her superiors when she could live a rich, fat life with us? Who is served by Commander Yang's misery, Sister Lin? Is she? Are you? Marshal Gao had her caned and force-marched hundreds of li into an exile post, all for the audacity of living through a storm that took all else. And now she was supposed to regain her rank with this doomed and wasteful errand, merely to feed a Chancellor's vanity?"

She'd begun to sound angry, the sort of righteous, frustrated fury at the world Chao Gai sometimes possessed. But Lin Chong's own simmering anger didn't have room for sympathy.

"You lied to me."

"Should we have told you the whole truth?"

Chao Gai's eyes had been on the road ahead, but now she looked over briefly to pin Lin Chong with that sharp, intelligent gaze. If they had shared everything—what would Lin Chong have done? She didn't like to ponder the answer. All of her other paths had been burned, too.

"Was this ever about the treasure?" she asked stiffly. "Were we after the gold, or Commander Yang?"

"Oh, we wanted the gold," Chao Gai answered. "But yes, we also wanted the commander. Life never has to be about only one thing,

Sister Lin. Sometimes we find cunning ways to make the puzzle fit more pleasingly . . . One arrow piercing two eagles, no?"

She sounded entirely too satisfied with herself. Lin Chong clamped her jaw shut. She didn't even know what she wished to say, only that this was wrong, even as each step seemed so easily explained by Chao Gai. Lin Chong had trusted her own internal moral ethic her whole life, and Chao Gai could explain for eight hundred and eight years, but that sting would never go away.

This had been wrong.

"We thought to spare you," Chao Gai said more quietly, after Lin Chong had not spoken more. "The Tactician was confident that if things branched as they did, you would play your part well and earnestly, and be spared any untoward motives we might impose on you. You are a haojie, Sister Lin, as is Sister Yang, and you spoke to save her. You did it not out of selfishness or duty in bringing her to us, but out of a true desire to offer her your hand and share our fortune with her—"

"Don't," Lin Chong interrupted. "Never again. Do you hear me? Or I'll walk and make my own way."

"I understand." Chao Gai sounded sincere, but also, *still,* unbothered.

"I'll make my own decisions," Lin Chong persisted. "I'll not have you make them for me, just because you think it would be easier. That's not what I've agreed to, it's not who I am, and how *dare* you and Wu Yong—"

Chao Gai held up a hand, nodding. "I take your points. A harder path, but one I admire. I promise that from now on you will know all. Does that satisfy you?" She said it without rancor, and waited for Lin Chong's cautious nod. "Good. Then welcome to the ranks of leadership at Liangshan, Sister Lin. I hope it fits you as well as we wish it to—and if not, I hope you will change us to match yourself, rather than leaving for elsewhere."

Lin Chong blinked, briefly wondering if her injuries had clouded her head. How had they gotten to—she had done no more than speak her mind, yet somehow, some way, Chao Gai had gotten to exactly the place *she* wished, with Lin Chong in the ranks of Liangshan's chieftains . . . Lin Chong marching in to set herself up as a force for change, as an exemplar among the bandits, exactly as Song Jiang had wanted.

And still Lin Chong could not tell if Chao Gai spoke sincerely, or only as manipulation. After all, Lin Chong had done no less than demand it, hadn't she?

Her heart felt shaken. She'd doubted Wu Yong's sincerity many times, but never Chao Gai's.

Lin Chong let her horse drop back again, away from Chao Gai, back where she could think.

By the time they arrived at the mountain, Lin Chong's whole body ached, as if she had fallen trapped into a whirlpool and been buffeted against its walls for days. They'd reached Zhu Gui's inn long past dark, and the Crocodile had taken their fatigued mounts for a rubdown and rest while the party fell onto prepared mattresses. Despite the burning ache from the wound in her side, Lin Chong slept like the eternal dead, but woke to a body that barely responded. Her side was tender under the bandages, all the way down to her hip and spreading front to back, but worse were the bruises—the fall had pounded her in places she would not have thought possible.

She was relieved they were almost returned. She would need—she would need the Divine Physician. And a bed. *Her* bed, now that this had become her home.

Fortunately, the first part of the day was on the ferries, where she could slump with her back against the railing. Seventh Brother Ruan seemed to have taken it upon himself to give Commander Yang the same tour he had enthused about to Lin Chong on the way out, and she let the words wash over her, glad there was no call for her to speak or interact. Lin Chong noticed with some jealousy that Yang Zhi didn't seem to be having any trouble standing, or joking around and thumping Seventh Brother on the back—although, to be fair, she hadn't been stabbed in the ribs as Lin Chong had.

Taking injuries might not have fazed Yang Zhi, but she was, apparently, very, very good at inflicting them. Wu Yong was in a similar state to Lin Chong, and had limped onto the ferry supported by Chao Gai's arm before also settling to the decking, eyes closed. Even so, a slight smile quirked the edges of the Tactician's lips.

Their ferry captains—the Tong and Mu sisters this time—took on the task of loading up most of the treasure, cheerful where the homecoming bandits were exhausted. Lin Chong listened to them crow about the haul every time they peeked into a saddlebag—they were already planning lustily what they'd do with their own shares of it. *Live a rich, fat life with us,* Chao Gai had said. Why should it be denied to people like Yang Zhi, to live as someone like Gao Qiu did every day, with his savory duck and fragrant, rich wine and silver chopsticks? The thought drifted through Lin Chong's wrung-out mind, innocuous and pleading and yet oh so dangerous. *Why should this be denied any of them?*

The ride up the mountain was agony; the world blurred together as Lin Chong leaned on the saddle and gave the horse her head as much as possible. Little Wujing was good at following the mount in front, and had left off the friskiness she'd danced down the mountain with—her nose had dipped down and her hooves plodded, kicking against the ground. Doubtless she, too, wanted nothing more than to rest—and roll in the grass—after the long and heavy journey.

But if Liangshan's heroes of the robbery were ready for sleep, the Tongs and the Mus were very much not. Even on foot after stowing the boats they easily caught up to the horses' weary pace. Their shouts and cheers rowdily surrounded the return journey along the path, and in between escorting they sidled up time and again for more peeks at the prize trove that lay in the packs, glimpses of the glittering hoards within. Lin Chong was not one to lose her head over riches, and her life had been lived in desire for security rather than luxury, but she had to admit that the giddiness was . . . infectious.

Despite everything, she thought she might rest well tonight. Other worries could wait.

As they rounded up the last turn to the settlement, the shouts and cheers echoed back and forth between their escorts and first the lookouts in the watchtowers, then those on the fighting ground who witnessed their arrival and sprinted to spread the word.

"They've returned! Sister Chao and the others are back!"

"They have the birthday presents! They beat Cai Jing!"

"They got it! Come see, come see!"

Eager hands offered to take Lin Chong's horse, and she gratefully slid off and passed everything over. Chao Gai became the center of the hubbub, calmly directing various bandits to unload, to unsaddle and care for the horses, to fetch the Divine Physician even though Wu Yong kept mumbling that it was not necessary. Somewhat to Lin Chong's surprise, though there was much crowing of delight over the goods and the occasional grab out of one of the bags to hold something aloft in excitement, none of the bandits seemed to be filling their own pockets or squirreling away ingots or gemstones from the others.

Either there were consequences for such things here, or it had become its own social taboo. Lin Chong knew vaguely that some amount would be kept for the group's treasury—as overseen by Jiang Jing, the Mathematic and accounting wizard—and the rest would be divided so that every member of the group got an individual share. Even split among the three-dozen-odd members of Liangshan, the wealth here would be sizable.

It had not occurred to Lin Chong until that moment that as a member of the bandits, she was about to be rich. Even a fiftieth of this treasure—even a *hundredth*—would be more than she'd held in her hands together at any time in her entire life.

The thought dizzied her.

"Sister Lin! Sister Lin, I heard you were injured—I've torn my very hair out. My Elder Sister!" Lin Chong turned toward the voice only to meet a crushing bear hug from the much larger Lu Da. Too crushing—she tried to push away, coughing slightly.

"Oh, Elder Sister, I've hurt you. Curse me and the next ten generations out of my loins. Sister An! Sister An, Sister Lin needs you! Er, again."

"See to Wu Yong first," Lin Chong grunted.

Lu Da took Lin Chong's shoulders and held her at arm's length like a prize. "Sister Lin. You have proven your worth here at Liangshan a thousand times over. Everyone sees it! The rumors of your feats are already buzzing in the whole camp, and the riches, hooo whee, the riches on this one. This is the greatest haul since Liangshan's founding, they are all saying, and Sister Chao says it's all thanks to you, that you saved them all!"

Chao Gai had said that? It didn't seem right, considering the parts the rest had played in taking out the soldiers.

"I did only what was needed," she mumbled. Besides, Chao Gai and Wu Yong had planned far ahead to engineer Yang Zhi into joining them . . . could Lin Chong truly be said to have accomplished anything of value, when she had only been playing their predetermined part?

More than the riches were dizzying her. Liangshan, the Empire, every step she'd ever taken, every choice she'd made.

"Elder Sister, you're swaying. Divine Physician! No, Sister Lin, this is my fault, I must prostrate myself before you—I deserve to be flayed, I am awash with guilt—I was unfair to your magnificence and it has been stewing in me like a pot of boiled pig stomach—and now you've been harmed when all you did was fight loyally for us here on the mountain. It will be my fault if you die, stand straight, Elder Sister, I beg you!"

Lin Chong would have chuckled if her ribs were not on fire. Whatever slight the excitable Lu Da imagined herself guilty of, it had doubtless been no more than a stray thought or minor misstep.

She reached out to pat her younger sister's hand. "Do not worry yourself, Little Sister. I'll be fine. Nothing some rest among friends cannot cure."

"And what's all this?"

The new voice cut across the cheering bandits and Lin Chong's own conversation. Wang Lun had arrived.

The joviality died down among the other bandits, and they drifted back a few steps, creating a clearing for their leader. So she might step forward to view the heavy packs stacked upon the ground . . . and the celebrated homecomers standing among their spoils.

But Wang Lun looked anything but proud.

She scanned across the seven returning bandits plus Yang Zhi, and her lip curled upward as if a fishhook had caught her in the edge of the mouth. "You brought someone back with you. Without permission."

"I gave it," Chao Gai spoke up serenely. "I'll vouch for Commander Yang. We are very lucky Sister Lin convinced her to join us. Sister Yang is a renowned military commander with untold years in the Imperial Guard, and will make a fine addition."

"'Sister Lin,' eh?" Wang Lun swung toward Lin Chong, the ropes of her hair sent flying with the force of the movement. "Sister Lin! I demanded you bring me a head to prove yourself worthy of us. I see no head!"

"I did bring you a head." In her exhaustion, Lin Chong did not even try to moderate her tone. Her arm snapped out to point at Yang Zhi. "I brought you a fine head of a fine officer, only still attached to her body. Send me away if you like, but if your jealousy is too great to keep someone with Commander Yang's skill, then you aren't fit to lead these people."

Wang Lun's face flushed bluish purple, and a collective gasp went up from the surrounding bandits, including from Lu Da where she still gripped Lin Chong's arm. Lin Chong's gut went hot and liquid, because when had she ever spoken such blunt thoughts? When had she ever spoken at all without careful consideration first?

Except she was a bandit now, and outside the law, and everything was back-to-front, and she would repent not one word of it.

Some of Wang Lun's most loyal lieutenants—Du Qian, Song Wan, Sun Erniang the Witch—had begun hurrying to her side, but she held up a harsh hand to them and they stopped. The leader of the Liangshan bandits stepped closer to Lin Chong deliberately, once, then twice, each footfall a threat.

Lu Da's grip had begun squeezing hard enough to bruise.

When Wang Lun spoke, her voice was like gravel ground under iron, but the mountainside had gone so quiet that she might as well have shouted.

"You challenge me?" she demanded. "You challenge *me*?"

CHAPTER 15

Challenge you? Lin Chong hadn't been trying to *challenge* her, exactly, and what did that mean, here on the lawless marsh? A moment ago she thought she had been about to rest . . . she was so tired, and sick of Wang Lun's antics, and done with moderating her words. About anything.

"No!" Lu Da cried, still clinging to Lin Chong's side. The shout broke into the tension as if Lu Da sought to tear it with her teeth. "Sister Scholar, Elder Sister Lin is only trying to help us, I'll swear it on my god's tooth. Is this about what I told you? Don't listen to me, I'm a dullard, a jealous dullard, I never meant for—"

"Look how you come and rip us apart," Wang Lun hissed, never taking her eyes from Lin Chong's. "You've got no place with us. All you do is make everyone het up and fighting each other. Well, we won't have it here. I'd've let you walk out of here free and clear, take your chaos with you, but you humiliate me—in front of *my* people—and that's got to be answered. Your challenge—is—*accepted*."

She reached a hand back behind her, palm open. Du Qian sprinted to put a long single-edged saber in it. Wang Lun swung it a few times, whacking the air in front of her. Her technique was clumsy, as if she chopped at wood rather than toward an opponent—not that Lin Chong was in any condition to school her, even if she *wanted* to do such a thing, which she didn't. Did she? It might give momentary satisfaction, yes, but what would that do to the governance of the bandits here?

"Well?" Wang Lun slashed the saber again, in a move she clearly thought looked intimidating. "You gonna insult me and then turn your back? Think I'm below you, do you? Does the arms instructor have no honor?"

"I—" Lin Chong started, but a different voice spoke up instead.

"Of course Sister Lin is honorable! Scholar, you didn't see how she was such a great help in this recent quest of ours," Chao Gai said earnestly. "I'm sure this is all a misunderstanding."

"She's the *most* honorable!" Lu Da tacked on in fierce defense.

"They're right," called Wu Yong, from a position propped against some of the stacked packs of treasure, with An Daoquan crouched alongside and carefully prodding at her patient's joints and pressure points. "Whatever your differences, no one here could claim Sister Lin exhibits anything other than perfect uprightness. I speak with every respect due you, Sister Wang, but you underestimate her—she saved us all out there. Had our backs."

If the three of them were trying to help her get out of this peacefully, they couldn't have said anything worse. Wang Lun's expression sucked inward as if her whole body were about to shrivel in rage.

"What seems to be the matter?" a new voice asked.

No. Song Jiang had arrived on the scene, tailed closely by Li Kui. The poet was the last person Lin Chong would trust to defuse a conflict against Wang Lun, whom she thought so little of . . . this was spiraling . . .

But Song Jiang's presence was, shockingly, calming. Not enough, not to stand in the path of whatever tide was happening here, but Lin Chong felt the other bandits tilting back from the precipice. They looked to her, this beacon of charisma and Benevolence—they did not know what she'd said to Lin Chong behind closed doors, about their beloved founding sister.

It hurt Lin Chong's head.

"I issue no challenge," she tried to assert. Speaking was painful, her damaged ribs sparking with each breath. "We have our differences, but I issue no challenge—"

"You refuse to answer! You mock me!" spat Wang Lun.

"She does not, I promise you." Song Jiang had somehow drifted into the middle, and she raised unarmed hands to both Wang Lun and the surrounding bandits, quieting their shifting murmurs.

How was this happening—Lin Chong was trapped—if she said she would leave, Wang Lun would take it as insult; if she insisted upon staying, even more so; and any violence here seemed likely to cause civil war on the mountain; *how was this happening?*

"Sister Lin will answer your challenge," Song Jiang said to Wang Lun soothingly, with a reassuring glance toward Lin Chong. "She would never dream of so insulting you. This quarrel is honorable on both sides." She'd raised her voice now, addressing the rest of those gathered. "We all know the laws of this life. We all respect them! Neither of our sisters here will break that covenant, and nor will any of us. We are above that. Better than! Let the challenge be decided honestly, in fair combat between the parties, and we shall all respect whatever determination comes. Let the heavens judge!"

"The heavens will judge!" The cheer rose from the bandits raggedly, but with an enthusiasm that was sliding away from mistrust. If there was one thing Song Jiang could do, it was quell minds with a pretty speech.

The speech had even affected Wang Lun, if not returned her to reason. She passed her saber hand to hand, a feral grin growing on her narrow face, but the murderous glint in her eyes had turned to hunger. She wanted to be seen to do this right and properly, as Song Jiang had declared; to be seen as acting within the boundaries of these lawless laws; to emerge victorious in a manner that could not be reproached. She would kill Lin Chong in a way that was unquestionably moral.

"Oh, Elder Sister," Lu Da moaned against her. "I've contributed to this, I have. But you're so injured; why did you have to challenge her now? Aiya, I love you, Elder Sister, I love Sister Wang too, but I've got to stand by you as this is my fault—it is—how *dare* I! Letting my mouth leak farts again, I should be whipped!"

Lin Chong had no idea what Lu Da was going on about, but she could at least feel grateful the Flower Monk seemed duty-bound to stand in support of her. *That's one.*

Song Jiang gestured sharply to Li Kui, who sprinted off and returned with a fine two-handed sword, which she brought over to Lin Chong. "Poke her full of holes like you've got an overactive dick," the Iron Whirlwind said, not bothering to lower her voice, and Lin Chong wasn't sure whether she was also trying for supportive or aiming to inflame everyone further.

"Wait a drop, I owe this woman. I owe her my sword," Commander Yang proclaimed suddenly, from where she stood back on the sidelines. "I gave it, and she gave it back, with my life and a chance at coming to you all here. Arms Instructor, you'd clear that debt if you'll borrow my sword for this here duel of yours."

And she drew the blade so sharp it could cut hairs, so keen it could kill a man without leaving a trace of blood.

Lin Chong took the offered hilt automatically. Her body ached enough that it was hard to hold straight. *I don't want to kill her,* she thought numbly. But what was the better option? Boxed into single combat, unable to walk away without making it worse, and Wang Lun certainly planned to kill *her.*

She stepped apart from Lu Da. The sword weighed heavy in her hands. Her tunic on the left side had gone soggy again, despite Zhu Gui's bandage job at the inn.

On a normal day, Wang Lun would have been no match for her.

That was probably why Liangshan's leader had pushed this now. When her enemy was weak. Easy pickings.

Lin Chong raised Yang Zhi's sword. This close, its blade sang through the air, its sharpness a hum every time she moved.

Aiya, but it hurt to breathe. She was so tired.

The other bandits retreated still further, forming a rough open circle around her and Wang Lun, one that seemed to be holding its breath.

With a great yell that echoed down the mountainside, Wang Lun raced at her, saber raised, ready to end this threat to her standing once and for all. Lin Chong lifted the singing sword.

Later, she would think back to this moment and remember the thought crossing her mind that she could likely defeat and disarm

Wang Lun without killing her—that she could both end this ridiculous, unwanted conflict and also show mercy. It would take more finesse, more energy—it would mean more danger to herself, already in such a weakened state—but she would have a reasonable confidence of success, if she made the effort.

Perhaps she should have done so. But she was so tired.

Lin Chong had made choice after choice to be here. Fighting back against Gao Qiu, confessing to a crime she was innocent of, running from his assassins and accepting Lu Da's offer of help and home, agreeing to stay in this one place that would have her, and as part of that, committing to the protection of its people and a respect for its laws. None of those had seemed very much like choices at all, when she made each of them, each knocking her toward this eventual end, when she had to choose one more time, her bone-weariness and anger rubbing her to rawness far past endurance, out here in this place where the first law was that of martial skill, and why should she reject her own dominance, her own hard-earned training?

She chose one more time.

She chose, this time, not to give in to one more person who only wished her ill, who was corrupting this life where she might find a place, a person who was a clear and current danger to all those she oversaw, whose presence only tore down and poisoned and whose absence would mean a better world.

Lin Chong chose.

Wang Lun lunged at her with a battle cry only just leaving her lips, and even weakened as Lin Chong was, it was no contest. She sidestepped, circled the singing sword up with what felt like lazy slowness, and met Wang Lun's clumsy charge—not very hard, not with the brute strength that would have sent the singing sword slicing through Wang Lun's own weapon, but just enough to turn the blade and send her own point past it directly at Wang Lun's heart.

Once committed, Lin Chong's skill was too great for the sword not to proceed exactly where she sent it.

Wang Lun's momentum carried her all the way up so she was nearly face to face with Lin Chong, the heaviness of her body weighing down the hilt in Lin Chong's hands. Wang Lun's own saber thunked to the ground beside them, her face gone to thwarted, raw surprise for one brief moment before death clutched her away.

Then she fell. Slid off that quicksilver blade to become a motionless lump on the ground.

Yang Zhi had told no lie. The blade was still clean.

Dead silence fell heavy across the mountain, as if even the birds and animals had frozen in place.

Then a voice—was it Wu Yong's?—cried out from behind Lin Chong. "All hail the Arms Instructor! All hail the new leader here at Liangshan!"

And Lu Da, picking up the shout in almost a chant: "Sister Lin! Sister Lin forever!"

"I don't want—" Lin Chong began in a mumble, but the other bandits were beginning to take up the cry too, not Wang Lun's most dedicated lieutenants yet—they still stared in shock—but some of the others, doubtless in an immediate judgment of where this wind blew. Song Jiang had stepped forward again too, repeating a proclamation of how this combat had been fair and decisive.

Li Kui lumbered up to where Lin Chong still stood over the body. "You gotta chop off the head. Declare yourself!"

"I don't—I'm not going to do that," Lin Chong managed, as the hubbub rose around them. She had no desire to be leader here. This had never been what she wanted . . .

"Well, then I'll do it," Li Kui declared, and heaved one of her enormous battleaxes to bring it down in one clean sweep.

Lin Chong would not have said she felt ill, exactly—she was far too experienced for that, and far too numb.

Li Kui scooped up Wang Lun's head by the hair and heaved it aloft. "Wang Lun's dead as a smashed rat! All hail our new leader who chopped her down fair and square!"

Cries of even more enthusiasm rose in response—"Arms Instructor!" and "Sister Lin!"—and this, finally, was enough to shake

Lin Chong out of her stupor. She had chosen here and she could choose again. She did not have to accept this thorny, unwanted power, over people who did not entirely trust her. If Wang Lun had not been fit for this position, neither was Lin Chong.

"Wait!" she cried. "Wait. Stop! I fought Wang Lun because—because someone needed to, and because she was wrong . . . I did not want it to come to this, but it did. I defeated her fairly—but I'm still new to you, and it would not be right for me to take on her role above the rest of you. There are many here who are senior to me. Let one of them lead instead."

"Such modesty." The words were said low, for her ear alone. Song Jiang had sidestepped over next to her, just at Li Kui's shoulder.

"It's not modesty. I shouldn't lead here," Lin Chong insisted. The aftermath of the fight was leaving her weak. All she wanted to do was lie down for a long while and not worry about being murdered in her sleep.

"If you refuse, there will be bloodshed," Song Jiang said. "You must take the mantle or pass it to someone else, and you must do it now. Or we will not survive. Do you understand?"

"And I suppose that someone should be you?" Lin Chong did not attempt to keep the coldness from her tone. She'd had no intention here of enacting Song Jiang's coup for her.

"I would never presume to put myself forward for such a thing," Song Jiang answered, her expression tight. "But you must decide, and quickly. Be warned—not all here would be better for us than Wang Lun."

Whatever else Lin Chong thought of her, Song Jiang was right. Wang Lun's death—it would create a sucking emptiness here; it already had. One Lin Chong was responsible for, even if she insisted to herself that she must not regret, she *would* not regret—but if she did not speak, she risked being the cause of more bloodshed.

It must end here . . . I must end it . . .

She refused to crown Song Jiang as the successor, though. Or any of the bandits she'd learned to trust even less in training them, the ones who cheated, or gloried in their opponents' pain—Song

Jiang was correct in this too, damn her, that many here would only follow in the same footsteps as Wang Lun, and Lin Chong would not be a party to that, either.

She tried to think quickly, even as her brain felt mired in sluggishness—the energy of the fight seeping away, and the stiffness of her injuries reasserting their drag on her muscles. Still, there was only one choice here, wasn't there? Someone all would respect; someone who would make the best choices for the bandits; someone who was kind, and moral, even with Lin Chong's still-raw sourness and nascent doubts.

Not being able to think straight was all right, when no other answer existed to make her second-guess.

"Sister Chao!" she called, mustering up the strength to raise her voice over the buzzing spectators. "Chao Gai! Come forward!"

A rustle of movement off to the side, and Chao Gai hurried up to her. "Sister Lin," she said softly, urgently, "If you're about to do what I think you are, I must advise you that Sister Song would be by far the better—"

"I won in fair combat over Wang Lun," Lin Chong proclaimed to the rest, not letting her finish. "It had to be done. You all know this, and you know I won fairly, and in so doing, I declare to all of you: our new leader must be Chao Gai. She has long watched over all of you, counseled all of you, and she has proven herself a master here at Liangshan by bringing back victory and wealth." She waved a hand at the mounded saddle packs behind her, with their gleaming contents. "To Chao Gai!"

To Lin Chong's surprise, Song Jiang was the first to raise a fist to the sky. "Chao Gai! Our rightful leader! Our Heavenly King!"

"Sister Chao!" other voices called—among them, Lin Chong was pretty sure, Lu Da and Wu Yong. And Li Kui, following Song Jiang's lead. "Chao Gai! Sister Chao! Heavenly King!"

Somewhere among the bandits, a new chant started, hollering Chao Gai's nickname to the sky. *"HEAVENLY KING! HEAVENLY KING! HEAVENLY KING!"*

"You had better options," Chao Gai murmured wryly, low

enough that only Lin Chong could hear below the chanting. "I am not even here all the time."

"So when you go back to your village, you'll deputize," Lin Chong said. "Welcome to the leadership of Liangshan. I believe those words were spoken to me only yesterday."

"I deserve that." Chao Gai smiled ruefully. "I would not have asked for this, but I would die a thousand deaths before I would let the smallest harm come to Liangshan. Sister Lin, I will use every part of my meager skills to ensure your confidence in me is not misplaced."

The bandits' chants had turned to a roar. Chao Gai stepped forward, apart from Lin Chong, and raised her hands until they quieted. "My friends! My sisters, brothers, kindred. You know I would cut my heart into pieces and divide it among you if I thought it would bring us health and success. I have no great talent, but every share of it is yours. Together we shall rise into a force even the rot in the Empire cannot deny, a force that stands for justice, for mercy, for Benevolence in every action we take. We are heroes—we will be heroes—and in return, every richness and triumph will come our way. I have no doubt of it. Join me in looking forward to the future!"

A great cheer rose up among those assembled. Lin Chong found Wang Lun's most loyal lieutenants with her eyes. Song Wan and Sun Erniang had already joined in on the acclaiming of Chao Gai, with Sun Erniang throwing her fist over and over in enthusiasm. Only Du Qian, who had been Wang Lun's second, still hesitated, their face twisted in discontent.

Their eyes met Lin Chong's, and then slid to Yang Zhi's singing sword in her hand, the same blade that had killed Wang Lun with a single stroke. Then their gaze crept to Song Jiang, and Li Kui standing before her with Wang Lun's head, thrusting it in the air repeatedly as she shouted Chao Gai's name—and all the other bandits, who had accepted the nature of this change in power. And Du Qian, too, opened their mouth to shout Chao Gai's name with all the rest.

It was a look Lin Chong had seen before, when a recalcitrant soldier bowed back and yielded to the chain of command. There would be no trouble from Wang Lun's lieutenants. They had accepted the new order.

"A FEAST IN HONOR OF SISTER CHAO!" Li Kui yelled.

If there was one thing the Liangshan bandits loved, it was feasting. Cooking fires roared up; jugs of wine began flowing without restraint. Which meant at last Lin Chong could stumble back and slip away, leaving the spotlight to Chao Gai, to Song Jiang's loyal support, to Li Kui and the head she seemed disinclined to let go of. Lin Chong could return Yang Zhi's sword with the low bow such a favor deserved, then fade back to her own bed here, her bed that would be hers for as long as she wanted it after what she'd done. She thought about calling for the doctor, Sister An, but none of her wounds felt mortal, only . . . seeping.

Once she had lain down, she was loath to rise again, even to procure herself medicine.

Besides, An Daoquan was probably tending to Wu Yong. Lin Chong could wait.

She closed her eyes, and again felt the slide of Commander Yang's sword into Wang Lun's chest, so smooth on the blade's keenness that it was barely a whisper, only the sudden weight pulling the hilt against her grasp. And Wang Lun's face, gone from this life too fast to register anything more than bewilderment.

The Transcendentalists taught that everything a person did in life molded their next lives, cycles upon cycles a person's souls would pattern through, each life building on the last. Perhaps she would meet Wang Lun again someday. Perhaps Wang Lun would have her revenge.

Lin Chong would not begrudge her that. But she would also not regret.

They're coming, Sister An signed.

"Good," Wu Yong answered. "Wake me when they get here, will you? If I drift off."

I will.

"Thank you." Wu Yong didn't think the maw of unconsciousness would rise again soon, not with the wild carousing of the feast outside that had now lasted well past sunset. But head injuries were not unfamiliar, not in their line of work, and drifting in and out was . . . not unexpected.

It was truly irritating that these injuries had led to bed rest. Wu Yong reveled in a good feast, and tonight especially would have been the perfect time to raise a cup and celebrate the sweet tang of victory. Not that anyone else would have known why, precisely, except for those who did know, but Wu Yong had never needed the adulation of others. It was satisfaction enough to see the wheels line up exactly, after being so cleverly set in motion so many weeks ago, and now to fall to conclusion just as they had been so carefully and brilliantly designed.

Well. The Liangshan bandits did like to party—it wasn't unlikely the feast would stretch not only all night, but out into several days. Maybe Wu Yong would be recovered enough by then to drink with the best of them.

The door curtain pulled back, revealing for a moment the clear night of stars off the mountain. Chao Gai stepped inside, followed by Song Jiang.

"How is our Tactician?" Chao Gai asked.

I expect a full recovery after sufficient rest, An Daoquan answered. She turned back to Wu Yong and made the final few signs more emphatically, smacking one hand against the other. *After. Sufficient. Rest.*

"You're the doctor," Wu Yong groused. "I'll be good, I promise."

You do?

"I promise! When have I ever—"

An Daoquan's hands came up energetically.

"All right, all right, stop! I suppose it's true, I'm not very good at staying down."

"Sister An is right." Chao Gai came over and leaned against the rough-hewn table abutting Wu Yong's bed. "You may enjoy being in the center of the web, my spider-like friend, but I hope your feelings are not too wounded if I assure you it is unnecessary."

"Things go smoothly with the rest, then?"

"Very. Sister Song's speeches put them in the right mindset, I think, and the contest was fair. No one can deny it."

A smile touched Wu Yong's lips. "Not quite the result we were aiming at, eh? But close."

"Sister Song would be a far better leader than I," Chao Gai said with a chuckle. "Ridiculous that the renowned Spring Rain would follow a simple village chief. But I will do my utmost, and she will help me—won't you, my friend?"

Song Jiang smiled back. "You speak such rubbish. You are far better suited. It's not a position I ever coveted for its own sake anyway; I only wished it to be done right, and you, *you,* my Elder Sister, will bring us to heights we never imagined. No, this is the perfect result."

This was why Wu Yong loved these people. If only the Empire could be run by those like them . . .

Wu Yong might not have the control yet to make that happen. But enough dedicated cunning and enough time, and the world could be made to inch closer.

"I've put the Mathematic on the treasure," Chao Gai said. "Sister Jiang is like a hog in mud, she is so excited by the accounting of it. Individual shares will be prepared by tomorrow, and our treasury is bursting."

"That will make them all happy," Wu Yong said. Good, very good, that Sister Chao's first act as leader was to be distributing great spoils. Nothing manufactured loyalty—or drained resentments—faster than gold.

"I'll be taking my share back to Dongxi to give to my people," Chao Gai continued. "Sister Song, you can oversee things in my absence?"

"Of course. I think everyone already expects me to act as an extension of your will, and I'm glad to be. Let me know what you'd like completed while you're away."

"I think nothing too ambitious, for now—while people become used to this transition. A fuller training schedule, and bring Commander Yang in on that—I suspect Lin Chong will work well with her. Once Sister Jiang has the final numbers, we'll assign some supply runs. I want any purchases to make wealthy those who need it most, the overtaxed farmers of Ji Province and the small farriers and blacksmiths and tailors of the northern villages who have been sucked dry by the military governments of the penal colonies. It's the justice of poetry, is it not, Sister Song? Taking back from those who squeeze the ordinary people and enriching those same ordinary folk in acquiring our other supplies."

Just don't bring the chicken stealer, An Daoquan said.

Chao Gai's face went dark. "Shi Qian has promised never to do such a thing again. Neither the thefts nor the burning nor the lies to us to cover her tracks. She knows well that if she were to step wrong again, I *would* insist she leave us by the sword—with great sorrow, but we cannot have such things here. It would poison both the others and our own reputation."

"See? You will be exactly the type of leader songs are written about." Song Jiang placed a supportive hand on Chao Gai's arm. "I might ink some of them myself. You have this within you, Sister. Even the parts that would be most painful."

Chao Gai breathed in deeply, resettling herself. "I thank you for your confidence. And make no mistake, I shall be leaning on you—all of you," she added to the rest of them. "Sister Song, I shall sit down with you in the next few days to make a list. Nothing too dramatic yet, as I said."

"Do you think anyone harbors suspicions?" Wu Yong asked.

Suspicions that this was all by design, that Wu Yong, and others Wu Yong had directed or manipulated or allied with, had been planting the seeds of this for weeks and months. Suspicions that they'd planned every eventuality, just like always, and how to best take advantage of each; that they'd leveraged Lin Chong's arrival and Wang Lun's jealousy, pushing both women slowly and subtly toward some climax that one way or the other could not be returned from; that even today, when these long-pressured cracks began to fracture, they had instantly worked in tandem, with nary a glance toward each other, to speak the right words to ensure the result would be accepted by all.

It was a magnificent game. One best kept in the shadows, however. Not all of the others would understand.

"Lin Chong might suspect," Chao Gai said. "I don't know if you were sensible on the road, but she approached me about Yang Zhi. She knew it was too much of a coincidence, elsewise, and concluded we had planned it. She got it quite correct."

"Will she cause trouble? She doesn't like *me* very much," Song Jiang put in ruefully. "And she's clearly willing to . . . assert herself."

"Ha." Wu Yong coughed a bit as an aborted chuckle set off the damned bruised ribs. "That's why we needed her for this. That and the fact that she'd win the fight, of course."

"I think she's practical," Chao Gai answered. "And lawful to the extreme, though what that means for her here at Liangshan remains to be determined. But I believe if we ourselves stay on the path of justice, she will remain an ally—if not by intention, by her own morals aligning with ours."

Good, Wu Yong thought. Chao Gai's assessment could be trusted. Which meant all was in place.

For now.

"Speaking of Sister Lin, why don't you go bother her injuries for a while?" Wu Yong made it a tease, waving off An Daoquan. "And Heavenly King, while she's gone, sneak me in a jug of wine—"

Absolutely not, An Daoquan said, laughing silently. *I did minister to Sister Lin, before the sun set. She was asleep, but I've rebandaged her wounds. She will be fine as long as people stop trying to kill her.*

"Not much chance of that here," Wu Yong said. "All right. Good. And what of our new Sister Yang?"

Hale and hearty and feasting. I tried to poultice her bruising but she told me gnats had given her worse.

"We need more like her." Wu Yong had begun speaking half in

a mutter, mind now racing ahead toward what came next. "People like her and Sister Lin. Disciplined. Fighters. Masters from the martial arts scene, itinerant heroes, military fugitives. Thieves and exiles are all well and good, but difficult to mold into an army."

None of the four spoke for a moment. Then Chao Gai said, "An army. That's a dangerous thought."

This time Wu Yong's smile bent feral. "We're dangerous people."

"Only to those who would oppose what the Empire should be," Song Jiang affirmed, with her usual calm poetry. "What the Empire's heart *can* be. To all others, we shall be what stands between them and the rising waves. We shall be the storm of silk and steel that shelters all those in need."

It was a magnificent dream. A worthy dream. Even if it would take much more blood before it was done.

Today had been the first step toward making it truth.

CHAPTER 16

Buried in darkness, deep within one of the secret cracks of the Imperial City of Bianliang, the eighth man's screams drew out long and longer. More unearthly howling issued forth than should have been possible for a human body to hold, heartbeat upon heartbeat, turn upon turn. The man clawed at his face—his hair—tearing its locks from his scalp so hard they came away in bloody clumps. His fingernails opened deep gouges behind.

Reason had left him. Which made him uninteresting and pointless. Cai Jing turned on his heel and left the dark stone hole of a room, the diviner scurrying after him.

The screams muffled themselves behind the thick wooden door but didn't stop. Would never stop, not while the man lived, and that would not be long.

As was deserved. The soldier had failed—furiously—mightily.

He and his compatriots had counted on mercy if they prostrated themselves before Cai Jing in the ashes of abject honesty, after they had the gall to continue on to Bianliang stripped of both cargo and commander. Mercy they might have gotten, if they had been able to provide him with anything useful at all.

Instead, the incompetent north country louts moaned only of having awoken bound in a grove alongside the road. No knowledge of how they had come there. No memory of their missing commander's certain betrayal, no consciousness at all of what they had done or failed to do after laboring up Huangni Ridge under the weight of Cai Jing's treasure.

No reason or explanation. No usefulness.

As if that would gain them any leniency. Their service was an assault on the dignity of the Empire.

More—it was an affront to Cai Jing personally.

Hot irons had not retrieved their memories, so Cai Jing had been forced to fetch the diviner, an oracle whose hypnotic treatments were sworn to be the best in the land. So far the dolt had proven almost as useless. His skills had drawn a single vague recollection from only one man, the fourth or fifth one they had interrogated—something about drugged wine on the road, as if the bottom of a bucket was all the infuriating sot could remember.

For the rest, their minds had become mashed pulp before they could divulge even anything so vague.

The incandescence of Cai Jing's rage burned through him, white-hot with the injustice. Someone had taken from him what was rightfully his. Again.

Worse, others in the Court refused to see the principle of it. *Gone,* they said, brushing off that this was Cai Jing's own property. *Give it up, not worth pursuing, these hills are filled with bandits, the task is impossible.* Never uttered where he would hear directly, of course. But Cai Jing knew.

He would not yield. Not this time. He would find those responsible for this blight on the Empire and sear them from the face of the earth.

Let the Court whisper that he chased dragons. They already whispered about his "secret project," sowing cracks in his reputation with their giggles about the old man clawing for impossible powers. Gao Qiu had flapped his mouth with unfortunate predictability—Gao Qiu, the one man who both knew a few specks of truth and whom Cai Jing could not order put to death. It was beyond enraging.

The Court would see. They would all see. His antagonizers would eat their laughter like oil-soaked rags stuffed up their throats, which Cai Jing would light aflame and walk away.

He refused to let the project's recent failures make him doubt that certainty.

He'd dealt with those failures as well as such things could be dealt with. As Lady Lu Junyi's punishment for her disastrous and wasteful initial test, he'd selected one of her team of scholars at random, a slender man with the shaven head of a Transcendentalist monk. Then he'd shattered the monk's hands with an iron hammer in front of her and dispatched the man back to his monastery. A woman of Lu Junyi's temperament was easily shocked by such things, and incentive was important.

Despite his anger, Cai Jing's expression had been cool as still water. He'd ordered her back to work and informed her that for her next failure she'd be forced to choose the man and wield the hammer herself. Then he had repaired to his sanctum and forced himself to copy out Qu Yuan's Heavenly Questions, all hundred and seventy-two of them, until the strokes flowed even and calm. Letting the heat of his choler seep away until any emotion sank to indiscernible beneath the smoothness of ink and poetry.

Cai Jing did not enjoy failure. Particularly not his own.

He refused to dwell, however. One god's fang had been wasted, but Lady Lu swore they had gained information from its demise. She'd gone on to describe an intricate understanding of alchemy that truthfully exceeded Cai Jing's own study. He made certain not to reveal his ignorance; she would do well to think he could catch any misstatement or error. Paradoxically, it made him rather pleased with how the frontier of the project's knowledge was progressing.

His current investigation had no such redeeming qualities.

Behind the wooden door, the howls and moans began to taper off. "This one's mind. It's irretrievable?" Cai Jing demanded of the diviner.

He knew it to be true. They had run up against seven other miserable dead ends already.

"Yes, Grand Chancellor." The man spoke in a perpetual bow, bobbing up and down with every word. "Once again, the drugs the bandits used stole every memory of the encounter. I found none to recover. Like the others, I needed to scrape so deep to be sure, the process took his sense and reason. It is most unfortunate."

Cai Jing had half a mind to have the diviner himself sliced up for his failure. The only reason he refrained was that they still had two of the drugged guards remaining to interrogate. Scraping the minds of the first seven—now eight—may have provided only crumbs, but every man would be checked.

If the diviner failed on the last two, then Cai Jing would exact punishment.

"Might I suggest . . . these bandits were very thorough," ventured the man, unaware of how close he hovered to death. "Your men, the Guard, they may find more in other ways . . ."

Soldiers already scoured the countryside on Cai Jing's orders. Company upon company, crawling every insignificant rural town with orders to question the common people to exhaustion. Technically Cai Jing had bypassed the Chancellor of the Ministry, but no one had challenged his fury, not even those who whispered how he squandered the Empire's resources on the impossible. *Drugged wine* was so little a clue as to be nearly nothing for the men to go on—yet, in a sudden pearl of good luck, Cai Jing had received a communication only this morning with the report of a lead.

Not a promising lead, but a lead nonetheless. The runner was waiting even now for an audience with him.

This was what the whisperers of the Court did not understand. Impossible was only so until it was achieved. This was why they would never climb to the ranks that Cai Jing had and would.

Cai Jing would find what he sought. It was inevitable—because he would force it to be.

Others' lack of faith did not excuse the diviner's impertinence, however. Suggesting military directives as if he had greater wisdom than Cai Jing himself! Yes, the man would definitely have to die. Cai Jing would make a note of it for later.

For now, he turned his back on the diviner and strode to his chambers.

The waiting soldier was on one knee, head bowed, the dust of the road that covered his armor showing how urgently he had treated his errand. Good. Someone who knew his proper job. At Cai Jing's arrival, the Guardsman bowed even lower, pressing his forehead to the floor.

Cai Jing forced himself to settle, calmly, into a chair, to take eight slow breaths before continuing. No matter what happened, he would not lower himself to the mien of a fatuous cretin like Gao Qiu.

He would be in control. Today and every day.

It was why he would succeed.

"Tell me," he said to the runner, "about this wine merchant you found."

CHAPTER 17

“You want me to come with you to Dongxi?” Wu Yong asked. Not in surprise, exactly—but Chao Gai had always returned alone before.

“I want them to become familiar with your face. Now that I shall be spending more time on the mountain, it may be that I have to send people in my stead at times,” Chao Gai answered, twisting the straps down on a sack of rice to bind it tightly for the journey. “Besides, it’s not only my share of the treasure I’m bringing back. I could use the extra hands, if Sister An says you’re well enough.”

“Pah. Sister An couldn’t keep me in bed another day if she offered me the nightly ‘treatments’ she gives Sister Song.” Wu Yong let the jest go slick with innuendo. Not everyone in the camp knew Sister An and Sister Song were burnishing each other’s weapons, so to speak, but Wu Yong had special talent at picking these things up. A nose for it, as the saying went. Especially when people tried to be discreet.

Now Wu Yong levered up from sitting, ignoring the slight ringing that invited comparisons of one’s skull to a vibrating gong. “We’ll depart on the morrow? Good, that will leave me the afternoon for some exercise. I was ready to flay our Divine Physician in the night to escape her ministering clutches.”

Sister An had thrown up her hands today and declared in nearly violent gestures that she was done trying to keep Wu Yong at rest. But in truth, Wu Yong never would have dared cross her. The Divine Physician might not have some of the others’ martial skill, but she could be frightening in her own way.

Very frightening. Wu Yong thought again of those stories as to how Sister An had become wanted in Jianye, the tales of her family dead and the floors awash with blood. Nobody's business what the truth was, not here on the mountain, but . . . Wu Yong had theories.

Not all of them involved innocence from all parties.

But again, it was nobody's business unless Sister An wished to say. Such was the redemption of Liangshan. Wu Yong would keep such musings internal, and continue to be nothing but obedient to Sister An's medical instructions.

Well. Most of the time.

As always, the Divine Physician had been wise in the timing of her recommendations, neither too early nor overcautiously late. Once Wu Yong made it all the way down to the practice yard—having refused all help—and began stepping through drills, the movement felt marvelous and at the same time proved nearly too taxing. Weakness dragged heavy, and sweat poured until Wu Yong's soaked clothes flapped with wet, but damn the heavens if this was not more invigorating than the doctor's prescriptions.

Wu Yong cycled through the whip-chain forms again and again, muscles both aching and luxuriating in the stretch of each strike and lash. As usual, the forms became a kind of meditation, mind matching each precise snap of body and limbs. Drifting through the future and the past. Planning, reviewing, reassessing.

Fitting together new intelligence with old clues. Reaching toward ever more lofty goals as the chain reached for earth and sky.

So far, word had reached them of a far more intense investigation into the birthday treasure heist than even Wu Yong had anticipated. The Imperial Guard was not known for its discipline these days, and that the time and manpower even existed for several companies to traipse the countryside for weeks . . . it was frankly astonishing. No such high-powered investigation had been launched when highwaymen had waylaid the similar birthday convoy last year. Wu Yong was not one to skimp on research, and that tidbit had been known and factored in before they ever began planning this robbery.

With military resources weakening all over the Empire and

more and more requests from the northern border, how did Cai Jing see any profit in going after this paltry shadow that had insulted him? *It must be exactly that insult,* Wu Yong thought, whirling to land in a forward stance and letting the copper chain spin out and then back. *He must have taken this as a personal offense.*

True, they had meant it that way, but the Chancellor was well-hated. It was somewhat . . . flattering . . . that this had managed to cut him so deep. Flattering, and worrying.

Wu Yong dropped, and the copper chain snaked fast in a circle, brushing the grass and sweeping the legs out from beneath seven imaginary opponents.

Personal revenge changed the calculation. If Cai Jing became determined to point the entire strength of the Imperial military at Liangshan . . .

It was a fight they didn't seek, but they weren't ill prepared, either. This mountain was as defensible as an encampment could be, and all here would protect it with their lives.

Wu Yong would have liked to think that Cai Jing would never be able to dig far enough to identify them as his targets. The Empire did, after all, stretch many sunsets across. But the Liangshan bandits were acquiring a reputation in these parts—one Wu Yong appreciated, usually. People heard Liangshan's name and cowered. Travelers whispered tales of them in front of fires at inns, casting skittish glances at the door. The manor houses bolstered their guards and kept on alert every time they heard tell of another of Liangshan's deeds. It wasn't as if these hills did not house other mountains with other bandit encampments—too many to count, and Liangshan had cordial relationships with some of them, if not all—but the other piece of gossip people whispered about Liangshan was that they were the fierce bandit group of *women.*

Not strictly true, but not strictly false, and probably enough to be identifying. In addition to the sheer hopelessness of the search, the drugged wine should have taken most if not all of the soldiers' memories, but if Cai Jing managed to retrieve even the most muddled story . . . if he used it alongside the rumors of the countryside to make an assumption . . .

Wu Yong had thought the ruse a clever and well-suited one, to travel in the guise of an unthreatening group of women. It was still clever—but they should have sliced the soldiers' throats instead of only leaving them bound and drugged. Wu Yong was not morally opposed to such a move, merely found it distasteful . . . stooping to such tactics was a concession of skill, the overkill of the artless, which didn't deliver nearly the same satisfaction.

All signs had pointed toward it not being needed, either. Until now. When nothing could be undone.

Wu Yong snapped out the chain and threw it, racing to dive into a somersault on the grass and then stick perfect balance on the catch, one hand thrust out in an Earth Shifting Palm, the chain swinging deadly from the other.

Even if it was impossible for the Chancellor to be certain of Liangshan's guilt, it wasn't as if the Empire would balk at mistakenly wiping out the wrong bandits' stronghold on a guess. The government considered banditry a scourge on the people, and had only ignored them thus far because the government ranks themselves were the scourge, choosing to stuff their pockets rather than defend the villages against the Empire's supposed villains.

Liangshan had removed—or converted—far more evildoers than the magistrates ever had.

Of course, that was only reason for those magistrates to hate them more.

Arc the chain around this opponent's throat, wrap it to strike, bounce off one's own body to whip out and catch limb and joint. Wu Yong breathed deep into tight lungs, pushing through fatigue that rang as lightheaded as the good mushrooms.

If the Guard marched on the mountain, Liangshan had the strength and the tactical position to fend off even a reasonably competent assault. Wu Yong was certain of it—almost. It would be worth checking with Sister Lin and Sister Yang before leaving here, just in case. Make sure their two best military assets were alert and ready.

Sending runners to those members who were off the mountain would not be amiss either. Only as a precaution—no matter how many assumptions Cai Jing made, it would be an improbable feat to discover the *names* of all Liangshan's members—but Wu Yong had not gained the reputation of Tactician by being uncautious. It would be easy to notify the Crocodile to retreat into the marsh at the first sign of trouble. A messenger could be sent to Noblewoman Chai, though even if Cai Jing uncovered her name somehow, Noblewoman Chai had that special iron tablet . . . a carved document from three generations back that exempted her from any prosecution. Such was the reward of an ancestor who had saved that Emperor's life, and Noblewoman Chai used its powers well, to provide aid and safe haven.

Wu Yong carefully ticked through any of Liangshan's other allies and affiliates, making a mental list, assigning runners and composing messages. Perhaps the most vulnerable of those names was Bai Sheng—it would be worth telling Chao Gai they should detour to visit the Sunmouse on the way back from Dongxi. Wu Yong was not overly worried; after all, they had guarded hard against Bai Sheng being discovered . . . they'd sent her to a town three dozen li away from her usual haunts to show her face to the soldiers the day before, so even if the drugged wine failed to properly scramble the men's memories, it would take combing through half a dozen nearer villages before Cai Jing would have a chance of happening upon anyone who knew Bai Sheng's name. Even then, it would be like fishing for a needle in the ocean. Cai Jing would need not only every investigative resource at his disposal, but a thousand ingots of luck to fall directly on his white head if he was to track her down successfully.

Still. The Sunmouse had been on the heist with them. Best to check in with her, set all minds at ease.

Wu Yong landed in a low, twisted stance, the chain held taut in a tension strike. Sweat dripped down onto the metal links.

Cai Jing was proving a more surprising opponent than expected. Worrisome, yes, but also . . . strangely thrilling.

Wu Yong's lips formed a sharp, private smile. The pieces were all on the board.

Time to play.

"You take being stabbed very lightly," Lu Da scolded Lin Chong. "Elder Sister, if I didn't know better, I would suppose you wanted festering scars instead of healed ones. The better for showing off your prowess, isn't it? Oh, yes, I've done that. I thought about stabbing myself once—"

"My prowess shows off itself, thank you." Sister Lin toweled off her face with a rag while the students collected weapons and headed off the training ground in a desultory fashion. Before Lu Da could follow them, however, Lin Chong caught her arm. "Sister Lu. Please, walk with me a moment. I would speak with you."

"That's never good," groused Lu Da, but turned to follow Lin Chong up one of the side paths that snaked through the forest instead of returning them directly to the encampment.

A stone hardened itself in Lu Da's stomach. Sister Lin had found out at last—about what Lu Da had said to Wang Lun, while stewing so ungratefully about her god's tooth. Sister Lin would be angry. She had every right to it, too. Lu Da's careless words, provoking Sister Wang to be so rash—and damn Sister Wang for her poverty of either temper or patience! But it had been all Lu Da's fault in the end, her careless mouth farts provoking Wang Lun against her sister whom she should have protected at any cost, and then poor Sister Lin left with no honorable choice but to kill Sister Wang, and Lu Da might reluctantly agree that Liangshan looked to be shaping up stronger now and Sister Chao was the best person who had ever existed and of course was noble and good and would be a magnificent leader, but *still*. Sister Wang would probably come back in the next life very disgruntled. Or maybe haunt them. Haunt Lu Da. Because it was all her fault . . .

"I wanted to speak to you about Wang Lun," Lin Chong said, as if she augured what was in Lu Da's mind. "You mourn her, don't you?"

Damn it all. Of course Lin Chong was so selfless as to ask this.

"Only as I would mourn any of my kin here!" Lu Da declared. Too hotly. The guilt was strong. "The Scholar built this mountain one stone at a time—succored us from nothing in its bosom—anyone here would speak the same. Oh—dear sister—you're so kind to ask about our grief—and when you were the one forced to deal such an awful final blow!"

She flung her arms around Lin Chong's neck with a sob, momentarily forgetting about her sister's healing injuries. Again. But who cared, Sister Lin treated all wounds so lightly—she was a quarter Lu Da's size and would probably rise from being bristled with arrows to shake them off the way a dog shook off water.

After a few moments, Sister Lin gently detached them, keeping a grip on Lu Da's forearms. "Sister Lu, I . . ."

"Yes?" Lu Da bawled.

"I am not . . ." She cleared her throat. "Sister Lu. I beg your pardon. I am not—good at this. Here, sit with me."

She moved them over to sit on a wide, mossy log that was halfway overtaken by the forest floor.

"I . . . with my own blood family, I was never good at . . . I would like to be of comfort to you." Lin Chong's eyes held hers, shining and serious. "I beg your forgiveness. I—I am embarrassed, as my question is not what you think, but was borne out of self-centered thoughts. What I wanted to ask is if the residents here forgive me . . . but I see now it was the wrong question. How can I help you, Little Sister? Do you hate me for it?"

Did she hate *Sister Lin*?

"Of course not! You did only what you had to, and it was my fault, all mine. I told Sister Wang . . . I was so angry with you, may fate strike me down for my pettiness . . ."

"You were angry . . . with me? Before?" Lin Chong asked, her face creasing in confusion. "Why?"

"Pah. It's not a reason worth mentioning."

"Did you tell Sister Wang to insist on facing me the way she did?"

"No!" cried Lu Da. "It was very noble of her to choose that, but I never wanted it . . ."

"Sister, please. I . . ." Lin Chong reached up tentatively and touched Lu Da's shoulder. "I've never had a younger sister, and my own family—this is, it's new, and I—I want to do right by you. Please tell me. What offense did I commit?"

"No offense at all. It was only because I . . ." Lu Da didn't know how to admit it. *Selfish, selfish . . . the monks told you to wait. You didn't listen to them just like you didn't listen to Lin Chong.* "I saw you training with Chao Gai," she blurted. "You won't let me use my god's tooth, but you won't teach me to use it right either! I've been so good in drills but you could teach me after, or at night, or even early in the morning, I could get myself up for first watch, I swear. But you won't. You don't even have a god's tooth and you . . ."

The memory of Lin Chong and Chao Gai sparring danced through her mind again. It wasn't *fair.*

Lin Chong was a long time in answering, long enough for Lu Da to berate herself all over again for her lack of character. When her older sister finally did speak, it was very soft.

"I'm sorry." Her hand tightened on Lu Da's arm. "I didn't realize—I'm so sorry, Little Sister. I ask your forgiveness."

"You're the teacher," Lu Da grunted. "It's not for me to question."

"But I was a—bad teacher," Lin Chong said, with an apparent effort. "I was so wrapped up in my own . . . I . . . this is difficult for me to . . . I have not told anyone so, but this new advancement scares me. It's not something I understand. I don't know what it means, or how to control it."

Her gaze had fallen to the log between them.

"You're already loads better than me," Lu Da said. Not without that bite of envy. "I know you're an arms instructor and not an abbot, but I've got no one else to teach me, and you're already loads better. Sister Chao's never even tried to help me either."

"Chao Gai's understanding of it is, is different, I think. At least, that's how she's explained it to me, that this is not her realm either, but she helps me in meditations and the like that allow for greater control of—of whatever this is. I'm sorry, I—I am no spiritual expert; I never thought—I thought you were asking for me to teach you how to *fight* with your god's tooth. Martial skills are all I'm expert in, Sister Lu."

"Well that, too," Lu Da huffed. "But you don't need to be a forty-year expert. We could learn together even."

"Together." Lin Chong's head moved in a small nod. Her eyes had squinted closed. "Yes. All right. I will try. I've never been very good at being . . . unsure."

"How do you learn anything new, then?"

"How indeed," Lin Chong answered wryly. "You are far wiser than you are given credit for, Reverend Monk."

"Abbot Zhi would be glad to hear you say that. He said he hoped the other monks' wisdom would rub through from them, but all I got were some itchy warts."

Lin Chong coughed. "Let's, ah. Shall we try now? Together? Why don't you . . . why don't you reach through your god's tooth now. But do nothing with it? Just seek a state of meditation."

"Boring," Lu Da grumbled, but she also sat up straighter, excitement fluttering. As always, the power of the god's tooth seemed to vibrate just below the surface. She let herself sink into it, let it rush through her without moving, trying not to be swayed, as if she sat in rushing rapids and gulped water into her lungs to breathe.

"I don't know . . ." Lin Chong murmured. "I don't know if this is right, but . . ."

Suddenly Lu Da could feel her. Really *feel* her, alongside, seated together on the log with Lin Chong's hand on her arm, but also sitting in this rushing river. But Sister Lin wasn't touching any god's tooth! Lu Da's was tucked well inside her tunic, lying warmed among the folds of her skin.

"How are you doing this?" she whispered. The words weren't quite audible, whisked away as soon as they were spoken.

"I don't know—"

Other shapes flashed around them, too fast to see. People, whole worlds, whole civilizations rising and falling in the space between the movement of a moth's wings. They sat very still.

The shapes shaded darker somehow. Threatening? Lu Da's heart beat faster. She didn't have her staff with her, but her fist tightened against itself. She didn't understand.

A scream. Lu Da jumped where she sat. In the physical world, Lin Chong's hand clenched on her sleeve, pinching the skin beneath. A face, a familiar face, screaming forever—and now more people, screaming and dying, the pain everywhere, everywhere, an enemy she couldn't fight—*and was that voice Chao Gai's . . . ?*

Lu Da gasped, snapping out of the power of the god's tooth, back to the bright and too-green forest at Liangshan. Sister Lin was breathing hard, leaning on her grip upon Lu Da's arm to stay seated upright.

"What was that?" cried Lu Da. "Was that—some sort of augury? But my god's tooth can't—that's not what it—was that Sister Chao? Is she about to be in danger?"

The face loomed again in her memory, screaming and screaming, distorted and transparent as smoke on smoke.

"I don't know . . ." pleaded Sister Lin. "I don't know. I saw her too. And others—but I don't think it's augury; this didn't feel like the future . . ."

"When did Sister Chao and the Professor leave for Dongxi?"

"This morning . . ."

Lu Da leapt to her feet, leaving Sister Lin to catch herself against the log. "We have to tell Sister Song! Right now!"

They clambered up the path back into the encampment. Heads turned at their sprinting hurry, but Lu Da paid no mind. "Sister Song! Sister Song!"

Song Jiang had heard their cries and was rising from her seat when they burst into the meeting hall. Li Kui stood behind her, at her shoulder, battleaxes secured across her back, and a mess of papers was spread on a table between Sister Song and Sister Jiang with some sort of accounting figures. But Lu Da didn't pay mind to any of that either. "Sister Song, Sister Lin and I had a vision, I can't explain—I think Sister Chao is in danger! Right now!"

"Slow down," Song Jiang urged them, as Li Kui swept out her battleaxes with a mighty yell. "Sister Li! Pause a moment! Flower Monk, please continue. What vision is this? And what kind of danger?"

"I—I don't know," Lu Da gasped unhappily. "It was all foggy and unclear. But it *felt* very sure. Sister Chao is in terrible danger."

"Do you have any further details?" Song Jiang looked to Lin Chong, whose face was pale, her eyes as glassy as when they'd come out of the vision.

"No, I—I only had a strong impression of the same, and that it is happening now, or very soon from now—If we ride immediately—"

"We can't catch them," Song Jiang said, tight-lipped. "They'll be close to arriving in Dongxi already. But we can't desert them, either. Sister Lin."

"Yes. Here."

"I'm taking Lu Da and Li Kui, as soon as we can saddle the horses." She gestured sharply to Li Kui, who saluted and ran to obey. Lu Da's heart trampled like a rampaging army, kicking her with urgency—they were going, they were going now, and they would ride so hard they would scorch the earth . . .

Song Jiang turned back to Lin Chong. "You're in charge until my return."

"Me? But people won't—"

"You would have been leader if you hadn't abdicated, and all respect you in the daily drills now. You and Sister Yang must keep on alert. If anything happens while we're gone, it will be a military matter."

"If Chao Gai is in trouble, wouldn't it be best for you and I to switch—"

"I may not have your skill, but I know the road they took. Besides . . ." Sister Song cast a glance at Lu Da, and reflected in her eyes was that same souls-deep certainty, the conviction that they would tear through all obstacles, even their own flesh. "I'm not coming back without them. Are you prepared, Sister Lu?"

Lu Da felt her spine straightening. "I only have to grab staff and sword, Sister Song. We'll blast any enemies from Sister Chao if she lives and avenge her if she's dead."

"Good woman." Song Jiang swept her coat from the back of a chair and began to hasten out of the hall, then paused to turn and put a hand on Lin Chong's shoulder. "I trust you to defend the mountain. Keep them safe."

Sister Song strode out into the gathering evening, and Lu Da hurried after, only one thought ringing in her head: they had to get to Chao Gai and Wu Yong. The only way they would fail would be to die.

Chao Gai's distorted face blanketed her mind's eye again, screaming and melting into a haze of nothing.

CHAPTER 18

Lu Junyi's body wouldn't stop clenching, as if she were trapped in a frozen tundra, everything in her twitching and curling away from exposure. She couldn't seem to stop it, even when her hand closed on one of the chunks of raw lodestone in a grip hard enough to cut her.

She rinsed off the jagged piece of ore and wrapped her hand so tightly it hurt, as if it would quell whatever thrashed inside of her. Ling Zhen glanced over but offered no comment or comfort.

Why should he?

She closed her eyes for a moment and went back to her simmering crucibles holding yet another try at the cooling elixirs, yet another mark of her deficiency when they cleared and congealed but then had no effect. *Concentrate on the work.* The work was difficult enough. Blank out any other thought.

She was the head of this endeavor. All results were her responsibility. All results, all consequences.

Her fault, if they could not make this work.

Her fault, if any more of her men bore the punishment.

Jia had tried to comfort her, at first, when Lu Junyi came home terse and hard-faced—as much comfort as could be offered when no information could be shared. Jia had held her hands, played for her on the lute, brought plates of finely prepared food that Lu Junyi only picked at while she sat long into the night staring out at the garden. Jia had even, tentatively, suggested she run one of her salons again.

Lu Junyi had refused, saying she was too busy now.

She spoke the truth. She was too busy.

Her stomach cramped at the thought of how brazenly they had

flung ideas about her little groups. Ideas with perilous edges to them, ideas that could fall and cut and kill.

The last few days Jia had not come to her. When they'd crossed paths, like two creatures strange to each other and only occupying space in the same house, Jia had seemed drawn into her own quietude, her own sadness.

Lu Junyi could not blame her for that, either.

"From childhood I studied classics and history . . ." Ling Zhen read softly, in an odd, singsong voice. As if trying to collect an understanding that lay scattered in wisps. He was looking down at an ink-filled paper that had been left by Fan Rui—husband and wife were still forbidden from direct communication. Her write-up had been vetted by several people, people who were not Lu Junyi, people who scanned for seditious content and only allowed it to change hands when they were satisfied.

The page was mostly about lodestone, along with some of Fan Rui's ever-present rambles.

"That line, does it mean something?" Lu Junyi asked.

"Oh—" Ling Zhen's head came up in quiet despair, his eyes wide as if he'd been caught in a lie. "No meaning. It has no meaning."

She could not fathom what he felt, reading it. He hadn't been with his wife since her imprisonment. The textual evidence of her unwellness must be . . . a shock.

"She still has her mind." Lu Junyi struck for comfort, but missed. "She . . . if you and she can earn clemency, I think she may yet recover."

Ling Zhen glanced behind him at his ever-present escort of Guardsmen, then dropped his eyes and straightened the paper from nonexistent crookedness. "I have trouble deciphering her hand, is all." He said it too quickly, defensive. "She always, she writes too quick. Confusing."

Lu Junyi did not know what he meant by that. Fan Rui's ink was chaotic and slashing, but perfectly decipherable, just the same as on the alchemical recipes she'd written out for Lu Junyi. Her words were what sometimes wrought the confusion, not her hand.

In the brief she'd left for her husband, *From childhood I studied classics and history* lay sandwiched in the midst of an instruction about properties of lodestone, and later something about people sinking drowned and dyed in a river that Lu Junyi was nearly certain was not supposed to refer to the god's fangs. Or to anything else in the real world.

The god's fangs. Ling Zhen had been told of them, now. He had to be, to follow his wife's directives.

When Lu Junyi had informed him of the truth, he had shrunk into himself, a tortoise flinching back into its shell. As if the weight of the knowledge had the potential to injure him. His reaction was wiser than hers had been.

Focus on the work.

She turned away from her own inadequate mixtures. "Explain to me better the lodestone procedure she suggests. I know the otherworldly properties of lodestone—it can sense the greater seats of power embedded in the universe, so spins always to the south and thus can guide travelers in straight lines. It is also known to draw materials together through space without anything touching them . . . surely a powerful mineral, but I have not heard of any scholarship relating it with god's teeth or scholar's stone."

"Maybe nobody has attempted. Save for my Chaos Demon . . ." Ling Zhen kneaded the knuckles of one of his hands with the other, not meeting Lu Junyi's eyes. "She was always braver than I. If Benevolence will let me live up to her example . . . what does she want me to do?"

"Concentrate, Scholar Ling. She talked of using lodestone to 'reverse the flow.' What does that mean?"

"When applied repeatedly to materials—this was something we discovered together." His face lit with the happiness of some long-ago memory, only a shadow now. "When applied repeatedly, modified lodestone can reverse the . . . for lack of another word, the direction of the energy. In many materials, but my dear one, she thought—god's teeth, scholar's stone, my wife's Renxia philosophy considers them as puzzle pieces in discovery that only time and research keep us from understanding fully. She believed them to be a conduit, one opening in some untold dimension that we cannot sense, its energy and strangeness flowing into ours. Very similar to the life energy that each of us carries within us."

"'Reverse the flow,'" Lu Junyi quoted. "That would mean—"

"Sending it away from us. Yes. Forcing the material to become—an absorber, a sinkhole, for the energy. Rather than its source."

"Then what she's proposing—it's to modify one of the god's fangs to become a siphon. Draw in through one, release through the other. You agree with her?"

"If we can reverse it . . . I will have to work with the lodestone. Purify it. The raw ore does not produce the necessary effect . . ."

He sounded lost.

"How can we know?" Lu Junyi asked. It was the important question. The only one that mattered. "How can we know whether it's succeeded, whether the god's fang has been—reversed?"

"If it hasn't . . ."

Ling Zhen trailed off, and then his shoulders began to shake. It took Lu Junyi several heartbeats to realize he trembled with silent, frenzied laughter.

Lu Junyi reached out and took Fan Rui's instructions from him. Near the bottom was scrawled, *"If it screams in your own reflection, over and over and over."*

Reflection . . .

"What happens?" she pressed. "What will happen, if we try this siphoning and the god's fang is not sufficiently reversed?"

"What happens when you bond with two armies, both determined to go to battle?" The words hitched out, barely decipherable among Ling Zhen's choked hysteria.

She had read so many scrolls, so many folios now, had been observing the enigmatic properties of scholar's stone up close for long enough that her eyes bled with it and her dreams burst in too much dangerous knowledge. Everything she knew about the power of a god's tooth, or of scholar's stone . . . if it was ever directed at itself . . .

Or if scholar's skills hit the unrefined stone—which was what the Pit was built to guard against, since scholar's stone might not be predictable but in this one way it was—in one way it was so predictably unpredictable.

One of the scrolls from Cai Jing detailed a monk who had been about to experiment with the bonding of two distinct god's teeth. That scroll had been one of the ones to end abruptly. Lu Junyi had inquired after more historical writings from that monastery only to find it had wholly vanished from the record.

Your own reflection, Fan Rui had written.

"It will reflect instead of absorbing." She said it as she realized. Once it did—

God's teeth had to be too rare for many people to have tried it. Very few people ever possessed more than one. The Emperor himself was the only personage she could think of.

She would—she must—ask Cai Jing. Surely the traditions of the Imperial state would have kept a record, a warning, that not more than one of the god's teeth could ever be used at once. Surely they had some information on what would happen, what *could* happen.

She thought she knew.

"A reflection of a reflection of a reflection," she murmured. If the partnering god's fang was not fully reversed . . .

Each feeding off the other. It fit, fit with everything she knew of these deep powers, every unexplained interaction. Reflecting again and again and again, with no end.

Until . . .

The size of that buildup of energy could potentially become enormous, before it escaped any pretense at control. Escape it would—the energy from god's teeth always went *somewhere;* an immutable law. That energy would either go somewhere in a controlled way, or go uncontrolled.

The world had seen it with single god's teeth, in how even the weakest could unleash turbulent peril. A skilled user might wield them as an aid or a weapon, but an unskilled one might bring only a ball of chaos into the world around them, like grabbing up ten snarling wolverines by the necks and then losing any grip, letting them free to bound in every direction.

With the vastness of the power locked in the god's fangs . . . even a single stabilized fang under the control of its wielder would hold potential for immeasurable risk, and would require training and a learned hand. The chain reaction between two . . . from what Ling Zhen and Fan Rui were saying, it would become uncontrolled by nature. And quickly.

Unpreventable. Spiking to far more than double what level of destruction one god's fang alone might wreak.

If they failed at this test, it would destroy more than a single volunteer.

The Chancellor would have to be told. If they erred—this could level the building. The Palace. The entire central district—half the Imperial City—

They wouldn't be able to test it here. Somewhere far away, deserted of people, out in a rural expanse with no one to witness or be hurt. No one but them.

"We must find a way to be more certain," she said faintly. "Before—before."

The god's teeth of the Emperor . . . nobody said it very loud, but it was rumored they were of minimal strength. The god's fangs would be many, many times more powerful. Perhaps the Emperor's weaker god's teeth could be—utilized—? Before they tested the improved, artificial god's fangs—

You would dare to ask the Chancellor to demand something from the Emperor? Was her mind thick with wine?

Besides, the Emperor's god's teeth would resist bonding with a different human host. She must think of another choice. Then she must explain all this to the Chancellor; make him understand what consequences they risked . . .

The Chancellor. She could never say, when she approached him, whether he would grunt in kind understanding or—or—

He would understand. He had to. She would come up with every possible safeguard and alternative to present to him. Punishment came only because he wanted to see success, because she had failed him, failed his expectations of her. Because he had raised her up, and she had disappointed him. When she spoke to him about what was needed—when she asked, when she explained—he was receptive, always, the gentleman scholar . . .

Her eyes fell to her own failed alchemy attempts. Fan Rui had been too busy with greater possibilities to produce these herself. Lu Junyi might have to give up and require it of her, even if both the priestess and her husband thought lodestone the better chance. After all, should they not try everything else before Lu Junyi approached the Chancellor with a request that might gut a city, if it went wrong?

A sharp bang echoed from one of the outside doors—then a voice, raised to tempest, a roar of fury that stole all breath and air—"*Where is she?*"

Lu Junyi stumbled back and cracked her hip against the shelving. The Chancellor. In the first reflexive, nonsensical moment she was sure he somehow knew all her fears and reservations—that he considered it another failure—

No, no, impossible. They had barely started work on this—and they had done nothing wrong, not since—but he was angry, why was he angry? She had been working so hard to make no other error, never again, she couldn't, she *hadn't*—

Cai Jing descended on their research space, backed by his ever-present personal guard. His gaze targeted Lu Junyi alone. All she could see was his eyes, and in his rage they seemed to be pools of red and black, ready to swallow her whole.

He strode over, his presence towering, consuming all thought, until his face eclipsed everything else. His hand shot out.

Those long fingers slammed her throat back against the shelving behind her, her head ricocheting and his rings crushing against her jaw. She choked and clutched at his hand without meaning to. What had she done—she had to soothe him, get him to see reason or compassion—to forgive her—*what had she done* . . .

His hand tightened, and Lu Junyi felt her throat bowing in

under the pressure. It hurt, a deep, wrong pain that wasn't only a lack of breath. Tears blurred her vision. She tried to beg and couldn't.

"Where is she?" he hissed in her ear.

Who . . . Her mouth formed the word, but not the rest of her.

"Your *friend.* The one you lied to Grand Marshal Gao about. Where. Is. She."

Grand Marshal Gao?

What friend?

What . . .

Her memory dragged back, back and back, so long ago and yet not long at all. Lin Chong? He was asking about . . . Lin Chong? What? Why? Why *now*?

The pressure on her throat abruptly loosened. A thunderclap went off in Lu Junyi's head with the sudden gulp into her lungs. Her throat couldn't handle it either, closing in a cough that wouldn't stop until she retched.

Her head snapped back with a sudden crack, a blow from the Chancellor she hadn't seen coming. Pain blossomed in her cheek.

She raised a trembling hand to her face. Cai Jing's rings had shredded her skin.

He had never touched her before. Not ever . . .

"I knew you held back and I chose not to care. This is how you repay me? Your *friend* was seen with that treasonous Blue Beast commander on the road, after they and the other traitors took what was mine. *They took what was mine.* You think the Empire would lack the resources for this search? You thought I would not find out? Where is she!"

"I don't—I don't know," Lu Junyi got out, between ragged coughs. Something in her throat felt alarmingly wrong, all catching against itself the wrong way. She didn't understand half of what the Chancellor said—a blue beast? Taking what was his? Lin Chong, somehow mixed up in this, but how . . . "I swear, I swear I don't know . . ."

She knew so little. Not worth hiding, not worth this—*It's not betraying her to speak the truth, it will not give her away—only crumbs you kept in your heart like hope, only small suspicions—*

Cai Jing's hand came back again. This time she saw it fast enough to shrink away. She half slid, half fell to the floor, trying to make it an act of supplication.

A dagger appeared in Cai Jing's hand, and in a sudden whirlwind of motion he dragged a trembling Ling Zhen in front of him, blade to his throat. "Tell me what you hid or you both die now. First his head, then yours."

Cai Jing—he would know whether she lied. He could always tell.

Lin Chong was far from here—safe—likely among those who protected her . . .

Forgive me, Sister . . .

"I don't know, I don't know where she is," she gasped. "I sent—I sent a woman monk to protect her in case of danger, that's all I hid, I swear it. The monk was supposed to see her safely to Canghu. I meant no harm, I didn't know . . ."

She'd hoped so hard that it was Lu Da who had rescued Lin Chong, as brash as such an act would have been, as much as she wished for their own lives and safety that Lin Chong had gone on to serve out her exile in Canghu as planned. As much as she worried, as much as she brooded on the ill wisdom of such an escape, she'd let herself fancy the two of them banded together, roaming the hills northeast of Bianliang, meeting up with Lu Da's friends . . . friends whom Lu Junyi strongly suspected to be operating outside of lawful society . . .

How could she have pictured such a thing so blithely! As though it was a playful dream and had no consequence!

Cai Jing threw Ling Zhen back at his guards, then stabbed a hand at his own entourage like a knife. "Bring her."

Impersonal hands grasped Lu Junyi by the arms and shoulders, dragging her up and along in their wake. She stumbled, still struggling to breathe without pain, the world going by in blinks. She shouldn't have said—but if she hadn't—her fault—no matter what, someone would suffer because of her . . .

Cai Jing led them to an unfamiliar building and then down twisting corridors and stairwells. Was her fate to be a prison as well? Trapped in a cell, degraded, tortured? Had her life spiraled away so fast, in the turn of a coin today?

A wild rushing filled her mind until her thoughts fragmented. She'd railed against the unhappy arrests of so many others, but she'd never understood—

Instead of a dungeon, however, the passageway dead-ended in a round stone room. Guards stood along the sides of it, and against the opposite wall, a woman's body was bolted against an upright wooden pallet—ankles fastened tight to the wood, wrists secured up next to her face. She was an older, plump woman, with a tumble of gray hair, and her head hung to the side, as if she could no longer hold it up. Ragged patches of red and brown stained her face and clothes, and where her weight sagged against the manacles, the flesh was scraped to bloody rivulets.

This was a chamber of torture.

Cai Jing turned back to his followers. "Hold her. And fetch Marshal Gao."

Several of the guards pinioned Lu Junyi's arms behind her. Others hurried to follow Cai Jing's second order.

Cai Jing went up to the woman bound against the wall and reached up a hand to touch her hair. "Only a simple wine merchant," he hissed. "This picture becomes clearer. These thieves dared to attempt defiance of me. Me. That beast with the blue face, Commander Yang of Daleng, she ran like a coward after robbing me—ran with the traitor Lin Chong who was banished from these very walls. They conspired with conniving merchants, and now I learn of a monk. And you, their used and abused wine seller, whom they did not care to protect. Of course you would be recognized. Of course you would be found. It was your friends who did this to you. The reach of the Empire is inevitable."

"I didn't . . ." murmured the woman. "Not me. I wasn't part . . ."

Cai Jing paced to the side of the room and picked something up off a tray held by one of the Guardsmen. "As I said, the picture becomes clearer. This is the work of some bandit stronghold. You will give me names. You will give me their location. Once you do, I will let you die quickly."

With that, he took the metal spike in his hand and drove it straight through the woman's shoulder.

She howled, her body twisting sharp against the restraints. Lu Junyi's joints jerked in sympathy and she tried to turn, to hide her eyes, but the guards held her in place. A forced audience.

"Where can I find them?" Cai Jing's voice had gone back to his genial, conversational tone, and that was almost worse, a screeching nightmare of contradiction. He stepped over to the guard and lifted another one of those metal spikes. "We have plenty of time, my little wine seller Bai Sheng. My men tell me some call you Sunmouse. Well, little mouse, tell me. Where can I find your friends?"

He stepped back over to her. The woman called Bai Sheng dragged her head up, and it seemed she was gathering herself to speak.

Instead, she spat in his face. The blood and saliva landed across Cai Jing's neck and collar.

A shallow gasp squeaked out of Lu Junyi. She couldn't help it.

Fastidiously, Cai Jing took out a hand cloth and wiped it away. Then he said, "Very well" and slammed the next spike through Bai Sheng's hand.

This time she didn't scream, only bucked hard against the wooden frame, her eyes rolling back in her head.

Lu Junyi had begun shaking, her whole body one weak shudder. She was having trouble standing straight, her weight sagging against the Guardsmen without meaning to. Two of Bai Sheng's fingers were twitching like they couldn't stop, her ruined hand the wrong shape now against the wood.

Lu Junyi was here to—what—Cai Jing was going to force her to watch this woman murdered, slowly, and then—and then she would be next? But she knew nothing else, nothing . . . surely he believed her. Even notwithstanding his position over her—his punishments when she erred—they had still shared a mutual respect; he knew her; she had not lied to him . . .

Bai Sheng's head lolled against her neck. She didn't seem sensible.

A Guardsman burst in and took a knee. "Grand Chancellor, they found the husband."

"Bring him in. Ah, Marshal, come join me."

Gao Qiu had appeared at the entrance to the chamber. He glanced around at the scene before him, his face going revolted, like someone had asked him to eat from a latrine. He brought his hands up as if to prevent his embroidered tunic from becoming sullied by what he witnessed. "What is this? Why have you summoned me here?"

Cai Jing had retrieved another of those metal spikes, and he toyed with it in his hand, tapping it in Gao Qiu's direction. "Do not forget yourself, *Marshal.* As it happens, I have very good intelligence on a matter of great personal importance to yourself, and I thought to share it with you, as a favor. If you had rather I did not . . ."

"No, no, I—thank you. Chancellor. Grand Chancellor."

"You might approve of my methods more, once you know. I am in the process of extracting information about that troublesome former arms instructor of yours."

"Lin Chong." Gao Qiu's face creased itself in frightful, dark fury. "You found her. Tell me. Tell me now!"

"Now, now, Marshal. Calm yourself, or I'll have you removed. You are here as my guest."

Gao Qiu's color was going past red to a purplish, bottled-up rage, and he visibly forced himself to step back from his superior, toward the edge of the room. Lu Junyi did not think he had seen or recognized her.

She kept her head down. She was not sure Cai Jing would protect her, not again, not now that he had decided to take her to task for her deception. *I should never have done it . . . he knew, he knew from the beginning. Of course he knew.*

Two more guards hustled into the room, dragging a peasant

man between them. They shoved him to the ground in the center of the circle, at Cai Jing's feet.

The old man was cowering. Near weeping in fear. But the bound woman's face came up at last, roused, somehow, by his presence, and she let out a low cry.

The man risked a glance upward from his kneeled bow, and he flinched as if an arrow had struck him. "I beg you, I beg you, mercy . . ." He broke down in sobs.

Cai Jing stepped over and pushed at him with one foot. "You are the husband of our little wine merchant."

"Y—y—yes, Grand Chancellor. Please, I beg you, whatever we've done, mercy . . ."

"Your name is Huang Wenbing."

"Yes, Grand Chancellor, you know all . . ."

"Not all. Not yet. But as her husband, you are as guilty as your mouselike wife."

"Yes, Grand Chancellor, all is as you say, Grand Chancellor . . . please show mercy, please . . ."

"You have no idea what I'm talking about, do you," Cai Jing said down his nose. "The whipped dog, to your wife the calculating thief. *She* had the audacity to steal from me."

"No, Grand Chancellor—I mean, I'm sure it was a mistake, Grand Chancellor, please, punish me instead, forgive us—"

"Pathetic little worm of a man. And yet. You can save your wife."

"Yes—please—anything—"

Cai Jing meandered back over to Bai Sheng, reaching out with the metal spike he held to drag it across her neck and cheek. "Tell me. Who was your wife conspiring with? Where are they?"

"I—I don't know, I swear it. My Sunmouse, tell him, please, just tell him!"

"You have the bravery in this family," Cai Jing said quietly in Bai Sheng's ear, when she had said nothing. "But also all the foolhardiness. Your husband in his cowardice is much more clever than you."

On the last word, he thrust the spike hard through the side of her abdomen.

Lu Junyi could not tell if Bai Sheng made any sound, because her husband wailed so loud it echoed against every stone.

"It's not too late." Cai Jing raised his voice above the man's sobbing. "A doctor may yet save her before the festering devours her body. You can still have your wife back, minus the use of a hand and arm, I think, but this is a small punishment, is it not? Now tell me, whom did she conspire with?"

"I don't know!" Huang Wenbing screamed. "I don't know! I swear on the lives of our families. I would tell you, Grand Chancellor, I would give you any clue, I would tell you anything. Anything you want to know, ask, and if I know then it's yours, please!"

"You expect me to believe you don't know what goes on in your own house." Cai Jing took his slow, deliberate stride back over to the guard holding the tray of metal spikes, lifted yet one more, and tapped it against the stone wall. "Almost two weeks ago your wife robs me of everything due me, and where were you, good Uncle? Drunk, perhaps, or bedding another woman. Or you are only trying to protect your malefactor wife and her ill-gotten riches."

He began pacing back over. But Huang Wenbing's head came up, his eyes suddenly wide, his beard soggy with tears. "Grand Chancellor! Two weeks ago—but I remember—my wife, she had unexpected visitors—"

Cai Jing whirled on him with such speed the man fell backward. Cai Jing advanced and kicked him hard, once, in the chest, so that he sprawled on his back, the Chancellor looming above him, metal spike poised high in his hand.

Everything inside Lu Junyi had gone numb, a terrible cold stealing over her. Everyone in this room had their fate sealed, including her; she knew it with the certainty of death. Huang Wenbing knew something that would take still others to the grave with them . . .

Lin Chong and Lu Da and whoever they allied with now, this man knew something, and Cai Jing would wipe them all from earth and time.

"There were horses," the man wept. "I saw horses. My wife, she said she had friends visiting who had stepped outside. I remember thinking it odd, because we'd not expected anyone, and so many horses, as if it was very many people, but my wife said it was just an old friend from her village, where she used to live in Dongxi . . ."

"Quiet," whispered Bai Sheng, though it did not seem possible she had the strength for words. She tried again to speak, and a bubble of blood formed on her lips and then dribbled down her chin. *"Quiet, husband. I lied, I lied to you . . ."*

"Ah," Cai Jing said. "So helpful to have confirmation that this was exactly what you did not wish me to know. Elder Huang, you have saved your wife."

He drew back that metal spike, and with a mighty thrust drove it straight through Bai Sheng's eye.

CHAPTER 19

". . . And then the monk said, 'So that's where my staff went.'"

Wu Yong waited for a dutiful chuckle. Chao Gai unfortunately had very poor taste—she was not the most appreciative audience for raunchy jokes, however well-crafted.

But Sister Chao wasn't paying any attention at all. Instead she sat her horse abstractly, staring into the setting sun as if the flat and deserted road before them were about to reveal a secret.

Abruptly more alert, Wu Yong twisted around in the saddle, absentmindedly correcting the horse when he gave an unappreciative skip at the shift in weight. The road behind them stretched empty, too. Rutted dirt with the hardened tracks of boots and hooves and wheels, bracketed by grassland and dotted groves. Their own three packhorses were strung out in single file, piled high with the provisions Chao Gai was bringing back to grant her villagers. But the animals' heads were down and their ears relaxed, with the lead mare's rope looping tensionless to Chao Gai's hand. The animals heard nothing, either.

Even Wu Yong's horse, a spirited gelding they called Dancing Leaf who spooked at dragonflies, was showing no skittishness.

They couldn't be very long from Dongxi. Chao Gai had said they would arrive by nightfall or not long after, and they only had about one watch of the day left before they'd begin to lose the summer light. No ill had befallen them on the journey today, no sign any evil dogged their steps—in fact the ride had been downright boring, save for Wu Yong's excellent repertoire of jokes.

Now Wu Yong imagined the air pricking with some unseen tension, something only Chao Gai could sense . . .

"Heavenly King! What do you see?"

"I don't know." Chao Gai's horse began sensing his rider's distraction and slowed, the packhorses slowing in turn behind. Wu Yong pulled up to match. The horses had begun to pick up on the mood and tossed their heads with disquiet.

Chao Gai's posture tightened suddenly, and her mount danced to a stop in response. "There. Someone comes."

Wu Yong whipped around to follow Chao Gai's pointing hand. This time the landscape was not so empty. A small figure, racing toward them from far across the grasslands, but approaching fast.

"Ally or enemy?" One of Wu Yong's gloved hands tightened on the reins, the other reaching for the whip-chain. They were only two out here, but the figure was alone, so should not pose too much threat . . .

"Ally," Chao Gai said. "It's Sister Chai."

Foreboding crept up Wu Yong's spine like the hand of a too-dangerous lover.

Noblewoman Chai? Why here? Galloping at them, alone, without the multitudinous retinue that much more often accompanied her . . . and across the grasses no less, shortcutting the road from her estate. A dangerous proposition if her horse's thundering gait hit an animal burrow or partially buried tree root, and not a move that would have saved her very much time at all . . . not much time at all . . .

Wu Yong knew the instant Sister Chai saw them, because her horse wheeled in its pounding pace, and she centered arrow-straight on where they waited in the middle of the road. Rider and mount drove faster and faster, heads lowered, an oncoming storm.

She hadn't been riding at them initially, Wu Yong realized. She had been riding for Dongxi.

"Sister!" Chao Gai called. Noblewoman Chai's horse barreled into the road, its hindquarters dragging hard into a stop and kicking up a whirlwind of dust from the hard-packed track in a small version of Sister Chai's cyclone namesake. She pulled her recovering mount into a turn so she could face them. Both she and her horse were blowing mightily, the beast's nostrils flaring with froth as its sides heaved, dark with the pouring sweat of a panicked ride.

The Cyclone couldn't get her own breath for a moment. She tried to speak only to choke on wild gasps.

"Haojie—breathe!" Chao Gai cried. "What ill wind brings you here?"

"Dongxi," gasped the Cyclone, leaning hard on her horse's neck. "You have to get to Dongxi—warn them—it's Cai Jing, he knows. He knows the person who stole from him is of Dongxi, he will raze the village—"

Chao Gai did not wait. With a shout, she spurred her horse into a leap forward, galloping away down the road toward her village and her people. She'd dropped the packhorses' lead. A moment of panicked milling ensued as the horses tried to follow until Wu Yong spurred in and managed to grab ahold of the lead mare's bridle to bring them around. The poor beasts pulled and stamped, sending anxious whinnies into the evening.

"I have to go help her," Wu Yong called to Sister Chai. "Rest here. Stay with the horses!"

Noblewoman Chai nodded rapidly, clumsily catching the lead rope that Wu Yong threw.

"Speak quickly, is there anything else you can tell me?"

"It will be bad—go! Go now, get the villagers out. My estate, they will be safe—go!"

Wu Yong nodded and leaned low, heels squeezing against Dancing Leaf's flanks. Even after a long day's ride, the gelding reacted with the friskiness of a foal, leaping to obey and run, run, running for the edge of the world.

Wu Yong's body moved with the gallop, flying into the sunset as if they were one beast. This was good luck, wasn't it? With fresher mounts, they would reach Dongxi a hair faster than the Cyclone would have. Noblewoman Chai had half killed herself and her horse on their breakneck ride, and it was a good trade for Chao Gai and Wu Yong to continue on in her stead, as she could have warned but they could also fight—the Cyclone was not helpless in her martial skills, but her training was more art than brutality, so it was lucky she had met them, very lucky, because if they didn't make it to Dongxi before Cai Jing's forces . . .

Lucky, lucky, lucky, beat out the hooves of Dancing Leaf.

They *must* have some luck here; it was an indisputable law of the game. After all, how had Cai Jing made this sort of connection? It must have been through extraordinary luck of his own, scavenging the countryside without rest. Their plan had left no easy stepping stone, Wu Yong was sure of it, but luck was always what could turn the game—luck—and Cai Jing had stumbled on more of his share. So it was only right for Wu Yong to come up lucky next, just a touch, the smallest touch, to make up the balance. Noblewoman Chai finding them before they'd reached the village, spurring them faster, it was lucky . . .

Sister Jiang the Mathematic joined Wu Yong in number games sometimes. She always laughed and mocked if Wu Yong claimed a balance of destiny would come. "Nature scorns your balance," she would say, in that gravelly voice of hers. "The future cares not for the past, only for its own randomness. You lost six times to me because nature *laughs* at your idea of balance."

Wu Yong was firmly of the opinion that Sister Jiang cheated. Of course, Wu Yong cheated, too, and had gained the title of the only one in the encampment who sometimes beat Sister Jiang's numerical riddles. The better title was that aside from the number games, Wu Yong beat everyone else in games of strategy *every* time.

Even with the element of luck in play. Tactics just had to put you far enough ahead that bad luck could never catch you . . .

Cai Jing's luck can't catch me. Can't catch us. I will not allow it.

Wu Yong leaned lower, urging the horse faster, as if together they raced the Chancellor himself along this lonely road. Out ahead, the sun dipped below the horizon, the sky becoming a husky gray speckled with the early dimness of stars.

Wu Yong had only been to Dongxi a handful of times before, always to visit Chao Gai during the latter's tenure as village chief. It was a night not unlike this one when Wu Yong had first raised a whiff of the Liangshan bandits in conversation with the chief, a seemingly careless testing of waters that Chao Gai had jumped to eagerly. The two had stayed late with their heads together, refilling their cups and plotting ways they could better the world. The very next week Wu Yong had brought Chao Gai to the mountain.

During that Dongxi meeting, a drunken beggar had come pounding at the gate, and Chao Gai had sent out five jin of rice for the man without a second thought. Such was the magnanimity of Dongxi's village chief, as all its people knew.

Luck. We had luck tonight. It won't be too late.

How many people lived in Dongxi? The village was not small—perhaps two hundred lives, by Wu Yong's estimate. Upward of fifty households, surely. Families. Children . . . Most eking out a living on the land, or through livestock. Chao Gai tried to shelter them from the never-ending grind of tax extortion by the local military governor, or rackets by the county and provincial magistrates, and had largely figured out how to finesse such a feat. More than that, Chao Gai had fostered good feeling between the residents, a neighborliness. Forever setting an example by giving to any who struggled, with no expectation of return, and forgiving just as generously. Over the years such leadership had brought the villagers to a state of . . . perhaps not outright prosperity, but comfort. Safety.

Wu Yong was fairly sure Sister Chao knew every one of the damn residents' names.

How long has it been, since she landed here originally and they called her chief? Fifteen, twenty years at least—an age had passed while neither of them noticed. Back then, Chao Gai had been a young and headstrong ghost hunter, fresh from studies at the monastery, eager to prove hero. The odd haunting had so far ranked as no challenge to her and had only tempted her appetite for more.

Dongxi had defeated far more experienced exorcists. The land under the village was plagued with spirits, ravaged by the restless dead. The people soldiered on, exhausted, hateful, as they woke to mutilated livestock or had their children fall to frightful accidents. Some tried to relocate elsewhere, but where could they go? No one would buy the land their fortunes were staked on; even traveling peddlers avoided the festering boil that was Dongxi, leaving its people scraping in poverty.

Only the tax collectors were undeterred. They could not be forestalled by ghosts.

No benevolent spirit had ever visited. Somehow the land had been poisoned into a cesspit of ancient villainy, every one of its phantoms so far from any humanity that they were no more than manifested evil made real. All collecting at the bend in a stream where the village called Dongxi withered but failed to die.

Until Chao Gai had come.

Wu Yong had not been witness, but the way Chao Gai told it, the battle had been one of legend. One by one, Chao Gai trapped each of those spirits beyond the physical plane, walling them away as if behind seamless stone and inscribing their own names and natures against them, until every single beastly emergence was bound thrashing and furious—forever. The feat had minted her a new and indisputable hero. The shocking side effect was that after Chao Gai had emerged victorious, it was to find the people begging their savior to become chief.

She'd proven even better at that than as a wandering champion. *Heavenly King,* they'd called her.

Two hundred lives. Children and families.

Noblewoman Chai's offered sanctuary at her estate would host them easily. They would be inconvenienced, greatly inconvenienced, but saved. The sprawling lands belonging to the Cyclone had more than enough space and rooms to house them temporarily, and Liangshan could offer a helpful expansion of that hospitality with a little lead time for construction and logistics. Noblewoman Chai was well-known for the safe haven her family lands offered, and her own lifelong amnesty meant she could walk very close to every law—even cross them now and again—and the Emperor could neither condemn nor even pursue her without abdicating his family's own honor. Noblewoman Chai would shelter all of Dongxi until . . .

Until Wu Yong found the next move against Cai Jing. There was always a next move.

Wu Yong's horse caught the scent first.

The gelding's rhythm skipped and bucked, and Wu Yong was barely able to keep a seat in the saddle, thighs clamped hard, hand and booted heels forcing the little horse to firmness. *Go, go, keep on, we had luck and we can't be too late—*

Then Wu Yong smelled it too.

The acrid sharpness of a camp's cooking fuel. A neighboring house's stove when standing out on the street some cold night.

Fire.

Dancing Leaf shied and balked. Wu Yong fought his jerking and drove them faster, faster; they had to help, had to warn . . . Darkness had begun gloving the sky, but the night was not full. Yet somehow Wu Yong could still not see ahead, as if the world were shrouded in a veil of fog.

A fog that burned and blurred. Gradually joined by a muted, monstrous glow.

Wu Yong lifted a glove to wipe away the tearing. Tears had no meaning, spur the horse on, force them both forward, even as every instinct in both horse and rider shrieked to flee. The rolling miasma clouded everything before them, a towering and too-final claim.

The first buildings rose up suddenly out of the smoke, shadowy charred spikes of the reeking and ruined. Glowing embers helped outline the destruction against the dusk and clogged air. Other shapes moved—ran—screamed—until still others followed, men on horseback in a cavalry of death, who cut down the screamers into silence.

No.

Wu Yong made no coherent decision. Horse and rider plunged after one of those deadly shapes, and Wu Yong's copper chain whipped out.

Now one of the Imperial Guardsmen screamed.

The blow smacked him from the saddle to plunge off his horse's back. The riderless horse reared, eyes rolling, and thundered away. Wu Yong's horse, driven by heels of stone in his flanks, kept plunging on, his hooves churning over the injured man who had fallen stunned to the ground. An iron-shod beast weighing a thousand jin was as good as a weapon, anvils that crushed throat or groin or sternum before Wu Yong rode hard after the next.

Chain met skull—another soldier fell. Chase down the next—he galloped away, but metal cracked out and smacked the hindquarters of his horse, who bucked and bolted. The rider grasped at air and found nothing, his mount racing out from beneath him.

No decision. Trample forward and finish it.

The soldiers were becoming harder to see. Darkness and smoke and streaming tears that Wu Yong tried to ignore even while coughing out of lungs filled with tar.

More screams, muffled and swallowed by the smoke. From where? Where?

A farm was ablaze off to the right, a full inferno, the flames licking up to the night sky. As Wu Yong rode toward it, a girl who looked about twelve or thirteen crashed from the collapse in a disintegrating wall. She fled, bawling, nightdress still aflame, her hair blackened and charred away.

Another one of the soldiers pounded in. Before Wu Yong could close the distance, he'd struck from the saddle, sword cutting the girl down the way a man might chop at troublesome brush.

Wu Yong still wasn't close enough. But someone else was.

Chao Gai galloped in at right angles, straight at the soldier, letting loose a shout of pure pain.

Her sword flew. The man's head separated clean off his shoulders and bounced to the ground in his wake. His headless body rode on for several paces more before creaking slowly out of the saddle, but its foot tangled in the stirrup. The panicked horse dragged the corpse away into the night, bucking and kicking against this burden it didn't understand.

Chao Gai wailed another bloody, grief-stricken cry at the soot and sky, but two more riders appeared out of the smoke, upon her at once. They met their ends just as fast. Chao Gai's staff and sword slashed brutal, no finesse, only death.

This time Wu Yong had drawn close enough to help. The soldiers fell lifeless in moments.

"Where to?" Wu Yong tried to ask, but the words became nothing more than a hacking choke.

Chao Gai didn't answer anyway. She screamed again, wordless, coughing, broken, vicious and fury-filled. Then she thrust her weapons back into the saddle and twisted abruptly to slide from her horse. Wu Yong spurred closer and barely caught hold of the bridle in time—both horses wanted to bolt, flipping themselves against the reins and twitching their heads as if to shake off this nightmare. Juggling a grip on both sets of reins, Wu Yong managed a clumsy dismount as well.

Chao Gai had swept the dead girl into her arms, pressing their foreheads together—and heedless of the way the girl's body fell nearly in halves. Her small frame had been cleaved so deeply that it folded open, blood and bone and a warm mess of organs ballooning into the night.

All backlit by her family home in flames. The house she hadn't been permitted to escape from.

Wu Yong looped the horses' reins forward over their heads, one hand reaching above and behind to keep a grip, and went to one knee next to Chao Gai. The smoke scoured their faces and throats. The heat from the house fire scorched through their tunics even at this distance.

Chao Gai's eyes were wild, streaming from smoke or emotion or both, her face smudged dark with soot. She raised her head from the girl's, her anguished gaze going to the abstract distance.

"None of them," she rasped, barely audible. "None . . ."

Even lacking Chao Gai's further senses, Wu Yong had seen enough to take her meaning. The villagers burned in their homes, anyone fleeing becoming victim of the sword instead.

"Trapped . . ." Chao Gai whispered. "Tortured and then trapped them . . . to die alone . . . the pain, I can feel—so much pain—too late. Too late. Only the dying left . . ."

Her voice scratched like rusted metal. Wu Yong reached out and gripped her arm.

Chao Gai . . . she was feeling her own people massacred.

A startling darkness seemed to overtake her eyes. As if liquid ink replaced her tears, her eyes becoming black diamonds in an inhuman face.

She whipped to face Wu Yong. "Run."

"I'll stay—"

"I can do one thing for them. I can end it. *Run.*"

Clarity began to dawn, but still Wu Yong hesitated for one fragile extra instant. Chao Gai's expression went closed and altered, drawing into something unnatural. Otherworldly.

"Now," she hissed, and Wu Yong ran.

In the moment it took for boot to hit stirrup and for Wu Yong to land hard against Dancing Leaf's saddle, the ground began to shake.

No. Not the ground. The air. Vibrating in every direction, overwhelming every sense. Jarring Wu Yong's body apart from the inside.

This time the *horses* screamed. Dancing Leaf reared at the same time Chao Gai's mount bolted. The second set of reins tore out of Wu Yong's hand and was gone, and it was all Wu Yong could do to stay in the saddle, *hold on, hold on, hold on and run—*

On the ground, Chao Gai had her fingers spread, palm up. She stood very straight, no longer reacting to the smoke, the dead girl at her feet. Her robes were soaked dark with other people's blood.

Wu Yong did not wait to see what she did next. The instant Dancing Leaf's hooves hit ground again, they shot away through the trembling air like a bolt from a crossbow, running, running anywhere but here, out of this village that was about to become nothing but death. The smoke had cloaked all sense of direction, but Wu Yong bent low and let the horse run straight, straight in any direction that would take them out and away—

The world seemed to cleave against itself. Not the earth, but reality itself, everywhere, shuddering through every nerve and joint and limb. Wu Yong knew, suddenly with a terrible certainty, what this village's chief was doing to save it, one last time.

Chao Gai was releasing the ghosts.

This place. This place that had been plagued by spirits that Chao Gai herself had trapped somewhere just beyond. She was cracking apart her own impenetrable seal, breaking them loose, all of them and more, calling on everything ancient and evil.

And they were hungry.

Shapes burst forth, out of the ground, out of the air, from cracks in the sky. Visible darkness, rupturing through into the world with only a mind to devour.

Wu Yong yanked hard on the reins, forcing Dancing Leaf to spin away and avoid, to wheel in the sharpest of turns, leaning so hard they both should have driven into the dirt. He tried to buck against the bit, to throw the vise of pressure off his flanks—but Wu Yong forced his head, forced with the certainty of life and death, because that's what these shapes were, *death*—

Several of the soldiers rode by at a distance, shouting to each other in panic, slashing swords at the empty air and finding nothing. One of the shadows rose behind them, for a single heartbeat billowing up ever taller and darker and more vicious.

It plunged with all the speed of a raptor. A raptor the size of a house.

The soldiers tried to flee. The shadow tore into them, *through* them, bone bursting as if their flesh inverted from the inside out, human faces exploding into skulls and then into nothing. Slivers of meat and skeleton whipped like daggers to smack Wu Yong across the cheek from fifty paces away.

Where men and horses had ridden only a moment ago drifted fine mists of blood and the echo of agony.

Don't stop. Head down, ride harder, get out, get out, don't touch them—don't get close—

Reality shook again, harder, juddering against itself in fault lines, evil seeping through from every crack.

Could Chao Gai control this? Did she even want to?

No time to think about it. Run. Twist away. Rear back from the yawning cracks where this world collapsed into darkness, force Dancing Leaf through a wildness he didn't understand to save them both, zig and zag and bite hard down on any possible scrap of luck because if one of those burst through in the path ahead—or if one were to burst through on them, *in* them, devouring animal or human with no quarter . . .

If that happened, all would be done. Ended.

Wu Yong could not feel the dying and dead as Chao Gai did. Yet somehow, in this fracturing world, for a handful of moments everything seemed to be as one. The devourers pouring from their prison, called forth by Chao Gai to this fertile ground, multiplied a thousandfold in number and hunger in their decades of imprisonment. The soldiers, crying out in fear now, for mercy, for forgiveness, for their mothers and grandmothers, and disintegrating before they could flee.

And the people—the villagers—barred or bound in their homes, pleading for death as they burned . . .

Death heard their pleas, and came.

Their screams stopped, too.

Wu Yong rode and rode and didn't look back, far past where the world stopped cracking and the unnatural shadows grew sparse and sparser and then were left behind. Far out under the stars, with the air clear and the earth still and reality knit together again.

Dancing Leaf stumbled to a stop. Wu Yong sat in the saddle for a long moment. Then another, and another, unmoving.

They were on a road, but not the one they'd come in on—this one stretched in a narrow dirt track that formed a trough between banks of tall grasses. Wu Yong kicked the stirrup off on one side and slid down, ankles almost folding against the ground. Every bone felt shredded, every breath a knife.

I'm alive, though. Alive.

Wu Yong's mind leapt to the rest of it, to Cai Jing, to Chao Gai, to whatever Noblewoman Chai had learned that had sent them racing into this bloodbath. Had Cai Jing discovered—? Was Sister Chao still—? *Leave it. Not yet. Leave it!*

With difficulty, Wu Yong tamped down the chaos of questions and the reflexive grasp for strategy and reaction. It was like swinging a bat against one's own self.

Dancing Leaf's head hung low in clear exhaustion, his eyes lidding closed, sides fluttering shallowly. Wu Yong sank down against the bank of grass, head fallen back, gazing up at the stars and letting them both rest.

Breathing was difficult, but possible. Wu Yong's focus came and went in shards that cut and bled.

Direction. Find a direction, use the stars . . .

Don't think yet. Don't think about Chao Gai.

There. The pole star, the North Celestial, glittering calmly as if it oversaw an ordinary night. This track was leading southwest, then. And they'd come in roughly from the east.

When Wu Yong rose again, unknotting joints and straightening in pops of dull pain, a nervous Dancing Leaf twitched away from being touched. With leaden arms, Wu Yong lifted the water skin from its thong on the saddle and drank against a throat that stabbed with every sip.

Half only, the rest went to the horse. He shied away, again, but Wu Yong caught at the bridle, steadying him and turning the waterskin to let it dribble against his tongue.

"Drink. A bit longer, and then we can both rest. Drink."

At least the horse let himself be mounted. Though swinging up into the stirrups was almost too much to ask of Wu Yong.

Sit. Breathe. Vomit if you need to. Nobody here to see.

Don't think about Chao Gai, or what Cai Jing knows. Not yet.

The right direction. That was all.

Wu Yong managed to rouse and coax the horse to slow action. Up into the grass, even as he balked, hooves pawing against the uneven ground.

"No, we're not going back by the road. That way lies . . ."

Something. Would Chao Gai lock away the spirits again, after everything was done? Or leave them to roam, devouring Dongxi off the map forever, a no man's land where no one ever dared step foot again?

Would Chao Gai even be able to re-imprison them, if she wished to?

Had Chao Gai even planned to save herself?

Wu Yong guided the horse in a wide berth of where the village had been. They kept farther than they needed to, plodding slowly over the rough grasses in a distant arc. But they'd galloped in and were meandering out, and an estimation of the distances was difficult . . . better to overshoot for safety than to happen back across the fringes of Dongxi.

Wu Yong shuddered.

Dancing Leaf's hooves dragged, tripping on the earth. Wu Yong let the poor animal set his own pace. A slow walk was more than enough to handle from the saddle right now anyway. The smoke had been its own poison even before the fighting and the horrors and the breakneck ride, and Wu Yong's mind slid in oily circles, tinged with sick.

The landscape rolled on beneath them, step by exhausted step. Mostly grasses, but some thickets of forest, here and there another farm track or a stream. Wu Yong let the horse drink his fill, and dismounted to do the same, rinsing and spitting. The taste of the fire still lingered.

It must have been half the night when Dancing Leaf's hooves stumbled out onto a wide dirt road again. Wu Yong's head tilted back, taking in the stars. Was this the right road? The one they had ridden in on? Impossible to say for sure, until they hit an inn or a post marker. It seemed right . . .

East, it was going east, roughly. That had to be right.

The horse stumbled again and listed to the side. Too tired. Too much. Wu Yong shook one foot loose, body barely responding, and slid into an even more graceless dismount than before. Dancing Leaf tossed his head and nosed a question.

"You got me to the road. Let's see if I can stay upright for a while. Mind you, you might still have to carry me if I can't."

Wu Yong took hold of the reins in one hand and turned eastward.

One foot in front of the other. One at a time. *If this is the wrong road . . . at first light I can find an inn, surely. Or, failing that, a farmhouse. Ask them where I am. They can tell me in relation to Dongxi.*

Warn them, too. Warn them never to go near Dongxi again.

Wu Yong couldn't have said how long they walked that way, horse and rider a reflection of each other, feet dragging in a rough staccato, heads lolling downward as if their necks could not hold up the weight.

"Wu Yong! Professor!"

The shout had to be repeated three times. *You're lucky no villainous attacker has found you here,* Wu Yong thought. *This is no good state of alertness.* And then: *At least it's the right road.*

Wu Yong tried to turn toward Sister Chai's voice, but ended up folding to sit on the ground instead. The horse wandered a few steps to the side and then stopped and blew out a breath, head hanging low.

The Cyclone's hands. Grasping at Wu Yong's head, wiping at the soot and sweat and heedless of how it stained her silken sleeves. "Professor. What happened? Where is Sister Chao?"

Wu Yong couldn't speak.

"Is she in trouble? Should we ride to aid her?"

"No! No. No riding. Dongxi is—" What? Dead, blackened, a pit that would devour any souls that wandered through and add them to its ghostly number. "It's over."

"Is Sister Chao—" Noblewoman Chai stopped, clamped her lips together.

"I don't know."

The Cyclone sank down to the road also, their shoulders touching. They sat that way for a time before Wu Yong roused to ask her to see to Dancing Leaf. Sister Chai brought him over to hobble with the others and took down the saddle and tack, giving him a careful rubdown and another skin of water.

It surprised Wu Yong slightly that she knew how to do all that. Her estate was not lacking in well-gilded servants. But Sister Chai was independent, and a fighter herself, and perhaps she had learned for just such a situation as this.

She came back and resumed sitting next to Wu Yong, offering another waterskin. She didn't appear to have changed for the frantic ride out—her clothes were of their usual fine quality, lavender silk trimmed with midnight, though torn and dirty now. But she did not pay the damage any heed.

It was far too long before Wu Yong's mind began to work well enough—or at all—to ask the important questions, the obvious questions. "How did you know? Wait—Liangshan, are they—"

"I sent a trusted runner to Zhu Gui at her inn. I did not have time to find another to ride for Dongxi, so came myself, as fast as I could."

"What does Cai Jing know?"

"I'm not certain I discovered everything. But I was told the greatest threat was to Dongxi. I don't think he is aimed at the mountain yet, but . . . it's surely only a matter of time."

Wu Yong nodded. Tortured, Chao Gai had said of the villagers. Doubtless the soldiers had squeezed all the information they could from Dongxi before laying it to waste.

"He had his investigators scour the countryside day after day for any clue. Professor . . ." Sister Chai hesitated, then drove on. "He found Sister Chao's friend. Bai Sheng."

"She's dead?"

"So I'm told."

I failed her, Wu Yong realized. *I should have, could have anticipated an eventuality such as this. Even the most rudimentary caution of bringing her back to the mountain . . .*

Sacrifices sometimes readied the whole board for victory. But unnecessary sacrifices, senseless ones, sacrifices that happened because Wu Yong had not properly prepared, had left something to chance—sacrifices that gave the enemy an advantage—

Two hundred people in Dongxi. And one wine merchant who had been a sister to the Liangshan bandits. Cai Jing had killed one of their own.

Maybe two.

"You're swaying." Noblewoman Chai's hand stretched supportive against Wu Yong's back. "There's more for me to tell, but it can wait for—when should we—? We can get you to an inn. There must be one not far from here."

"No," Wu Yong said.

Sister Chai nodded. They sat. Waited.

When hoofbeats came, however, they were not from Dongxi, but from the east.

Sister Chai drew a dagger. "Quick. Back by the horses."

Wu Yong's copper chain was out, swinging from one gloved hand, but this night had already wrung out everything possible and left nothing behind. *How effective can I be, now? Will I fail again here?*

They retreated off the road, back by the packs and the hobbled, sleeping horses. Noblewoman Chai was gripping Wu Yong's arm.

She was the one who saw the truth first.

"Oh, grace be to the Emperor!" She let go and dashed forward, shouting out into the night. "Sister Song! Haojie! Stop!"

Sister Song? Sister Song was—here?

And she was riding for Dongxi—the galloping hooves hadn't paused, they hadn't heard Sister Chai—

Wu Yong's body lurched into stumbled action without any conscious direction. Down into the road, in front of the sprinting horses like a drunkard, *they can't go toward Dongxi, stop stop stop stop stop—*

One of the horses whinnied loud at the sky, front hooves coming off the ground close enough for Wu Yong to feel the wind of it.

"Mother of a cunt!" bellowed a familiar voice from the rearing horse. *"What in a stinking demon's foreskin—"*

"Professor!" Song Jiang made it sound as harsh as one of Li Kui's curses.

Wu Yong couldn't draw a breath. The world spun, narrowing to a point. *Hands on knees. Try to breathe. Don't fall . . .*

That dictate failed. When Wu Yong was next sensible, the stars wheeled above again, the hard-packed dirt of the road below.

Breathe . . .

"Professor. Speak, please. Are you all right? Where's Sister Chao?" Song Jiang crouched down, her face eclipsing the sky, her hand pressing Wu Yong's. The figures of Li Kui and Lu Da clustered behind her, bulky shadows in the night.

"Sister Chao," Wu Yong tried. "She . . ."

"We knew trouble had found you—we rode to help," Song Jiang explained. She gestured behind her. "Or—Sister Lu knew. What befell you? Where is Chao Gai?"

"You can't go after her." Wu Yong's elbows pushed against the ground, aiming for something close to a sitting position. "You can't go. Nobody can."

"I don't understand. Is she still in Dongxi?"

Wu Yong's mind tried to answer that, and failed. "She . . . we need to wait for her. Here. You can't go . . . it's over."

"Oh, that makes perfect sense," Li Kui said sarcastically. "'S why we call you the Professor, sure. Sister Song, our Tactician is addled in the headmeat. Let *me* go to the village. I'll bring Sister Chao back if I have to knock her out, truss her up, and throw her across my saddle, see if I don't."

"*No.*" Wu Yong groped to physically stop her but found only air. "No. Nobody can go. Chao Gai sent me—sent me away. I said I would stay, I said—But she sent me—It's finished."

"I'm afraid the Iron Whirlwind speaks the truth tonight, Professor," said Song Jiang. "You're not making sense. You know we won't leave Sister Chao behind—what happened? Where is she? Professor. *Concentrate.*"

"Yeah, concentrate!" Li Kui roared, and reached forward to

smack Wu Yong across the face. "Where's Sister Chao? Did you kill her?"

"Shush," Song Jiang hissed over her shoulder, before turning back to add, "but you must speak, and quickly. *Where is Sister Chao?*"

"Here."

Everyone but Wu Yong stood or turned suddenly. Wu Yong managed to twist around, too, only more slowly.

Chao Gai stood on the western tract of road, on foot. Her robes were torn and black with smoke and blood, her eyes spiderwebbed with red, the veins of her face blown into indigo bruises.

"Sister Chao!" Lu Da and Noblewoman Chai cried her name at once, both hurrying to support her. But Chao Gai shook them off.

Song Jiang stepped forward. Met her eyes. "Dongxi?"

"Gone." Chao Gai said it without emotion.

"Cai Jing's doing?"

"Yes."

"How?"

"Sister Chai said he killed Bai Sheng." With the help of some elbow work, Wu Yong managed to push up to stand with the rest of them. "That's how he knew . . ."

"It was her husband, Huang Wenbing," Noblewoman Chai added quietly. "I'm told he was the one who talked. Bai Sheng protected you to the end."

Li Kui drew one of her battleaxes and roared, slashing the weapon down to thump into the dirt of the road, with such force the axe head buried half its blade in the hard-packed clay. "He talked? He dies! No one crosses Liangshan!"

"She's right," Chao Gai said. Soft. Deadly. She turned to Noblewoman Chai. "Do they still hold him?"

"No," she answered. "Once he gave the Chancellor the information, he was granted clemency."

"Then Bai Sheng must be avenged. Tonight."

Silence, with nods from some of the others. Everyone understood how this night must end.

Wu Yong surely did. The certainty had been waiting all along, behind smoke-riddled wits and the breath-stealing scent of their own failure. Before anything else, before the next move of the game could be conceived—the move that would lead to the crushing destruction of Cai Jing and everything he touched—this part must be finished.

It was only right.

"I have more," Noblewoman Chai put in quietly. "Rumors, mostly, but I believe them to be important ones. This merits a longer conversation—we should get off the road."

Song Jiang reached over and touched Wu Yong's shoulder. "You're not well. You need to get back to the mountain. Sister Chai can accompany you and await us there."

"No." Wu Yong pushed her hand away. "It was only some smoke. I ride with you."

"Sister An would have our heads," Song Jiang said gently. "You weren't at full strength before tonight. Let the Cyclone take you back. Tell everyone else what's transpiring here, and make sure they're on highest alert."

"Spring Rain." Wu Yong said her nickname so coldly that Song Jiang drew back slightly. "You mean to help me yet you would castrate my dignity forever. The only way to stop me from coming is to run me through on the side of this road. Do it, if you dare."

Song Jiang stared for a moment, then turned helplessly to Chao Gai. "Sister Chao. Make the Professor listen to reason. As Liangshan's leader—"

"Our Tactician has the choice to come," Chao Gai interrupted. She wasn't looking at Song Jiang, but at Wu Yong, eyes hooded and red. "Every hero of Liangshan has the right to sacrifice for vengeance. I honor that right."

Wu Yong nodded at her.

Song Jiang made a frustrated sound, but she didn't argue further. "As a practical matter, Liangshan must still be updated as quickly as possible," she said instead. "If something should happen to our party . . ."

"Sister Chai. May I ask you to ride for the mountain?" Chao Gai said. "We'll leave some of the rice and you can return with two of the packhorses—I won't deprive Liangshan of those resources. I'll take the third to ride. Don't rush or overspend the horses—take every precaution and you should still arrive by early tomorrow. You know the road from here?"

"Yes, Heavenly King."

"Thank you for riding to warn us. I owe you a great debt."

Noblewoman Chai lowered her head in a regretful bow. "I'm afraid I was not fast enough."

Not for us to save them, Wu Yong thought. *But fast enough for Chao Gai to avenge them.*

None of the crimes tonight would go unanswered. Liangshan's fury would be known. Cai Jing had made this a mortal battle, and Liangshan would return with no quarter.

Blood and death would be answered in kind.

Lu Da was not sure she understood what had happened to Sister Chao's village. Something bad. Something so unspeakably awful that nobody was talking about it straight out.

Lu Da was normally one to make a blunt demand for straight talking, but even a tongue like hers felt bound by the tension. Or, not so much the tension as Sister Chao's face, which looked like it had repeatedly been pummeled by a goat's horns, or a whole herd of goats, and their hooves too, but which still wasn't as bad as her expression, which put Lu Da in mind of when Abbot Zhi had caught Lu Da smuggling in meat, except a thousandfold worse.

Lu Da hadn't known Bai Sheng. Bai Sheng, the Sunmouse, friend to Chao Gai and a key part of the birthday present heist. But Chao Gai spoke of her like a sister. Like one of them.

She had died for them.

That was enough for Lu Da. Bai Sheng would be avenged. Simple. A law of nature.

The idea that the haojie of Liangshan would work any other

way—*could* work any other way—would have shocked her to the cores of her souls.

They parted with Sister Chai and turned to ride for Bai Sheng's village—not quickly, but steadily. Lu Da's hand stayed clenched against her heavy metal staff. Nobody spoke, except for Li Kui's occasional muttered curse if her horse skipped or shied.

In the quietest part of the night—long after midnight had been struck but still well before the east began to fade to gray—Chao Gai led them up a path off the main road and to a cottage that seemed just like every other. They dismounted in silence and tied the horses. Then Chao Gai nodded to Lu Da and Li Kui.

The crash of a battleaxe and the slam of Lu Da's staff, and the front door splintered and fell inward. The bandits marched over the shards.

The man Huang Wenbing was only just waking startled from slumber, his face drawn and bruised and his eyes haunted even before he focused on their presence.

Fitting, Lu Da thought.

He had killed one of their sisters. He had killed Chao Gai's village.

Everything to follow was only an expected result.

Lu Da began to march on him, but Chao Gai was faster. She swept forward, flying at the man, twisting in the air, her slight frame coming down in an arc that focused all its energy directly at his throat.

Bai Sheng's husband ricocheted from the bed. His body crashed into the cottage's living space, snapping against the edges of table and chairs.

Lu Da strode over and grabbed him by the shirt. He still breathed. She slammed him up against the wall, staff across his chest and neck.

He made a small sound, like a dying bird.

Now in no hurry, the other haojie drifted to form a semicircle around him. Shadows, gathering in the night, as if they meant to perform some dark ritual.

Wu Yong moved to the fireplace to start a low blaze, which threw the tiny cottage into dancing shadows.

"Bai Sheng deserved better than to be shackled to a worm like you." The voice was Chao Gai's. The firelight cast her bruised face into terrible red planes. "You are responsible for her murder."

"I . . . I tried . . ." the man wheezed against Lu Da's staff. "I tried to protect her. I did all I could . . ."

"Coward," spat Chao Gai.

"You're right." Tears had begun seeping from between his swollen eyelids, his chest heaving and hitching against Lu Da's hold. "You're right, I'm to blame. Kill me quickly, please . . ."

Somehow, his wretchedness only lit Lu Da's anger.

How dare he. How dare he *beg*. Her staff tightened against his throat until he gurgled and choked.

"Easy," murmured Song Jiang, and Lu Da made herself, *forced* herself, to draw back a hair.

"You will not die quickly," Chao Gai announced, in that same dead fury. "My only mercy tonight is not burning your entire village as was done to mine, nor bringing slaughter to everyone you have ever cast your eyes upon. You alone will suffer—you will suffer for each life in Dongxi. Only then will you be allowed to die."

Li Kui threw her battleaxes to the cottage floor and drew a dagger, one so sharp its point disappeared to nothing in the dancing light. She tossed it from hand to hand and barked a laugh. "I know just the thing. Professor, find us some wine. I'll slice a piece of this bastard off for every bit of vengeance you want to taste, Sister. We'll feast well tonight!"

Lu Da jerked around to find Sister Chao with her eyes. Killing a man was one thing, killing *this* man was right and proper, but could this be the way? Could this be righteous?

"Sister . . ." Song Jiang murmured, stepping toward Chao Gai, but Wu Yong held up an arm to stop her.

"Not tonight," the Tactician said in a low voice.

Chao Gai waited a long, long moment before speaking, a moment that stretched as wide as the heavens. Then she said, "Let it be done."

Later Lu Da would feel what they did that night like a fulcrum in her mind, a balance point of before and after. Like the first time she had killed a man. Only this time, she was with others, her kindred, and she would sense the finality of being sealed to them after this, as one, forever.

For Lu Da learned several things that night—

She learned that every idea she'd had about how loyal the Liangshan bandits were, their fury if one crossed them, had been a droplet of nothing compared to what was real. She learned they would do the same for her—and that she would, unequivocally, do the same for them, again and again, forever, as many times as she was called to.

She'd known they were willing to die for each other. As it turned out, dying for each other was nothing.

She also learned that Li Kui was right: human flesh, roasted over a fire and consumed with wine, tasted very much like pork or dog. Only seasoned with vengeance.

And she learned that a man could live an awful long time with piece after piece of him carved out, until one of those pieces was his heart, which Wu Yong boiled into a soup as the sun rose.

It restored them all for the journey back.

They rode into the rising sun without much speech among them. If Chao Gai's eyes still had a deadness to them, at least they had calmed from a rage that threatened to burn anyone nearby. It ground at Lu Da's heart that she could do no more to banish the exhaustion and grief from Sister Chao, nothing to unmake what had happened tonight. Nothing beyond what they had done already, and what they would still do. For this would not be the end of Liangshan's vengeance—Lu Da knew it without asking. This was only enough to start.

Lu Da would stand by every one of her Liangshan family, for however long it took.

CHAPTER 20

Cai Jing's brush swept across the fine calligraphy paper. Not smoothly. Not calmly. The edges of his flourishes wobbled intolerably. The ink spat at the ends of his strokes, the finest spray of black misting in between the characters.

Unacceptable. It was all unacceptable.

An entire regiment, destroyed, and nobody could yet tell him why. Incompetence. Sheer incompetence.

Whoever these villains were, they brought horror to the Empire beyond all consideration. Willing to cross any boundary, blacken anyone with the most vicious, violent acts of barbarism—up to and including himself. Likely they would even enact their blasphemy against the Emperor, given the chance. These bandits were supported, too, by the manpower to swallow nearly a thousand trained Guardsmen so thoroughly that no one could find Cai Jing even a crumb of information.

This entire investigation had been incompetence and chaos from the beginning. Either Cai Jing was surrounded by fools, or these bandits were more cunning than any in the Empire's finest—neither something he'd prefer to believe. He was keenly conscious that it was only a few pearls of purest chance that had led them to the wine merchant. Likewise, it had taken scraping the countryside with hundreds of interviews with travelers to find one who remembered the blue-faced commander on the stretch of road adjacent to where the men had woken—and only the traveler's lucky recall of a criminal tattoo had identified Commander Yang's companion as the former arms instructor Lin Chong.

Who had apparently, somehow, become party to people who could send a full regiment into a deadly trap.

Still, the longer this went on, the more Cai Jing knew. The more he discovered about those who would defy him.

The constable in front of him fortunately seemed to have a speck of intelligence. Cai Jing continued his strokes, ordering his hand to relax, forcing his brush toward steadiness, and throttling every shard of fury into listening to the constable's report from elsewhere in the region—a report the Guardsman seemed to think bore some relevancy here. A sliver of capability from his military would be a welcome shock.

"Continue, Constable."

"Everywhere we ask, we have learned this group has been quickly gaining notoriety across the countryside." The man kept himself in a low bow as he spoke, as if he feared Cai Jing's reaction. Rightly so. "Peasants and magistrates equally quail at their name. Very few landowners have dared to mount any offensive against them, and those that have, have failed."

"You have told me nothing. What makes you think these Liangshan bandits are the ones I seek? The mountains are rife with highwaymen. They are a scourge."

"Because, Grand Chancellor, the Liangshan bandits are . . . it is said . . . Chancellor, I report only what I hear. But the outlaws you have said you are seeking . . . the Liangshan bandits are said to be made up mostly of females."

Steady. Steady on the brush. Compress any rage to perfect sharpness. Rage means nothing if one cannot strike.

Lin Chong, and the monk Lu Junyi had sent after her. Commander Yang Zhi . . .

Even so, Cai Jing had assumed their costumes to be mostly a ruse. It seemed not.

He felt righteously justified in ignoring the whispers of the Imperial Court, those that wondered if the Grand Chancellor had discarded all reason in his quest to dismantle the countryside in the search for such petty thieves. No, he'd been right to pursue this. A conspiracy with this reputation—this gross entitlement—was worth rooting out from their lands if he had to bloody his own fingernails to rip these women from their arrogant perch.

"Speak further," he ordered. "What else is known of these Liangshan bandits?"

"They gained their name because their base is at Mount Liang, at the edge of the marshlands," the constable continued. "Their headquarters are rumored to be—ah—impregnable, although I am sure that is not true with your own resources, Grand Chancellor. We heard tell that the famous poet Song Jiang is another of their number, after she fled punishment as a murderer—she may even be their leader."

"And what connection have they to this village of Dongxi?"

"We think we have discovered that as well. Dongxi had a somewhat famed village chief, whose name has also turned up in connection to Liangshan. We think this Chief Chao Gai is one of their number."

"Chao Gai."

"Yes, Chancellor. Chao as for the dawn, and Gai as written in the Hundred Family Surnames."

Clever lad. He'd seen what Cai Jing was inking.

A list. One to be accompanied by drawings, as soon as an illustrator and sufficient descriptions for the rest could be acquired. Cai Jing added two more lines to the end:

Former Arms Instructor Lin Chong, Traitor to the Imperial Guard
Former Commander Yang Zhi, Traitor to the Imperial Guard
The Monk Lu Da of Qingliang Monastery
Wine Merchant Bai Sheng (captured and executed)
The Murderous Poet Song Jiang, the Empire's Dark Daughter
Chief Chao Gai of Dongxi Village

These Names Are Wanted for High Crimes Against the Empire, Along With All Who Call Themselves the Bandits of Liangshan Marsh.

PART III

EMPIRE

CHAPTER 21

The day she returned from Dongxi with her skin mottled, bruised, and bleeding, Chao Gai called a council of Liangshan's chiefs.

Lin Chong had not slept for the full night and day that Liangshan's leaders had been gone from the mountain. Noblewoman Chai's messenger had arrived at the Crocodile's inn only shortly after Song Jiang's departure, sending the camp into a flurry of heightened alert. The messenger had brought news of Bai Sheng's death and the immediate imperilment of Dongxi—and of Chancellor Cai Jing's determination to bring the thunder of heaven down on the rest of them, as soon as he discovered who and where.

The runner had also shared news even more disturbing. Rumors, only rumors, but of research the Chancellor was engaged in to harness some great perversion of power. God's teeth and saltpeter and weapons no one had ever conceived.

An uncharacteristically selfish despair welled in Lin Chong. The rich and powerful and corrupt, those men of Gao Qiu and Cai Jing's ilk—did they have no weaknesses at all? Was it a law of the universe that if she ever dared fight back, if she clawed any power that was outside their grasp, then they had the means and desire to crush her like a flea?

Yang Zhi accepted the news much faster than Lin Chong. To the commander, it was one more piece of military intelligence to deal with as they must, and if they died facing it, that was the way of things.

"You won't have any trouble going up against the Guard if they attack, then?" Lin Chong asked her in an aside.

Commander Yang grunted something like a laugh. "Trust me, little panther. I was loyal to the Guard till the end, just like you, but that means I have a whole feast's worth of reasons built up to hate on them more'n anyone here. I chose my side now and that's done."

She made it sound so easy. So instant.

Whichever way they had each arrived here, however, they spent their night side by side bolstering Liangshan's defenses, scheduling the bandits into disciplined cycles of watch and making sure all knew their roles if an attack came. The others were respectful and pliable, calling agreements of "Yes, Drill Instructor" and "Yes, Commander" with no apparent resentment, even those who had been allies to Wang Lun. Lin Chong marveled at what less than two months of well-designed training could do. Would that the Empire had taken her advisements about military discipline . . .

Though she also wondered—silently—if all her nascent efforts here would be for naught. The mountain's natural obstacles were well-suited against an incursion from men on foot or horseback, and the bandits had built up an even more vicious defensive infrastructure over their years here, but if Cai Jing was developing some new weapon that could reach them from farther than arrows ever could? Their preparations might be nothing more than hopeless. A twig Cai Jing would step on to snap.

Lin Chong had argued for sending more haojie toward Dongxi, unable to escape the inky stain in her mind of Chao Gai screaming forever. Now they had verified intelligence of a threat—but Commander Yang pointed out they would be too far behind to help and would do better to fortify the mountain and prepare to launch a rescue effort. They made a plan to send scouts out in daylight, but before they could put it to action, a whistling arrow sounded across the marsh and turned out to be the arrival of Noblewoman Chai.

She brought the sobering news of the massacre at Dongxi.

Lin Chong's heart clenched. An entire village. Innocent families. Chao Gai's people.

She wondered, suddenly, what she would have done if she had ever been given such an order when working with the Guard. She'd heard rumors of similar actions among the military, but . . .

It had always been easiest to assume them the exception to the rule. Orders she might have preferred not be given, but the occasional blemish did not spoil the fruit. It was not her place to disagree with a general in the field anyway.

Dongxi had been made up of simple farmers. Neighbors, children, people Chao Gai had spoken of with a smile in her eyes. The only thing those people had done was love the hero who had saved them when the Empire hadn't.

Lin Chong and Yang Zhi kept the mountain on high alert until more whistles across the marsh told of the full party's return. The ferries were sent to retrieve them immediately, and Lin Chong climbed one of the watchtowers to see for her own eyes as they rode up the mountain.

More than a little relief when she saw Lu Da riding unharmed—but something twinged in her when Chao Gai came into clearer view. Even at a distance, the fierce recoloring of the ghost hunter's face and skin were vivid enough to steal the breath. Lin Chong could not picture what kind of injury might be the cause of such a thing. Her mind flashed back to sitting with Lu Da, the shadow they somehow knew to be Chao Gai contorting between them—*and pain, such wrenching pain . . .*

Lin Chong had not thought to see her alive again, after feeling that.

Upon their return, Chao Gai's military leadership circle turned out to include Song Jiang, Wu Yong, and Du Qian, who had been the secondary chieftain under Wang Lun. Plus, now, Lin Chong and Yang Zhi. Noblewoman Chai joined them as well so that she could answer any further questions about the intelligence she had brought.

They began with a moment of remembrance for Bai Sheng, the Sunmouse, who had been one of them. Who had died protecting the mountain.

"A true haojie," Chao Gai murmured, and the others nodded.

"She will be fully avenged," Wu Yong said. "We will make certain of it. Noblewoman Chai—these new weapons Cai Jing wishes to gain control of. What else can you tell us of them? Do you know how far along Cai Jing is in this research?"

"No certainty," Noblewoman Chai answered. "The rumors that came to me were tinged with some criticism of the folly, but that could be for either the danger or for Cai Jing's methods. It is said that he is using convicted seditionists in this project, while toying with extreme energies."

"Our defenses here might swallow hundreds or thousands of soldiers, but a power we have never seen before—this could end us all." Chao Gai's bruised face and quiet tone were carved of iron. "I will *not* oversee the destruction of Liangshan."

"We could move our base elsewhere, make ourselves more difficult to find," Song Jiang suggested.

"Ill-advised," Lin Chong said immediately, at the same time Wu Yong said, "No" and Yang Zhi said, "Bad idea."

Yang Zhi waved Wu Yong on in explaining. "The military advantages of this outpost are considerable, and would be difficult to duplicate elsewhere against standard troops and weapons. Besides, the logistics of relocating a camp of this size would be significant. We didn't build anything here with an eye toward becoming nomadic."

"Take the fight to them, then," Du Qian declared. "Cai Jing gets what's comin' to him when he's right at the heart of Bianliang, and the whole Empire will learn not to mess with us."

"Stop such talk!" Song Jiang rose up, fire in her eyes. "Have you forgotten what we are? We do what we do *for* the Empire. We serve the Emperor in every action we take, better than any other citizens—we do not lust after that power for ourselves!"

Lin Chong kept her mouth shut. She was starting to see exactly how much of Song Jiang's idealism was shared here.

But to her mild surprise, Du Qian backed down, with a gruff and grudging "You're right, of course" before thumping back in the chair. Song Jiang resettled herself more sedately.

"We need our own scholarship," murmured Wu Yong. "Our own research into this type of power. Someone who can rival Cai Jing's knowledge and whatever he brings against us."

A quiet smack as Chao Gai's fist met her other hand. She rose to begin pacing. "I know a monk—we studied together at the monastery. So advanced in the philosophical paths as to have gained monkhood among both the Transcendentalists and the Fa, and I have never met anyone who understands as deeply the energies of this world, nor can wield such significant power without the aid of a god's tooth. Unfortunately, last I knew, Gongsun Sheng had retreated deep into seclusion in Fa study."

"We don't have gobs of time to go traipsing around tracking down some monk," Commander Yang said. "You got any idea where to start, Heavenly King?"

Chao Gai pressed her hands flat against the bruises blown out across her temples, as if she could finish splitting her own skin open and the answers would splay themselves out. "I don't know. With some weeks I might be able to find a location—with meditation, with the help of Sister Lu and her god's tooth . . . no, it's no use."

Something rubbed against Lin Chong's consciousness—something Noblewoman Chai had said. *Significant power . . . convicted seditionists . . .*

"A moment," she said. "What if . . . we know already where the best scholars in this area are? Not only scholars who study the learning of it, but experts in the very technology Cai Jing now manufactures."

It took a moment for the others to understand. "Whoa, what? You're not talking sense," Commander Yang said. "The folk working on the Chancellor's whatsit thing for him aren't going to help us."

"Noblewoman Chai told us they're seditionists," Lin Chong pointed out. "Their loyalty won't be secure. If we can find even one who would rather work against Cai Jing than for him . . ."

Wu Yong steepled long fingers in contemplation. "It might work. Heavenly King, I have many contacts in the capital. We could discover who would be weakest and where to find them. Then we could break them from this enforced labor."

"Bianliang has a great many free thinkers," Song Jiang agreed thoughtfully. "I've seen many who were erroneously painted with the brush of sedition, and that path leads only to execution. I cannot imagine any such who would not leap to join our cause."

"I had a friend, the Lady Lu, who would always tell me—much the same," Lin Chong said with an effort. "She would speak so angrily of when scholars she knew fell under suspicion of the Empire. If the people Cai Jing has employed are of this mold . . ." She flashed back, briefly, to letting Lu Junyi's vociferous rants wash past her. She had wondered, privately, whether any arrest and punishment of Lu Junyi's acquaintances hadn't been brought down on them by their own actions, through some recklessly taboo ideas or verboten scholarship . . .

Shame threaded the memory.

"Lady Lu—you speak of the Lady Lu Junyi? You were a friend to her?" Song Jiang sounded bemused. "I have been to several of her gatherings of the mind myself, and what she put out with her press was always good for shocking or lively stimulation. In fact, I have often thought she would be a tremendous addition to us here."

"No. May that never happen." Lin Chong said it so severely that Song Jiang's eyebrows jumped. "Lu Junyi has committed no crime. She has a good life in the capital, and I wish it never to be disturbed."

Song Jiang cast a short but significant glance toward Noblewoman Chai. "I meant no harm, Sister Lin."

Wu Yong's head had cocked to the side. "Wait. Sister Lin. Your friend has the means of a printing press?"

"It's hers," Lin Chong said. "She uses it for . . ." *To be disruptive, in her own spirited way.* "To spread ideas."

"A two-pronged defense," Wu Yong said. "Stealing away with Cai Jing's scholars—it is excellent, but in the long term we need more. The military path and the political. The knowledge of these new inventions might well place us in a secure position for now, but better if we combine it with yet another angle: Liangshan's reputation."

"Our reputation is fearsome," Du Qian put in. "Everyone is growing to know the name Liangshan."

"Everyone is growing to *fear* us," Wu Yong corrected. "We wish them to fear crossing us, yes. But if the common people also come to *love* us . . ."

Song Jiang had begun nodding along. "A man like Cai Jing maintains power only through fear. The common people are starving for saviors and heroes. We are in the perfect position to become his political nightmare, if we can be cunning about it."

"It may not work," Wu Yong cautioned. "But it's another way to add friction. Make every step he takes more difficult, until he is mired in the muck. Weaken him from multiple sides at once. The fact that his research is considered folly by some in the Court—that only makes him more vulnerable politically—"

"Stop." Dread had begun chewing through Lin Chong—she knew, she *knew* what the damned Tactician was about to ask. "We can't ask this of her. You'd be making *her* into a seditionist."

"Then she really can come join us here," said Song Jiang with a laugh.

"This is no joke." *If that was even meant as a joke.* "I refuse to ask that. I won't be a party to it."

"Party to what?" said Commander Yang. "Stop speaking around things. Come on, Tactician, lay it out so the rest of us can join the squabble."

"I suspect our Sister Lin has the right of it," admitted Wu Yong with that slithery smile. "The most stunning victories have been won not on the battlefield, but through propaganda. *That* is a war worth winning. A printing press is a magnificent invention, capable of distributing information more thickly than has ever been tried before . . . let Cai Jing risk great unrest if he comes up against the so-known *Heroes of Liangshan.*"

"Stop!" Lin Chong cried. "You can't use people like this. You call us heroes—you'd take a person's skills for your own ends and snatch away their lives—"

"I've read your friend's circulars," Song Jiang said calmly. "As I said, I've been to her salons. According to the dictates of our dear Imperial legal system, she's only sedition in waiting, once those with eyes notice. We may do her a great service by calling her to join us."

"No—no joining, no calling," Lin Chong tried to insist, with the mounting desperation of chasing a wild foal that has already broken free. "What you did—what *we* did to Commander Yang was bad enough. I'll not have you doing the same to my friend—"

"No grudge here," Yang Zhi put in. "There's a freedom in retirement, you know. Never was this rich as a captain."

"See? Your friend might want this," Song Jiang said, as if she spoke with perfect reason.

Lin Chong opened her mouth to tear into them—this was a line she wouldn't cross, wouldn't *let* them cross; loyalty worked in more than one direction—but Wu Yong held up both hands to calm the argument. "Haojie. This has an easy answer. We offer the good Lady Lu a choice—surely her *friend* would not deny her that. After all, Lady Lu may never forgive us, if we don't offer her the chance to be a part of the history we're writing."

Lin Chong didn't bother to try to keep her reaction hidden.

"Sister Lin, don't judge my lack of humbleness!" Wu Yong said. "I'm not speaking of myself, but of *us*. All of us. We're striving for a grand legacy, even as each one of us is only a tiny speck. Come now, agree for us to present the offer. You can come and do it yourself."

Lin Chong's instinct was to refuse. A proposal from her lips, a friend's lips, was liable to be *more* persuasive, and something this weighted should be decided without being swayed by old ties. Doubtless the Tactician knew that, and was manipulating her into being the one to ask.

But if she refused . . . no. She had to maintain control here, digging her fingernails in as a power among these bandits—ensuring it would be done her way or not at all.

She met Wu Yong's gaze levelly. "No undue pressure."

"I wouldn't dream of it." The Tactician's smile was all teeth this time.

"Good. It's decided then," Chao Gai announced. "Sister Song, can you use your songbird brush to provide the text?"

"Of course. I have always said that ink was the mightiest weapon of all."

Chao Gai turned to the rest of them. "Professor, Sister Lin, you will travel to Bianliang together. Today. Find us at least one haojie among the scholars who has intimate knowledge of this weapons research and who will break away to our cause, and present our other request to Lady Lu. This recruitment must not fail, you understand? Name whomever else you would take to assist you."

"Thoughts?" Wu Yong asked Lin Chong. "An attack of precision might be superior to the Iron Whirlwind's axes crashing through the capital, as effective as that can be."

With an effort, Lin Chong pushed aside her other misgivings. "I agree. Keep everyone else here. You may need them if the Guard is faster than we are. The Tactician and I will figure out a way."

She might not be as taken in by the so-called Professor as the rest of them, but maybe she had become as convinced as the rest that Wu Yong could always figure out a plan.

Lu Junyi pushed the door open and slipped into the shadows of her house.

As soon as the darkness swallowed her, she stumbled against the wall. Her body was all hollowed out, her skin a thin and cracked shell, the world a cacophony that was liable to cleave her open at any moment. Ling Zhen had spent much of the last two days unobtrusively gripping her arm or shoulder, with grim whispers that she must stay upright, that they had to keep going . . .

She was still waiting for the Chancellor's consequence. He'd thrown her back into their research building as if it were a prison and ordered her to return to work. She hadn't been beaten, or killed, or demoted—or chained to be tortured and have a spike shoved through her eye. She'd been allowed to go home, and then to come back to work today . . . each repeated reprieve like a knife carving into her flesh.

Cai Jing had even taken her report as normal, a report she

faltered through without articulation while trying to impress on him the dangers of the lodestone approach. He didn't seem as displeased as she'd feared—with the information, at least—but his mood did seem to be elsewhere, and he'd impressed greater urgency upon her even after she'd recommended every caution. She'd forced herself to push Ling Zhen and her scholars in as many small-scale experiments as they could quickly manufacture, with her mind rioting all the while, waiting for the Chancellor to come back and tell her it was time for her execution, or that all her friends had been killed, or one and then the other.

Cai Jing had revealed almost offhand that he knew the monk she had referred to was Lu Da. Her confession of a monk's involvement kept ringing through her with the loud clang of guilt. *How could you, you know how much the Chancellor knows, he knows everything, and even if he didn't it would only have taken trivial questioning—of my associates, of Lin Chong's students, of people on the street who saw us together. He'll kill them and it will be on my head . . .*

She couldn't figure out why she had faced no punishment yet. It kept spiraling through her, distracting her from cramming the alchemy principles into her head, or now the properties of the lodestone—its purification techniques, its careful application to other minerals until whatever strange field it exuded reversed their properties, she must understand everything. They had so many tests to run and so little time, and if Cai Jing demanded progress before they were ready it would be everyone's safety sacrificed.

Yet she could not stop dwelling on why she had received no punishment.

She deserved it for endangering Lu Da and Lin Chong. She deserved it for having kept anything from the Chancellor of the Empire in the first place. How could Cai Jing let this go? He couldn't, it wasn't right for him to, she deserved whatever consequence he decided she merited. He should order her to report to the Ministry of Justice and prostrate herself.

After all, she had betrayed his trust, too.

Lamplight sprang across the entryway as one of her maids, Jin'er, hurried to welcome her. The alternately yawing shadows were as off-kilter as Lu Junyi's whole life.

"Forgive me, Lady Lu! Forgive me. I didn't hear you come in, and since the Lady Jia—"

She stopped talking.

"What of Lady Jia?" The house was so quiet. Unspecified fear began to bite through her. What if Cai Jing had—*something*— "What do you speak of? Where is she?"

"The Lady Jia left a message for you, madam. She directed me to tell you it was in your study. I beg your pardon for not informing you as soon as you arrived—the household has been in a stir without her . . ."

Left a message. That meant she hadn't been snatched away for Lu Junyi's crimes.

The maidservant stepped up and gave her an unobtrusive hand, steadying her steps. At the door to her study, Lu Junyi paused.

"Thank you, Jin'er. You may retire for the night."

Jin'er passed her the light, bowed, and wished her good evening before retreating. Lu Junyi slumped against the doorway.

What awaited her in here . . . she both knew, and didn't. Briefly, she contemplated retiring without looking. She wasn't sure what more she could take, not without crumbling away forever.

Dust on the winds of time and Empire, nothing of herself left.

It was a long time before she moved, the bamboo curtain that set off her study whispering over her skin and clacking behind her. She raised the lamp and made her way to the study's carved desk, still covered in overlapping papers with arrays of formulas and half-finished scientific notes. The servants knew not to neaten up in here.

In a clear space in the center of the desk, a sheet sat in isolation, with Jia's neat hand inking two lines down the right side of the page.

Zhao Yuannu has recently borne her fifth child. I go to aid her during her confinement time. Jia

Lu Junyi sank down in her chair, her fingers touching the edges of the paper as if it would cease to be real if she let it go. She didn't recognize the name Zhao Yuannu. Perhaps one of Jia's tea friends.

Jia didn't have very many close friends. Not like Lu Junyi, who had too many.

Jia, so timid, who turned her face down in perpetual shame, forever carrying her family's judgment with her. She rarely thought she merited the approbation of anyone else, either, which served as a constant gentle disagreement between them . . . and she did not have close friends she would feel pulled to join in confinement. Not in any ordinary time.

The unsaid words of the message pulsed between the written ones, bleeding loneliness and accusation.

Lu Junyi's mind fluttered to try to retrace everything that had brought her here—the deep nights falling into obsession, day after day trapped in her own paranoia and nightmares, then up to yesterday, coming home a jagged wreck, and she'd refused to speak of it, of course she'd refused, how could she drag Jia into any of it, and when Jia had tried to reach out to her, to soothe and console . . .

She'd snapped. Shouted that she wasn't worthy of it, that Jia should leave, leave, that nothing could help. She'd felt so hot, like she would burn anyone who touched her.

Maybe it was better that Jia was gone. Maybe she should stay gone. She needn't suffer for Lu Junyi's sins.

Lu Junyi sat that way for more than a few moments, very still. The lamp illuminated only a small circle on the desk, the rest of the study shrouded in darkness behind her. Darkness and quiet.

Mostly quiet.

Lu Junyi's breath stopped in her lungs.

Only the smallest scrape—the whisper of movement—but someone else stirred in the room. Someone behind her. In the dark.

If it was the Guard—she couldn't fight the Guard—but why would they wait for her in the shadows, as a thief or blackmailer? They had all the authority to haul her out of here, beat her, chain her away in prison to anticipate only the executioner's sword, *why would they wait?*

Unless they only waited to torment her . . .

Inky certainty crept through every frayed sense. *This is the end. This is how I break. It is fitting.*

Still, her hand snaked out and closed over a slender wooden paper knife. Her heart fluttered, her souls floating outside herself.

She sprang up and spun, her left hand thrusting out with the lamp to cast its flare against the opposite wall, her right holding forth the tiny, meager paper knife. Her feet slid into a stance she wasn't sure she'd even be able to use, because if it was the Guard—

She froze, lamp flickering in her hand. The flutters of light showed Lin Chong's face in blinks, here and then not, bright and then dark.

Part of Lu Junyi wanted to lunge forward, the words *friend* and *safe* ricocheting in her head, but her feet stayed mired against the lacquered wood of her study floor. Something in Lin Chong's face—her expression, hard, pitiless, inhuman—and Lu Junyi had somehow forgotten the criminal tattoo scrawled in untidy inking down her friend's cheek, so different from Lu Junyi's own mental image. She wondered for one addled instant whether this was even the same person she remembered.

Besides—there was the other face next to Sister Lin's. A person with a thin, cavernous face, and strange tawny hair cropped close to the scalp.

Their expressions were still. Waiting.

Lin Chong finally pushed away from the wall and took one or two paces closer. "Calm," she whispered, one hand raised as if Lu Junyi were a wild deer who might bolt. "We're alone?"

"I—yes." Jia was gone, Jia was *gone*—and Jin'er would have been the last of the staff waiting up for her. The servants would all be in their own wing, asleep, unless she rang for them. "What—why are you—are you all right?"

The question came out something between an accusation and a gasp.

"Steady," Lin Chong said, and somehow she had closed the distance to slip a strong arm under Lu Junyi's weight. "Sit. Be calm."

"Forgive us for causing you such a shock," came the voice of the other intruder—who had not moved from the back wall. "We don't mean to frighten. I'm sure you understand why it is dangerous for Sister Lin to show her face in the city."

"Yes . . . of course . . ."

"Are you well?" Lin Chong's face seemed even harder up close, even more that of a stranger, but it creased in worry. "You're shaking."

Lu Junyi let her hand find the desk behind her. Her fingers slipped over the edge of the note from Jia and turned it facedown against the tabletop.

Lin Chong's eyes followed the movement. "I see your work these days is far above my understanding. What is it you are studying now?"

The question was friendly enough, a well-intentioned overture, but Lu Junyi cast a panicked glance back at the scattered formulas and numerical tables. She placed the lamp carefully on the flipped letter to buy herself a moment of time. How careless she had been, to leave evidence of a secret project for the Chancellor lying about, she deserved every punishment, every grief . . . "It's—nothing. A fancy. What—why are you here? If they catch you—"

"We know. We won't be long. We're here to ask your help, if you're willing."

"Mine? With what?"

"I am part of a . . ." Lin Chong paused. Her lips rolled against each other, hesitating. "Gao Qiu. He gave orders that I should be killed. On the road."

"Marshal Gao—what?" Lu Junyi's voice automatically went to a nervous whisper, her eyes darting about the dark room. "What are you saying? How?"

"He paid the guards to kill me. Lu Da was my savior." Lin Chong's eyes were dark and intense. "She brought me to join—a group of heroes serving the northeast countryside."

"We are much enriched by Sister Lin." Lin Chong's friend—colleague? Fellow traveler?—stepped forward. "Now, however, we are under great threat from the more corrupt elements of the Empire's governance. You could be of incalculable help to us in our quest to further justice and protection . . . we have heard of your intellectual crusades. We hope you will see it as a higher calling to join us in this matter."

The person spoke as if those words would only gladden Lu Junyi's heart, but her first, reflexive thoughts were only, *What—no—*

Her breath had begun coming in short gasps, because her mind knew the shape of what they spoke of without putting name to it. Shadows in the dark, a haven for convicts and outcasts, fighting *the Empire*—and she worked for the *Chancellor of the Empire*—and even if she didn't, how could they, how could they ask her to—

Too-familiar shame and guilt poured through her in equal measure. Along with resentment, anger, at herself, at everything. She recalled again with some hysteria how she had felt no grief at Lin Chong's escape, only a good bit of worry and that vein of sneaky satisfaction, like a schoolgirl who had gotten away with breaking a rule behind the teacher's back . . . hoping that Lin Chong and Lu Da were off riding to their own fortune among the lakes and rivers of the Empire's vast countryside . . .

In her flights of imagination, it hadn't seemed like treason.

How impossibly naive she had been.

"Sister Lin tells us you are the custodian of a printing press," the other intruder went on. "One you yourself know how to operate—"

"Wait a moment." Lin Chong held up a hand to her friend, her eyes on Lu Junyi. "Sister, are you all right? What ails you?"

Her hand touched Lu Junyi's neck and jaw, burning against her skin. Not quite against the plaster over her cheek, the place where Cai Jing had struck her—but close enough to ask the question.

Lu Junyi had forgotten. She jerked away, turning her face deeper toward the shadows.

"Nothing. I—it's nothing." She forced herself to take one breath, then another, and wished that they had never come.

Yet this had been her own doing, hadn't it? She had sent Lu Da after Lin Chong, a reckless pretense, all because she'd fancied herself enlightened, clever . . . she had been toying with consequences she'd never understood.

Then would you rather Gao Qiu have assassinated her? For shame!

She was trapped, trapped between a demon tiger with flame for eyes and a black pit with no bottom. How could she have helped them break every law of the Empire? How could she have refused?

Lin Chong's companion came further forward into the lamplight and went to one knee. "Lady Lu. I have heard much of your perspicacity, your far-reaching wisdom. Not only from Sister Lin, but from the poet Song Jiang the Spring Rain, who joins our cause in challenging any who would abuse those weaker than they. I am humbled to connect with someone who has so inspired and educated two leaders of our movement."

Lin Chong's hand tightened on Lu Junyi's shoulder, briefly and comfortingly. "Meet our Tactician. More names aren't wise, but it's true Song Jiang is one of our number—and beyond that, I'll ask my friend to keep that silver tongue sheathed. Sister Lu, we only request. You can refuse freely."

"Request what?" Lu Junyi asked faintly. Song Jiang? The Spring Rain had been inspired—by *her*? To do what?

Something that trod dangerously against those with power in the Empire . . .

She didn't want to know.

The Tactician drew a folded paper from some inner pocket. "We need all of Bianliang to be speaking of this."

Lu Junyi took the sheet with mechanical fingers. Held it in the wavering lamplight. Read it.

Read it again. The neatly inked characters unfolded with an elegant musicality, the words of high art. Their meaning, however—

their meaning fell against itself in discordant clangs, because this could not be, this was not to be believed . . . even her spiking dread had not imagined *this.* And signed with the revered name of Song Jiang . . . In her hand, the paper had begun fluttering, like an autumn leaf that refused its inevitable death.

"I can't . . ." She wet her lips. Tried again. "This is treason."

The statement felt both ludicrously dramatic and far too paltry. How could she respond with calm factualness to a request like *this*? How could she even acknowledge it in words?

"Treason? Or change?" It was Lin Chong who asked, low but tense, as though Lu Junyi's accusation had stirred some great reaction in her. "What Gao Qiu did—mine is not the only case. You always wanted me to see more clearly for justice."

"In hypothetical debate, but that is not—you're asking me to propagandize—against the *Empire.* That's not change, that's treason, it's—"

"Not against the Empire," said Lin Chong. "Not against the Emperor. The heart of the Empire is not the corruption that webs through its ranks. We must believe that. We must. You would be aiding in the just reputation of haojie who fight for the people."

Lu Junyi tried to speak. Her lips would form no sound.

"'Who is an Empire, but the people?'" Lin Chong quoted softly. "I believe you said that to me, once upon a time. Let the Empire be the Emperor and the people, not those others who would use their power to destroy everything civilized we have built over so many generations."

Those words. They had been ones Lu Junyi herself had been fond of saying. Shooting back at her intellectual fellows in spirited conversation, sometimes to be shushed by those less brazen, as their cheeks reddened and they made a show of glancing around for hidden eyes.

The Emperor himself would agree, Lu Junyi had been fond of declaring, upon receiving such a reaction.

Idealism was not reality. Reality was the Chancellor putting a spike through a woman's eye, was Fan Rui muttering in endless damaged obsession, was the constant hanging fear of powers that could pop her skull like it was a beetle's carapace, and not just her, but everybody she had ever cared for or spoken to, starting with Jia and cycling through every friend or attendee at her foolish, naive, infantile salons.

"I can't. I—I won't." Her hand crushed the paper in involuntary rejection, crumpling it to the rubbish it was. *Sister Lin, who are you now? What was I, all along?* "Please—please go."

Lin Chong pressed back from the desk, straightening up. For the first time, the scrawled criminal tattoo seemed to fit her. A new costume, for the person she had become.

"If you were forced to operate the machine, no one could place the blame on you," the Tactician put in. "We could offer you freedom from all culpability."

Lu Junyi moved her head in a small, mute shake. It was all the same. How could they not see that?

"You fear the worst excesses of the Empire," the Tactician went on silkily. "The people who taint what it could be. As so many people do. We can be very good friends—"

"Stop." Lin Chong's voice. She stepped back and away, her eyes still on Lu Junyi's face. "You agreed. We offered. She has refused."

"Come now," the Tactician said. "A civil discussion first—"

"In which you could doubtless convert the most stubborn mind to your view." Frost edged Lin Chong's words. "My friend is clearly unwell tonight. She received us graciously and has given us her answer. Let this go."

The Tactician glanced between the two of them. Hesitated.

"This is not our most important aim," Lin Chong said to her companion, pulling them both away. "We have more urgent business tonight."

Lu Junyi's eyes stared at nothing. Why had she never realized that the change she'd so agitated for—the reality of it was only blood. She had been such a child.

A touch on her shoulder.

"We stand for justice," Lin Chong said. "I promise."

"How can you know?" The question scratched, a hoarse whisper.

"Because it's all I have left." Lin Chong's touch tightened briefly, and then she and the Tactician moved together toward the door. Neither of them looked back again.

Lu Junyi sat in the dark for a long time, until the lamp began to sputter. When she rose, her joints had stiffened to clay and her fingertips were numb.

The paper the Tactician had given her was still crumpled in her hand. She picked up the lamp, made it over to the room's hearth, and slid to sit on the floor.

She held the paper for a moment, staring, as if its poison might have stained her skin. Then she touched it to the guttering lamplight.

The edge flared, hot and yellow. The page dipped against the sheen of remaining oil, and the fire raced almost to Lu Junyi's fingers before she dropped it to curl to ash on the stone.

She watched until it flickered out, then continued waiting until it was cool enough for her to crush her palm against the charred remains. She didn't stop until her hand was black and no sign remained of what Lin Chong had asked of her.

CHAPTER 22

Lin Chong kept her head bent forward under the shadows of the straw hat so her hair fell over her face. Every so often she rotated the bowl of wine on the table before her, or lifted it to touch her lips.

It wasn't so suspicious for a taciturn traveler to nurse wine alone this way, even one dressed as a Renxia priest.

Wu Yong had chosen the disguise for her. Renxia practitioners were the only people known for commonly wearing their hair loose, and that and the broad-brimmed hat helped keep Lin Chong's features hidden. Neither of them had Hu Sanniang's skill with makeup, and though they'd pasted some plaster bandaging over the tattooed cheek to pretend it was an injury instead, the placement would be suspicious for anyone savvy about the tricks convicts used to avoid questions.

Lin Chong could always try the lie and say she had served her sentence and returned, but with the ink still dark and sharp enough to scream its newness, only the greenest officer would be fooled by such a ruse. Besides, enough of the Guardsmen in Bianliang knew her on sight. Being detained and examined for even a few moments could lead to discovery.

Wu Yong, on the other hand, had no such difficulty.

Across the room, the Tactician shouted a drunken cheer, some sort of toast, and raised a cup to tilt it back sloppily. The soldiers at the same table echoed the cry and did the same, laughing and slapping Wu Yong on the back.

Apparently a master of disguise, Wu Yong had donned the uniform of an Imperial Guardsman—then folded open the tunic and tucked the empty sword ties back behind the belt, just as the

Guardsmen did when they loosened themselves off duty. With a felt cap in the military style to finish the ensemble, Wu Yong in only moments had become indistinguishable from a low-level officer ready to carouse with the men after a shift.

"How do I carry it off? Missing anything?" the Tactician had asked, turning to show off the costume to Lin Chong.

"Nothing," Lin Chong had answered. A strange resentment poked at her, reminding her how many years she'd given the Guard, and still it was a uniform she'd never donned. Yet in a mere instant, Wu Yong had transformed into the role, entirely unearned.

It's only a disguise, Lin Chong reminded herself. Besides, it wasn't only Wu Yong's untattooed, unrecognizable face that made the Tactician a better choice to play off-duty Guardsman. Lin Chong might know the slang, might recognize every repeated complaint the Guardsmen flung about in their late carousals, but even when she'd belonged among them she'd had to sweat hard to be so much as tolerated at the table. She had no idea how to act comfortable at it, no matter how she was dressed.

Wu Yong, on the other hand—a few drinks and crass jests, and suddenly the whole group was indistinguishable from longtime bosom friends.

What a perverse talent.

Sometime after the drums beat out the midnight watch, Wu Yong bid the others good night and staggered back to Lin Chong's table in the corner—though not until all the others had paid and ducked out into the darkness.

"What did you learn—be careful! Are you all right?"

Wu Yong had staggered into the wall, feet tangling with the chair. "Drunk. 'M very, *very* drunk. Hullo, Sister Lin. You need a nickname."

"Sit down." Lin Chong rose briefly to direct Wu Yong's body into the chair—achieved after only a brief battle of flopping arms and legs. "You're not faking? You were truly drinking?"

"Of course I was. Gotta be real," slurred Wu Yong. "Big gossips, those men are. Richer the wine, the looser their tongues."

"You got the information."

"I sure did." Wu Yong smiled that all-teeth grin. "Or, least as much of it as those lads were privy to. The innkeeper in the eastern ward had the right of it. This is *exactly* where the detachment for the black cells wets their throats."

"I assumed as much," Lin Chong said dryly. "Unless you decided you were only here to enjoy yourself."

"Oh, Sister Lin! You try to wound me, but it doesn't hit." Wu Yong wagged a long finger at Lin Chong. "By the by, how marvelous that our splendid Empire has a secret prison, isn't it? One not even overseen by jailers and wardens and magistrates, but the Imperial Guard itself. What politics must have ensued there, I shudder to think. Something like that, Sister Lin, means somewhere in history a minister or two fell in a sinkhole and ended up drinking poison as the only way out. *Fascinating.*"

"It's not a secret prison," Lin Chong said. "Everyone knows of it."

"Knows *of* it but not *about* it. A parent telling their child to obey or be thrown in the Pit is much different from ever meeting someone who has survived a stay."

"Because they're all executed," Lin Chong said bluntly. "There's no mystery here. The Pit is only reserved for the Empire's worst."

"Ah yes, says the arms instructor convicted of attempting to kill an Imperial Marshal. Have you ever wondered, my fugitive friend, how the Empire imprisons high-level scholars?"

Lin Chong paused. She'd never stopped to think about it. The Empire was . . . was the government. Was law. They had ways of enforcing that law. Monks and philosophers had been executed before, so clearly there was a way.

"There may be no more true immortals," Wu Yong purred, "but I've heard tales of some of the ascetics who have lived beyond two hundred, or heal from any injury. As a practical matter, Arms Instructor, how would you execute such a person? Removal of the head may suffice, but who can say?"

"I doubt many trained philosophers turn to crime," Lin Chong said, knowing she had already lost the argument.

"Luckily some did." Wu Yong grinned. "Including, let the gongs ring out, a Renxia priestess with some prodigious talent at alchemy, in whom the Chancellor of the Secretariat has taken a particular interest of late. She seems a magnificently likely recruit for us, don't you think? Now, my dear Arms Instructor, you say everyone knows of the Pit, but let me tell you something that is not well known, but that our friends who just departed for the night were gracious enough to share. The reason even the most dangerous priests and monks can be trapped within its depths is that the prison walls are threaded with scholar's stone. As well as being impregnable. It is quite a well-thought-out prison."

"I'm glad you're impressed," Lin Chong said. "I assume we'll be extracting her from somewhere other than this impenetrable prison. How often does the Chancellor's interest extend to removing her from it?"

"Frequently, I'm told, but not tomorrow. Tomorrow, in fact, some new orders are expected from the fine Chancellor Cai, ones specifically regarding this priestess . . . or so the rumor runs."

"You think she's about to be executed."

Wu Yong twirled a hand in a gesture that seemed entirely too cavalier. "Let's say I believe it wise to make our visit as early in the morning as can be managed."

"I see." Their visit—their visit to break into an unassailable stronghold of the highest security, deep in the heart of the inner city of the capital of the Empire. "I take it you have a plan."

"Of course I have a plan." Wu Yong cast a devious eye up and down Lin Chong's body. "Oh, Arms Instructor. How would you feel about getting a few more tattoos?"

As the sun rose and the drums beat out the first watch of the day, Lu Junyi forced her hands to tie a sash, to slide slippers onto her feet. To twist her hair back and secure it in her usual polished style. As if she could don a new skin firmly enough to howl another reality into existence.

Her feet took her presentable self all the way to the inner city, to the southern district, the central district, the research building that had flayed her over its stones these many weeks. The place that had at first seemed such a paradise, and now was only dread. She ducked through the gates and let her mechanical steps take her up the path, past the ever-watchful rows of guards, turn to the right, enter their research area, one foot after the other. Just like every other day.

Cai Jing was waiting.

Not like every other day.

This is my time, then, Lu Junyi thought. She wondered, much too late, if she should have tried to flee the city.

A retinue of servants and Guardsmen backed the Chancellor as if he stood at the head of a palace audience chamber. Ling Zhen was already present and bent over the lodestone and the tests they had left in progress, with more chaperoning Guardsmen arrayed behind him as usual.

Lu Junyi hurried forward and bowed, all the way to kneeling, head against the floor. "Honorable Grand Chancellor." The words were cracked as a drought-seared plain. "How may we be of service . . ."

"This operation is to be packed up to march," he replied, looking out over her head. "Today. You and the seditionists and whichever other scholars you choose will travel with the army starting tomorrow morning and continue your research en route. You have until we arrive at our destination to build me something deployable. No more than four days."

Lu Junyi sucked in a breath against the stone. "Honorable Grand Chancellor, we have many more tests to run before having a good guess of the safety—"

"Then we shall use it unsafely."

Contradictions collided through Lu Junyi's mind. She had explained to him that a premature test could lead, with this method, to a catastrophic overload of energy. Such a ruthless, foolish act on a field of battle might scorch far more of the Empire's own countryside than was ever intended, hurt so many innocent citizens; she wanted to remind, again, that the god's fang still must bond to its wielder, and that a lack of properly prepared control might burn that wielder alive from the inside out; she wanted to point out how even an ordinary god's tooth often took years of training to keep from causing collateral harm through an unskilled hand. She wanted to cry out that they needed so much more time, so much more information, and the slick taste beneath it all that she didn't want to acknowledge was that four days' march by foot wouldn't take them anywhere close to the Empire's borders.

None of it passed her lips. Cai Jing knew everything she could say. He had taken every one of her reports, and he had almost as good an understanding of the research here as she did.

He knew what he asked. He knew how the god's fangs might melt the earth if they went wrong. He wanted to use them anyway.

Against someone within the Empire.

"I have already dispatched orders for your seditionists to be prepared and chained for transport by tomorrow morning. Separately, of course. It would not do for us to lose our leverage over them. Stand, Lady Lu. I want a full update, and then you will inform the servants of what you wish transported with you and what precautions must be taken with the materials."

Lu Junyi pushed against the floor, trying to move her feet back under her. They were stumps at the ends of her ankles, as if her legs had forgotten how to support her. She swayed to her feet, keeping her eyes deferentially lowered. "Yes, Grand Chancellor."

"Good. Before the moon begins to wax again we will have seared the diseased pustule of the Liangshan bandits from the glorious face of our Empire."

The chains chafed Lin Chong's wrists behind her back, and the angle dragged at the still-healing cuts she'd sustained in her fight with Yang Zhi. How had it been so recent that she still bore the effects of it?

The greater discomfort, however, was the new marks snaking up and down her body beneath her clothes, spirals and geometric symbols and flowers and leaves, the ink so fresh it crawled like fire ants under her skin. The tattoo on her face was exposed now as well, the false bandaging torn away, but her hair still fell partially across it, matching the streaks of dirt and disarrayed clothes that shouted how viciously she must have fought before succumbing.

Wu Yong thwacked her against the back of the calves with the spear haft. Not gently, either. Lin Chong closed her eyes and sucked in a breath through the burn that chased its way all up and down her abused skin. She remembered Lu Da's full-body chaos of winding flowers—*Sister, you must be some strange masochist to do this by choice.*

Wu Yong's plans might be good, but apparently they were not guaranteed to be comfortable.

"Got a new prisoner for the Pit." Wu Yong's casual accent had dropped its usual scholarly diction, becoming indistinguishable from the speech of a common soldier. "Former Master Arms Instructor Lin Chong. Wanted for attempted assassination of Grand Marshal Gao Qiu, escape from custody, and treason against the Empire."

You're enjoying this too much, Lin Chong thought. She concentrated on keeping her wrists flexed so that the metal cuffs would appear properly attached. Wu Yong had fastened them just loosely enough that her hands could slip free.

The guards in the watchtowers shouted down, demanding evidence of the orders. Wu Yong reached into the fake uniform's belt and brandished an official-looking scroll, and the thick iron gates creaked open.

Wu Yong shoved Lin Chong between the shoulder blades—so hard she stumbled for real—and together they spilled into the top tier of the Pit.

Single-edged swords immediately surrounded them, the first

row of soldiers pivoting to block their passage. Lin Chong noted one of the boys from last night among their number, whose expression jumped when he recognized Wu Yong's face. He didn't look displeased, exactly, but not nearly as open and welcoming as at the inn, either.

Especially when he saw Lin Chong. Then his eyes got very round. She suddenly remembered, then—she had trained him, perhaps five or six years ago. The memory was vague, a cloud of fine dust that mingled with the faces of all the other trainees who had come through her drills on their way into the Guard. Of course *he* would recognize *her*, though. Similar startled familiarity painted the faces of at least half the soldiers holding them at bay, and an acute pain kinked through Lin Chong's heart.

They had trained under her. They knew her. And now . . . now they saw her dragged back to them as a convict and traitor.

She could remind herself today's arrest was a gambit all she liked, but the accusations Wu Yong proclaimed were real ones, noted down against her in the ledger of the magistrate of Bianliang Prefecture. Rumors of her downfall must have spread through the Guard in Bianliang like free-flowing water, but she would not have wished for any of her men to see her like this with their own eyes.

Tattooed and disgraced.

The Guardsmen parted slightly to allow through a grizzled soldier wearing the single tassel of a detachment commander, as he climbed up the tiers out of the central descent.

"Your orders, Officer," the commander snapped at Wu Yong. "This is the Pit. Your prisoner can only be directed here on the highest authority."

"I have it," Wu Yong answered easily, and passed the scroll over with a relaxed salute.

The commander perused the writing slowly. Lin Chong kept her breathing shallow and steady. He would see nothing but Cai Jing's famous, striking hand in the calligraphy, nothing but the Chancellor's intricate seal marking the bottom as proof of its veracity. Wu Yong's contacts here in Bianliang had seen to that.

Lin Chong had not been present to see which of threats, bribes, or persuasion the Tactician had used in acquiring the forgeries. Endless acquaintances and resources, for anything from extra props or costumes to imitating the Empire's most well-known calligraphist, all conjured from somewhere in the city by Wu Yong. Lin Chong, on the other hand, had instead spent nearly the entire night under the unrelenting painful tapping of bone and bamboo needles by five cowled apothecaries. They kept themselves in eerie silence, and she had asked no names, breathing deep into her center as the time drummed on and they worked through Wu Yong's full list of instructions.

The Tactician had a strange and exhausting list of associates.

The Pit's commander finished examining the forged orders, straightened, and saluted Wu Yong back. "This is all in order. You understand my suspicion. The Chancellor demands alertness from us all."

"Indeed," Wu Yong agreed.

The commander had no need to justify himself to a lowly junior officer. *You don't want your conduct presented unfavorably to Cai Jing,* Lin Chong thought.

Perhaps realizing how he had sounded, the commander cleared his throat gruffly and tucked away the orders. "Pass your prisoner to my men."

"Ah!" Wu Yong held up a hand, *just* genially enough to be deferential to a supposed superior. "A thousand pardons, Commander. I can't report to the Chancellor until I've seen this here prisoner bolted up in a cell with my own very eyes. Especially as she's already escaped the one time, and killed some very noble Guardsmen who were supposed to be keeping her licked. Crushed 'em like berries."

I didn't kill anyone, Lin Chong corrected silently. Although . . . she would have. She had fought those two constables with everything she had.

She understood, though, what Wu Yong was doing, and she marveled a little that she could see it. Preying on that same nervousness about the Chancellor that Lin Chong had noticed—but that she wouldn't have known what to do with, not like this.

The detachment commander slitted suspicious eyes at Wu Yong in a broad, paranoid face. But Wu Yong leaned in and added—not softly enough to mask it from anyone—"Commander, have a heart and save me my skin. If I tell the Chancellor I didn't see this prisoner sealed in, what do you think he's going to do to me? I can't lie to the Grand Chancellor, now can I, so it's a caning for me for sure either way. I know he'll be pleased with you, Commander, being so fierce not to let anyone pass, and doubtless he'll see how well that speaks of you and your men, but have pity on the messenger—"

"You'll tell him no such thing," barked the commander, who clearly knew it would *not* speak well of him if Cai Jing truly had given such an order. "The Chancellor will get his full report. Officers, escort them down and seal in the prisoner."

Several of the Guardsmen came forward and grabbed Lin Chong by the upper arms, yanking her forward, with more of them falling in behind. She sucked in a sharp breath at the pressure on the recent inkings and hoped it would pass unnoticed as she tried to propel her legs in sync with the guards' impatience.

They hiked down, and down, and down, stone tier after stone tier, each manned by another row of stalwart Guardsmen. As they reached the bottom, the prison itself rose up above them, an ugly pall that seemed to loom larger than its shape, shadows clawing out to weigh on their minds.

Or maybe that was the scholar's stone gnarled through its depths.

"Search her out here in the light," ordered one of the officers. Lin Chong felt herself yanked to one side. Multiple men's hands shoved against her body, painful against her unhealed skin. Up under her arms, pushing up her belly and chest, climbing her legs to smack against her thighs.

As impersonal as the men were, Lin Chong grit her teeth against the visceral flashback of violation, of Gao Qiu's drunken hands pawing against her . . . of the manacles that had clamped over her wrists for real as her life spiraled away. The weight of the cangue on her shoulders and neck. The constables' cudgels in Yezhu Forest when they beat her down and tried to remove her face for a petty tyrant—

Her fists knotted and clenched, and for one heart-stopping moment she lost the tension against the cuffs around her wrists.

She re-flexed almost immediately, catching the metal against the back of her hands hard enough to bite the skin. If the Guardsmen caught how loose they were—no officer would make such a mistake—her heart pounded like she'd crashed through the ice of a lake. How could she have let herself be distracted . . .

One of the Guardsmen grabbed her by the shoulder and spun her roughly, and she braced to jerk herself out of the cuffs entirely, if she'd just ruined everything.

But he only said, "Take her in," and turned away with disinterest.

Sword points pricked against her, prodding her toward the black maw of the prison entrance. A clammy sweat itched all over her body, mingling with the ink's hidden burn.

The entrance was more a hole than a door, through stone-laced black walls more than three paces thick. Lin Chong let herself be escorted down the narrow space, darkness cloaking them with the daylight a distant portal behind. The shaft ended in a door of wrought iron, lumpy with more chunks of scholar's stone belted into its depths.

The way was narrow enough that most of the Guardsmen had remained outside, and their escort thinned to only the young guard who'd been so chummy with Wu Yong the night before, and had been among those who accompanied them down. After his initial surprise—and a little distance from his commander—he seemed to relax back into friendliness.

"Ever been here before?" he muttered to Wu Yong impressively. He'd turned to some rough sconces next to the door, ones holding rag-wrapped torches that stank of dark honey. He pulled a sulfur stick from a holder next to them.

Wu Yong raised questioning eyebrows. "First time. Bet you could tell me all the secrets, eh?"

The guard chuckled. "You think it's a plum spot, getting trusted to see the beating heart of it, but three days in and it's boring as a one-trick singing girl. We gotta take shifts taking care of the inside, and this place'll drive you as mad as it does the prisoners. Least we've got torches, but I swear the dark gets tentacles in it, tries to reach out and murder us."

He lifted one of the honey-soaked torches in a practiced motion, but instead of striking the sulfur stick against the wall in front of him, he turned away carefully and struck it against the armored scales on the skirts of his uniform. A small fire sputtered to life and he held it against the rags well away from the wall to produce a low golden burn.

"Can't risk any fire against the scholar's stone," he explained affably to Wu Yong. "They send these torches to us made special. Burn low and near smokeless, so they say, though the air's so stale it's a shock this place don't stifle 'em anyway. Guess not many of 'em last to die of it. Hey, keep your spear on this one—the uncles like to tell tales about dishonorable lowlifes who wanted to flame out with a few of their guards."

He cast a baleful glance at Lin Chong. Grinning, Wu Yong obligingly stepped back and levied the spear point against her back a lot harder than necessary. "Don't worry, she moves funny and I'll spit 'er."

"Well done. Here, now keep this away from the walls unless you want us all dead quicker'n you can say it."

With that, the guard passed the torch to Wu Yong and pulled out a string of heavy keys. The door to the Pit scraped back, as thick as Lin Chong's two hands and heavy enough that their escort had to shove his shoulder against its weight.

They passed through into darkness.

The black was near-total, with only the single flame casting an eerie glow against a suffocating space the heavy walls begrudgingly made room for. Wu Yong raised the torch, limning the edges of a many-sided polygonal chamber, with rough, stone-laced walls coming to a pyramidal apex above them.

Here was where the Tactician's plan became more vague—*we won't know the best attack until we see the inside. Sister Lin, stop your fretting. Some thinking on the feet is good for the blood.* Lin Chong swept the area with a hooded glance, beginning to let the cuffs slip down against her knuckles. One guard alone was better than they had hoped for; Wu Yong might give the signal at any moment . . .

"Got sixteen cells here," the young soldier said, sorting through his keys. "Only about half of 'em full. They get processed through pretty quick most of the time. The traitor can have the one across."

"You've got some beasts right now, eh?" Wu Yong's voice tilted toward the deliciously conspiratorial. "You told me last night about that balls-out Renxia priestess . . ."

"Oh, yeah, she's right in there," their escort said easily, nodding over his shoulder. "Lemme tell you, when we first got 'er in here—"

The Tactician's smile dropped like a door slamming shut. The spear spun from Lin Chong's back, fast, so fast, over their heads in a flash of wood and metal to slash straight across the boy's throat. He had time for his expression to go wide in shock, one hand clawing at the blood fountaining up, before his bones went soft and he collapsed with a choking gurgle.

It was over before Lin Chong's manacles had hit the stone, before she had turned halfway to help. She froze. She hadn't known Wu Yong was going to do that.

But then, she hadn't known Wu Yong *wasn't* going to do that. This was why they were here. Casualties of war.

The boy's eyes stared sightless in the dim gold light, his blood creeping out in tendrils along the rough floor, seeping in the crannies of the same black mortar and scholar's stone that made the walls.

"No more than two turns before they come looking," Wu Yong

said quickly. "But I can jam them at the entrance for as long as you need. Take the torch!"

Ripping free of the manacles had scraped the skin wholly off the backs of Lin Chong's hands. She ignored the stinging dampness and moved fast, palming the torch from Wu Yong—*don't drop it, don't let it hit a wall*—and sweeping one fist down to scoop the string of keys from the boy soldier's lifeless fingers. The door he had indicated was as featureless as the rest, wrought iron in the same style as the entrance, lumpy with more bits of stone. And near-solid, with no barred window cut out to allow light or air or sound.

Lin Chong had fanned out the keys with her fingers as she hurried over. The large and heavy one on the end, that was the one the guard had opened the main door with—then came a jangle of smaller keys; each must go to a door here—*Most logical if the string is in order. Count over, one two three four five, try the fifth key—*

It jammed into the lock but wouldn't turn. Lin Chong twisted hard, twice, her grip slipping on her own blood from where she'd wrenched out of the manacles. Not the fifth key. Try the fifth in the other direction . . .

That one wouldn't turn either.

Nothing for it but to try each from the beginning. The lock gaped wide and loose, making it difficult to tell whether a key fit or not. She tried to balance certainty with speed.

From the entrance came a rustle of movement and then a shout.

Lin Chong didn't look around. Next key, next key. Grunts and thumps and the sound of Wu Yong's spear point burying itself in flesh. *The Tactician can handle it. Keep going. Focus.*

The seventh key turned.

The sudden movement almost made Lin Chong stumble, but she turned it into a heave, grinding the heavy door back against its ill fittings. Behind her, the clamor escalated—the clack of weapons and armor, screams and shouts and the wet smacks that silenced them.

Taking care to tuck the torch in close to her, Lin Chong ducked into the slice of pitch beyond the cell door.

A blanket of stifling, stale air and the scent of human waste assailed her senses. The torchlight slanted through the narrow space, bringing to life a tall, skewed cell, the walls pinching together high above. Standing motionless in the center of the space, unmoving and unsurprised, hulked the thin silhouette of a woman.

Her hands grasped at nothing at her sides. She neither spoke nor approached.

"You are Fan Rui?" Lin Chong asked urgently. "The priestess of the Renxia?"

"I am she." Her voice was a creak.

"My friend and I broke in to find you. Come with us and leave this place."

Fan Rui's head came up, very slightly, glittering black eyes meeting Lin Chong's.

"Two people?" Mockery shaded the question. "Breaking in is easy, but you did it to die. If you counted on the alchemical priestess to save you, they have made me nothing but an impotent earthworm, didn't you know? Smothered in cobwebs, every direction. Even if I were not, I do not have the might to defeat the swarm of cockroaches at the gate. You bet poorly. You are dead."

"Both doors stand open. We have a route through the scholar's stone to the outside," Lin Chong countered. "As for the power of an army—" One-handed, she yanked at the tie to her tunic so the collar began to fall open. "What if you had access to the most potent of all materials in alchemical science?"

Fan Rui's head snapped up. She stepped forward as if drawn by some unseen force, her hands coming up to hover close to Lin Chong's exposed skin—and the tattoos beneath it.

"The designs identify them." Lin Chong held the torch high, forcing herself not to flinch away from a stranger's hands. "Gold, cinnabar, arsenolite, oyster shells—twenty-two others, I can tell you—"

"No need. I feel them now. Like music—they sing." She laughed.

"Then quickly—"

"Yes." Fan Rui inhaled sharply through her nose, her mouth twisting up into something that, on another's face, might have been close to a smile. "Be warned. This will hurt."

She stepped back fast and hard, yanking her hands down and away in closed and grasping fists.

Lin Chong screamed.

CHAPTER 23

Lin Chong's world went the red-hot fire of being flayed alive, as the gold and cinnabar, the realgar and jade and croton seed and every other material they'd had the apothecaries mix with ink and etch into her flesh tore out at the priestess's call. Lin Chong knew she screamed, her throat ripping raw, she knew her body snapped and flailed as if in rigor, but haze and pain swallowed everything.

She had one lucid moment of panic as she began to fall—*the torch, if it scorches against the scholar's stone*—but a wind had begun to rise toward Fan Rui, swirling through the cloud of metals and salts and medicines, and the flame snuffed out before the torch hit the ground next to Lin Chong's face.

Above her, Fan Rui slowly brought her hands up and up, a monument of a woman come to life. The torchlight was gone but somehow everywhere was lit with a dim and eerie glow in the very air, even as her growing alchemical maelstrom formed a vicious darkness within it.

The cloud of power and danger and freedom writhed in front of her, around her, as Fan Rui stepped over Lin Chong's collapsed body and out of the cell. The whirlwind slipped through with her, without touching wall or door or floor.

Get up. Get up . . .

Lin Chong's thoughts began to pool toward that inner place, that dangerous place, the energy between worlds. *No. No* . . . not here, not surrounded by a trap of inert scholar's stone when she could control nothing . . . if she brushed the stone with her mind it could swallow her whole. A sharp mental jerk back, as she panicked that the mere thought had caused it to happen.

She had to move. Wu Yong would not leave her behind, but the priestess might leave them both—

Get up. She's the only way out. You will die here if you do not stand—now!

She would not give Gao Qiu the satisfaction.

Lin Chong's hands twisted against the rough mortar floor, clawing without bending the right way before she managed to get them under her and push. Her clothes slapped against her, wet with what must be her own blood, each scrape of the cloth bringing new agony.

The wall was near enough. She reached up and dug at it with her fingertips, hauling herself up. Her body had begun shaking, her mind liquid in the aftermath of too much shock, but at least she was gaining back control over her muscles. She pushed herself through the still-open cell door.

The wan, thin light and shouts and clangs of combat called her in the right direction.

She'd moved faster than she had credited herself with. Fan Rui was still inside, now standing in the center of the entrance chamber, a cyclone of fine particles swirling high and higher around her in a massive, deadly halo. At the entrance, backlit by the beckoning day, Wu Yong spun and slashed, each fresh corpse flopping higher to clog the narrow space. One of the Guardsmen threw himself at the door, attempting to heave it closed and trap them all inside, but his effort caught on the bodies. Wu Yong hurled the spear like a javelin to skewer him against the wall, then seamlessly drew a single-edged sword, one attack flowing into the next.

More soldiers swarmed in behind the fallen.

Facing the entrance, Fan Rui drew her hands up to her chest, fingers clawed open as if she were preparing to deliver a double palm strike. The air began to hum, twitching with static like just before thunder came. Her storm gathered up to her, the hum becoming a buzz becoming a painful whine that vibrated through Lin Chong's every bone.

Wu Yong roared a battle cry and opened the next man's neck—with no eyes for Fan Rui, who stood behind, with her mounting, dizzying power . . .

Lin Chong was still leaning on the wall next to the fifth door. Too slow, too far away to help. She sucked in a breath and shouted, the words instantly ripped from her by the crackling air and the clashing bloodlust of the battle.

"PROFESSOR! DROP!"

At that moment, Fan Rui thrust her hands forward.

Wu Yong—thank Benevolence, thank the heavens, thank any god or demon that might have seen fit to grant a favor—Wu Yong heard. Fast enough. And dropped without hesitation, without turning to look. The fall was inelegant, a dive made for speed that hit hard enough for the Tactician's body to roll against the floor. The soldier at the entrance raised his sword with a victorious yell, ready to plunge it down and end his fallen foe.

Fan Rui's attack hit.

Whatever alchemical cyclone she had created—it burst out with the speed of a typhoon, funneling down the entranceway in a great smoke-like column. The men in the way ripped into pieces in its path, bodies whipped against one wall as detached limbs and scalps hit the other. Fan Rui took one step forward, then one more, her long and vicious rod of swirling darkness still held against her tense and open palms.

Wu Yong belly-crawled out of her way and bounced up by her side. Lin Chong hobbled to join them.

"I say we follow the priestess," the Tactician shouted. Had to shout, because Fan Rui's focused storm still sucked every sound from the air. "Can you fight?"

"If I have to," Lin Chong shouted back.

Fan Rui stepped almost delicately among the piled bodies, placing her feet to stay steady at the same level. Her attack, Lin Chong noticed, never touched the stone.

She was excellent. She was terrifying.

Lin Chong and Wu Yong followed, picking their way through

the carnage. Wu Yong grabbed the spear and passed it to Lin Chong. She took it, even as every movement made her wince.

May Benevolence grant me one more bout of strength. She tightened her grip against the spear haft, raising it in preparation.

She need not have bothered.

Fan Rui reached the edge of the tunnel, where it opened into the outer courtyard sunk deep within fat walls, the tiered courtyard which had previously been so filled with well-disciplined troops. Now those troops all faced this one point, swords drawn, every eye, every will, bent toward killing them.

Fan Rui threw back her head and screamed the cry of an angry raptor. Her arms flung out, one to either side.

The storm followed.

Some of the men tried to attack. Some tried to flee. None made more than two steps before the monstrous maelstrom punched through armor and flesh, their own screams choked off before they started. Yells erupted from up in the watchtowers, with one desperate crossbow bolt loosed before spikes of metallic darkness split off from Fan Rui's artificial gale and swooped upward. Projectile and watchmen were skewered through and snuffed out in less than an instant.

Above them, the clear sky cracked in response, lightning ripping through the blue and tinging it in otherworldly colors that flickered and rolled over the carnage. Fan Rui's malignant, stained wind swirled between earth and heavens in discontented eddies over the slaughter it had left behind. It was the only thing that moved.

Lin Chong flexed her fingers against the borrowed spear, staring out over a field of battle that had just become a debris heap of flesh.

Fan Rui pulled her roiling cloud of death back to her in long strokes. It seemed to have thinned some. She gathered the remainder around her as if it were a magnificent, towering cloak and turned to look back over one shoulder.

"Follow me," she said, and she began to run.

For someone who had just come from being locked away in a pitch-dark coffin of stone—for anyone of her age, even if showered with exercise and sunlight—the priestess moved blindingly fast. Her long strides loped straight up the tiered rings that stepped up from the prison, straight up toward the bulbous walls that cupped this place in their indomitable grip, her grand black cloud of power buoying her from behind and her feet barely touching the ground.

Perhaps they didn't.

Lin Chong and Wu Yong scrambled after, a skipping hop through the bodies that crisscrossed their path, the soles of their boots smacking in blood and seeping innards. The violence in the sky had calmed some, though it still glowed in strange colors, the type of gray-gold and ill green that whispered to the hindbrain of cyclones or typhoons or icy hail the size of a man's fist.

They gained on the wall fast, its inky blackness looming as if it intended to keep them trapped, its iron gates shut fast and solid. The tiered incline began to steal the breath from Lin Chong's lungs. The rush of the battle and of their escape coursed through her, letting her ride its wave of energy, keeping her abused body awake and fighting . . .

They were almost at the gates.

Fan Rui raised her hands and shouted, "Leap!" before thrusting her palms straight down at the ground.

The intent was clear in an instant—wild, delirious, unbelievable, but perfectly clear.

Without stopping to think about it, Lin Chong delved inside herself for every scrap of remaining strength. She and Wu Yong grasped at each other, and they leapt.

The last of Fan Rui's manufactured cyclone rushed up below them.

Together with the priestess, they shot high into the air as if loosed from a crossbow themselves. The air rushed by in a wind that snatched at their clothes and hair and the breath of their lungs, with their legs and feet pedaling uselessly below. Lin Chong and Wu Yong fell against each other in the air, bereft of any control, buffeted into that eerie sky by this swooping, grainy gale that would take them where it would.

They arced high over the wall, so high, soaring over the span of wooded land that surrounded this prison. Before them, the city of Bianliang stretched out in breathtaking miniature: buildings and trees and streets lacing through, all made tiny, crawling out until it sprawled from below the shadowed sky back into blue sunlight. For one gossamer moment they existed as tiny specks in the high heavens, free of the grip of the earth below.

Then they fell.

The wind that had propelled them so high began to flicker out, dissipating to weak tendrils. The ground rushed back toward them, faster and faster, the alchemical support provided by Fan Rui collapsing out from around them, leaving no cushion, no remnants.

Too fast. Too hard. They plummeted toward a road, the pavement coming to crush them with a mace the size of the earth.

Automatically and frantically, Lin Chong reached for all her vast skill in fighting and falling, all her training that allowed her to treat the ground's pull as a friend she could dance with lightly. Even as she knew this was too large, too inescapable. She could fall from a horse unharmed. Not from the sky.

In that one instant of clarity, however, her mind fell again into that space between worlds. The twist of energies from nowhere and everywhere. The portal of the god's teeth.

She had failed to control it every time before—but holding back now would be pointless.

In the blink of time before they hit, Lin Chong *reached.*

Instant hyperawareness of Wu Yong and Fan Rui tumbling through the air beside her, of the sky and ground and trees and wind and air, of the city below teeming with life and the country stretching out green and full in every direction. *Do something. Protect us—*

With no time to think, Lin Chong's long-ingrained training instincts decided for her. No fanciness. No creativity. She simply saw them landing as lightly as she always did after a jump and kick in the midst of a fight.

A vision she cast out among the three of them, a bending of the world. To alight with perfect control, with the feet of a butterfly and the nimbleness of a mountain goat.

They hit. Much, much harder than that.

The landing that should have been a feathered drop to the soles of their feet jarred Lin Chong up through her legs and knees, snapping hard and unforgiving through every tendon and spiking pain in her ankles that made her momentarily fear she'd shattered them. She fell forward, hand tearing apart from where she and Wu Yong had held each other. The road hit Lin Chong's elbow, shoulder, hip, her skull ricocheting only just gently enough that her mind sloshed against itself instead of going black. The spear cracked out of her grip against the pavement.

She lay still for a moment. Moving seemed . . . unwise.

"Are you all right, Sister?" Wu Yong's face filled her vision, cap lost, blood trickling from some unseen head wound. Dust and bruising and a torn uniform reflected every pain in Lin Chong's body.

Wu Yong's hand reached out bracingly. Lin Chong grasped it. Pulled herself up.

Her own clothes were patched with seeping red. Where the skin had scraped free on her hands, the abrasions had become packed with caked dirt.

Despite it all, a lightness floated through her, a fragile knowledge of accomplishment. *I did it. I did it . . . ?* Not beautifully or gracefully, but she had saved them . . .

She reached for that meditative state again, but it had receded along with the focus of battle. She wobbled against Wu Yong's arm.

A few paces away, Fan Rui sprang up to her feet as if she were a child who had fallen while playing in the street. "My mistake!" she said to Lin Chong, and laughed. The laughter was a trifle too long, and a trifle too loud.

Lin Chong and Wu Yong did not join in.

Lin Chong limped to gather back her weapon. Her fingers were numb, her grip weak.

"The Guard will be on this position soon," Wu Yong said. "Time to go. Follow us, Priestess."

Fan Rui tipped them a salute and turned in sudden hurry—but not toward the city wall or the gates to the outer city, but inward, scuttling away from the prison straight back into the central district.

"Wait!" Wu Yong cried, scrambling a moment before giving chase. Apparently even the ever-prepared Tactician could be surprised. "That's not the way!"

Lin Chong was a moment behind, her feet and knees crying out at every pounding step. They'd done the hardest part—they'd rescued one of Cai Jing's seditionists. If it went wrong now . . .

Wu Yong's long legs managed to catch the priestess and stumble in front to cut her off. "Stop! This road leads back into the central district. You don't want—"

"I know what I want when I want. Roads go where I want. Let me by!"

Wu Yong dodged to stay in front of her. "Priestess! This is only the path to re-arrest and death. We can get you out of the city. We came to offer you a proposal—heroism, riches, and all the revenge against Cai Jing you could yearn for—"

"Get off!" barked Fan Rui. "Revenge, ha! My vengeance is come today. Let go!"

"Revenge will mean nothing if you fail in it! Go back now and the Guard will take you! If you come with us to Liangshan, I promise you, we will go after Cai Jing, and your revenge will be all the sweeter for its victory—"

"It never will be! Not if I kill him. Now that I am free we both can be. Let me go!"

Wu Yong had gripped her wrists and arrested her struggling. "Calm. Calm! You don't talk of Cai Jing, do you—who is it you speak of? Quickly, Priestess, please."

Whatever Wu Yong had picked up on, Lin Chong had missed it. But as per much-vaunted reputation, the Tactician had hit the target.

"My own one . . ." Fan Rui stopped moving abruptly, her face sagging in sadness. "He always had so much more joy than I. How could I kill him? The Chancellor said, if either of us . . . we'll be good, we agreed, until we can be butterflies together in a later life . . ."

"Your husband?" Wu Yong said, apparently recognizing the folklore reference. "You and your husband—you were going to take your own lives . . ."

"To destroy Cai Jing's weapon," Lin Chong realized. "Destroy it before your work could be used."

"And him!" Fan Rui cackled. "And him, he knows too much, the Chancellor does!"

Sabotage and assassination.

"A good death, we agreed, we agreed, we spoke through the work we left each other. I told him it was right, hide it, hide it all, continue for each other until it was done. Dying is good, living is better. It's happening now, today. I must hurry—"

She began fighting against Wu Yong again, this time with the furor of a wildcat.

"Wait! Stop! Priestess," Wu Yong tried, wheezing as one of Fan Rui's inexpert kicks landed. "This is what we want, too. This is all we want! Let us help."

Fan Rui stilled. Her eyes found Wu Yong's for the first time. "You would?" she said. "You would . . . Are you heroes?"

"Only according to some," Lin Chong muttered. "Tactician—a word—"

With Fan Rui momentarily calm, Wu Yong allowed Lin Chong to tug the two of them away from her, to the side. "What is it, Sister Lin?"

"We can't." The truth of it tasted sour, but part of knowing the battlefield was understanding when the odds were too great. "The entire Guard will be on alert now. We're wasting too much time here already. If we lose in Bianliang we imperil any chance Liangshan has—"

"But if we can steal or destroy Cai Jing's weapon?" Wu Yong's eyes narrowed. "Then we protect Liangshan not only from this upcoming battle—but from *every* battle."

"Going back into the central district is suicide," Lin Chong argued. "We have to get back to the outer city, and we have to go *now*—"

"Learn to toss the coins, Sister Lin," Wu Yong said lightly, and spun back to Fan Rui. "Priestess, we'll help you destroy the weapon, and we'll bring both you and your husband with us in the wake of it. Lead the way—aiya, quickly!"

Lin Chong heard it, too. Shouts and the clatter of fast-moving men in armor. In moments the entire inner city would be bristling with the Guard.

Wu Yong and Fan Rui turned together, gloriously, fatally, to run straight into the beating heart of the enemy.

Lin Chong had no choice but to follow.

In White Tiger Hall, Cai Jing sat at the head of the long table and steepled his fingers in front of him, showing no outward sign of his deep annoyance. His deep personal annoyance.

The Emperor, may Benevolence shine upon him, was not in attendance, leaving his chancellors to sort this out among themselves. Which meant Cai Jing had to be affronted with the presence of the Chancellors of Ministry and State. The Chancellor of the Ministry in particular liked to heave his political weight about, just to show that he could—particularly when he opposed Cai Jing. Unfortunately, the Imperial Guard was technically in his chain of command.

He'd brought the Minister of War to back him, too, who displayed his god's tooth prominently in a medallion around his neck, like the stuffed head he was. Minister Duan was not, unfortunately, an incompetent—alas, as that would have been easier to deal with—but he had shown the audacity to refuse all prior opportunities to align himself with Cai Jing. Besides which, he had a certain self-centered perception of his own uprightness that caused him to get in other people's way. Like a child who preened at tattling on others.

The War Minister was joined by three of his generals, also, in what Cai Jing thought was a frankly embarrassing brandishing of power. Generals would do as they were told, if their superiors commanded. No general loyal to the Emperor would balk at being ordered to march against bandits.

Finally, rounding out their conference, and overreaching from his station as always, was the creeping contagion that was Marshal Gao Qiu. Gao Qiu's presence was all the more irritating because he was so firmly and loudly on Cai Jing's side in this matter. Though useful when going before the Emperor, Gao Qiu's support in front of the other chancellors . . .

Cai Jing wasn't the only one who viewed the man with disgust. No one ever dared say so, of course. Not with Gao Qiu so favored by the Emperor, may he live forever.

No, the other chancellors' undermining was much more subtle. At this moment, it was taking the form of refusing Cai Jing his troops.

"Preposterous," spat the Chancellor of the Ministry, not even bothering to hide his temper. His small black beard whipped and flipped with the force of it. "You would take ten thousand troops and mire them in rural swamps? And to do what? Bandits are like fleas. Stomp on one, a hundred more pop up. A pestilence, but not one to drain good resources over."

He was only being so impolitic because Cai Jing had attempted to go around him. A miscalculation, in retrospect.

"A pestilence, yes," Cai Jing said calmly. "I applaud your foresightedness in calling them such, Chancellor. If we do not rout them from their foothold and tear out their roots, that pestilence will take hold and begin corrupting the Empire from within."

"You keep sounding warnings of incursions to the north." The Chancellor of State took a more delicate and doubtful tack, rubbing a hand across his thick jaw. "Your energy has been persuasive, Chancellor Cai, although I admit many of us have been slow to have the same stomach for conflict. Committing so many troops to a domestic matter instead, when the northern threat looms—I would sound a note of caution in such a risk."

Cai Jing managed not to grind his teeth against each other. "Ah, but it *is* a domestic matter. As I have pointed out several times to your gracious excellencies. Which makes this decision my sole purview, gentlemen."

"Ha!" The Chancellor of the Ministry's hand came down on the table, a flat slap. "I beg the esteemed Chancellor's pardon, but *nothing* is solely your purview when it involves the Imperial Guard. I can give you five hundred troops, Chancellor Cai, and consider that a generous bequest."

"Five . . . hundred," Cai Jing said coldly. "You vastly underestimate the terrain of their stronghold. *One* man could hold five hundred in the marshlands, if the day brings him luck. Ten thousand may not be enough."

"Against a handful of backwater bandits?" scoffed the Chancellor of the Ministry. "You insult the military of this Empire, Chancellor."

"My men are well-trained," the Minister of War put in, with a coolness that annoyed Cai Jing far beyond his superior's choler. "They will march in any terrain and see victory. It is only a matter of whether that victory is worth the cost."

"The person who trained *your men* is now training the forces at Liangshan," Cai Jing snapped back. "As is one of your commanders. Might I remind my esteemed colleagues that twice five hundred troops were somehow devoured wholly when they went after these bandits in Ji Province at the village of Dongxi? The augurs have determined that the place now festers with evil. Whatever dark strength these swamp bandits possess, the reports of the countryside are that the nobles and magistrates antagonize Liangshan at their peril, cringing at their very name—"

"Exaggerated," scoffed the Chancellor of the Ministry. "Half the Empire in fear of a handful of *women*? Absurd."

Cai Jing considered it a testament to his great control that he did not strangle his colleague at the council table.

Of course, Gao Qiu could always make things worse.

"Gentlemen, gentlemen," the marshal cut in smarmily. "It's not only what's for the benefit of Empire—remember, these upstart whores insulted both myself and the good Chancellor personally. It's weakness to let that go unanswered, isn't it!"

Cai Jing wished the earth would swallow him in disgrace. The others averted their eyes and deferred response. They knew, of course, how Cai Jing had been insulted, and they breached all etiquette by not rushing to avenge it, but to wave that flag himself was the height of ill breeding.

As Marshal Gao should know.

"There's no need for this conflict," the Emperor's favorite marshal continued, with all the oblivious crudeness of a man who would pick his feet at a dining table. "If we take it before the Emperor, we'll get a definitive answer. He'll want these pests stamped out, and the best way to do that is with one swift stomp."

He smacked his fist against his other palm.

Everyone else was silent.

The Emperor had ordered his chancellors to resolve this matter and not bother him with it again. If Gao Qiu decided to whine about it to the Lord of Heaven, *Gao Qiu* wasn't the one who would feel the political fallout. Fortunately, the other chancellors wanted that as little as Cai Jing did, which gave him another angle.

Before he could begin to leverage it, a shout and a noise sounded at the front of the hall.

Cai Jing looked over, irritated. A messenger bowed his way in, bent nearly double with the cringing of someone who knew he risked death with his entrance.

"Who dares!" the Chancellor of the Ministry barked, and the messenger flinched. "This conference was not to be disturbed."

"What is it?" Cai Jing called. "Speak, man."

"Forgive me, Your Excellencies," the man said, hunched in perpetual obeisance. "There has been an incident at the Pit. A prisoner has escaped—"

Minister Duan reacted fastest, to his credit, leaping to his feet and dashing for the doors to the hall. "Marshal! With me, now!"

Gao Qiu's languid expression went wide with clear shock at being called into action before he scrambled to his feet and followed. Cai Jing and half of the others had begun to rise as well, most of them paralyzed partway from their seats in a disorganized confusion.

Including Cai Jing. The Pit—the Pit—*it can't be. Impossible.*

He spent a precious handful of heartbeats refusing to believe what he already knew to be truth. Then, cursing himself for the delay, he hurried to the front of the hall himself, ignoring his fish-mouthed colleagues.

The doors had been flung wide by Minister Duan's exit, and he and Gao Qiu were visible grabbing weapons back and racing down the steps into streets that bristled with burgeoning chaos. The generals, who were not technically of the Bianliang garrison and had hesitated in whether to race after their superiors, rushed past Cai Jing to join in the fray, leaving only the other two chancellors cowering in the hall. Cai Jing reached out and grabbed the messenger by the layered cloth collar of his uniform.

"Who was this prisoner?" *You know, you know who it is . . .* "Who escaped? Speak as if your life depends on it!"

The man's teeth clattered. "I d-d-don't—forgive me, Grand Chancellor, I don't know yet. The Guard at the Pit—they were all killed, every man. Nobody has been able to say what happened—"

"Was it a woman!"

"I don't know, I swear it! Please, Grand Chancellor, I can go to find out—"

Cai Jing shoved him away. The messenger cringed to the ground, falling to kneel and grovel against the stone stair, but Cai Jing had already set the man from his mind. He swept out and down toward the street, his steps quickening with urgency.

He didn't bother to gather his daggers from the guards. The vials of poison in his sleeves he had neglected to consider weapons and never surrendered to them.

He must get to the building he had assigned to this research, the heart of the project he had fought so hard for and that he truly believed might someday save the Empire. If the priestess had escaped . . . correction, he must assume she had escaped. The least damaging result was if the Guard killed her. He could not count on it. The second least damaging was if she escaped the city.

If she fought her way back to find her husband . . .

If the two of them took this opportunity for a monstrous assault on the research Cai Jing had so carefully, beautifully curated . . .

That was not an outcome Cai Jing could permit.

The priestess must be stopped.

Wu Yong yanked Lin Chong and Fan Rui back and between two buildings as a full platoon of soldiers raced past, armor clattering and swords in hand.

Lin Chong took a breath and tried to concentrate, to see if she could feel the presence of the Guardsmen as she'd increasingly been able to do when practicing with Chao Gai. But she could barely stand and keep the spear hefted without swaying; any further skills seemed beyond her right now.

At least she could still fight. As long as she could stand, she could fight . . .

Not that it would save them.

"We won't make it." She let the wall take her weight while peering through chinks in the masonry of its corner. More Guardsmen at the intersection they had just run from. "We need to go back. We might be boxed in already."

Wu Yong put a hand on her shoulder. "Sister Lin, if your strength is flagging, we can have you run for the wall, and no shame in it—"

Lin Chong shrugged off the gesture. *Yes, there would be.*

With their three skills together they raced toward near-certain oblivion; without her it would be absolute. Returning to the mountain and reporting that she had lost not only Liangshan's chief strategist but their only hope of defense against Cai Jing—the object of their entire Bianliang mission—it was unthinkable. Wu Yong knew it.

"You know my objections," Lin Chong said coldly. "We need a plan."

A plan to avoid death by sheer numbers. Three people, charging into the inner city with the Guard on full alert. This was no strategy—only arrogance.

"How far do your scholar's skills extend?" Wu Yong said.

"To nothing, right now. I . . . it comes and goes." She was ashamed to admit it. What use was this new talent without access?

Wu Yong turned to Fan Rui. "How thoroughly could you hide us?"

"Hiding is easy," cackled the priestess. "Dust is everywhere."

"If we could find an apothecary, we could get you more than dust," the Tactician muttered. "With only what's available in the streets, how far does your materials skill reach?"

Fan Rui's fingers twitched at her sides. "I shout, the dust obeys. It hears me."

Wu Yong gripped Lin Chong's elbow. "If the range of her skills is only the distance a person can shout, we can't use cover for long. Any cloud that hides us will only bring the rest of the Guard to surround that space. We would need to obscure the whole inner city to get through."

"We can't fight our way through, either." They would be impaled on sword and spear within moments. Even if they took ten times their number in Guardsmen with them, it would be no win. "You suggested splitting. We should. As a diversion. I can lead them away."

Wu Yong's eyebrows went up. "You're rather eager to throw yourself on a sword, Sister Lin. I prefer not to create martyrs."

"Then what?"

The Tactician's eyes went between them, then over Lin Chong's shoulder to the street. "A diversion, yes. But it's not one of us who will play the bait."

A few moments later, the dust began swirling up in feathering eddies from the cracks between the stones of the streets. No one noticed at first—any civilians on the streets had scurried from the multiplying Guardsmen to hide behind walls and doors, and the soldiers themselves were stirring up enough dust with their boots not to notice. At first.

Until it became inescapable.

The dust simmered up until it was at knee level, then above that. Some of the rushing Guardsmen began to trip; others batted at the rising cloud as if they could smack it away from themselves. Yells of consternation rose up as they tried to figure out what was going on.

Either not all of them knew a Renxia priestess was one of the fugitives, or the connection took a while to penetrate. Longer than Lin Chong expected. The dust rose thicker and higher until the men began to cough and panic, and only as it swallowed their heads and they began to stumble and flee did the shout gain traction: *"It's the priestess! Find her!"*

"Good," Wu Yong murmured, watching from the alley. "Now send it away."

Fan Rui muttered and stirred her hands in front of her. Her fingers stretched straight at angles with so much tension they near bent back on themselves. The enormous dust storm began to sweep down the street, picking up speed as it poured away from them. Guardsmen spun in disorientation as it rolled off them and left them behind.

Again, it took longer than Lin Chong expected for the obvious conclusion. Finally, the rallying cry came down, *"She's hidden somewhere in the dust! Find her! Find her!,"* the orders echoing through the streets and Guardsmen reorienting to pound after the cloud.

Truly, the army lacked discipline.

"Let's go," Wu Yong said. "Carefully, now."

They slipped out of their hiding place and hurried down the street, keeping their passage behind the backs of the rallying Guardsmen.

"Where to?" hissed Lin Chong.

"His heart in the knowledge," Fan Rui murmured. "My Thunder God, he will be there today. Oh, my husband . . ."

She turned and began striding at a rapid clip, not looking behind her to make sure her companions followed. Lin Chong and Wu Yong matched her pace a step behind, weapons out, eyes scanning for danger.

They made it three streets into the central district before they turned the next corner and ran straight into an entire platoon of Guardsmen.

The soldiers skidded to stop their rapid march, but their shock didn't last long. They rushed to surround Lin Chong and her companions at a few paces away, spears and swords bristling in a deadly cage and cutting off escape. Among them, in the lead, stood the Minister of War himself, his cape billowing behind him and his hand locked upon the god's tooth around his neck.

Lin Chong barely registered his presence. Because beside him, in an embroidered coat and loping along with the naked steel of his drawn sword gleaming in the sun, was Gao Qiu.

CHAPTER 24

Wu Yong did not, at first, assume they were finished.

They had two excellent fighters—even if Sister Lin was slightly battered—and a priestess of the Renxia who had just murdered far more soldiers than this in a truly worshipful display of blood. Wu Yong had been pleasantly impressed. Even though Fan Rui had used up the volatile materials of the apothecary they had brought her, they should have had a chance . . .

Until Wu Yong recognized the man leading the Guard against them.

The War Minister.

He wasn't familiar enough for the connections to be instant, but it only took a moment to put together who he must be—or to know what the man must be gripping in his left hand. The Minister was famous for his possession of a god's tooth. One on the weaker side, as such artifacts went, but a "weaker god's tooth" was like a "less predatory tiger" . . .

Both would devour a mere human.

Two options. Run or fight. Running would only get them spears in their backs.

Before Wu Yong could move, Fan Rui threw back her head and screeched at the sky, then flung her hands forward. The dust storm flew from every direction and streaked straight at the soldiers.

Minister Duan kept his left hand on his god's tooth. The other held a two-edged sword, and he thrust out both fist and sword as if warding off a demon. A wind surged up from behind him, flapping sleeves and skirts of armor and whipping the Minister's hair about his hard-planed face. Wind met dust, and Fan Rui's attack scattered in all directions, pattering to nothing.

Before he had finished the motion, Wu Yong pounded forward, sword raised. *Take him by surprise—*

The move failed. Laughingly, obviously, when Wu Yong had cleared barely half the distance.

Minister Duan spun up and forward on his mighty wind, flying into the clash, his sword executing perfectly with the movement, his cape flaring like wings behind him. Wu Yong tried to skid around and attack at an angle, but the Minister's sword stabbed in and knocked the attempt aside like it was the flail of a child.

Wu Yong twisted to recover. Not fast enough. The Minister's foot lashed out in a kick so fast it was like the flash of water flung through the air—seen but unstoppable.

The impact was a blast of colors and light. The world flipped a dozen times before the crack of a collision against the ground, limbs and joints smacking and bruising.

Dust and stone. It was difficult to keep a grip on the sword. Wu Yong tried to push back up and gagged, coughing blood onto the paving stones.

A shadow flickered above, and Wu Yong fell into a roll, swinging to ward off the coming death blow. But sword met air, with the whisper of a cape flickering aside. Wu Yong dredged up every reserve of spirit and flipped up, feet slapping the right way down with only a little sway—a spin to see where the Minister had gone—

But the other soldiers closed in, their steel a crowd of deadly spikes. Wu Yong parried only just in time, but found more flocking from behind, no space to retreat . . . Blade after blade, they kept coming, cornering their prey, hungry to pin and kill.

Wu Yong kicked off the ground and leapt vertically, high, so high, climbing ever so briefly over the sword blades swiping below, a spear stabbing through so close that Wu Yong's boot kicked aside the haft. The small moment of weightlessness at the top of the jump was enough to look out across their heads . . .

Sister Lin, hair and bloody clothes flying, had knocked the Imperial Marshal to the ground, his sword lost off to the side. He gazed up in glazed horror as her spear whipped back into the arrow-straight drive of a killing blow.

The Minister of War barreled into her from the side, spinning them both in a whirling cyclone of bodies and weapons into the wall of the nearest building. Wood cracked and several shingles fell off the roof.

Wu Yong had no time to see more. Dropping back into the fray was an instant storm of fury, blows too fast and hard for anything but pure reaction. Wu Yong blocked eight, twelve, sixteen times.

A hit broke through, a tag to the small of the back, then to the shoulder. A spear haft hooked around horizontally from behind, jerking hard enough to choke. Wu Yong tried to writhe out from behind it but lost footing against the street. Hands clamped down, too many hands, twisting Wu Yong's arms back while blades came up fast and close enough to prick at the sensitive skin of neck and chin.

Wu Yong's head stiffened upward, fingers losing the sword hilt. The blade clattered to the stone.

The cacophony of the fight had dampened enough for Minister Duan's voice to be heard shouting over all the rest of them. *"Alive! Take them alive. They must go before the Emperor!"*

The Emperor?

Think fast, think fast—we must make it back to Liangshan—I shall not allow this mission to fail—

Had they failed already? *No. Brook no thought of it. There's always a way. You have lived your life knowing there is always a way.*

The Guardsmen manhandled Wu Yong to the side of the street. Slammed up against a building, limbs held fast in place, Wu Yong managed to contort enough to get eyes on the situation. A dazed Fan Rui was being held securely by more Guardsmen, one of them behind her with a gloved hand clamped tight over her mouth. Her eyes rolled wildly above it. And to Wu Yong's right . . .

Even more soldiers trapped Lin Chong. The former arms instructor still fought, weapon lost now, blood sheeting down the side of her head and matting her hair against her neck. Every time the soldiers pinned one limb, she yanked another free to strike out viciously at whichever skull or groin or hand was closest.

But it was over. The cursing Guardsmen managed to hold her, finally, pinning her against the wall next to Wu Yong.

The man wearing the surcoat of an Imperial Marshal ambled over, wiping blood from his face and neck with a fine hand cloth. He turned and spat bloody sputum into the street. At least one tooth came with it.

Wu Yong winced.

The marshal came right up to Lin Chong's face, his sharp profile staring down into her wild one. With a grunt, Lin Chong made another good attempt to yank herself free, sending one of the Guardsmen sprawling before they subdued her.

"Former Arms Instructor Lin Chong," the marshal purred. "Traitor to the Empire and fugitive from the law. I shall take very great pleasure in witnessing your execution. I think I shall request to carry it out myself. By the sword, or perhaps the dog's head guillotine would be most appropriate. You are only a jumped-up peasant, after all."

He reached out and brushed his fingernails almost silkily against the skin of her neck.

Lin Chong snapped her head forward, sudden and brutal, her forehead slamming into the marshal's mouth and nose. He reeled back, cursing wildly, and spun with instant fury to slap her across the face. Then he grabbed a sword off one of his men and struck her in the side of the head with the pommel. Again. Then again.

"You *dare*!" Spittle flew, peppering his men with blood, every word a shriek and accompanied by another blow. "You dare—you *dare*! Sniveling wench!"

Wu Yong struggled against the Guardsmen, kicking and shouting, but could move none of them for more than a breath. It was Minister Duan who pulled the marshal away, dragging him back by the arm.

"Calm yourself, Marshal Gao. The criminals will see justice. Calm yourself."

Lin Chong's head lolled against the wall, her face a mass of blood and bruising.

So this was *that* marshal. Gao Qiu. The marshal who had so conveniently shredded the lives of both Lin Chong and Yang Zhi. What a perfect epitome of everything that could be wrong with man or Empire.

Wu Yong mentally added him to the list of people who must be excised. For the health of the land and the people.

The Minister of War released Gao Qiu, who did not approach Lin Chong again but sneered at her from afar, wiping his bleeding face on his sleeve. He seemed to have lost his hand cloth. Lin Chong sagged, too still, unable to provoke him further.

Minister Duan scanned the rest of them. "You are the priestess, aren't you," he said to Fan Rui. "The one working for Honorable Grand Chancellor Cai Jing on his, eh, his little project. Keep a tight hold of her hands and face," he added to his men.

"Throw them in the Pit," Gao Qiu spat. "Throw them all in the Pit! We'll schedule a public execution within the day."

Wu Yong thought fast, read the Minister's contemplative stance, and shouted out above the soldiers' heads. "Go on, then. Do it!"

Minister Duan turned. Studied Wu Yong with the attention of a man who considered before he acted.

"You're awfully eager to be locked away, Soldier. Marshal Gao, I think it would be wise to discover how these criminals escaped with such—thoroughness—before we lock them into the same place, don't you?" Without waiting for a response, he turned to the man on his right. "Lieutenant. Get me an update from the Pit. See if they know yet exactly how this ill-advised jailbreak was achieved."

The man saluted smartly and hurried off. Minister Duan continued to survey them thoughtfully, while Gao Qiu swiped more at his bleeding face with muttered curses. Whatever happened next, it was clearly the Minister's decision, not the marshal's.

If Wu Yong could tweak things just a little further . . . reading people was a longtime skill, and this Minister was reasonable, and clever, with a clear head and a strong loyalty to his duty. Exactly the type of rare official the Empire could be proud of. His cleverness could be used for their benefit.

"Do whatever you like," Wu Yong called, purposely returning to an accent closer to the upper classes, a more educated cadence. "Our execution will be only martyrdom. You cannot stop this!"

The Minister's eyebrows beetled together, and he took a step forward. "Stop what, Soldier?"

Wu Yong made a show of not answering, lips pressed together, nose raised in fierce arrogance.

Don't oversell. He must think the conclusion is his own . . .

The scene teetered on the point of a needle.

"You escaped in a way we have not yet determined, and then you come to re-enter the heart of the city," the Minister said slowly—piecing together the facts, fitting bits of the puzzle others might have missed. Oh, yes. He was just as clever as Wu Yong had hoped. "We also have no word as to whether you had any compatriots who may be using you only as a diversion . . . for all we know here, you may have been on a mission to assassinate the Emperor himself, may he live forever."

Gao Qiu looked up at his superior in resentful shock. *Ignoramus*—clearly not one used to thinking ahead of immediate satisfaction. But Minister Duan hadn't taken his gaze from Wu Yong, nor his hand from the god's tooth. Wu Yong met his eyes, betraying nothing. *He wants us contained under threat of his god's tooth—yes, perfect. If he thinks we may hide an even greater danger . . .*

"No missteps can be made here," the Minister announced. "I shall not let these prisoners out of my sight until my superiors have determined the best course. The chancellors must be consulted."

He turned to his men. "Bind the prisoners, and stay alert. There may be others."

The Guardsmen shoved Wu Yong forward, twisting the ropes

tight enough to bite into the skin and turning every elbow and shoulder joint to fiery discomfort. Wu Yong suppressed any expression. *Good, good . . . now for the last turn of the card . . .*

"I can already tell you what the Emperor will want." Gao Qiu spat blood in the street again, his words not quite a sneer. "We execute traitors here."

"And so we shall. But we may want more information first." The Minister raised his voice. "Follow and bring them. I know where Chancellor Cai Jing will be."

Yes! Benevolence smiles! It may be a narrow crack, but good fortune still shines through.

Of course, they still had the Minister's god's tooth to contend with, a barely conscious Lin Chong, and a rapidly multiplying guard escort. Rather large wrinkles, but if Wu Yong could find a way around them . . . the ever-so-responsible Minister of War was about to take them exactly where they had been aiming to go.

The game wasn't over yet.

Liangshan. Cai Jing was planning to use the god's fangs against Liangshan. Before yesterday, the name would have meant little to Lu Junyi. She might have recalled a whisper of it here or there—rumors that the mountain and its swamp were becoming infamous as the stronghold of bandits—but so were many such mountains and swamps in the rural stretches of the Empire.

After reading the page Lin Chong had brought last night—the frightful, soul-searing page—she knew a great deal more of what Liangshan was. What they thought they were.

What they thought the Empire was.

More than that, she knew that Lin Chong was among their members now. She knew Lu Da always had been. And the poetic descriptions had been signed—boldly, so boldly—by none other than the poet Song Jiang.

A blight on the Empire, Cai Jing had called them, among many other colorful names.

Lu Junyi forced her mouth around orders, her tongue as thick as if she'd bitten through a fistful of numbing peppers. Servants and scholars moved to do her bidding. She was not even certain what she asked for.

She took a moment to lean against one of the long stone countertops, its coolness soaking against her palms. *What am I doing? What should I be doing?* It all felt like a dream, one funneling to a single point with no escape.

Shouts went up outside, and some of the supervising Guardsmen pounded out of the building. Lu Junyi noticed, but distantly, like a far-off sea breeze whispering against her skin. Her mind and heart were too full to wonder.

Heavily, she peeled herself upright and set back to work. If she concentrated on her duties—that was the answer. Don't think outside of what she had to complete today, in this moment. Her hands fumbled for ink and brush. Lists. She would make lists. Ensure she was not forgetting anything, not making any mistakes that would get her killed, her or Ling Zhen or Fan Rui or any of the scholars or soldiers who might become Cai Jing's next example. Her hands shook, grinding out the lampblack unevenly and spilling it across the inkstone.

Servants came up and bowed for instructions. Lu Junyi gave them. Her souls floated outside herself, refusing to feel.

Ling Zhen had not looked up from his work, sequestered off in a corner with the lodestone and the last two of the god's fangs they had here on site. With Cai Jing's deadline they'd had to jump straight to the artifacts themselves—ludicrous, like learning to walk one day and leaping a gorge the next. Four days, Cai Jing had said, until he needed the god's fangs to murder Lu Junyi's friends . . .

She'd retrieved both the remaining pieces for Ling Zhen, as he claimed the need to sense the reaction of the altered one to the other. Using tongs, he ran their purified ore over their chosen god's fang again and again, keeping its partner carefully separate, all with a single-minded intensity as if demons dogged his hands. Guards surrounded him as usual, but this time their alert was even more heightened, since he worked with the most precious of their materials.

Lu Junyi should check in with him. Pull him away for a moment to consult, make sure she was accounting for everything he might need on the road. Ask him to pause with her and plan. The volatility of the items they transported—and the goal Cai Jing forced them toward, to make this weapon work or risk destroying so many innocents—on top of Lin Chong and Lu Da and Song Jiang and the others the Chancellor targeted—

The dizzy, impossible thought reached her, that if an accident happened on the road, and they never reached the mountain . . . if she *made* an accident happen on the road and they never reached Liangshan . . .

The fact that she would even have such a notion stole breath and thought.

No. Even if she would—even if she could—scholar's stone and god's fangs were too unstable to destroy intentionally without risking unfathomable loss of life. *I loved Lin Chong like a sister—but the reality of it is that she is a bandit—is it not? She chose that life; she knew what she risked.* Would it not be unforgivable to let the Empire's ire against the mountain and its brigands extend to the blameless countryside?

She hated that thought, too.

Not for the first time, it crossed her mind that the only noble choice might be to go home and drink a draft of some delicate poison tea, lie down, and let an endless sleep come on her. Unfortunately that had the same result as her failure: more of the Empire's citizens massacred, and on her head.

Only duty remained.

Lu Junyi slipped through the ranks of Guardsmen to join Ling Zhen. The Thunder God did not acknowledge her. She busied her hands behind him, on the basins that still held her own paltry attempts at alchemy. Unhelpful, all, but still too dangerous to dispose of casually, with mercury and orpiment, tortoise shell and vermillion and sulfur and more, all combined within their depths.

She pressed the back of one hand against her forehead. Fan Rui had brushed off her struggles with these—rightfully. They all knew the priestess's best ideas were what drove them; Lu Junyi's contribution was best confined to leadership and management. Enough scholarship to understand, but not to discover.

Still . . .

Some sensation tickled her mind. One that disappeared if she attempted to look at it directly, but one she couldn't shake.

Have I missed something . . . ? But what?

Everything the priestess had said about what they prioritized had seemed to make sense with what Lu Junyi knew. Fan Rui had been the one to mention these elixirs in the first place, but then she had so quickly discarded the attempt as unlikely to be of help . . . Even when ordered to, she'd dragged at instructing Lu Junyi, dancing instead with her heavy metals and lightning and lodestone. She'd claimed basic elixirs were nowhere near as promising as the far more dangerous methods, and indeed it had seemed to be so; the priestess had decades of instinct . . .

Lu Junyi had done these herself on the principle of efficient exploration, and upon testing them with the scholar's stone, Fan Rui's sense had proven right. Why, then, did Lu Junyi feel as if she'd put a foot wrong on shifting sands?

She set aside the ill-fitted thoughts and turned to inventory the lodestone spread across Ling Zhen's workspace, taking notes with brush and ink. "I shall tell them this packs up last," Lu Junyi murmured to him. "We can continue till the last moment. Are you all right, Scholar Ling?"

He looked up. His eyes were black pools of pure fear.

Lu Junyi nearly took a step back. She reached out a hand to stop his fevered movement with the lodestone. "Scholar Ling—"

That was when she realized the second god's fang he worked on was far too close, within the field of the lodestone, just the same as its partner.

She froze. Her hand stilled where it reached out, brushing the little old scholar's arm.

A mistake. He must have made a mistake. But she had never noted any carelessness from him, never, and now his expression had gone wide and naked and cracked, realizing she saw, and he knew, he knew—but what was his aim? Did he attempt to turn *both* god's fangs into energy sinks? Perhaps as a way to make one more of the artifacts harmless, only usable with a second, so that . . . so that . . . what?

Such an act would have no effect. Cai Jing had more of the god's fangs—albeit limited, but it would be no successful sabotage.

Sabotage—

If Ling Zhen meant sabotage . . .

Lu Junyi's frozen thoughts spun into frantic, shattering denial. Only one other possibility made sense. No—it must be something else; she must be missing something—

Because the one possibility she could think of was—was appalling, unthinkable—the one possibility that made sense was that the lodestone did not work fully, would never work fully, and *Fan Rui and Ling Zhen both knew.*

They both knew, and this had all been one long ruse to string her along with information that made just enough sense until husband and wife could complete their true objective. An objective that wouldn't be limited only to sabotaging the value of the research.

If the lodestone didn't work—then right now Ling Zhen's worktable held the means to destroy them all.

"Scholar Ling—" She should have called immediately for the guards who stood next to them. Her sensibilities were taking too long to catch up with her eyes, danger shrieking in the back of her head for far too long before she could flatten it into words. "Scholar Ling, why do you . . ."

Several of the soldiers must have caught her tone, and they turned, beginning to rouse to the fact that something was wrong.

At that moment, however, the ruckus outside reached a sudden fever. Guards poured in, Chancellor Cai Jing in their midst, descending on the room and barking out orders. "I want men surrounding this building ten deep. Add another perimeter outside the courtyard gates. You! Take him and bind him!"

Ling Zhen's guards lunged forward instantly, no hesitation left. They dragged him back, yanking his arms behind him. Lu Junyi stumbled against the table in something that felt like relief but wasn't.

"No!" Usually so cooperative, Ling Zhen tore against their grip in a frenzy. "Not now—let go!"

"No chance of that, seditionist," Cai Jing said, and spoke to the guards. "If his criminal wife appears, we must be ready. Keep a blade on him."

One of the soldiers obediently grabbed Ling Zhen's hair and placed a sword up against his throat. The little old man arched away from it, sweating and hyperventilating, and Lu Junyi felt trapped in a nightmare.

His wife—did that mean Fan Rui had attempted an escape?

Had they both been planning this from the beginning?

Lu Junyi couldn't take her eyes off the double god's fangs. Bile collected at the back of her throat. Cai Jing had not yet noticed, and if Lu Junyi spoke, she would seal Ling Zhen's death sentence, as sure as if she'd opened his throat herself.

As he might have been about to do to her . . .

The hubbub around the building hadn't died down. Guardsmen pounded back and forth, sealing off entrances that had already seemed unassailable. No one looking their way. No one suspicious of a threat here in their midst.

Ling Zhen and Fan Rui—if she had escaped, could this instead have been some part of a larger plan that merely aimed to secure their freedom? If the lodestone worked as they claimed after all, if Ling Zhen believed their reversed god's fang to be ready and that all he need do was snatch one of the others to have power so great he could drive through the guards and run, along with his wife the moment she burst in here . . .

Except he had been too sloppy. He had not been applying the stone in a way that agreed with how it was supposed to work. How any of it was supposed to work. Besides, when Lu Junyi had caught his eyes, he'd frozen like a rabbit in the path of a hunter.

He knew. He knew what he did.

Her gaze flickered back up to Ling Zhen's, above where he was held at swordpoint, his eyes rolling in the guise of a strangled animal until they locked fast on hers. He glanced down at his workspace, then back up to her, and he seemed to be begging.

More commotion sounded outside. One of the Guardsmen raced in and bowed to Cai Jing with a fast salute. "Minister Duan has caught them, Your Excellency!"

Caught whom?

On the heels of the message, the soldiers at one of the doors parted, and Lu Junyi's legs went numb beneath her.

The Guardsmen who entered were holding captive Fan Rui, Lin Chong, and the so-named Tactician who had visited Lu Junyi's house only the night before. The Tactician was the only one of them mostly upright and walking, though bound and flanked by soldiers like the others. Fan Rui was held fastest, her hands and mouth fastened tight, at least a dozen weapons trained in a careful circle around her and with the Minister of War—the *Minister of War*—towering up behind her. Marshal Gao stalked alongside, considerably more bloodied than his superior, his face twisted in a scowl.

Two other soldiers dragged Lin Chong. She seemed barely conscious, her face an almost unrecognizable mass of bruising and blood, her hair and clothes a tangled mess.

Why? Sister Lin, why did you come back and do this?

Lin Chong had been free—free, and away, and innocent of any true crime, and yet she'd returned to stab the Empire in the eye and become the very criminal they accused her of—*why?*

This must have been the "more urgent business" she and her colleague had been planning, what they had so obliquely referred to while trying to convince Lu Junyi to join them in treason. She couldn't even fathom how they had known of Fan Rui, or had any motive to break her from prison.

"Grand Chancellor," the War Minister declared, stepping forward to salute and bow to Cai Jing. "Information is still being gathered, so I have not called off the search. Catching these three is but a small contribution, but I thought it best to bring them before you and my other superiors immediately, as their criminal intent should be divined by those with greater foresight than I. I have dispatched messengers to have the other chancellors meet us."

Something was happening that Lu Junyi did not understand—the Minister's speech had been flattering and humble, if also clearly abdicating responsibility for some cryptic reason, but Cai Jing's face had begun to shade with fury. Not at Fan Rui's escape, but at the Minister.

"Marshal Gao," Cai Jing said, not taking his eyes from the War Minister. "Be so good as to meet the esteemed chancellors and accompany them to White Tiger Hall. Tell them we shall conference there instead."

Marshal Gao glanced between his superiors. Wisely deciding that he didn't want to stand in the way of their spitting match, he ducked out and left with no protest.

"Now, Minister Duan." Cai Jing's tone went silky, dripping acid beneath its purr. "Keeping these prisoners within the oversight of your god's tooth is shrewdly done. Far better, however, would have been to contain them within the walls of a prison while you provided that oversight."

The Minister's eyes narrowed. Cai Jing might be his superior, but some power struggle reverberated between them—or possibly between Cai Jing and the man one rank above the Minister, who was one of Cai Jing's fellow chancellors . . . the Minister of War had brought these dangerous prisoners here, to Cai Jing's secure research sanctum, like a challenge . . .

"This is your pursuit, Grand Chancellor," the Minister answered, his tone pegged exactly to what was respectful—no more and no less. "I merely thought to bring to you what's yours, as it is not for me to say what should be done with your things."

The tension stretched taut and thick. Cai Jing seemed to swell, becoming taller, his face going to such an aggressively neutral expression that it was worse than anger. Uncertainty flickered in the Minister's eyes.

At that moment, while the Empire's eyes were on each other, Lin Chong's friend the Tactician gave a mighty yell and kicked out hard against a bench that stood before one of the countertops.

It flew across the floor as if wings took it, directly into the legs of the guards who held Ling Zhen. Hard and fast enough to send the soldiers collapsing into each other with shouts of agony.

Ling Zhen did not wait a blink.

He tore from their grasps and lunged forward. The sword that had threatened him left a long slash along his collar and shoulder, but he dove through, straight for the god's fangs.

Lu Junyi was closest. She tried to move—to stop him? Even she didn't know. She wasn't fast enough.

He snatched both of the god's fangs off his worktable with his bare hands.

Reflection. Insufficiently altered by the lodestone, they would reflect against each other, over and over to infinity—

His motive was not escape. Not escape.

Energy pulsed out from the little old scholar, sending Lu Junyi tumbling to the floor and the soldiers tripping backward against each other. Ling Zhen straightened slowly, one god's fang in each fist, a white brilliance beating in the air between them.

"No! Stop!" Lu Junyi threw a forearm in front of her eyes, the glow had become so searing. She tried to claw her way back up toward him and fell again, though what she could do at this point—what anybody could do, what even Ling Zhen could do—"Run—everyone run!"

They wouldn't get far enough. Nobody would.

The soldiers began moving in panicked confusion, to protect the Chancellor and the Minister, to drag their prisoners away and escape themselves . . . but they moved as if drugged, flopping in abortive attempts, limbs fighting the very air. Even if they had been able to run—the calculations her scholars had done on the few much smaller tests they'd managed, the numbers all flashed through Lu Junyi's mind and she knew. Nobody could move that fast. Nobody could escape.

Ling Zhen planned to murder them all, them and all of Cai Jing's research and also Cai Jing himself—this was about to be an assassination of *a Grand Chancellor of the Empire*—

The explosion might even reach the Imperial Palace itself. The Emperor.

This was not Ling Zhen alone, either. The realization cracked in Lu Junyi's memory—the messages left by Fan Rui. What Lu Junyi had taken to be nonsense rambling . . . *From childhood I studied classics and history.*

It was the first line of a poem by Song Jiang.

Lu Junyi hadn't recognized it. It was not a poem Song Jiang had ever performed, only passed about among friends who gasped and giggled at its audacity. Its rebelliousness.

Fan Rui had spoken of dye in a river. In the poem, the river was dyed with blood.

Ling Zhen and Fan Rui, they had planned this together. Without ever being permitted to speak to one another. They had waited only for the right moment.

Ling Zhen had known Cai Jing would return today.

Light and sound rippled between the god's fangs, faster and brighter and higher, the hum beyond hearing until the air vibrated with it. How long before it broke free—before the god's fangs could no longer contain it? Ling Zhen's body had begun to twitch, racked with waves of tension, the surface of him becoming brightness chased with shadow and flashing in colors too fast to see. His flesh convulsed like worms burrowed in its depths. The god's fangs were consuming him from the inside—just as they had the men at Anfeng—the only question becoming how much destruction he could wreak with them before they did . . .

Then he would die, martyred for his cause. Fan Rui would die. Lin Chong and her friend would die. Lu Junyi would die . . .

Grand Chancellor Cai Jing would die too, no doubt as intended.

Every one of Lu Junyi's senses rose to a piercing scream. The energy seemed to saturate the air, filling not only their eyes and ears but teeth and mouths and buzzing across every patch of exposed skin. An acrid scent burned their nostrils with a charged sharpness. Several of the Guardsmen were trying to fight toward Ling Zhen but kept skidding and slithering to the floor, and when Lu Junyi tried to move, her limbs pushed as though through thick syrup, miring them in time.

She was still the closest to him. In splintered desperation, she pushed up and shoved herself forward.

For all her training in the martial arts over so many years, the move was graceless, slow, through a reality that had gone heavy.

She didn't lurch straight at Ling Zhen. Instead, she clawed for the shelves behind him, grasping for one of the basins that sat holding her own sad pretense at alchemy. The too-heavy air dragged at her movements, straining her hands far more than seemed possible for such a small pot.

She heaved her momentum around and flung herself at Ling Zhen in a lumbering tackle. The pot came with her like a clumsy weapon, and she aimed its contents at the god's fangs, hoping for some effect—any at all.

The liquid mostly hit Ling Zhen instead. So did she. Everything seemed to be happening in stalled increments and yet also at a fever pitch. She collided with Ling Zhen, and the impact of every elbow and knee crashing into the other went magnified in isolation, reverberating a thousand times before they smashed hard into the floor together. The pot shattered, spattering them both with its shards, along with the remainder of the elixir that had already sloshed to soak Ling Zhen.

The god's fangs skittered out among the mess.

A dazed Ling Zhen tried to grope for them. He wasn't moving faster than anyone else. Lu Junyi kicked out with her foot, and the drunken motion connected, sending the two tiny artifacts skimming away, under one of the heavy counters and out of his reach.

The painful vibrations in the air suddenly undulated. Not

much—only granting relief for half a moment before another wave came, but then a dip again—the acceleration had eased, somehow; she could feel it. The energy still mired the atmosphere but had stopped building . . .

Lu Junyi's mind worked too slowly. God's teeth needed the contact of skin to be wielded—Ling Zhen would not be able to keep pushing their escalation—but that power still oscillated, now disconnected from him. Nor would breaking the contact have unbonded him completely; the men from Anfeng had proven that when they flung the god's fangs aside and still burned . . .

Except Ling Zhen wasn't burning.

His skin had gone raw red or rotted black in places, but the spasms had ceased, and he gasped against the stone floor of the research building, in pain but not death.

The revelation plunged through Lu Junyi like she'd been submerged in an icy lake. Every time they had attempted to infuse a god's fang to make it more stable, they had failed. They had not thought to consider that like a god's tooth, the fang had to be bonded to a person.

A person would always be the other half of its power.

Infusing *the person* was the secret they had missed. The secret to control over the weapon.

Or—partial control. Two god's fangs still magnified each other beyond any attempt at stability. Ling Zhen could no longer stop this, even if he desired it. She had saved him, momentarily, but not the rest of them.

The rule, the rule of god's teeth, always, was that their power would never dissipate, the energy must go somewhere. She may have stopped his chain reaction early, may have prevented a city-ending catastrophe—maybe—possibly. Might have bought them a few more heartbeats of time before it all tore free. No more than that.

"Get out," Lu Junyi tried to warn again, but it was as if her lungs had been squeezed flat of breath. "Run . . ."

She tried to suit her own words to action by pushing herself away from Ling Zhen. Moving had become easier, just a little, enough to shove herself in between the pulsating beats, to her feet, trying again for shambling movement. The Thunder God curled on the floor, not following. The guards around the room were likewise struggling to stand back up from where they had tumbled against walls and corners and each other, through the all-pervasive keening of their rapidly impending doom . . . it had begun to build again, the god's fangs reflecting in their nightmare destruction, now desultory and untargeted, and almost ready to fling loose, she could feel it, they could all feel it . . .

A shout—then more—came from the end of the room the other prisoners had been held at, but Lu Junyi's vision was too blurred to make out what was happening. *Fan Rui—maybe she can stop this. She is the only one who would have a hope.*

If she even wanted to.

The Minister of War had his hand clutching at a necklace in a pose Lu Junyi recognized—he had a god's tooth, that was right, and his other hand thrust out as if he could fight this, as if he could save them. He would have had no chance before, but maybe he could blunt this lesser explosion, if he threw everything he had into it, if his god's tooth was powerful enough. They should all run anyway, at least they had a chance now—if they ran—

Cai Jing reared up before her, shaking off the soldiers who had fallen together while trying to protect him. He tried to roar a question at her, but it was becoming hard to hear again. The vibrations were reaching a throbbing zenith—too painful, too overwhelming, to mean anything but a final release that would tear them all to nothing. Lu Junyi didn't think, only threw herself at Cai Jing, at the Grand Chancellor of the Empire, shoved him with her in a staggering stumble toward the nearest door, out of the building, onto the stones of the courtyard and then away, away, as far as possible away.

A great rumbling began to boil up from the room they had just left. Lu Junyi yanked them both down hard behind the very same plinths she had used for protection when running their experiments here before, so many times, so many dangerous times. They hit the loose stone pavement too hard, face-first against gravel and earth, filling their mouths and nostrils.

At that moment, a thunderclap roared up from Cai Jing's research building, out and over and through them in a deafening cacophony of pure destruction.

CHAPTER 25

Lin Chong was not unconscious when they were all dragged before Cai Jing. Not quite. She'd been moving under her own power, mostly, even if her boots turned against the ground every few steps and the soldiers had to drag her up from falling. Her head thumped, her vision hazy and red and partially crusted over.

The rage hurt more. Sharp and hot enough to scald her from the inside out.

Gao Qiu had bested her. Again.

She had not thought to prepare for seeing him again. She'd almost succeeded in killing him. Next time she would. She'd make sure of it.

She had met the Grand Chancellor before—enough that she recognized him through the haze of pain and blood and noise. She found she barely cared. A personage like Cai Jing once would have loomed so large in her mind, the right hand of the Emperor, nearly a god among men.

Not anymore.

He was only a man. A man who wanted to use his power to crush them.

He drifted from her attention as irrelevant. Somewhere in her semi-lucidity, something far more important was tugging at her senses. At first she couldn't tease it out. That feeling, of different worlds being too close, of ragged jigsaws of life and energy and untold layers of the vast unknown, all tickling for reach . . . like when she and Lu Da had been experimenting with the god's tooth . . .

She thought at first it must be the Minister of War's god's tooth, but she had felt that open up in the street, weaker and more . . . strained . . . than Sister Lu's. She wondered, suddenly, if she could have countered it somehow—she'd been racing for Gao Qiu, everything blurry with rage, and she hadn't tried . . .

She should have thought to try.

In any case, she could still feel his tooth, localized near the Minister as he kept his hawk's eyes on his prisoners. What she sensed now wasn't that. Something far larger, and not staying localized, but spreading throughout the room and the building and out into the adjoining streets—

Before Lin Chong could figure it out, the strange feeling rippled up into a thundering storm without any warning at all, bowling her and everyone else to the floor. She thought she heard Lu Junyi's voice, but no, that must have been a hallucination. Staggering spikes of sensation crashed through her, tearing against each other in ways that they shouldn't, searing and overwhelming.

Do it—try this time, you must try . . .

These scholar's skills, she must stop fearing to use them. *Refuse to be helpless. Defend yourself—defend your friends—defend Liangshan.*

She sucked in a breath, reaching for that inner center Chao Gai had coached her to find. The effort was weak, risible—but still, somehow, the world seemed to rebalance, ever so slightly. The intersecting energies in the room became easier to differentiate, though when she tried to push back against them, her consciousness slipped, like greased fingers against a spear haft.

She recentered. Reality bucked and heaved around her. Lin Chong concentrated not on pushing back, but on letting the chaos flow past her, a rock in a whitewater river. As if in a dream, she was able to flow to her feet. To look across the scene and see.

To her shock, Lu Junyi *was* here—she hadn't imagined it—Lu Junyi, diving at a man who stood in some brutal ecstasy, a short graybeard scholar who was the vortex of everything. Through him, out of him, burst so much that shouldn't be, uncontainable.

In that moment, Lin Chong was not only able to see, but to understand.

This was the weapon. This ugly, jagged, volatile power. So like a god's tooth, and yet not, burning higher and higher but with no aim, no direction.

Lu Junyi shouted, attacking the man before falling away. The surging intensity snapped off but didn't quiet, a lashing that had come loose in the wind.

The world sped up again, if only in staccato patches, drunk and off-kilter. Lin Chong was still standing—but she couldn't fight this, not in time, not enough. *Don't try to fight. Use it!*

Most of the guards still writhed on the floor or slumped against walls. Lin Chong gathered herself and let her mind sink further into that liminal space, resisting the urge to flinch away from the rushing, roaring *power* that poured around them. It buffeted her, spun her about until she nearly lost orientation—she breathed it in, leaned into it without resisting. It buttressed her strength even as it threatened to bowl her over and crush her.

She would not be able to maintain this for long.

All she needed was long enough to save them.

Riding the borrowed wave, Lin Chong let her body fall into moves of long-trained comfort. She spun and slid into what was almost a full split, her arms still bound behind her but landing exactly against the hilt of a dagger carried at one of the soldiers' waists. Flip it up, free herself. Wu Yong was attempting to use the chaos to stagger upright, to writhe away from the guards. Lin Chong whipped in and the Tactician was freed as well.

Lin Chong instinctively pushed a bubble of protection around them both—fragile, imperfect, but enough to regain sense and balance.

Cries and movement had begun to trickle up from the soldiers, where one or more managed to buck against the energies that beat at them. Some roused enough to try to flee, running for the outside in steps that yawed and stumbled. A few Guardsmen still reached for fractured duty and made as if to restrain their escaping prisoners.

Elbows met faces, newly stolen blades opening necks, and Wu Yong and Lin Chong stood free, the world tilting around them.

"We have to get out!" Lin Chong shouted. She had to shout. She wasn't even sure if Wu Yong heard.

"Help the priestess!" Wu Yong yelled back, the words tinny and very far away, though they were right in Lin Chong's ear.

The directive was unnecessary. Fan Rui had broken apart from the guards as well—enough, at least, to render her once again a capable alchemist.

Unnamed minerals flew from the shelves of the room, and the remainder of the priestess's bonds disintegrated away. Wu Yong tried to grab at her, to get her attention, shouting something indecipherable before straying too far from Lin Chong and losing balance to wheel and fall to one knee.

Fan Rui ignored everything but the man in the center of the room, the man who was on the floor now, curling in pain or shame. The Renxia priestess sucked the whole room to her in a last red wedding veil of power and death, and ran to him.

Wu Yong still tried to follow, to drag her back. Lin Chong grabbed the Tactician's arm. "We can't! Run, now!"

Wu Yong pulled in opposition, stubborn, mouth forming something like the words *we need her*—

"We'll die!" Lin Chong shouted. Her mental balance shuddered, teetering. They needed to get away—as far away as possible. Lin Chong could protect them, she thought, she hoped, but every moment she strained more, struggling against the maelstrom.

Fan Rui's scholar's skills were far in excess of Lin Chong's—she needed no aid. She had made her choice.

"Professor!" Lin Chong forced the Tactician around to face her. *"Trust me!"*

Wu Yong acquiesced, finally, tripping against Lin Chong as they began to run. The world felt out of sync, blurring while the ground came up to meet their feet too slowly and never exactly as they expected. The door seemed to loom so close and yet constantly retreating, a nightmare mirage until they were falling through it. Lin Chong had some peripheral awareness still—of Lu Junyi dragging the Chancellor out by another entrance, of the Minister of War standing strong, brave and futile with his god's tooth, so tragically unaware that he had nowhere near the power to stop this.

And of Fan Rui, twining across the man who must be her husband, adding her power to his as it soared to its peak to erupt outward in blazing brilliance. Two bright doomed butterflies choosing to stay and die, as they lay one last claim to their massive, brutal final act.

CHAPTER 26

The explosion tore out behind them like the earth being rent open, smacking Lin Chong and Wu Yong hard against their backs. Not one blast, but a world-ending thunder and then a cluster of others that only prolonged it, like a building that brought down all its neighbors before going silent. Lin Chong thrashed back against it with every piece of inner strength she could dredge up, shoving clumsy protection over them with equal parts instinct and desperation.

She managed to push back enough to keep their bones from being flattened, but still pitched forward and almost fell, saved only by her grasp of iron around the Tactician's forearm. Debris rained around them in a deadly hail. Lin Chong regained her balance and continued to haul them away, out of the courtyard, down into the road.

Run, run, farther, faster—any guards that lived would be confused and fleeing, but they still had to get to the city wall as fast as possible . . .

"Wait!" Wu Yong yanked hard enough on Lin Chong's grip to bring them stuttering to a halt. They'd made it out to a side street on the outskirts of the Imperial City, between civilization and the city walls, an empty place in these more decadent grounds near the Palace. They ran along a low curved wall that abutted only stretches of garden and rock sanctuary.

No one was about. Yet.

"We have to go back," Wu Yong panted. "We failed—"

"Of course we failed!" Lin Chong's throat was raw. Her ears rang. She didn't think she was still shouting anymore, although maybe she was. "We never had a chance. Getting away at all was a miracle!"

"We said we would bring the priestess," Wu Yong snarled. "We said we would save Liangshan. We have to go back. You can run, but with or without you—"

"She's dead!"

Lin Chong knew it to be true, a certainty straight to her bones. She hadn't felt the deaths, exactly. But she had . . . understood, somehow. Understood exactly what was happening in that moment, and what they planned, and what they did.

The same way she had understood what she saw, what she felt, what Cai Jing did in the secret, transgressive darkness of his research.

Building god's teeth. Power that snatched her breath away. Power for any who would construct it, as many times as they might tap into it. An army of gods and demons.

The Tactician leaned down against the wall, face contorted in pain, and Lin Chong could tell—it was not for any injury, but for their failure. "You're certain?"

"They sacrificed themselves. To destroy their work," Lin Chong answered. As Fan Rui had said they would.

Wu Yong scrubbed a hand over face and eyes. "That was the weapon, wasn't it? Did they? Did they manage to destroy it?"

"No." It was worse than that. Lin Chong was still piecing the memory together, a puzzle of tiles where some were enameled bright and clear and others still obscured. "I think what they . . . I think this has only helped Cai Jing's efforts. Whatever those are."

He was still alive. Lin Chong had no preternatural certainty of it, but she could not believe otherwise.

Wu Yong apparently felt the same. "He'll be coming. For us all. There must be a way—if we go back, I could get close to Cai Jing. I would—I would need only a moment—"

"Get close to Cai Jing? What lies are you telling yourself?" Lin Chong didn't try to hide her anger. "The whole city's on alert now!

You're Liangshan's chief strategist. Go ahead and tell me you think that's possible!"

"We have to protect the mountain—"

"By getting back and warning them of what we've seen!"

Wu Yong wheeled around, right in Lin Chong's face. "Fan Rui's husband could have succeeded, could have saved us, every life on the mountain. He was stopped, wasn't he? By your friend, your precious Lady Lu! She's the one who made him fail—she blocked him, she's complicit—don't tell me you didn't see!"

Lin Chong had seen. "She saved our lives as well—"

"Why? Why would she do that? We should have died there! Died, in an act that protected our kindred, and it would have been glorious! Instead we are saved only to march back and tell those we would fight and die and kill for that *we* are the reason the storm will destroy them—not only did we not prevent it, we let it free to devour them!" Wu Yong took a ragged, heaving breath. "We would have been glad to die for them. Your Lu Junyi should have known."

Lin Chong wanted to retort, but the thoughts broke brittle in her mouth before she could voice them.

Wu Yong was right. Lu Junyi should have known.

How was she involved in this? What did she think Cai Jing was building this weapon *for*?

Did I ever know you at all, my friend?

Wu Yong slumped, turned away. "There must be something. We must be able to do something . . ."

Lin Chong put a hand on the low stone wall to steady herself and closed her eyes. She thought it might be becoming easier, this access to other senses. Or perhaps the pattern was that every time she was around a god's tooth, or anything similar, her mind opened more . . .

The inner city seethed as if they had kicked over a mound only to find a hornet's nest boiling out from the ground. Guards and officials swarmed in patches, seeking leadership to follow, seeking fugitives to seize. An explosion, a great explosion near the Palace . . .

escapees from the Pit . . . the Emperor himself potentially in danger . . . Panic oozed in disorganization, and in fear-driven paranoia.

Within half a watch of the day they would lock down the whole inner city for this. Maybe all of Bianliang.

"We have to go." Lin Chong charted the distance to the city wall in her head. Wu Yong had hidden Guard uniforms for all three of them on a route out of the city, but that was on the other side of Bianliang, an impossibility away. They could try to get to the outer city and then blend with the populace, but doubtless those gates were shut fast and guarded too now.

"A fire," Wu Yong said dully. "We can start a fire as a distraction, and to throw the guards at the wall into confusion. I've done it before."

Of course you have, Lin Chong thought.

"You should return and give them this intelligence. I . . . I have failed Liangshan. I will offer to the Heavenly King to swallow my sword."

Chao Gai was unlikely to accept it, but Lin Chong stayed silent. She wasn't about to pretend she thought Wu Yong's errors here were anything less than monumental.

They should have dragged Fan Rui to the mountain with them. Convinced her, ordered her, threatened her if they had to. Instead, Wu Yong had capitulated to her fatal demands. With glee.

Lin Chong touched a hand to the side of her own head, fingertips grazing over where the flesh swelled and had begun crusting over. She didn't remember everything. Only the image of Gao Qiu's face, contorted in a snarl, as he raised his fist and came at her.

Wu Yong had made the wrong call. Disastrously wrong.

The scene scraped against itself like shattered ceramic, pieces of it not fitting in with the others. The bodies on the floor made sense and didn't, Ling Zhen's form half burned and half buried, with Fan Rui lying atop him, so still, her face so peaceful, a crimson halo expanding around them with the sheen of art.

Not real, Lu Junyi begged—of herself, of the world, of some otherworldly power she wanted to believe could invert this day, this week, these months. *Not real* . . .

The rest of the building reinforced her lack of comprehension. The entire back wall had been mutilated, transformed, with stone and brick hanging in impossible pendulums or spiraling up toward the sky as if flash-frozen. Heavy rubble piled in boulders, slabs of wall and roof larger and heavier than a human ever could have broken or lifted alone—the amount of energy that must have taken, the enormity—Lu Junyi closed burning eyes against the Guardsmen's boots that protruded out into the dust, or the odd hand and wrist of an unlucky dead soldier.

The far wing of the building, the one that had housed her scholars, had collapsed like wet paper. The store of scholar's stone that had been brought by Cai Jing—it had been locked in one of the rooms adjacent to that wing, and she thought she had felt it burst into even more destructive power, set off by the god's fangs, sucking everything surrounding into its implosion.

She did not know exactly who had been inside. Some of the men had been engaged in errands today, told only what was needed for the frantic preparations of the morning. How many had still been here?

At least Lin Chong and her friend had gone. That was good. Wasn't it? Wasn't it? Lu Junyi had stopped Ling Zhen from his more catastrophic destruction in time for them to escape, at least. She had done that; she'd helped save them. She'd *saved* them.

Just like you thought you saved Ling Zhen and Fan Rui, when you had them recruited here. You never saved them, you never came close, we were all toys this whole time, toys to be prodded and used and discarded.

Shouts and pounding feet sounded outside the courtyard, the entire Bianliang Guard rushing to their location . . .

Then a much closer footfall behind her.

She turned. Cai Jing stepped up from the ruined courtyard into the rubble.

He didn't walk as if he had just regained consciousness behind a stone plinth, dust coating every eyelash and hair of his beard, blood in a small trickle down the side of his face. He carried himself as if he occupied a great throne in a great hall and had all the power over life and death for a vast distance.

As he always had.

Numbly, Lu Junyi crouched to kneel in the debris.

He would be so angry with her, she thought mechanically. She shouldn't have—he was the Chancellor—he would be angry that she had presumed to grab him, to push him down, and he was right to be. More, she had been the one to request Ling Zhen and Fan Rui to the project in the first place—her reputation, her life, tied to them . . . Cai Jing had been right about them all along . . .

They had tried to assassinate him.

Attempting to kill the Grand Chancellor, the man one step below the Emperor, the *Emperor*—it was more than treason, more than murder, it was on the level of a coup. In any rational society, such a crime would merit execution; it couldn't not. How could Lu Junyi say they had deserved anything other than what they . . .

"Why, Lady Lu." Cai Jing sounded mildly surprised. Mildly pleased. "You have acquitted yourself as a loyal citizen of the Empire in saving your Chancellor's life. What a fascinating development."

Lu Junyi stayed slumped amid the wreckage, her eyes unfocused on the cold limbs of too many corpses. He wasn't angry—how could he not be angry?

"I believe this day is greatly to our benefit," Cai Jing continued. "What a fortuitous occurrence. If this incompetent seditionist had not attempted his ill-fated treason, we would not have been provided such an effective demonstration of this other use for the god's fangs."

Other use . . . ?

"Begging your pardon, Chancellor . . ." The words croaked in Lu Junyi's throat. She was not sure they were fully audible. She could not grasp his meaning—this was what they had been trying to *prevent*. All the testing, all the careful development of boundaries and safeguards, all to make the god's fangs more controllable . . .

"You can be excused for not seeing it," Cai Jing said. "Not being a party to the field of war. I shall still require you to work toward completing your more directed option. What we have just seen, however, is a magnificent alternative, when brute destruction is desirable. Send an officer up a mountain with this power in his hands, and no bandit would escape. A very complete solution."

Lu Junyi's mind stuttered. He wanted to—*intentionally*—

Perhaps he doesn't understand—he can't know what he says; he can't—

She tried again. "Begging your pardon, Grand Chancellor . . . what we saw here . . . it was interrupted; if the reaction were to continue to multiply—planning for any precision would be folly. Forgive me, Honorable Grand Chancellor, but I do not think, we could not predict, the loss of innocent life would—it could be beyond calculation . . ."

She'd worried that she would fail, and that large swathes of the countryside would burn because of that failure.

She had never imagined the Empire might do it on purpose.

"Grand Chancellor, I beg you, let me finish our work here. When I tried to stop Ling Zhen, I realized, the alchemical elixirs—we never considered making changes to the person. If we improve upon the host before a bonding to the god's fang, it can, it can be done, I can give you what you want . . ."

The dust that coated her mouth and nose made the words stick. Pleading. Pleading to be allowed to complete a weapon that would be used against her friends, because the alternative was unimaginable.

She wondered if Fan Rui had realized from the beginning. If she'd instantly seen that applying an elixir to the person must be the way forward to control the god's fangs, and if that was why she'd retracted the suggestion and retroactively scorned it before guiding them all toward disaster. When Lu Junyi had insisted on doing it herself, Fan Rui had never once talked of the host, only of applications to the god's fangs themselves . . . had it all been misdirection? In contrast, in the page she'd written to Ling Zhen . . .

People drowning in a dyed river.

It was possible. She might have known the whole time. Conspired with her husband to put everyone else off of it until they could wreak their plans.

Cai Jing lifted the hem of his robes and began picking his way through the rubble, stepping delicately over debris and bodies alike. He approached Lu Junyi and stopped, gazing down at her. The dust and dirt caking him to the eyebrows somehow made him even more fierce.

"An alchemical means of control, through the wielder of the god's fang," he mused. "Another most fortuitous discovery. Precision is indeed my preference. After all, as powerful as this demonstration was, the long view requires a directable, repeatable weapon to protect against the Empire's enemies."

Lu Junyi had barely taken a breath in relief when he continued, "Either way, Mount Liang will provide rich opportunity for a battlefield test. Provide me your best attempt, Lady Lu. We will either prove a working god's fang, or show a glorious Imperial recreation of what these traitors attempted here. One after which no citizen will dare rebel."

Lu Junyi had no response. Her tongue curled in her mouth, becoming one with the dust.

Cai Jing did understand. He understood exactly what that latter choice would mean, every objection she might raise, all of its promised collateral harm against citizens of the Empire.

He understood, and he would do it anyway.

He is a madman.

No. Not a madman. Fan Rui had been mad, but she had in her own way been rational and righteous, even as she betrayed her land and Emperor. Cai Jing revealed only cold calculation.

Not a madman—a tyrant.

He'd begun moving again, walking among the destruction as if on a stroll in a museum. Beyond the broken walls, Guardsmen were bursting into the courtyard, calling to each other, orders ringing out to find the Chancellor and the Minister.

Cai Jing stopped to gaze down at the dead Minister of War. The Minister's motionless hand still gripped his god's tooth, but his fingers and palm had blackened and burned. The god's tooth itself . . . Lu Junyi's breath caught in her throat. It had crumbled to ash.

What kind of power can do such a thing . . .

She raised her eyes to Cai Jing again, and she would have sworn that a ghoulish smile touched the Chancellor's mouth.

"A serendipitous day indeed," he said, almost too softly to hear. "A strike like this will remove all objection. The Emperor will have to grant me my troops now."

CHAPTER 27

Cai Jing strode past the retinue of serving men and women, up the Imperial Stairs to pause at the threshold of the audience chamber he had frequented a thousand times.

He had bathed and changed from his ruined clothing before responding to the summons. Now his fine padded robe of gray and blue silk was belted with an embroidered sash beneath meticulously groomed hair and beard—just as polished as he always was when waiting on the Lord of Heaven.

His garb matched his confidence. The Emperor would of course have received full and immediate reports of the day's events; the Emperor would have realized that Cai Jing had been correct all along. As Cai Jing always was. The Emperor would have called him here to grant exactly those edicts of fire his Chancellor had so wished for.

The Court, those who had derided him behind closed doors—they would be strangling on their own misplaced arrogance.

Cai Jing waited for the silver rods to clang three times, and for those waiting in attendance to assume their positions, divided by civilian and military authorities. A herald proclaimed, "Long live the Emperor! Long may the Empire prosper!" three times in succession, and those in the audience chamber knelt.

Only once the Emperor ascended to the throne and took his place did the herald announce the Chancellor of the Secretariat.

Cai Jing stepped forward with his head respectfully lowered, traversing the long audience chamber on silken boot soles until he was at the center of the shining floor. He swept his robes aside to fold elegantly to the ground, pressing his forehead to his hands, murmuring the requisite words.

"This servant is unworthy to be in the presence of your Imperial Majesty."

The Emperor usually invited him to rise at once.

The moments dripped past. The Emperor said nothing.

Why does the Lord of Heaven not speak . . . ?

Cai Jing's thoughts cleaved against themselves. The Emperor—did the Emperor, his Imperial Majesty, did he blame—

No. Impossible. Cai Jing had *never* been in disfavor with the Emperor.

He had worked very hard to ensure it.

His tongue leapt in his mouth, yearning to put things right, back the way they ought to be, but he could not speak until His Radiance the Emperor allowed for it . . .

"Tell me." The voice came at last, from far above. "Tell me, my Chancellor. What would you do with an official who let free two traitors of the realm, handed them a dangerous new invention, then stood by while they placed the Imperial City and this palace at risk? What would you do with such a person . . . Chancellor?"

Cai Jing's prized calm teetered. The endless eyes of those in attendance at the Court today seemed to drill into his skin, seeing the bones of his shame.

No. He would not bear it. *This is what you are made for,* a whisper reminded him. *Convince the Emperor, then protect the Empire. This is only another challenge. Nothing more.*

The Emperor would not wait much longer for his answer . . .

Cai Jing kept his head down, his eyes on the polished stone, his beard pooling in snowy white beneath him.

"I would kill him, Radiant Majesty," he said.

A beat, as Cai Jing fancied he could feel the Emperor shifting above. Certainly muted shuffles came from the sides of the chamber, though no one would be so disrespectful as to make any other noise. Cai Jing waited just a hair beyond the peak of shocked tension, then continued.

"Your Imperial Majesty's grace and mercy has always far exceeded my own, and I do not deserve its light. If I am spared by

Your Majesty today, I will have eaten a cake of ash and humbleness in learning the wisdom of the Lord of Heaven's generosity. If I fall for my errors, I ask only to be remembered as a loyal servant of the Empire."

He fell silent. Waited. He thought he had thrown correctly. The Emperor always wished to be loved.

Always wished to be generous and merciful. To be *seen* as generous and merciful.

Cai Jing had served for so many years . . .

The idea that this might end ill for him—it was too large to fathom.

Finally—finally—the Emperor spoke.

"Rise."

The tension folded away, and Cai Jing knew he had moved correctly.

He stood. His robe fell smooth. His hands clasped each other in serenity. He was calm.

The Emperor sat on his throne above, rich red and gold robes dripping against it, his great winged headdress spreading a pace on either side. Lines of stress carved themselves deep in his royal face.

The Lord of Heaven carries a great burden, Cai Jing reminded himself.

Cai Jing rarely doubted his own correctness, but he did not carry an entire righteous land across his shoulders. He waited.

"You wish an army to go after these bandits at Liangshan," the Emperor said.

"I do, Your Majesty."

"I am told you asked ten thousand men."

"Their stronghold is said to be extremely well-fortified, Your Majesty, and we know not the full extent of ill powers they traffic in. My reports are that the countryside cowers in fear of them, and they murdered an entire regiment at the village of Dongxi in Ji Province. I believe the seditionists who attempted to attack Bianliang today to have always been among their number, and this was some culmination of a conspiracy of theirs. Their sickness has vast tendrils. A fungus that must be rooted out."

The Emperor's head bowed over steepled fingers. "Your troops are granted. Take General Guan."

Cai Jing took care not to show it, but his heart danced for joy.

General Guan Sheng's renown rang across the forty-five prefectures. The descendent of a god of war, he had a fine ruddy face and a peerless beard, and he wielded a long-handled, moon-bladed saber with a hilt as long as a spear haft.

"I also have fortunate tidings that have come out of the attack today," Cai Jing reported, emboldened. "In their failure, the traitors revealed secrets of the research I have been pursuing for Your Imperial Majesty. I believe we have learned what we need to build the Empire a devastating new advantage. In addition, this Scholar Ling demonstrated a great weapon in his uncontrolled use of our materials—this too can be a magnificent boon to the Empire, and may even serve to secure our interests forever."

The Emperor studied the tips of his steepled fingers. Then he said, "No."

The word struck Cai Jing in the middle of the chest, a nearly physical blow. "If Your Imperial Majesty would allow an elaboration on my counsel—" he began.

"No." The Emperor's eyes came up, then down, resting on his Chancellor. "The heavens have spoken. You will cease all such research immediately. These realms are not for men to meddle with."

But what of the Jin, Cai Jing wanted to cry. *The northern armies stand poised to invade. The omens in the blood and bones . . .* did His Majesty the Emperor forget why they did this?

The spectacular progress on the god's fangs—it was the Empire's great chance. They could solidify the safety of the entire land and all its borders, even take back territory that should rightfully be theirs. Having another cunning advantage against these Liangshan bandits and any like ilk was only a secondary bonus—the possibilities here were so much larger, so much farther-reaching . . .

Inside his sleeves, Cai Jing's hands curled against each other. The Emperor had never wanted absolute power. He wanted safety.

He refused to see that the one could not be had without the other.

"We shall speak no more of this," he announced to Cai Jing now. "You have your decree."

Dismissed, Cai Jing bowed his way out, the motions rote and barely with the proper obeisance. He returned to his own chambers and paused, stomach churning, knives slashing in his gut.

He never should have worried for his own fate. The true threat was to the Empire, and Cai Jing would give his life a thousand times to protect it.

He never should have lost sight of that.

He would not forget it now.

He had one last chance. The Emperor had halted any more use of the god's fangs, but not everyone would know of his decree, not yet. The army would march soon to a place a full day's ride from Bianliang, a place Cai Jing would have absolute authority for as long as it took news to travel to and from the capital.

The one way, the only way, to convince the Emperor would be to prove the accomplishment and ask forgiveness afterward. A stabilized version of the god's fangs. Not the superweapon that so scared His Majesty, but a calm, brutal, controlled power Cai Jing would place directly in the Emperor's hands.

They were so close. Lady Lu was not one to exaggerate or falsify, and she said it could be done. She was sufficiently in fear of what the uncontrolled god's fangs might wreak to ensure her continued pliability; she need not be told of the Emperor's decree. She also need not know that this must now be a final, leaping attempt, one that, if it failed, would surely mean Cai Jing's death.

That did not matter. The Empire was all.

Gao Qiu would be the key. Grand Marshal Gao Qiu, who so coveted this power that Cai Jing would easily be able to manipulate him into claiming this test for himself, with no sense for how they sprang forward untried. If they succeeded—surely they would succeed; they must succeed—Gao Qiu would serve to save Cai Jing from the Emperor's wrath.

Gao Qiu and his newfound glory.

If they failed—Gao Qiu would die, most likely, and Cai Jing would face execution.

He felt very calm about it. He had tossed the coins before. This would be no different.

Gao Qiu, of course, was not a reliable military mind. Cai Jing would send in General Guan to annihilate the bandits, with this experiment held back for the final dramatic victory. In one move, the Empire's Chancellor of the Secretariat would wipe out a plague upon the land and prove the method of raising a new god.

The Empire would burst into glorious strength as had never before been seen, an era of gods and dragons made from men. It would be safeguarded forever, able to deal a harsh hand against any who rose in defiance—whether inside or outside Imperial borders. The Empire would be able to gain any resource, stake claim to any land, and prosper as never before.

A golden stability that none could threaten. It would become an era of wealth and security, and would be Cai Jing's legacy.

Liangshan would be the perfect testing ground.

For the first time in many days, Lu Junyi arrived home before dark. Her workspace and research in the inner city were gone, with nothing left for her to stay and oversee. Those of her men who did not lie dead or injured she'd dismissed back to the safety of their homes. If Cai Jing asked, she would say they had too little expertise on their own, absent their superiors.

It was not a lie. The people who could most help her were the ones who had destroyed everything.

She might have considered keeping one of the alchemists to consult, as she herself barely qualified, but there had only been two, and both men lay buried beneath the rubble. She would have to make every dangerous guess on her own, and hope. The impossibility of the task yawed, like a tower that leaned and creaked above her head, ready to collapse and crush her.

If she could not satisfy him . . . how much of the Empire might Cai Jing destroy, in the name of his revenge?

She'd written out more lists with numb fingers, ores and powders and extracts of animal and plant, plus gathering every possible scroll or treatise on alchemy and every tattered instruction of Fan Rui's that could be salvaged from the ruins. She could do this. She *must* do this, and she must do it without aid. She felt clumsy and full of gaps in knowledge and instinct, but tried to remind herself that she'd read up on the alchemical theory for years . . . *but I only played at knowledge then.* What a naive dilettante she had been.

Still, as new as she was at the practice and as much as Fan Rui's motives had lay hidden, Lu Junyi had been learning from no less than a master of the craft. Her knowledge had multiplied quickly. She might succeed.

In the end, she had no choice in it.

She'd given what additional orders she could pry out of her haze, pretending an authority she did not feel. Then she'd returned to her empty house to pack her own personal sundries for the journey.

Not truly empty—the servants rushed to greet her at this unaccustomed time. Without Jia, however, their respectful queries seemed to echo softly off a dead space where nothing lived.

My dear Jiajia, I did you wrong. I'm not sure how or when or what I might have done to move down a different path, but you would have known. You could have told me, if I had let you. I was such a fool, thinking I had everything under control.

Thinking I had anything under control.

She'd brushed Jia aside and now Jia was gone. Maybe forever. Even if she intended to return . . . chances were not poor that Lu Junyi was the one who would not be stepping across this threshold again. Armies and war and desperate battles and god's fangs that would tear off the face of the earth unless she stopped it from happening, and even if she did prevail, might tear only a little less and take only the lives of her friends instead of innocent farmers and villagers.

Her lips moved against each other, instructing the servants to pack for a weeks-long journey with the calm of one already dead. One of the older maidservants inquired discreetly about drawing her a bath, and it was only then that Lu Junyi realized she must look a ghost—torn clothes, grime still crusted over her hair and skin.

The water and clean clothes did not wash away the guilt that caked her.

With nothing left to do, her feet found their way to her study. Jia's message from last night still lay on her desk, turned so the blank obverse stared up at her.

If she was not to return . . . she should write a message of her own.

She swept her robes aside to sit. Took up a bar of ink to grind it in careful, detached strokes. Mixed it to a liquid, took up a slim brush between her fingers. The soft animal hair hovered above the black.

She sat frozen. She who had written so many words, so many times.

Finally she dipped the tip of the brush and wrote only: *Forgive me.*

She sat back, perspiration prickling her skin as if she'd just run to exhaustion. It wasn't enough. It was all she had.

She stayed motionless, staring at what she had written, hoping wretchedly that the few characters would say more to Jia than their meaning, would say every thought she couldn't form. She stayed that way until her eye fell on the study's hearth, the accusing smear of ash and soot from the night before, yet another way she'd failed someone, failed a friend, and somehow again today even as she'd helped save them, because she'd done it only to kill them. She'd been trying so hard not to betray someone—anyone—anything—friends, her own ideals, the Empire, the Grand Chancellor—but she'd betrayed them all anyway, at every turn.

The words from the burned page sang through her mind again, telling a tale of freedom. Of a crusade for justice and heroism. Of escaping the harsh strictures placed by gender or social class, of defying marriages that were prisons, authorities who were jailers, or creditors who would gleefully sink their teeth into any suffering.

Of a wild and beautiful place, filled with riches and excellence, where true rightness ruled the day. Where a person didn't have to decide between infinite betrayals, but could always be secure in rewarding truth and being rewarded in turn.

The imagery had been painted as written by a poet. But Lu Junyi could remember enough.

She pressed her palms to the desk, heartbeats thumping loud through her head. Then she carefully moved the note to Jia to the side and slid out a fresh, clean sheet. Ground more ink, slowly, as if in sacred ritual, then mixed in the water. Her brush dipped into it, precise and calculated, then hovered above the blankness.

She stayed poised that way, a carved statue, for a long rivulet of time. She told herself the first touch of the brush was no inevitable decision, that she would have a thousand more opportunities to turn back. But she knew, at the root of her souls—the moment she let ink brush paper, she had committed.

Once she started, the words came slow but rock-steady, as if a ghost guided her hand until the last definitive stroke.

She sat and stared at what she had written. Quietly. Unmoving. Like sinking into a serene pool with the full intention of letting the water close over her head forever.

Then she powdered the wet page, folded it carefully between several others, and went to dismiss the servants. Only after she was truly alone did she take the paper into her back rooms. It burned against her hand.

Her press had lain silent for weeks now. Lu Junyi lit the lamps and settled between the vast circular typecases, spinning them to draw and sort the carved wooden blocks she would need out of their depths. She was practiced enough at it that collecting all the tiles barely took her into evening.

She loaded the press. The backward characters stared up at her out of their orderly rows, like carven soldiers at attention.

She deliberately did not read back the meaning in their order. Only symbols, symbols she arranged in the same sequence as her page.

She ran the press frequently enough that she had a storeroom full of neat stacks of paper already cut. Thousands of blanks, ready. The wide brush dipped in wet ink, painting over the prepared blocks until they gleamed black. Press the first page down, rolling it end to end before peeling it off with care.

That was one.

She wiped the ink from her hands and prepared to see how many she could print by morning.

The quiet span on the wrong side of dawn found her in the back room of an inn, passing ingots of silver and thick stacks of printed circulars to a woman in a patched apron. Then in an alley with a grinning, toothless man helming a porridge cart. Then breathing incense in an alcove of a monastery, then in a smoky gaming room, then in the silken and bejeweled presence of the madam of a brothel. The papers would go out via every tavern keeper, every child on the streets, passed with proclaimed innocence until the Guard realized the festering treason under their noses and cracked down—and then, like anything else not permitted, the circulars would be passed far more zealously, secretly, with the most delicious curiosity. Copied in brushwork, too, most probably, the more the originals were confiscated and burned.

Cai Jing would know it was her. If the army left too soon for the report to reach him immediately, then certainly when they returned from Liangshan.

By then, all the bandits of Liangshan would likely be dead, the mountain nothing more than ash. This last act of hers would have become meaningless. Making legendary the haojie who'd already burned, and scarring her with the same culpability in the process.

Cai Jing would execute her no matter what. That part was not in question. Only whether any of Liangshan would still be alive to benefit from her sacrifice.

CHAPTER 28

"Boats. He'll need boats." Wu Yong turned from staring out at the stars, back to Chao Gai and Song Jiang and Commander Yang, three of Liangshan's sharpest leaders here in Loyalty Hall. "The boats will delay him."

The other haojie were gathering, but Chao Gai had wanted to take the report from Bianliang in private first. Wu Yong and Lin Chong had made it back to Liangshan just fast enough to be able to guide their stolen horses through the marshlands in the deepening evening.

Zhu Gui's inn was shut up with the Crocodile herself hunkered behind the mountain's defenses, but Seventh Brother Ruan had come in stealth through the dusk in answer to their whistling arrow. In returning back up the mountain, Wu Yong's shame dragged as never before in memory. It weighted every motion, every step, every word in confessing failure—even in offering a final sacrifice, one Chao Gai refused, saying tersely that they needed their chief strategist for the upcoming battle.

Wu Yong would offer again after, if they both lived.

With no defense against Cai Jing's new god's tooth–like weapon—nothing but whatever Sister Lu and Sister Lin might muster up—Chao Gai intended to give all the haojie the choice of leaving the mountain before the battle descended. Wu Yong did not think any would take her up on it. Some because they had nowhere else to go, but most for loyalty—even in the face of known defeat.

They stood with each other. As haojie. Not only the heroism of intention or convenience, of rising to a storied champion of poetry—but justice, honor, commitment to one's chosen bonds.

Fighting with those sworn kindred to the end, even as the world crushed against them. Even when no one would know.

Liangshan was the home they would fight and die for. Just as Wu Yong would.

Think hard. You must surrender everything of mind and sword until there is nothing left, if you are barred from surrendering your life.

Marching an army took longer than travelers riding hard, longer even than those same travelers on foot. Add time to mobilize and equip the troops—add time to seize every fishing vessel along their way. The Empire may have a mighty navy, but not one that could be transplanted over land to come here, nor one designed to fit the nooks and narrow waterways of Liangshan Marsh.

Seizing boats would stall them. Two days at least, then, before the army was at Liangshan's doorstep. More likely four or six. In that time, the bandits could at least plan a strategy against any traditional attack . . .

"We'll be manning the watchtowers," Commander Yang murmured.

"I want us to be readier than that." Wu Yong felt through the tactics aloud. "Our traps might drown or crush a thousand men upon landing, but once we've used them, combat on the ground will be our only defense. We need to challenge them farther out."

"How many paths are there through the waters of the marsh?" Chao Gai asked.

It was the right question. "Safe ones—perhaps a dozen. I'll check with Second Brother Ruan. I believe they all cross some of the same points."

"A dozen . . . we could field a dozen boats," Song Jiang said thoughtfully.

Indeed they could.

"A three-fold defense." The instinct rang right. If, for any Benevolence-granted reason, Cai Jing attacked only with his army, and not this new power . . . it might grant them an outside chance. "We can have a line on the water, to trap and pick off the Guard before they can ever cross. Our members with the greatest brute strength will lie ready to loose the dam and release logs and boulders upon the enemy the moment they begin flooding our shores, with everyone else standing by to dispatch any who escape the traps."

Chao Gai nodded. "Good. You and I will command the defensive line on land and coordinate from the watchtowers. Commander Yang can lead the release of our prepared protections, and Drill Instructor Lin the boats—I believe she'll be able to utilize a particular skill that makes her ideal for coordination on the water. It's a strong plan."

Not strong enough, likely. But it was all they had.

"Where is Sister Lin?" Song Jiang asked. "Shouldn't she be here as well?"

Wu Yong grunted. "She's with the Divine Physician."

"She'll be able to fight?" asked Commander Yang.

Wu Yong had no doubt. Sister Lin was one of them now. One of them—to live, or to die, on a toss of the coins.

"It's only scrapes," Lin Chong tried to protest, but An Daoquan shut her down with several very definite gestures. Lin Chong still couldn't catch the meaning of more than one in ten—she glanced over to where Lu Da stood watch like an overactive guard dog. "What did she say?"

"She says it's your whole body, ass to toe," Lu Da answered, in what was clearly not a literal interpretation. "Sister An says, if you leave so much blood open to the air and dirt and stuff, it'll creep in and rot you all black from the inside out. Let 'er poultice, Elder Sister."

Lin Chong let her protests lapse, watching Sister An's sure fingers wrap the medicated bandages and secure them tight against her skin. At least they would be bound up for whatever fighting was sure to find them soon, here, in this last refuge.

Lin Chong should carve out some time for sleep. She'd caught bare moments of napping over the last two days.

Maybe it didn't matter. A much longer sleep might be about to claim her, after all, once Cai Jing came for them.

The Divine Physician finished another set of bandaging, hiding away where the lines of the tattoos had left their bloody shadows. She turned and motioned to Lu Da.

"She says not to worry, they won't scar or nothing. Unless you didn't want them to get gone, then I guess you should worry—me, I say it's downright tragic to get inked so much and not keep it!" Lu Da thumped her own chest, where her intricate floral designs wound against each other under her tunic. An Daoquan snapped fingers at her. "Oh, and she also says that if we all survive, now the one on your face is all the way healed, she can scrape it off with a good old gold and jade poultice if you want. Takes a whole season and your face is all red and blood while it's being done, but after there's no mark left. She's done it on more'n a few of the others, you know."

Lin Chong hadn't known. She'd spent so much time these past few days with deep consciousness of the brand on her cheek, the inelegant scrawl marking her a criminal forever. Now it turned out she could . . . erase it? Just like that . . .

It seemed too easy. Or maybe she had begun to think of the tattoo as a part of her. This strange new identity as a hero of the hills.

"I'll think about it."

"Loud and proud, I say," Lu Da said. "But I guess I served my time, so it's not so much a bother. Anyone gives me mouth about it, I punch 'em."

An Daoquan's fingers began to explore the more serious cuts and swelling across Lin Chong's temple and eye. She paused to say something else to Lu Da, who snorted and guffawed.

Lin Chong glanced between them.

"How long would it take me to understand you the way they do?" she asked the Divine Physician.

"Real soon, if you keep getting injured this often," Lu Da translated, with another barked laugh. "You'll learn it fast, don't you worry. Weren't more than a few months for me before I could tell nearly all of what she said. Easier too on account you can read and write, so's if you miss something she can finger-draw the word for you. She does that sometimes if you're not getting it."

Lin Chong rather thought Lu Da might be underrating herself—or overrating Lin Chong, considering how many weeks she'd been among the bandits already.

Sister An seemed to agree. Before beginning the next bandage, she looked up and made a few amused, almost conspiratorial motions that made Lu Da's chest puff out. "She says I'm remarkable quick. Says our sister the Mathematic still always asks her to slow down and she has to end up writing everything down on paper. I bet you get it way sooner though."

Soon. The word tumbled against the ugly wall of what was to come, dread settling heavy across Lin Chong's mind again. She tried not to wince away from the Divine Physician's ministrations, tried to reach for a calm beyond the dull thud of pain in her head that had been Gao Qiu's gift to her this time.

Soon.

A nice fantasy, pretending they all had a future together.

The curtain at the door pushed aside, and Song Jiang slipped in. "May I join you?"

Lin Chong motioned her to enter. The movement didn't sting like she expected. Shining Benevolence, but her skin already did feel better.

"We've been in consultation to prepare our defense," Song Jiang said. "Sister Chao will want to speak to you when you're done here. We don't know how likely it will be for Cai Jing to use these new god's teeth of his, though. The Tactician says they still appear very unstable?"

Lin Chong let the memory wash over her, the oscillating energies, wild and overbalanced. "Yes. It seemed so."

"If he does bring them against us . . . you are the only two who can effectively counter such things." She turned to include Lu Da as well. "Sister Chao says if you sense them coming, don't wait. Do whatever you can."

"Understood," Lin Chong said.

"I'll smash Chancellor Cai and his fake god's teeth into the ground," volunteered Lu Da. "And if I can't, Sister Lin will. She's getting to be an all-experted master now."

Her confidence made a small, sad smile come to Lin Chong's lips. She had felt Cai Jing's new god's teeth—she knew how far they measured beyond her every capability. How far they measured beyond even what Lu Da's god's tooth could draw. She'd told the Flower Monk this already, describing it in great seriousness, and Lu Da had merely smacked a fist into her palm and said their righteous cause would protect them. Then she'd called Lin Chong a fighting god again.

Lin Chong knew the truth of it. She'd *felt* the truth of it. Her nascent skills had no chance of victory, not in a fight against that. Lu Da's sisterly faith in her, however . . .

It made her want to believe. It made her want to rise up, and fight with hope, and call success possible.

"Everything we have is Liangshan's," Lin Chong told Song Jiang.

With a strange sort of peace, she found herself thinking that as deaths went, this would be a proud one.

Lu Junyi carried the pot carefully between folded cloths. Its heat still poured through and warmed her hands. Steam escaped the tight-fitted lid, enough so that its metallic, earthen scent lingered in her senses.

Not a pleasant scent. Reminiscent of burnt coal and noxious, bitter roots.

When she arrived at the Chancellor's tent, one of the soldiers stationed outside saluted and went in to announce her. She tried to blink the grimy exhaustion out of her eyes, the full days of reading nearly a library's worth of alchemy in the carriage as they traveled, then nights spent bent over the crucibles . . . only her, now, working alone. She had half expected Cai Jing to leverage his Imperial power to find other alchemists, to insist on bringing greater experts on this deadly march—or even to overrule her decision to send all her scholars home. But he had not.

She did not question it. Better for this to be on only one person's head.

She shifted on tired feet and gazed around the campground as she waited to meet with him. She had never traveled with an army before, and the visual was—imposing. Overwhelming. The soldiers who moved in lockstep, the cavalry of fierce horses with plumes and bells, the colored pennants and flags flying over different divisions of the undulating sea of troops . . . she could not pretend to understand the organization, but their numbers stretched like a great shining ocean across the land, the edges invisible in any direction. Even the smallest or clumsiest soldier became formidable in polished armor and clutching a spear or sword or halberd that was brightly tasseled to match his fellows. Then each one marching among so many like him that together they became as a swarm of bees, each individually armed but together a colossus no one would choose to face . . .

From here she could see where the front edge of the camp came up near the shoreline. Guardsmen moved in formation to secure boats in the water, mostly fishing vessels they had requisitioned on the march and carried over land in mass parade formations. Other men worked to erect a tall command platform, shouts echoing in unison as they heaved each piece. Colorful banners already fluttered from its wooden skeleton.

Lin Chong had mentioned her dissatisfaction with the Imperial Guard's discipline. Not often, but even once was remarkable from a woman who had kept her criticisms of government and officers so close . . . at least back then. Lu Junyi's untrained eye, however, could see no lack, only a fitted mosaic of well-oiled men.

Whatever her part here, she did not think it would make any real difference. Even without the god's fangs, the bandits of Liangshan could not win against this.

The same soldier who had gone in to announce her returned and lifted the flap to allow her entrance. She turned and stepped into the Chancellor's command tent, a colossal structure of heavy material the size of a building. Inside, rich carpets layered the floor, with furnishings equal to an audience chamber in Bianliang. Cai Jing was seated in a grand, carven chair, one of his generals attentive before him. Marshal Gao Qiu lounged off to the side, looking bored.

Lu Junyi missed a step before she caught her balance. Other than the brief appearance of the marshal's bloody visage in the chaos preceding Ling Zhen's sabotage, Lu Junyi hadn't crossed paths with him since before that fateful late-night visit from Lin Chong.

He paid the guards to kill me, she had said. Too calm. Matter of fact.

Lu Junyi realized she had never asked what started this vicious vendetta of the marshal's, that day in White Tiger Hall after Lu Junyi had left and Lin Chong had been called back to remain. Lin Chong, who not moments earlier had been defending her superior from even the mildest criticism. It had been natural to assume some pointless, fabricated charge by a mercurial official, which surely it was—but chasing her down for assassination? What could *Lin Chong* have said or done to become dragged as a pariah, targeted for execution and then murder?

"My counsel is for us to wait until dawn," the general was saying. Guan Sheng was his name, a great fierce lion of a man who was said to be descended from a god of war, famous enough that even a civilian like Lu Junyi knew of him. Strong, dedicated, loyal, well-loved, as far as anything she had ever heard spoken.

"This marsh is treacherous," he continued. "It would pick off our soldiers before we even make the shore, and if the bandits see us coming, they will wreak worse. We'll still lose some in daylight, but the tradeoff will be much more favorable to us."

Gao Qiu snorted. "Spoken like a coward. Do you presume Chancellor Cai doesn't know this? This is the bandits' terrain; you want them to see us coming? We're far better off slaughtering them in their beds."

"You're right, of course," General Guan said, with the patient politeness of a man whose superior is very dull. "If we could be certain of surprising them, I would agree wholeheartedly. Chancellor, by all accounts these bandits scheme well tactically, which is why I recommend as I do. I do not think we can count on a lack of vigilance from them."

Cai Jing's hands steepled before him, gazing at his general and ignoring Gao Qiu. It was clear his voice would be the deciding one.

"Your recommendation is noted," he said to General Guan after a long pause, quiet and deliberate. "My own assessment would be the same, *if* we had a full accounting of what dark energies these bandits draw on. Recall that they slaughtered a full regiment of men with no survivors, then broke into the Empire's most secure prison, assassinated your superior the Minister of War, and attempted to strike at the heart of Bianliang and the Emperor himself . . . These are the people you wish to give the advantage of daylight, General?"

His white eyebrows lifted. Mildly, oh so mildly.

General Guan shifted slightly, sensing the rebuke. "You are wise in your assessment, Chancellor," he settled on.

Lu Junyi wondered if the Chancellor truly saw the Liangshan bandits as such demons, something imagined out of a nightmare. Lin Chong, Lu Da, even the strange Tactician—they were only humans. Capable fighters, but surely no more than the Empire's generals.

It was Cai Jing's own research that had enabled the disaster in Bianliang. He must know it. He wanted the appearance of a crushing victory for his own reasons, and he was shaming his general into giving him one.

"Lady Lu."

Lu Junyi jumped, worried for a moment that her suspicions were written on her face. "I am here, Grand Chancellor."

"You bring the elixir?"

"Yes, Honorable Grand Chancellor, but . . ." She glanced at the others in the tent; wet her lips. "Your Excellency knows I would prefer more time."

"Now you'd rob me of my god's fang? Lazy witch!"

It was not Cai Jing who had spoken, but Gao Qiu. He stepped forward to loom into Lu Junyi's space, raising a fist as if he intended to backhand her. His face was still mottled purple and black with healing bruises.

Lu Junyi couldn't help it. She shifted to retreat a step, her eyes going to Cai Jing for help.

"Now, now, Marshal. Lady Lu intends no such thing." Cai Jing turned back to his general briefly. "General Guan, go select your commanders for the crossing. You are to lead the vanguard behind, once a safe path is found. I expect your men to stand ready by midnight."

Guan Sheng saluted and bowed his way out of the tent.

Cai Jing turned smoothly back to Lu Junyi.

"Lady Lu, as I'm sure you have surmised, Marshal Gao has a determination to test this version on himself. He knows what a breakthrough you have discovered."

Was Lu Junyi imagining it, or did a small smile play around the Chancellor's lips? He had to know how dangerous this was, how untried. To select a high-level military officer for such experimentation . . .

Lu Junyi had already known she must not fail here, for a multitude of reasons. If the elixir did not have sufficient efficacy to keep the god's fang from destroying its host—if that host was someone of Gao Qiu's stature—

If he died, someone would have to answer. For his assassination, she would be summarily executed. It wasn't even a question.

Instead of being executed for your failure, or for your sedition, or for your role in allowing Fan Rui and Ling Zhen the access for their treason? Incongruously, she wanted to laugh. How many times could they condemn her?

It was a type of freedom.

She gave the marshal as deep a bow as she could over the pot and spoke calmly. "Grand Marshal, I beg your pardon. I only wish for your gain here to be smooth and free of complication. As you see, the Chancellor chastises me for being too cautious—it is only my own weakness, and no comment on your valor."

Gao Qiu snorted something that sounded suspiciously like "*women.*"

Lu Junyi wondered, somewhat ludicrously, how he could say that here, now, standing on this shoreline with ten thousand troops to back him.

She did not point it out. "May I give you counsel on the elixir?"

Gao Qiu waved her ahead, but dismissively, turning away. Lu Junyi wanted to ask if he harbored a death wish, but again refrained.

"Please continue, Lady Lu," Cai Jing supplied. "I, too, have studied some of these matters. Marshal, I will tell you if I find her judgments accurate."

He smiled at her. As if they conspired. As if she was his partner in a joke, telling Gao Qiu what he wanted to hear so that he'd listen to her. Her hands tightened against the warm pot. Cai Jing was not her benevolent friend. Had never been, no matter how she had fooled herself into forgetting.

A ruthless, rebellious hope rose in her that the bandits might win.

She did not see how, and such a victory would likely kill her too, but she would consider it worth the price.

She coughed. Spoke. Her words came out unruffled, summarizing the material she now knew by heart.

"Marshal, it is my belief that the most efficacious method for protecting yourself will be ingestion." All feeling receded from her, burnt away until she fluttered free, unable to be hurt. "This elixir is one made to draw out hot energies from the body, and it should allow you a balance with the god's fang instead of being consumed by its heat. I must warn you that given what we know of these forces, it is impossible for this balance to be a peaceful one. The elixir will not calm the god's fang to a comfortable median, but rather constantly pull against it while it pulls back. I expect the effect to be less like coming to rest in a valley and much more the experience of being atop a steep hill with forces pulling from both sides, barely staying atop. It will be fatiguing, and with no way to unbond you unless you pass the artifact on to a willing heir."

Despite himself, Gao Qiu seemed to be listening. Cai Jing certainly was, with a disconcerting intensity. "If the marshal finds adjustment difficult, can the dosage be modified?" he said.

"In fact, it must be," Lu Junyi answered. "This elixir wears off after a time, so you will need to continue taking drafts of it, and I expect it will take practice to find a timing and amount that provides evenness. Depending on how you respond to the god's fang, Marshal, the potency can also be adapted."

"It takes half a day, doesn't it, to reach full potential," Cai Jing pressed.

"Yes, but you will largely feel its vigor right away. I would certainly counsel taking that delay into account when making your adjustments, however."

"Perfect," the Chancellor said. "Treat Marshal Gao now, and be back at dawn to observe the bonding. Marshal, this will be the ideal timing for the vanguard to go ahead of you and dispense with any initial messiness. By dawn we shall have a path through the swamp, and you can lead us to glorious victory."

Lu Junyi opened her mouth to clarify that she had not actually suggested a delay.

But if the Chancellor wished to, why fight it? Nor, she realized, did his words match what he had just told General Guan about obtaining a crushing and clean victory instantly in the night . . . not to mention that a newly minted wielder, particularly someone with the temperament of Gao Qiu, would surely not be expected to have precise control immediately even if this worked . . .

Cai Jing must want a dawn timing for his own reasons.

Reasons she had no desire to know. She swayed on her feet, so very tired.

The marshal began ordering her to get on with it, his impatience plain. She thought about stressing to them, one more time, that no one had ever tried this before. That she had neither the expertise in these potions that a Grand Marshal might wish nor any confidence in the outcome. That they ran headlong into the unknown, plunging toward the temptation of power without seeing the equal parts danger.

They knew. She'd spoken her warnings. Cai Jing had some agenda of his own, and Gao Qiu wanted to grab at godhood in any way he could. They knew everything she could say, and they demanded it anyway.

With a strange tranquility, Lu Junyi placed the pot on a table and measured out a small cup of its contents.

She tried not to let any vindictive feeling show on her face when Gao Qiu sputtered and spat it out before choking it down.

In the space of a night, he would either gain ultimate power, or he would be dead. Despite all the possible consequences, Lu Junyi could not be sure which she rooted for.

CHAPTER 29

On an unexpectedly cool summer evening in the Empire of Song, Cai Jing's army of ten thousand gathered at the border of Liangshan Marsh.

Lu Da watched from a high outcropping, along with three dozen of her fellows gathered across the various vantage points and watchtowers. Far across the water, the army's camp stretched like rows of tiny bugs, the subtle ripples of its movement a disturbing reminder of its contained power.

"So many men for us piddly little spitwads," scoffed Li Kui the Iron Whirlwind.

"They must be very afraid of us." Hu Sanniang's eyes narrowed, her hand spinning one of her sabers in long habit.

"Not saying I mind," grunted Li Kui. "More men for me to kill. This'll be glorious. They'll write poems."

For once Lu Da didn't disagree. She stretched her fingers against her iron staff.

"Quiet," called Commander Yang. "Stay ready. Drill Instructor, what do you think?"

"If they cross the marsh in the dark, they'll lose one in ten men," Sister Lin said with a frown. "Dawn is the tactical play. They must know we have the advantage of terrain."

"No." Wu Yong stepped forward between them, gaze piercing, as if fire could shoot from a person's eyes all the way down to where Cai Jing made camp. "They'll attack tonight. Cai Jing will take any risk for a cleaner victory. He doesn't care how many men the marsh swallows, if he has a chance to cut our throats while we sleep."

The others all oriented on their chief strategist, silence falling over the group on this outcropping. A flutter of excitement flicked up Lu Da's insides.

This was no longer a ponderous possibility, but real.

They were going to battle.

I wonder what it will be like, Lu Da thought. Not very different from raiding parties, probably.

The excitement burned hotter. She thought it likely she would be *very* good at it.

Wu Yong nodded to Sister Lin and Commander Yang. "Take your people now. When they come, we'll be waiting."

Lin Chong gathered the haojie under her command on the bank of the water, where the mountain descended into the marsh. Liangshan's naval chieftains, as it were. A number of them had come to the mountain as families. The Ruan brothers, of course, then the Tong sisters who had been salt smugglers or the Zhang siblings who had run a murderous ferry to steal their fares' treasures . . . Mu Hong the Unrestrained and her younger sister Mu Chun the Slightly Restrained, then some lone miscreants like Li Jun the River Dragon, who had been a friend of the Tongs . . . an eclectic group to be sure.

In the short time Lin Chong had been here, she had come to know every one of them. Thieves, killers, and heroes, all rolled together in a chaos that no longer seemed to contradict itself.

In the days they'd had to prepare—their small, precious delay before the army arrived—these haojie had all proved thirsty students and ready warriors. Lin Chong was proud to have them at her back.

Proud to be one of them.

"Remember," Lin Chong ordered her unlikely navy. "Any time you can avoid engaging, do so. The marsh will do our work for us. You know the bird calls for the formations. You'll hear Sister Chao's whistles from the mountain, but let me worry about those. Listen for my signals only."

The bandits—the heroes—all nodded and gave each other too-hard slaps on the shoulder for luck. Lin Chong still had some bandaging under her clothing, but she joined in anyway.

Wu Yong had provided wooden whistles to the three commanders, since they would be so many spans of distance from each other. In their brief preparation, the coordination had somehow fallen out naturally, as if they were all organs of one body. Now, as dusk dusted the reeds and lilies along the shoreline, Lin Chong's haojie all slipped eagerly into small fishing sculls that could zip in and out of the Liangshan waterways.

Each of these bandits knew those waterways like a map of their own skin. Each knew the position they would start in, the places their other boats lay hidden in waiting, as well as the combustible traps they'd set and the underwater paths these fishlike haojie could traverse even in the dark.

They would flay the threat to Liangshan until they could do no more.

Lin Chong, not at home on the water herself, had chosen Seventh Brother's boat as the one she would join and command from, a decision that made the young man puff up with pride. She stepped onto planks that bobbed beneath her, and Seventh Brother pushed them off with the excitement of a boy about to attend his first Lantern Festival. He was stripped to the waist, feet bare and sure on the planks, all the better for flitting in and out of the water with the speed of a salamander. Most of the water captains were similarly attired. Lin Chong wore a light battle dress and carried a short blade and a crossbow, the better for the type of fighting most likely to result out here, though with any luck, they wouldn't engage the enemy directly at all. The more important consideration was for nothing to weigh her down if she met the water.

"Do you swim at all, Drill Instructor?" Seventh Brother had asked during their practice.

"Not well," was Lin Chong's answer.

"Don't worry. If we capsize, I'll pull you out!"

Lin Chong had permitted herself a small smile. She did not

think drowning was the way she would die tonight. Besides, she had not been assigned to the water for her swimming abilities.

Trust yourself, Chao Gai had urged. *Do not fear your own skills.*

They pushed out under Seventh Brother's sure hands, out onto the twisty, hungry marsh that so protected its nest of outlaws. Soft blue-black crept over the water as the sun set, the insects phasing from their evening chitter to the buzz of the nocturnal. The moon lay absent, the stars brushed bright against the black like crushed diamonds. Down in the boats, the darkness became almost total.

They waited in the boat, rocking gently in the bosom of the marsh, staying quiet and still, until somewhere past midnight. Then the expected whistle rang out from the mountain—high and short, and then long and low.

Cai Jing's army was coming.

Whoever commanded the soldiers had good instincts. Lin Chong had seen no torches glinting through the night, heard no massive shuffle of troop movement from the far shore. If the army had decided to sacrifice all in the deadly darkness for the dubious advantage of a surprise ambush, then any light or sound would render that pointless.

Of course, the bandits up on the mountain were watching closely for any sign, and someone—likely Wu Yong—had seen them anyway.

Lin Chong began to count. Slowly. One number per heartbeat.

They had timed, yesterday, how long a boat took to cross, either at speed or with caution.

"There," whispered Seventh Brother, hearing the same muffled splash and curse Lin Chong did. She let out a cautious coo across the water, the call of a wood pigeon and the signal to wait.

Close now. Very close.

She might not have the skills of underwater action, but in their practices she had managed something equally important, exactly as Chao Gai had urged . . . She closed her eyes against the night, breathing in the marsh air. Cool humidity filled her lungs. She felt Seventh Brother's wiry presence beside her, the beat of his heart as he thrilled to defend his home. Insects trilled to each other, calling mates to them, while small fish flicked below the surface and larger ones lurked in the muddy depths. Snakes and turtles and frogs and the nests of small birds, all packed hiding among the dense clusters of swamp vegetation that weighed into the water on all sides, roots tangling in mud. Some of those tiny animal heartbeats fluttered in fearful sleep, still alert for predators, and others twirled in their nightly romps.

Then—very still among the wildlife, twelve boats with a different haojie's heartbeat on each one.

Lin Chong's senses stretched further, and found the oncoming wall of humanity. Pressing inexorably forward, the smaller critters going silent and diving deep out of the way from this unknown and monstrous wave. Oars dipped and splashed, hurriedly muffled. Hot sweat beneath armor. Prickles of fear at this place they did not know, where they kept having to turn back at blockades and dead ends, where it was so easy to lose their fellows and commanders. Two boats right next to each other might become divided by a mudflat or a stand of reeds and in navigating around it, be lost from each other completely . . .

Several already spun in darkness, separated, mud sucking up against them. Lin Chong felt the distant panic of their oarsmen, the desperation as they turned, and turned again, always moving in the wrong direction somehow, always further lost in this great wetland wilderness.

The marsh was many li wide and many long. Even in daylight, one shore could not be seen from the other, and a boat stuck in its maze might circle in endless dead ends forever, no matter whether sounds of battle shouted the way.

One in ten boats lost might not have given the marsh enough credit, at least on this initial foray. On the other hand, once the soldiers found a path . . .

The haojie were here to make that prospect as painful as possible.

Closer. Closer.

Now.

Lin Chong filled her lungs and belted out her best imitation of a loud green frog. On the boat nearest to the approaching vanguard, Second Brother Ruan sprang up and shouted.

The approaching army realized immediately they had been discovered, and abandoned stealth. Shouts rose up, and bowstrings twanged as arrows flew to thunk hard into the wood of Second Brother's boat.

She had already jumped off the side, diving into the deep waters of the marsh, swimming through known tunnels in the reeds and roots to take up her next post.

A block of the army's boats broke off in disarray, following the bait.

Farther down, Li Jun the River Dragon did the same. A shout, a dive, arrows. On the right flank, the army had dissolved without help, losing itself among the deep, hidden waterways in that section of the marsh, but on the left flank, Mu Chun the Slightly Restrained and her older sister baited still other boats into a large lake. They would be swimming to climb up on Fifth Brother Ruan's boat behind, while the Guardsmen shouted and slashed at the water, flailing for this unseen enemy . . .

This time the signal was an approximation of the northern whistling duck: two notes, sharp and long. *Light it up.*

Out in front of the army's vanguard, Zhang Shun, the best swimmer in all of Liangshan, plunged toward the straw floats they had set the day before. Lin Chong motioned to Seventh Brother, and he carefully began poling them crossways, in case their position was suspected.

On the right, immediately in front of the vanguard—sudden, startling fire leapt toward the sky, flames licking up against the darkness. Men shouted—in shock, then panic.

Lin Chong whistled again.

The Tongs had the left flank, where the Guardsmen had been lured to circle on a great glassy lake, trying to find their way out. Those soldiers, too, spun to find every side suddenly become a wall of fire.

Lin Chong could not read their thoughts. Only emotions jumped at her, their heat and fear, but she knew the story of what they must see. Fire all around them, scarlet and gold against the oil-black water of the night swamp, heat flashing against their faces—and then not just around them but approaching them, the hungry floating bonfires pushed from beneath by bandits who could swim like eels.

Men began to scream. Splashes sounded through the crackling flames as soldiers dove out of doomed boats, wailed as they tried to tear off armor first and didn't have time. Splashing, more splashing, desperate pleas for help—many who couldn't swim at all grasping for aid and finding nothing but fire. Even the ones who could swim breathed heat and smoke and flame and began to tire, struggling to peel helmets and boots and clothes from themselves before the muck swallowed their exhaustion.

In every direction the marsh became clogged with pain and bodies, fire and water and men dying in the night. The corpses went silent and swollen in droves, floating down into the deep where the bottom feeders would feast.

Unfortunately, behind the first wave came another. Steadily, inexorably. Never-ending men on never-ending boats, rowing and poling through every crack they could find, turning from the fire to find another way, loosing hailstorms of arrows whenever they caught the fleet limb of a bandit disappearing below the surface.

Lin Chong gave the signal to retreat to their secondary positions. The way through for their foes would be harder now, choked with their fallen brethren along with abandoned boats and burning debris. Their only chance across had narrowed to a mere handful of safe paths, ones they still had to find. Ones where Lin Chong and her haojie would be waiting in ambush.

The first boat that struck through to their secondary line was met with Li Jun bursting out of the water like her namesake the River Dragon. She somersaulted up among the soldiers, her knife flashing to open throats before she dove off the other side.

Coming on a boat just behind, the division commander shouted for men to get overboard, to grab and end her. A disorderly exodus followed, the men who could swim stripping down but then hesitating in anguished fear, the dark waters waiting to eat them in every direction. The commander yelled again, hurling imprecations at his men.

"Get down there! Finish off the swamp bandit or don't come back at all!"

Lin Chong was close enough to see and hear through the reeds now, the boats backlit by the fires they had escaped. Still the men hesitated, their bared feet shuffling on the planks of their boats, until one stepped off and plunged, then another.

Zhang Shun was waiting for them beneath.

When the first men did not surface again, the others began bleating in fear. Their commander railed, lashing out with his command staff and knocking two more of his men into the water.

They, too, did not resurface.

Lin Chong did not have to reach out with her other senses to know Zhang Shun wielded a dagger down in the dark with the fluidity of a creature of the deep. Blood would flow free until the waters of Liangshan swelled with it.

As the next boats broke through, the two eldest Ruan brothers attacked as Li Jun had done, rising from the black like swamp creatures of legend. The commander who had so shamed his subordinates lost his throat and his life, his corpse falling to splash with the rest. Down at the next passage, the Tongs and the Mus led the other half of the water bandits in a similar gauntlet.

They could not hold forever, however. More and more boats were breaking through. In moments the wave would overtake them, blanketing the water with their numbers.

Lin Chong could feel the turning of the battle, the teetering point at which the enemy would flood through. Stay much longer, and they would be overrun.

Time to return to the mountain.

She raised the wooden whistle to her lips and sounded the piercing notes for retreat. Up on the slopes, the acknowledgment echoed back from either Chao Gai or Wu Yong.

"Get us to the rivulet," she ordered Seventh Brother, scooping the crossbow from the bottom of the boat. They would reconvene with the other water bandits there, then take a twisting back route all the way around to where they could land the boats and climb a side path to come up behind the action on shore. The aim was for them to move fast enough to join the fight on land.

Seventh Brother gave their boat a mighty heave, guiding it expertly among hazards in the dark, now complicated by floating oars or boots or corpses. Lin Chong spread out all her senses. Six of her people on a far boat—already out of the army's clutches, far ahead as they zipped into secret paths. The older Ruan siblings closer at hand, pausing to let Li Jun flip up on board before they too whisked backward and away. Zhang Heng alone on a third vessel, but where was Zhang Shun?

Emboldened by how natural it was beginning to feel, Lin Chong leaned hard into her newly developing scholar's skills, plunging her senses out beneath the surface.

Zhang Shun was still underwater. Slipping between boats. Capsizing one and then yanking soldiers into the deep from another.

They had tested whether the whistle could be heard underwater—but that was without the noise and chaos of battle, the fury of bloodlust—

"Stay low," Lin Chong warned Seventh Brother, and gave the signal again. Zhang Shun was either too far out beneath the enemy boats to hear, or was ignoring it.

"Who's missing? Who's still out there?" whispered Seventh Brother, tension in his voice.

"Only Zhang Shun. Can we move in without being spotted?"

"Always, Drill Instructor," Seventh Brother answered. He maneuvered them back and then inward, the little boat flicking through reeds and roots as fast as a fishtail.

Lin Chong stayed hunched low, crossbow loaded in one hand.

The enemy was on three sides now—before, behind, crossways. Buoyed by breaking through the bandits' line, they shouted to each other in robust accomplishment, pouring past the halfway point of the marsh.

"Get ready to move fast," Lin Chong ordered, and raised the whistle to her lips again.

This much closer, the sound struck across the water with the force of a stone arrowhead.

Lin Chong *felt* the soldiers orient on them. Felt every hostile energy turn their way.

More importantly, she felt Zhang Shun hear—head coming around where she swam in the deep, spinning and whipping about only to realize the enemy was on all sides . . .

Seventh Brother had begun moving the boat before Lin Chong gave the order. Arrows splashed against the black water where they had just been. "Inward. Toward them," Lin Chong directed. Theirs was the only boat Zhang Shun had a chance of reaching.

Shouts up ahead. Someone giving the command to root them out. Seventh Brother twisted their path, zigzagging them into the dizzy and unexpected. More arrows missed, but the edge of the next volley grazed the boat, two arrowheads socking into the hull right next to Lin Chong's foot. Seventh Brother ducked down and poled faster.

Up ahead—there, between and below the chaos, a white streak zipping beneath the surface of the water, pale as the underbelly of a fish—Zhang Shun swimming for them with impossible swiftness. A little closer, only a little . . .

More Imperial vessels honed in, this time from behind and to the side. One grounded against some reeds, but the other burst out toward them, its oarsmen stroking hard, with discipline and skill and speed.

Too much speed. Zhang Shun wouldn't make it before the enemy was upon them.

"I've got this, Drill Instructor!" cried Seventh Brother Ruan.

By the time Lin Chong called for him to go, he had already

dropped his pole across the boat and disappeared beneath the surface, his dive so smooth it barely rippled.

The man acting as the boat's captain shouted an order to the archers. Lin Chong threw herself flat, but an arrow still would have speared her thigh had not some sixth sense yanked her into a roll to the side. The tiny craft rocked beneath her. She came up to one knee, bringing the crossbow around and loosing three bolts that found three oarsmen.

This time she was close enough, the flames still bright enough, to see Seventh Brother's performance in glorious detail.

His hands came up on the rim of the boat, dagger in his teeth, and he burst out of the water in a flip that took him exactly where the soldiers thought he wasn't. The archers scrambled for swords; the oarsmen scrambled for any weapon—not fast enough when their colleagues' corpses fell heavy across them. Seventh Brother Ruan danced the dance of a demon, flitting between the fighters as agilely as he swam through the waves.

Lin Chong helped him out with another two bolts from the crossbow.

By then Zhang Shun had reached their boat. Lin Chong reached out to help her slide on board while Seventh Brother peacocked amid the carnage he'd just completed.

"Get back here!" Lin Chong shouted, her hands slipping on Zhang Shun's wet forearms and water sloshing to soak her front.

Seventh Brother dove back into the water just as gracefully as before.

Another boat broke through behind the one he had just leapt from.

"Down!" Lin Chong yelled to Zhang Shun, tackling them both to the side before the arrows had even loosed. "Get us to Seventh Brother!"

Zhang Shun snatched up the pole, but it was unnecessary. Seventh Brother had reached them. Zhang Shun kept the pole thrust down ready to push off while heaving Seventh Brother into the boat with one muscled arm, and Lin Chong let fly again with the crossbow. This time the men ducked and threw up shields, and no silhouettes went down.

Lin Chong heard the next command too late.

She spun back to Zhang Shun and Seventh Brother. The arrows thudded into the wood of the boat, one at the bow, one into the hull near the stern. One whistled past Lin Chong's face so close the fletching slashed her.

And two more slammed into Seventh Brother Ruan's back where he climbed half in, half out of the boat.

"Brother!" Zhang Shun cried.

"Get him in!" Lin Chong ordered. Fury swirled up in her, and she let fly more bolts, but the other boat was coming at them at speed. Steel flashed in the men's hands, the crew bristling to meet them. Lin Chong drew her long knife, and all she could think of was the arrowheads burying themselves in Seventh Brother's body, Seventh Brother who was her kindred here on Liangshan, and him and Zhang Shun here on her boat and she had to *protect them—*

The knife came up and she ran.

Ran without thinking about it. Ran without questioning. Ran without doubting whether she could race across water.

Without falling. Without sinking.

Her boot soles barely splashed against the surface. The other boat saw her coming, but too many of the men froze in momentary shock, and before they could recover, Lin Chong was among them. Her knife danced. One soldier, two, three. She ducked and spun, kicking off the swaying planks of the boat's hull to smash a heel into an oarsman, sweep an armored officer off and into the water. The power of her strikes landed before she connected, crushing into skulls and ribs and taking men overboard, each move bursting in fundamental energies and righteous rage.

In one final spin her knife thrust out, one foot stretched back against the rolling boat, her stance wide, her steel stabbing straight up into the base of the commander's throat.

Blood welled up and down his armor. She slid the blade out,

and his body fell to bounce off the boat's edge and splash flat in the black.

Lin Chong turned back. Across the water, Zhang Shun's white face stared at her, slack, Seventh Brother Ruan cradled in her arms.

Lin Chong did not pause or blink. She ran lightly off the boat and skidded back across the water to land alongside Zhang Shun. Their boat did not rock at all when she placed her feet down.

"Get us to the rendezvous," she ordered a still-staring Zhang Shun, and crouched to take Seventh Brother Ruan.

Seventh Brother Ruan's body.

His spirit had fled. She knew. Without checking, she knew. She curled the fingers of her other hand next to his nose and mouth anyway, but no air tickled the skin.

She let his blood make her battle dress sodden, holding him while Zhang Shun steered them unerringly into the narrow back waterways, the ones the Imperial army would never find.

CHAPTER 30

So this was what it felt like to be in a battle, thought Lu Da.

As yet it hadn't been very exciting. A lot of waiting. And itching. Lu Da adjusted her position for the thousandth time, the brush squashed flat in a small circle around her.

"Stop fidgeting," hissed Shi Qian, she of the sticky fingers, the thief of the Three Fleas. Doubtless Shi Qian was used to hanging upside down from rafters until a family was asleep and then prancing away with all of their valuables. *She* wouldn't be bothered by squatting in the undergrowth for half the night.

"'S not like they can see us up here," grunted Lu Da. "There's no need for stealth."

"Let's hurry this up!" groused Li Kui. "I want to get down to where I can start upping my kill count. Not letting those prissy-foots beat me just because they get to start sooner."

Another one of the Three Fleas snickered—Yang Xiong, it sounded like. "You could always add an extra thousand for everything we drop on Cai Jing's army now."

"Nah, wouldn't feel right. Gotta get the bite of my axe in flesh," Li Kui said.

"Hush," snapped Commander Yang. Not for the first time. The bandits quieted.

They crouched high up on the mountainside, just at the edge of the fissure that led straight down to the shoreline where the army was sure to land. Long before Cai Jing had decided to pick this fight, they'd built sensible defenses here, ones that would protect the mountain from any enemy that dared cross the marsh. Barriers held back immense stacks of logs and boulders that, once released, would thunder down to bury whoever set foot on the shore. Even farther up, several seasons had been spent gradually damming the waterfall that had helped carve this gully, and all that water was now packed into a large crater about three-quarters of the way up the mountain.

Releasing it would not go well on whoever was below.

Lu Da would have thought that sufficient, but Sister Lin and Commander Yang and the Professor and everyone who knew better, they said it would take out a bunch but then even more would swarm over the corpses like roaches. That's why they'd have a third line, led by Chao Gai, where Sister Hu and Sister Song and Sister Sun and all the rest would be waiting. They'd dug a bunch of pits and other traps and would hold the mountain against any who survived those. Lu Da and the rest of Commander Yang's group would rush down to join them, and Sister Lin's group would be making their way around from the water to back them all up too.

That was probably where things would get more battle-like, Lu Da expected.

A sharp whistle echoed across the mountain. Commander Yang sat up swiftly, gazing out in the direction of Chao Gai's group.

"It begins," she said. "To your positions."

Commander Yang didn't make extra words when she meant business.

Glad to be moving, Lu Da lurched up on tingly legs from sitting too long and hiked up to the position she shared with Shi Qian the master thief. The next post above them was the Xie twins, their outlines tall in the dark, made more towering by the ferocious tiger skins they wore as cloaks and the gleam of their iron hunting tridents. Lu Da couldn't see anyone else, but at the next post up would be Li Kui and Yang Xiong, with Du Qian and Song Wan across the way, and so on and so on, all the way up until the dam. That bit wasn't manned yet—once they let loose their avalanche, Commander Yang said they'd have time to reset at the dam to pour down on the next swarm of newcomers.

All very impressive, in Lu Da's opinion.

She craned her neck to try to see out on the water. Was that a gout of flame she glimpsed? Or were they too far? But it seemed very fast before more whistles rang out and Commander Yang was telling them to *stand ready, won't be long now, vigilance!*

Lu Da laid her staff aside and gripped the heavy wooden pins keeping the barrier in place. Across from her, Shi Qian did the same. Shi Qian was all lightfooted and wiry, but strong, as thieves who hung from building rafters probably had to be. Still, if she couldn't pull her side, Lu Da had once uprooted a willow tree with her bare hands, so they would be all right together.

The mountainside seemed to hold its breath.

Then, so suddenly it seemed surreal, Commander Yang yelled, "*Heave!*"

Lu Da wrenched the first heavy pins free. The barrier began cracking outward with a terrific groan. Shi Qian struggled a moment longer, but within a single turn they were kicking out the support struts, one then two then three, the monstrous load stacked behind chewing to get free. Lu Da reached for the last one, only for it to crack with the clap of one of those exploding rockets.

The first mighty rock barreled straight at Lu Da's head. She dove to the side and it clipped her shoulder instead. The load roared from its prison, gargantuan logs too huge to fit one's arms around, boulders and chunks of mountain even larger than Lu Da, all emerging in a storm of chaos like a dragon disturbed from the deep.

With Shi Qian still right in its path. Too far away for Lu Da to reach.

Lu Da groped for the power of her god's tooth, knowing she'd be too late, but the thief yelled "*Ai!*" and leapt straight up, kicking off one of the emerging boulders to make it to the lower branch of an enormous pine, one that leaned out of the slope above them. She dangled there, the rush of rock and stone and wood crashing by not a pace below and thundering into the fissure and down the mountainside.

Lu Da grinned. The chicken stealer did have skills, didn't she!

One of the bandits upslope was not so lucky.

Lu Da was barely aware of Commander Yang's orders anymore over the chaos and noise—*"Heave, weaklings!"* and *"Prove your sorry worth!"* and the like directed at some of the haojie who still worked to release their traps. The mountain began to shake, the manufactured tumble becoming an avalanche, and somehow Lu Da still heard one of the Xie twins shout.

A shout of wrongness. Of anguish.

Still clutching her god's tooth, Lu Da snapped her gaze up. The Xie twins were both upright, dancing upon an outcropping above the fray, leaning out with their massive tridents to reach for . . .

Yang Xiong. Caught in the avalanche, clutching onto a huge log that plummeted right in the center of the crush, at any moment to be smashed flat by the rest.

Lu Da wasn't going to let that happen to a Liangshan sister. Not in a thousand years.

Despite any recent practice, her god's tooth was still far more of a hammer than a delicate needle. But she grabbed that hammer anyway, ready to slam it right in the middle of anywhere she could. She ran for the lip of the fissure that had become a demon-choked waterfall—and jumped straight off its edge.

She landed in the avalanche, *fell* with the avalanche. Armored by the god's tooth, she punched her way clear of everything that struck at her, a melee fight that was Lu Da the Flower Monk versus eight hundred and eight roaring objects instead of people. She tried to claw her way toward Yang Xiong, but everything was moving too fast, and she could only get her fingernails into the edge of the giant log the other woman clung to.

Without any plan, Lu Da dug in and hauled, letting the full power of her god's tooth howl behind.

Her feet kicked out against falling boulders that gave no solid foundation, but she shoved off them nonetheless and swung the great tree upright, in a wild circle, Yang Xiong still clinging to it like a beetle, and let fly.

The rush of the god's tooth fluctuated through her consciousness. She was starting to lose control, she knew it, she could tell. The power went slippery in her senses, like oil-soaked fish scales. With one panting, final effort, Lu Da screwed up every bit she had left and did as Commander Yang had ordered.

She *heaved.*

She burst out of the avalanche in a high arc above the slope. Pine branches whipped at her and twigs left bloody smacks on her face. She wasn't ready for the ground when it slapped up against her, either.

When a very bruised Lu Da finally rolled to a stop in a clearing not too far from where she'd left, it was to see Yang Xiong dragging herself up in an injured—but living—floppiness.

Lu Da sat back and gave a very pleased grunt. She'd done it.

Footsteps hurried from above. Commander Yang, along with the Xie twins and Shi Qian, who must have dropped down from the branch once the full load had rushed by below. Shi Qian ran to duck under the arm of her fellow Flea and support her up.

"We've got a problem," Commander Yang said loudly. The thunder they'd released was beginning to recede down the mountain slope, but it still dominated the air, enough that it needed shouting over. "One of the high posts didn't fall right. Blocked the path. We can't get up to the dam."

Lu Da shoved herself to her feet. "We'll just get it unblocked, then!"

Her legs went all to wobbles. She had to sit down very suddenly on the log Yang Xiong had ridden.

"In just a heartbeat or two, we'll get it unblocked," she amended, shamefaced.

"Iron Whirlwind's trying. I've got some of the others looking for another way around, but it's all sheer stone above. Thing is, we can't wait. The timing's gotta go right or the haojie down at the bottom, they'll get overrun. Reverend Monk, how long before you can give us some of that god's tooth action again?"

Everything in Lu Da wanted to leap up and cry, "Right now!" but she didn't even know if she could do the leaping up part, let alone the rest of it. "A few breaths' rest before I can heave more boulders, Commander."

She cringed inside as she said it. What if Cai Jing descended on them now with his fancy new unnaturally made god's teeth? She should have thought things through better. *Impatient, reckless Flower Monk . . . you're always too impulsive . . .*

Yang Xiong moved her drooping head to tilt up at Shi Qian, and her expression went all shifty-smiled, probably the same way it did before she stabbed someone. "How many does it take to free the dam?"

"Ha!" Shi Qian cried. "You're right, just one of us vixens could do it with a little grit. Commander, sheer stone's nothing to *me.* Same as prancing down the street for you lot."

"Even you would need more time than we've got, little Flea," Commander Yang said. "You'd have to snake all the way round—"

"Then have the good monk throw me!" Shi Qian flung one arm so wide that Yang Xiong winced and staggered against her. "Sister Lu, hurling a little light flea up the mountain has gotta be easier than moving bits of that mountain, right?"

"It's not *hard,* I could do it right now," Lu Da scoffed. "But I'd splat your face on the rocks for sure. My god's tooth is like me, all the way down. We punch through skulls, we don't pick up rice by the grain."

"You couldn't splat me if you tried," Shi Qian said. "The day *I* don't land on my feet is the day I want death to catch me! Send me up, Flower Monk. Right now!"

"But—" Lu Da looked to Commander Yang, because—because Lu Da would cheerfully risk her own life, but she wouldn't be responsible for splatting one of her sisters, she *wouldn't.*

Except Commander Yang went all grave and said, "Heavenly King and the others need us," and that was that.

Lu Da tottered to her feet and dubiously called up the rushing power of the god's tooth. Shi Qian helped Yang Xiong sit down and then danced forward.

Lu Da looked to Commander Yang one more time.

Then she let go.

The push was bigger and faster and harder than she'd meant—of *course* it was, it always was, and she'd warned them, too! The wiry little thief soared up and away, high over their heads, speeding toward the mountain plateau where their last main trap waited to be sprung.

Or—approximately that way. As much as Lu Da screwed up her face and concentrated on shoving in the right direction, her whole body tensing from crown to bowels, she wasn't sure she hadn't missed the mountain entirely.

Maybe she'd thrown too far, and Shi Qian would wing through the stars forever.

She slumped down on the log in the dark, now truly wrung dry.

"Up you get, knaves," Commander Yang ordered. "If Shi Qian has taken the dam, it's time for the rest of us to have the others' backs down at the shoreline. They'll need all the help if she can't move fast enough."

Lu Da rolled back up, weaving slightly, and cast about to find where she'd dropped her staff.

"They're late!" In one hand Wu Yong's chain snapped out, in the other a blade slashed forth. Two more enemy soldiers fell. "There must be a problem. We have to fall back!"

Chao Gai dispatched another Guardsman of her own, then backed toward Wu Yong in temporary reprieve. "A little more time. We can hold them!"

Wu Yong was not certain that was true. Once pieces of the Imperial army had begun making it through to the shore, the next of Liangshan's defenses had worked perfectly, a sweeping avalanche that buried at least a battalion or so. The men had sobbed out in fear when they realized the trap, loud enough to hear over the mountain shaking itself apart.

Not that anyone heard them for long. Not for long at all.

The next group had swarmed ashore more cautiously, climbing

over the graves of their fellows, bearing an inferno's worth of torches since the only result of their stealth had been for so many of them to be murdered in the dark. The rush of released floods from above should have buried them in the same grave as their predecessors, but it had failed to come, and they began crawling up the ridge in a rapidly multiplying horde toward where the haojie waited. The terrain delayed them still further—alternately sinking them in mud and forcing them to push through dense undergrowth or over rough boulders—but inexorably they advanced, up from the shore, slithering toward the first fold of high ground where the haojie had staked out their defensive line.

Meanwhile, Yang Zhi's sharp whistles came down the mountainside, always the same one, *working—working*—they were working on it—

Something's gone wrong.

The government soldiers climbed up the slope in handfuls and then packs and then mobs, swollen with fury and with bloodlust in their eyes and hands. Chao Gai gave the signal and the haojie burst from the brush to defend their home. The battle was joined in a fever of speed and blood and silhouettes in the night, as Wu Yong and the others, everyone who was not on the water or far upslope, they slashed and stabbed and hit—*keep them back keep them back keep them back, corral them below, just a little more time for those above to finish, keep them back to where death can rush down from above*—but something had gone wrong.

Song Jiang appeared beside Wu Yong and Chao Gai, a two-edged sword in one hand, blood sheeting down one full side of her face. She didn't seem aware of it.

"We have one more pit," she reported in a pant. "Sister Hu's taking it."

Wu Yong turned just in time to catch hurrying torches and shouts, and a flitting shadow that must be Sister Hu, racing a winding dance through the forest as bait. The men who tried to follow had their thirsty yells of pursuit turn to shocked terror as the ground gave way beneath their feet and swallowed them.

That was the last prepared ambush they had set. Down to their hands and steel now . . . and if they let the army become uncontained . . .

If they yielded, it would be over. If they yielded, Yang Zhi's haojie up on the mountain would have no chance of stopping this wave of the incursion with the release of the dam. The bandits would be pushed up the slope in retreat, their base raided and torched. The heroes of Liangshan would become no more than a small guerilla force in hiding, reduced to attacking from pockets of the forest until either full defeat or unlikely escape.

Another group of soldiers struggled up to gain the top of the ridge. Wu Yong moved as one with Chao Gai and Song Jiang, together a bristling crab of six legs and hands, sword and chain and sword again, fists and feet and no mercy.

Song Jiang was the weakest fighter of the three, and she slaughtered seven of them. She had learned, since coming to Liangshan.

"We have to hold," Chao Gai said. In the night, her eyes were dark diamonds in her still-bruised face, unreadable. "We must hold. Commander Yang will succeed."

And then what? Wu Yong didn't say. Cai Jing could keep sending troops until their bodies filled the swamp and made it solid enough for more attackers to walk across. Did it matter if the bandits lost the mountain now or on the next assault?

Of course it matters.

It mattered to who they were. Because if they crushed another thousand troops here when they themselves numbered less than forty, that would become the stuff of songs. It would upend history, prove everything that needed proving, to themselves and to the people and to the Empire and its overreaching oppression of ordinary citizens.

It mattered because of the legacy they left.

Wu Yong whipped the copper chain back in readiness, gripped the sword with knuckles already split to mingle with other people's blood. A commotion came from below, shouted orders that were hastily muffled.

"They come," Song Jiang said.

Chao Gai's back was up against Wu Yong's. The Heavenly King stood straight as a blade, straight as her moral souls that would stab these Imperial worms through the heart, whether or not it would be enough to save anyone, in the end.

"Does Liangshan have any ghosts beneath it, by any chance?" Wu Yong murmured.

Chao Gai tilted her face away, her expression disappearing in the darkness. "If it did . . . you would not want to meet them."

They might add some here today. Wu Yong found appeal in the idea of haunting Liangshan forever. Such that even in death, the Empire might not succeed in removing them.

Sounds of movement, armor, feet tromping in unison, wetland mud slapping and sucking and plants crushed under too many booted feet. Wu Yong raised weapons, ready to die.

With a great unearthly yell, someone barreled from behind them straight down into the approaching mass of soldiers.

Wu Yong stumbled slightly. New shapes charged by on all sides. Wu Yong heard, "Take *that!* And *there!* The Iron Whirlwind comes for your heads!" and then the Xie twins had appeared too, racing in with their massive hunting tridents, and Lu Da with her iron staff and Commander Yang Zhi with that shining sword of legend—

"Hold the line," the Blue Beast commander shouted to them. "The water is coming. Faith! Hold them!"

"Hold. Hold!" Other haojie took up the cry, so many voices, and when Wu Yong turned, Lin Chong and Second Brother and Zhang Shun were all racing up too, leading an onslaught from those who had been out on the water. "We hold! We *hold!*"

With new energy, the haojie rushed the line, all united, with nothing in the world to lose.

Only a few turns later—enough for Li Kui to take twenty or fifty heads, enough for Wu Yong's battle dress to become soaked with enemy blood, enough for several ranks of the enemy to begin to break and scatter—the mountain began to shake one more time.

Chao Gai brought the carved wooden whistle to her lips and blew.

As one, the bandits retreated, slashing their way back. Their shocked enemy took a moment to react, failing to press the apparent advantage. Only Li Kui, in a haze of blood and decapitation, needed to be called again.

They ran together, scrambling back up the ridge, each giving a hand to the other, dragging up any who lagged or stumbled so that no haojie fell behind. The last bandits' boots barely skimmed over the top of the ridge when the water hit.

More overwhelming even than the logs and boulders, the pent-up springs and snowmelt from years of the ancient mountain poured down in a flood that smashed flat any in its path. The government soldiers flailed and were tossed like toys before being gobbled by its ravenous hunger. The troops had packed onto the shore with the density of an insect swarm, and now they were swept away just as insects would be.

Up on the ridge, the row of bandits cheered with lusty victory.

Spray misted their faces and it cleansed like the blood of their enemies. Hu Sanniang and Xie Bao thrust their weapons in the air repeatedly. Zhu Gui the Crocodile grabbed Sun Erniang the Witch in delirious embrace. Sister Mu the Slightly Restrained scooped up rocks from the ground and flung them into the maelstrom flood, yelling, "That's what you get, government curs! Just try taking the haojie of Liangshan!"

Wu Yong felt a wide grin forming, the peaceful satisfaction of singular accomplishment.

Maybe they would not win tomorrow. But they had won *tonight.*

From somewhere out in the still-rushing whitewater, a single unseen crossbow bolt speared out of the night and flew like a demon's hand guided it, straight and straighter, blown by some evil wind.

Wu Yong saw it too late, spinning in horror to block or tackle or move or do anything else at all. Across, Lin Chong moved faster than any human, and it still was not fast enough.

She was only in time to catch Chao Gai's falling body when the crossbow bolt winged in and shattered the Heavenly King's left cheek.

CHAPTER 31

Lin Chong ran with Wu Yong for the camp, their legs stumbling under the too-heavy burden they carried between them.

Chao Gai.

Lin Chong refused to think of it as carrying her body. Not when she still lived, despite everything, giving lie to the bolt standing straight out under her eye, embedded so deep it must crack the back of her skull. Half her face had sunk in bloody collapse, unrecognizable.

Do not think about it—the Divine Physician has many skills not seen elsewhere, it is not for you to say . . . she lives still . . .

Sister An hurried to meet them as soon as they stumbled up to the building she was using as an infirmary. Someone fleet-footed must have run to tell her—several bandits converged with torches, throwing the scene into the brightness of near-daylight.

Lin Chong had no trouble at all understanding the Divine Physician's gestures this time. They followed her to a comfortable pallet against the wall, lowering Chao Gai oh so carefully, Sister An working to stabilize her splintered face and head.

Time seemed to stutter at that point. Lin Chong would later remember a hurried consultation with Commander Yang, a rapid directing of which bandits would rotate through the watchtowers during what was sure to be only a brief reprieve, with the others ordered to take food and rest. The Blue Beast glanced at Wu Yong and Lin Chong and volunteered to take the command shift.

She must have left after that, to oversee the rest of the bandits, but Lin Chong had no recollection of it. Only of sitting numbly in a corner some time later, next to Seventh Brother's body where it was stretched out quiet and still. Second Brother and Fifth Brother wept quietly nearby, embracing each other. Seventh Brother wasn't the only haojie they had lost, either . . . Du Qian, Wang Lun's oldest and most trusted lieutenant, had fought to the last on the field by their sides. Now Du Qian joined Seventh Brother to be laid out here too, solemn and subdued as they had never been in life.

Several of the other haojie helped each other bind injuries and splint wounds while Sister An focused on their leader. Yang Xiong had more than a few broken bones. Noblewoman Chai, who had joined the defensive line as lustily as the rest, had been slashed deep across the ribs in the fighting. Song Jiang had to be bullied away from Chao Gai's side for someone to paste her scalp closed.

Sister An was still working on Chao Gai. That had to mean something.

Lin Chong had never seen anyone receive a wound like that and live.

Someone let out a low cry. Lin Chong looked up. Time had skipped again. The hall was mostly empty now, save for Wu Yong who sat by Chao Gai's bedside, head lowered and still, and Song Jiang, her forehead bandaged, stumbling against a wall. It was she who had cried out, in response to something the Divine Physician had said.

For the first time, Sister An had left Chao Gai's bedside. The expression on Song Jiang's face told everything about why.

Lin Chong rose stiffly and limped over to them. "Is she . . ."

Song Jiang glanced up at the Divine Physician. "Sister An says—she says . . ."

She couldn't finish.

An Daoquan moved her hands again. Gently, the motions small.

"She says Sister Chao can speak, that we can—we can hear her last words. Say our farewells, and our thanks . . ."

She moved as if to step toward Chao Gai's bedside, but had to be helped by Sister An.

Lin Chong followed.

Chao Gai . . . it was hard to believe she still breathed. The bolt had been removed, and Sister An's heroic efforts were visible in the strong-smelling poultices that drew poison from the wound, the inventive splints that attempted to keep fragmented bones from falling in, the mind-bending number of tiny sutures that strove to sew her face back together. Despite all, the Heavenly King's kind visage was—in pieces, now, like a shattered vase, all jagged fragments and pooling blood.

Even the Divine Physician's powers had not stood a chance.

Song Jiang joined Wu Yong at their leader's bedside, reaching out to clasp Chao Gai's limp hand. "It's Song Jiang, Heavenly King. We are here."

"Sister . . ." More fresh blood welled up from Chao Gai's mouth, drowning her speech. Song Jiang quickly reached for a cloth and tried to touch it to the edges of her lips, tentatively, as if unsure what might cause more pain. Lin Chong had remained standing behind her and glanced around for the doctor, but An Daoquan had disappeared.

Gone to tell the rest of the haojie that their leader was dying.

"You set us on the path," Song Jiang murmured. Tears dripped from her, soaking the edge of the pallet with the speed of a spring rain. "You turned Liangshan toward our purpose. We would follow you forever, Heavenly King, we will continue to follow, you have my promise . . ."

"Cai Jing . . ." Chao Gai's mouth formed the syllables, half inaudible. "He did this . . ."

"We will revenge you." Song Jiang promised it with a dead finality.

"Whoever does. Shall carry . . ." Small coughs racked her body, the tremors of someone who had no strength left. Then, with sudden energy, her hand snapped out to tighten on Song Jiang's, and the one eye that was not bleeding and swollen shut seemed to gain focus. "The haojie who does shall lead Liangshan to our future."

The statement had taken her last reserve. Chao Gai's body slumped back into the pallet, her face relaxing into terrible emptiness.

"Sister!" Song Jiang cried, clutching at the hand that had gone still in hers. "Sister, please, you cannot leave us—we need you—please—"

Others had begun filing back into the infirmary hall, somber and too late. When they saw Song Jiang weeping and broken, heads began to bow, some of the bandits slipping down to kneel, and then more, until almost all of Liangshan gathered here. Paying respects to their Heavenly King.

Lin Chong joined them, going to one knee, curling around a deep pain that ached within her. Seventh Brother's death had hurt; now Chao Gai's kicked her inside, down at the base of her souls, bruising everything she knew. Their long talks, Chao Gai's relaxed philosophy, her encouragement . . . the way she opened Lin Chong's mind to what was possible, and to what was possible to become.

Sparring together like they danced with the gods. Lin Chong had never felt more free. Like two phoenixes twirling high above the earth, any doubts left behind.

You taught all of us, Heavenly King. So much.

A gasp and a cry of denial rang out from the doorway, and Lu Da pushed into the hall, hobbling with fatigue or injury or both. She wobbled forward, shoving up to kneel right at Chao Gai's bedside, between Lin Chong and Song Jiang. "Sister Chao," she sobbed. "Sister Chao, Heavenly King, I'm sorry for anything I ever said wrong, anything I did that was unkind, I'm sorry, I'm sorry, come back to us . . ."

Lin Chong reached out to grip her shoulder, even though she doubted she could provide comfort.

"What do we do now?" wept Lu Da to Chao Gai's still form. "What will we do without you? How can we go on . . ."

Lu Da was more right than she knew. Losing a commander in the middle of a battle . . . how they went on was not merely an emotional question, but logistical. And urgent.

It was a question with only one answer.

CHAPTER 32

"You must lead them now." Wu Yong was the one to say it.

The Tactician stood with head still bowed, showing no emotion, not meeting anyone else's eyes. But Wu Yong had been the one to pry Song Jiang from Chao Gai's side, finally, and bring her back here to a conference with only the three of them: Lin Chong, Wu Yong, and Song Jiang.

Song Jiang. Who must become the new leader of Liangshan.

"What? No!" the poet cried. She backed away from them, her eyes large and filled with grief and now panic. Those eyes found Lin Chong. "Sister Lin—we're in the middle of a military crisis. You or Commander Yang—"

"We're both relatively new to the mountain." Lin Chong felt as if someone else said the words through her. For her, full grief could come later, and would. "The haojie don't need a fighter. They need a leader—someone to follow. They need you."

Song Jiang's jerking, stricken movements arrested themselves, her eyes tracking over Lin Chong's face. "Before. You never wanted me to be . . ."

"That was before." Lin Chong swallowed. "You're what the mountain needs. You can carry forth Chao Gai's legacy."

To lead them into a last, glorious sacrifice.

"Sister Chao said—" Song Jiang had to clamp down over her heaving breath before continuing. "The one who avenges her is the next one who will lead us. She said. We have to honor that."

Liangshan would not have a next leader, only a last leader. Lin Chong did not say it aloud. Song Jiang might not have the same experience with war or tactics, but they both must know.

Wu Yong had become very still ever since bringing Chao Gai

in, after that reckless, tragic hurry with Lin Chong, bearing Chao Gai's weight and covered in her blood. The Tactician had sat by her bedside as if carved from rock, not speaking, not moving, not weeping. And now standing as if under the weight of centuries.

"You know what Sister Chao would have wanted," Wu Yong said to Song Jiang, quietly. "You can lead in her same spirit . . . You're the only one, Spring Rain."

The slight lean on Song Jiang's nickname must have been intentional. The Spring Rain—always there when needed, somehow; generous to a level that left recipients in shock; healing and prosperity left in her wake.

Wu Yong was right. The bandits would follow the Spring Rain.

Song Jiang's hands came up to her face. "No. I cannot—Sister Chao's last wishes—if I play this role, it can only be temporary, you understand? You know I will always help, and whatever you say we need tonight I shall do—but when our next leader proves themselves . . ."

"Until then," Wu Yong agreed, face giving nothing away.

Song Jiang leaned up against the wall, her palms still pressing against her eyes, as if she had to hold herself in place lest she break apart at any moment. "They might be willing to follow, but I don't know what to do," she confessed to them. "I don't know what *we* can do . . . Chancellor Cai still has thousands more troops across the marsh. We have nothing left but ourselves . . ."

"He hasn't used his new god's teeth yet," Lin Chong added, grim. "We'll have angered him now. That may spur him, if he was reluctant before."

"Then we die two ways instead of one?" Song Jiang's despair was obvious. "Friends, I—I will lead the haojie where you tell me, if I must, but . . ."

"We have one chance," Wu Yong said.

Lin Chong looked over sharply.

Face drawn in deep lines, shoulders stooped, Wu Yong might have aged eight hundred years in a night. "There is the saying," the Tactician said. "'A snake with no head cannot move.' What foot soldier would wish to march where half of his fellows have already died? Only one ordered to."

"You intend us to go after Cai Jing," Lin Chong said.

"We must behead the snake and either loot or destroy his new weapons. Recall—the rumors said even the Imperial Court did not stand by his meddling with the powers of god's teeth. Even if we die, we shall take this oppressive new power of his with us, along with one of the most corrupt men in all the Empire. We must try."

"How?" Lin Chong demanded. *If it were as easy as that, we would have done it to start, and Seventh Brother and Du Qian and Chao Gai, none of them would have been lost.* "You know as well as I do, Tactician—if any of us dare cross the marsh, we'd be picked off before the boat reaches shore."

"Before last night that may have been true." Wu Yong at last looked up and met Lin Chong's eyes. "The answer is—we don't go by boat. Zhang Shun told of what you did out on the water."

What she had done out on the water . . .

"We don't go by boat," Wu Yong said. "We send you."

When Seventh Brother Ruan had died. She had walked, run, and not even stopped to ask how.

Wu Yong reached out and gripped Lin Chong's arm hard enough to be painful. "You must save Liangshan, Sister Lin."

"*How* many troops?"

General Guan stayed kneeling before Cai Jing, bowed almost to the ground, not leaving the humble posture but not flinching in his report either. "We are still accounting for everyone, Grand Chancellor, but initial estimates are that almost two thousand men have not returned."

Two thousand men.

Two *thousand* men.

You should feel vindication, Cai Jing told himself, bitterness dripping in the realization. *You informed the other chancellors it would take this many. They scoffed, but you knew better.*

He hadn't truly believed it, though.

This was supposed to be an overwhelming victory. The Court would happily forget who was right and wrong about a deployment size if the leader of those companies came back in full celebration. If they did not, nobody would care that Cai Jing had warned, only that he had failed.

"I do bring some good news, Honorable Grand Chancellor," General Guan said.

No good news could make up for this. The bandits had defeated him. Worse—they had embarrassed him.

Twice.

"Speak, then. Quickly," Cai Jing commanded.

"We have found and marked the way through the marsh," the general answered. "If the bandits come at us again, on the water, we should now be able to overrun them, especially in the daylight. The defenses that have been reported on the shore are not any from untold dark powers, but opportunities of the terrain they will not be able to reuse. They must be close to running out of such moves, and once they are, we can take them easily."

"I shall consider that your sworn word, General. You will attack at first light."

"I'll lead the vanguard myself, Grand Chancellor."

Satisfactory. As long as they brought victory. Victory would excuse anything else.

Erase everything else.

"You will have more than men this time," Cai Jing promised.

Time to bring out every weapon at once. Gao Qiu would get to show his prowess with a god's fang after all.

If the bonding failed, or if Gao Qiu failed . . .

If that happened, Cai Jing would have thrown and lost. The walls would be on three sides, the only avenue remaining Bianliang and execution. A deserved fate for defying a direct decree of the Emperor and—worse—not achieving success in doing so. Cai Jing would meet his end, and if the omens held true—and Cai Jing knew in his bones they would, without him and all his efforts to defy them, they would hold—then within a handful of years, the Empire would fall as well.

All was being torn from his hands, a future he had fought so hard for but now might not even live to see. Before his own death, however, he could do one last thing for his lord and Emperor.

He could wipe out these bandits who destroyed everything they touched.

That traitorous old scholar Ling Zhen had shown him the way. If their last try with Lady Lu's elixir did not work, if Gao Qiu died or lost control, Cai Jing would take up two more of the god's fangs himself.

He would take them in his hands, and he would draw in the purity of his cause, his loyalty to the future of his Empire. He would focus the rage at his disgrace on these swamp bandits who had caused it, these weeping sores in the Empire's heart who would rot it from within.

If Lady Lu was to be believed, he would be able to remove their putrefaction fully, along with their base, their mountain, and the little swamp they hid behind. They would be cleansed from the Empire with no trace left.

So might a wide swathe of other citizens in the surrounding county. But if they knew, they should be proud to die for their Empire. As Cai Jing would be proud.

Together, those citizens and Cai Jing himself would all soar into the next life with the highest of virtue, dutiful servants who had done everything in their power to make the land whole.

Lu Da hiked down to the shoreline, most of her strength recovered but her heart stretched and hurting like it never had before.

Dawn did not quite touch the water yet. The sky had tinted itself gray enough to wash out the stars, but the marsh still lay shrouded in shadow. Shapes bobbed in its darkness—a boot here, a corpse there, an empty, capsized boat that drifted forlorn and alone.

They deserved it, every one of them. Sister Chao's murderers.

Lin Chong was waiting, staring out over the water as if she measured it with her eyes. "Here," she called. "Are you ready?"

Lu Da was decidedly *not* ready to try running across a deadly moat of a swamp that was many li wide and could suck you right down into its maw if you fell in it. Her souls had nearly jumped out of her skin when the Tactician had told her to go meet Lin Chong, and what they planned and that Lu Da was to go too, at Sister Lin's especial request. They were to hare off toward the western reach of the marsh, where dense stands of wetland trees and clumpy muddy isles collected into a gloomy jungle no boat could cut through . . . the enemy would not be watching for anyone emerging from such a place, so Wu Yong said, and the vegetation would hide them from stray eyes until nearly on shore.

Running across water! Lu Da had no fear of being on a boat, if someone like the Ruans or the Tongs were captaining it, but a boat had a solid thickness of planks between her bum and drowning. No, she was not ready at all.

But Sister Chao had not been ready to die.

Sister Du and Seventh Brother Ruan hadn't been, either.

Lu Da was not ready, but she would do this. For them.

She came abreast of her elder sister, down on the muddy bank, and hefted her heavy staff. She wondered if she should leave it behind. It wouldn't make them more likely to sink, would it?

"I don't know how to do this," she confessed to Sister Lin.

Lin Chong turned to face her. "You can follow me. I trust you."

The statement was open, unvarnished, without hesitation or caveat. Despite everything, a warmth swelled in Lu Da's chest.

"We must hurry," Sister Lin said. "Take my hand. And open your god's tooth."

Lu Da did as her sister asked.

Just as when they'd sat together before, Lu Da felt—not only the rush of her own god's tooth's familiar power—but another strength here, intertwining with it, winding through each other until they could support more than twice what they might alone. Lin Chong's strength, from somewhere beyond, that she somehow drew into herself with no artifact to help. This time, instead of jealousy, Lu Da felt only a quiet awe.

"Are you sure this will work, us doing this together?" she asked. Her voice felt strange and far away. She had to raise it to be sure of being heard.

"I don't know," Lin Chong answered. "But we have no more time. Now *run!*"

They pounded forward together. Lu Da's hand clutched Lin Chong's, their souls embracing until they moved as one. They ran and ran and didn't look when they ran straight off the shore, when their boots began smacking the water's surface in beautiful ripples like a stone skipping across forever.

In the same gray predawn, Song Jiang gathered Liangshan's remaining haojie for a last stand.

Wu Yong had helped her, positioning each of their members in the strongest tactical location for the best possible defense. It might mean nothing, in the end, but neither of them would have brooked the thought of anything less than striving to their utmost for Liangshan.

At least Wu Yong had been right and the others followed Song Jiang's command, without question or challenge. Some of them may have already seen her as Chao Gai's second and assumed this would be the way of things. To others, following the Spring Rain was akin to the natural order. Li Kui and Hu Sanniang and the Xie twins, the grieving Ruan brothers and the Tongs and the Three Fleas, even the surly Sun Erniang and Wang Lun's old lieutenant Song Wan . . . they looked at Song Jiang and they saw Liangshan's leader stepping into place.

She fit that place perfectly. Poised and composed. Evincing confidence, even if she did not feel it. Inspiring every one of them through example.

"I should say something to them," she murmured to Wu Yong, as they moved to take up their own posts. "Something that gives them courage. That makes them feel—that they are part of this, something greater than themselves, a family and a mission of justice. I don't . . ."

"What is it?" Wu Yong asked.

"I've always had words. Always." She brushed a hand over her face and tilted back her head to take in the graying sky. "I have no right words tonight, Professor. I have no poetry for our kindred."

"Whatever you say will be right," Wu Yong said softly.

It was.

Song Jiang climbed to the top of a boulder on this wooded and rocky slope they'd chosen to defend with their lives. She stood straight, with the silhouette of a hero from legend, and she called for all the haojie to listen, one last time.

"Today, we fight for Chao Gai. We fight for everything she wanted us to be, everything she believed we could be, to better the Empire. We fight for Sister Du and Seventh Brother Ruan, and we avenge them—our battle is a righteous one, and our souls are clean. For our Heavenly King."

She raised her two-edged sword in the air, not with a punch or a yell, but as if it were fact.

All across the slope, the other haojie raised sword and spear and staff and trident, and in one voice they echoed:

"For the Heavenly King!"

CHAPTER 33

Lu Junyi was called to the command tent just before dawn.

She'd brewed a new batch of the elixir. Marshal Gao should drink of it again, to smooth his chances, even as he rode the peak of the dose from last night.

She wondered if they would listen to her when she suggested it. She found she couldn't care.

As she walked through the camp, soldiers were pouring out onto boats for another staggering assault. She had heard, filtering through the camp, that the first had gone less than well. A small jump of guilty eagerness had flipped over in her chest, though one quickly dulled. After all, Cai Jing still had most of his army—more than enough resources to throw at the bandits again, and again.

Plus, soon, a god's fang.

If it worked.

When a Guardsman accompanied her into the command tent, Cai Jing was waiting. Another ornate, carved wooden box sat at his feet, doubtless what he'd carried the additional god's fangs in for their journey. Lu Junyi knelt and bowed and said proper words, ones she didn't hear even as they left her mouth.

Gao Qiu stomped into the tent.

He was decked out for battle, in the full splendor of an Imperial Marshal marching to war. Given what she had heard of him, Lu Junyi had to wonder if Marshal Gao had even fought once on a battlefield himself in the past, or if he'd only bragged about it. He wore the armor with a strut, as if it made him more of a man.

"Well?" he barked. "Where is it?"

"Here, Marshal," the Chancellor said, and with one smooth move bent to open the chest. One of the god's fangs had been set in a chain to wear around the neck, like the one the dead Minister of War had used.

"I recommend a second draft of the elixir first," Lu Junyi spoke up. "If it pleases you, Grand Marshal."

"Get on with it, then."

She measured and passed him the cup. She could feel her hand shaking slightly, though she did not think it could be seen. The night before, standing over the crucible alone in her tent, she'd thought of Lin Chong and unwrapped a packet of poisonous zhen feathers, holding their violet and green deadliness and hesitating there in the dark for a long time.

In the end, her courage had failed her.

Gao Qiu drank the unadulterated draft and flung the cup back at her. Beneath the bravado, he seemed nervous. Probably less nervous than he should be, if he understood what he risked. Lu Junyi remembered again Commander Wen, howling soundlessly forever while trapped in his immortal prison, and Ling Zhen, burning himself from the inside when he first called upon the god's fangs, so bright it hurt even in her memory.

"Take it up at your pleasure, Marshal," Cai Jing said. "The power of the gods is yours. The men wait to cheer when you come to back them."

"When I come to *lead* them," Gao Qiu said pompously. He strode over and reached out a hand.

Hesitated.

A muscle in his cheek twitched, his expression going sour, a struggle showing bare on his face. His hand hovered just above the wooden chest, and he flexed his fingers.

The moment stretched, and still he did not reach down to lift the god's fang to possess it.

Somehow, hollowly, Lu Junyi was unsurprised. Gao Qiu had always been a craven man. Why should that change now, even when he was offered untold power? Why shouldn't he be frightened? He would find some excuse to refuse.

She wasn't sure what would happen then.

Cai Jing's fierce white eyebrows began to draw together. His eyes and mouth folded in, a compression of building fury.

At that moment, a shout came outside, along with the clash of steel, and something fell hard against the tent.

Gao Qiu and Cai Jing both spun toward the sound. Only the three of them stood inside, Cai Jing having dismissed all the Guardsmen for this delicate operation. Before any of them could make another move, the flap of the tent tore free.

It sailed off into the dawn breeze.

Cai Jing's personal guard lay littered outside, their corpses nothing more than a collection of limbs and armor. The morning sun stabbed into the tent, silhouetting two figures who stood in its rays, dressed in stolen battle uniforms to walk here among the camp and shining far too brightly themselves. One almost as tall and broad as the tent door itself, with arms that could crush a tree and brandishing a heavy metal staff, the other wielding a slender sword and somehow radiating just as much strength.

Lu Da and Lin Chong.

Everything flew from Lin Chong's mind in the moment the tent flap tore away and she saw Gao Qiu. Their mission, Cai Jing, the unnatural god's teeth, the haojie depending on them back at the mountain—everything.

She had never imagined encountering him here, again, so soon. Despite his rank, he'd barely ever marched with an army his entire career. She'd come in search of Cai Jing and his generals—to discover one of them was *Gao Qiu*—as if he insisted on embedding himself into every piece of her life—

Her vision filled with his narrow, pinched face, everything he had taken from her building up inside until it became a pressure that would have burst the very earth.

Her feet pounded against the ground, and she ran at him.

In the heartbeats it took to cross the space, Gao Qiu turned. He spun away from her racing attack, shot a hand into the open chest behind him, and swept something up out of it. Lin Chong didn't see, didn't care. She let the energy rush through her, balling up every reach of her developing scholar's skills with no other purpose but to smash him into the next life.

Just as she barreled forth to end him, Gao Qiu whipped back toward her and thrust out his opposite hand.

A thunderclap echoed through every fiber of Lin Chong's body. As if she'd punched a gong barehanded with all the strength she possessed. The force took her back and away from him, tumbling her against the tent wall, her bones ringing in pain.

How—Gao Qiu can't—

He couldn't beat her, he had never been able to beat her, twice she had proven it, and only with the intervention of others and his position had he been able to take *anything* from her . . .

Now he loomed over her. A sickly smile spread across his face so she could see all of his teeth. Lin Chong tried to push herself up and couldn't. Tried to take a breath and couldn't, her chest not functioning.

Gao Qiu stared down his nose at her, then looked approvingly at something in his hand and said, "As I deserve. Try to come at me now, *Arms Instructor.*"

She hadn't ever thought her title could become a sneer.

She gazed up at his hand, and then at him, and put everything together too slowly.

God's teeth. Cai Jing had been building god's teeth. Gao Qiu . . .

He had become a god.

She could feel the tooth now, a wild, pulsating *power,* so far beyond what even Lu Da had ever been able to draw with hers. Immense. Bottomless. Devastating. All in Gao Qiu's hand.

He could have ended her right then. Crushed her like a flea under his nail. Instead, he didn't use the god's tooth at all. He looked at her, and smiled, and drew back a boot to slam it into her ribs.

She curled against the ground, coughing, her lungs caving in around the pain. Any attempts to regain her breath had fled. Her concentration flickered, her own scholar's skills frayed and paltry in comparison to what Gao Qiu could now command.

Something crashed, back in the middle of the tent. Gao Qiu stumbled as if he'd been knocked from behind. A voice shouted, *"Marshal!"* in furious command.

Gao Qiu jerked guiltily and turned.

Lu Da whirled her staff in the center of the command tent, more energy rushing through her god's tooth than Lin Chong had ever seen from her, a bursting power, so much it threatened to sweep her away. She slashed her staff wildly, and a great cyclone tore at the walls of the tent, ripping free panels of its material to reveal squares of blue sky. Cai Jing had dived behind a chair, rolling away from her as her whirlwind shredded his clothes and beard, and it was he who had shouted. In another corner, Lin Chong registered Lu Junyi—somehow here, of all places, again, with *them,* and now also cowering from Lu Da's fury, hands over her head.

Through it all, Lu Da strode forward, struggling against her own power but with eyes and hands fully intent on the chest in the middle of the room.

The chest Gao Qiu had taken his god's tooth from.

Their mission came roaring back to Lin Chong's mind. Her own revenge had blacked out everything they had come here to do—what they *needed* to do.

She managed to push against the ground, to suck in a stuttering breath. She'd lost her sword in the fall but couldn't take time to look. Gao Qiu was turning on Lu Da, Lu Da who was heroically trying to carry out their mission alone.

He would kill her.

Lin Chong begged her broken body for a last jolt of strength, anything she could scrape from deep inside. She pushed up off the ground and launched herself between them.

For one heart-stopping moment she thought she would be too slow. That she would not make it, and Lu Da would die by Gao Qiu's hand.

Then his attack hit.

Instead of trying to fight back, she only reached to protect them, wrapping herself and Lu Da in a bubble of calm the same way she had with Wu Yong back in Bianliang. She was smoother at it this time. Gao Qiu's blast still took them back—they fell against each other and lost their footing, tumbling to the ground, but most of the violence rushed past them. More of the tent tore away, some of Cai Jing's furniture splintering.

He can't control it, Lin Chong realized. *Gao Qiu can't control it . . .*

On some level, though, he didn't need control. All he needed was to try to hit them with enough power, enough times.

Lu Da grasped at Lin Chong, and they helped each other up. Lu Da set her feet in a brave stance, holding her ground. Lin Chong did the same by her side, shoulder to shoulder, bolstering each other's strength.

Gao Qiu laughed, long and loud. He raised the fist holding the god's tooth triumphantly at the sky, and then he descended on them.

Lu Junyi crouched to the side of the tent, the fury of the battle raging around her, past her, stray blows catching her head or shoulder or leg so she fell and cried out in pain. The chaos snatched the sound away.

She had never thought to witness a battle of gods.

Never in her life had she seen a power like Gao Qiu's. The god's fangs—she had done this, she had made them, she had made *him.* Against all odds, her elixir had worked.

At least for longer now than anything else had—it worked. It *worked.*

She could scarcely believe it.

Gao Qiu smashed out at Lu Junyi's friends again, and somehow they again dodged the brunt of it. She could not have said how. Half the tent had gone, torn away by the battle. Others of the

Guard must be running for them, but they would be equally battered away.

Cai Jing hunched against the ground only a pace or so from her. Lu Junyi did not notice at first that he crawled to close the distance, not until his hand latched onto her forearm like a claw, crushing her flesh straight to the bone. He yanked her toward him so he could shout against her ear.

"You said he would have control!"

Lu Junyi turned to him, utterly stupefied.

How could the man talk like he had never seen a god's tooth? This was what they *did*! Even the least powerful among them took years of training for any sort of precision. This, what she had done, what she had *accomplished*, it was exactly what he had asked of her. This was the win.

He didn't even recognize it.

"This *is* control!" she shouted back. "It's this powerful!"

Cai Jing shoved her away from him, lamenting something that sounded like, "The Emperor will not be pleased . . ."

Somehow, ludicrously, Lu Junyi could have sworn that Cai Jing's voice had gone forlorn and lost and defeated.

She didn't see why. He had gotten his weapon; Gao Qiu would kill her friends and then kill *their* friends and become known as a living god; and Cai Jing . . .

Cai Jing was crawling for the chest with the god's fangs. It had spilled onto its side, the remaining precious pieces shining against the ground. He spit something to himself she couldn't hear—once, then again. She caught it that time.

"*I shall fix everything. It will be done. The Empire will remember.*"

He would fix . . .

Cai Jing was *crawling for the god's fangs* . . .

The realization collided into Lu Junyi's mind so hard it hurt. Cai Jing had not drunk the elixir; he could not take up a god's fang without being devoured by it in short order. He could only have one other purpose in reaching for them.

The one he'd threatened Lu Junyi with, if she failed. Take up two together, as Ling Zhen had, and erase from the Empire everything in a wide radius, in glorious light. The army, the marsh, Liangshan, its bandits—and as collateral damage, a good chunk of the surrounding country.

The battle in the rest of the tent stormed on, with no attention spared for Lu Junyi or Cai Jing, the man who would kill them all.

Lu Junyi felt herself moving toward him. A long-conditioned reticence made her slow, loyalty and position and power of the state all fighting through her. She almost wasn't sure she could.

Except . . . Cai Jing had no power over her anymore.

She was dead already. He was nothing.

The words from that last fight class with Lin Chong drifted back to her, from so long ago. *The control you have over yourself will equip you, unmatched, in any situation you encounter.*

Long-practiced fight moves flowed down her limbs, fluidity and balance, her muscles remembering forms and drills and sparring. Moves she'd trained to fluency in practice but almost never used against a true threat.

Until today.

Cai Jing was still close. Lu Junyi pressed her hands against the ground, pivoted, and brought her leg swinging. She executed it perfectly, with honed technique that would have gained her praise from any martial instructor.

Her heel came around and smashed straight into the face of the Grand Chancellor of all the Empire, the man second only to the Emperor himself.

Cai Jing flew like a thrown rag doll, his limbs flopping over themselves before he slid to a stop. His arms jerked, and he struggled against the ground, trying to rise, spitting blood from his mangled face.

Lu Junyi stared at what she had done. Her whole body cringed rigid in shock.

Before Cai Jing could react, however, the battle behind them rose to the pitch of demons, whiting out all of Lu Junyi's senses until she could see nothing at all.

"We have to attack him back!" Lu Da shouted. "Elder Sister, you can't keep this up forever!"

Lin Chong well knew that. Already tiring, she could feel her control slipping, rough and tattered around the edges as Gao Qiu's assaults buffeted them. She and Lu Da had pooled their forces together again, as well as they could, but even combined they were no match.

"Don't you think I want to?" Lin Chong ground out, smacking aside yet another blow that would have killed them. "That's Gao Qiu! What he did—*you* remember—"

"You can't worry about that right now!" cried Lu Da.

Lin Chong's mind kicked back in retort because *how could she not* except then Lu Da's words penetrated.

Revenge, her revenge, still consumed her.

She had to let it go.

For today. For now. So they could protect the mountain.

The aura of Gao Qiu's power flashed and flickered, spiking and diving. Not like a regular god's tooth. Far, far more vulnerable . . .

Lu Da had reached out a hand to grab her shoulder, shaking her, shouting something that sounded like *Liangshan*.

Lin Chong flashed back suddenly to the deadly, wild release in Bianliang, the one Fan Rui's husband had begun before he'd been interrupted. This didn't feel the same, exactly—not as powerful, not nearly as uncontrolled.

But what if . . . if she could *make* it more uncontrolled . . .

In that instant, she knew what she had to do.

She didn't only have to let her revenge go.

She had to let Gao Qiu go. Let him go free, unharmed, with no attack or consequence for anything he had done. She had to *not* fight him.

It was simultaneously the hardest thing she had ever done, and also the easiest. Because as much as she wanted to claim her right and end him, Lu Da had spoken true—between Lin Chong's revenge and protecting Liangshan, her revenge was nothing.

She swatted another one of Gao Qiu's attempts aside. Then she raised her voice, injecting as much of a taunt into it as she could manage.

"You can't kill us, *Marshal*!" She made his title as much of a sneer as he'd made hers. More. "You have the power in your hand but you can't handle it. Even with a god's tooth you're nothing but a coward. A coward and *weak*!"

Gao Qiu screamed out in rage and struck at them again. This time Lin Chong barely fended it off.

"What are you doing, Sister?" hissed Lu Da.

"Trust me." Lin Chong raised her voice again, her heart beating faster. "An Imperial Marshal who can't even fight! You had to find yourself a god's tooth to face me, and you still can't win. You're nothing!"

She was not at all sure this would work, but Gao Qiu's god's tooth indeed seemed to be beating in time with his fury . . . as he drew more and more into it, more than he could sustain, more than he could control . . .

She'd taught Lu Da back when they first met—a god's tooth alone could not compete with a disciplined mind.

Of course, she had not been thinking of a god's tooth with the sheer power of this one. She could only hope she had been more correct than she knew.

"Coward!" she called again, the words coming faster and faster. "Gao Qiu, the coward! Feeble, impotent, laughable—the whole of the Imperial Court mocks you behind your back. Your *troops* mock you—every lowly officer knows they have more bravery and military knowhow in one knuckle. Everyone laughs at you, *Gao Qiu the lazy, Gai Qiu the ignorant, Gao Qiu the ill-mannered lout, coddle him and then keep him out of anything important—*"

Gao Qiu opened his mouth and howled. Every insecurity, every resentment, Lin Chong felt it as they roared up in him like internal dragons. She felt it as he reached to tear open the floodgates, as he rent open the spaces in reality, intending to use every untamable wrath to draw on the powers of a thousand worlds and blast Lin Chong into nothing.

She ducked down and grabbed Lu Da.

Protect.

That was all she had to do. Only protect.

She reached out—behind them, across the camp, over the water, to where her haojie family rallied on the slope of the mountain in the morning sun, slashing back a limitless enemy with fierce desperation. She saw as Second Brother Ruan shouted a war cry and took off a soldier's head in one stroke, as Xie Bao leapt forward with that massive iron trident to stab another through the throat. She also saw, in some strange slow motion, as Hu Sanniang rose up with her lasso only to have an arrowhead bury itself in her opposite shoulder and spin her around to slam into the ground. As Wu Yong struck out with that copper chain only for a sword blade to stab in and slash red across the Tactician's neck and cheek. As Song Jiang erupted with a rallying cry, Guardsmen surrounding her with no way out, and Li Kui before her bellowing and swinging her double axes in a never-ending sea of red mist, an infinite battle that was already lost.

Lin Chong found them all, those minds that had become so familiar to her over weeks of training and living and having each other's backs forever. She gripped onto them and onto herself and onto Lu Da, and in the last moment found Lu Junyi as well, her friend who maybe wasn't anymore, but who couldn't be left behind.

Protect. Protect us all.

Far easier than attacking, than killing, than meeting Gao Qiu head on to *fight* as every strand of her still yearned to do. She had done this in Bianliang, she had done it today, and she could do it one more time.

Protect.

Gao Qiu's unstable god's tooth rocketed into a monstrous, uncontrollable storm. The instability vibrated against Lin Chong's defensive layer, forces crackling out and around them. In front of them, in the visible world, Gao Qiu's thin body jerked taut, his back arching, every one of his limbs and bones racked with a suddenly explosive strain. Tendons stood out in his neck, along his hands, blood vessels bursting in small spatters across his exposed skin.

He was losing his grip on it. Losing any semblance of stewardship or restraint.

Lin Chong knew it, as firmly and deeply as knowing a law of the universe. The tooth was too unstable, and he had drawn in too much, so lost in his reckless need to end her. The buildup wasn't as great as the one at Bianliang had promised to be, if Lu Junyi hadn't turned it—not nearly that large—but it would be enough.

More than enough.

Lin Chong held on to the people she loved as tightly as she could, and braced.

Raw, overwhelming power burst forth from Gao Qiu like the breach of an ancient volcano. It flashed out faster than a man could run, faster than sound, faster than thought, mowing down everything in its path without discrimination or mercy.

Lin Chong clung to Lu Da's arms with hers and clung on to everyone else with mind and spirit.

The massive wave rushed across the whole army camp in the first thunderclap, then outward, ever-expanding, rippling across the marsh, crashing into the troops that climbed the shore, men tumbling to the ground as if a horde of demons had bowled straight over them. The energy swept up the slope, swallowing the advancing army, splintering trees and snuffing birds out of the sky, until it climbed straight up toward where Liangshan's haojie spent everything of themselves in the midst of battle, fighting and dying for their home.

Protect . . .

That was when Lin Chong lost her grip on everything.

She scarcely knew what was happening. She wasn't in the camp anymore, everything rushing by the wrong way round, tumbling in a whirlwind of chaos, as if a cyclone had snatched them away into storm-filled heavens. Her hands tried to keep hold of Lu Da, but her sister, too, was torn from her, both of them swirling separately into unknown darkness.

CHAPTER 34

"Wake up."

Lin Chong did not want to wake up. She was finally comfortable.

Resting.

Waking would ruin that.

"Wake up, Sister Lin. It's time to go home."

Her eyes fluttered open, reluctantly. She was lying on a bed of soft plants. Some sort of grass—but with tiny round leaves instead of blades, ones that crushed easily and cushioned her head. Trees arched overhead, and a brook trickled by close enough to where her left foot lay that her boot was wet.

Sitting serenely about half a pace away, on a softly green moss-covered rock, was Chao Gai.

Lin Chong sat up. Stared around the clearing. They were the only two here.

"I . . . you're . . ." She struggled to gather scattered thoughts, remnants on the breeze, reality confused with nightmare. "Am I dreaming?"

"What is a dream, but a reality invented by the mind?" Chao Gai asked, with a small smile. "You can call this a dream, if you like."

"Where am I?"

"About two dozen li northwest of Liangshan." Chao Gai's smile had a touch of pride—as for an accomplished student. "You've improved yourself, Little Sister. Look how you landed unhurt."

Gao Qiu's god's tooth. The surge—Lin Chong remembered now. She'd provoked him, on purpose, and then that unfathomable power . . .

"Lu Da? The rest of the haojie?" she asked urgently.

"Sister Lu landed unharmed only a few li from you. I believe if you walk south you'll find her. You and she managed to keep hold of each other until the last moment."

Lin Chong tried to calm her suddenly pounding heart. "Everyone else?"

"You protected them well." Again, that beatific smile. "All similarly scattered, but most not so far, and unharmed by the energy. They suffer wounds from the battle, no more, and are regrouping at Liangshan."

"What about you?" Lin Chong asked softly.

"Oh, I won't be here long."

Emotion soaked Lin Chong's throat. "I . . . we . . . you did so much for us. For everyone. I don't know how we'll . . ."

Chao Gai reached forward and touched her shoulder. Lin Chong twisted to look. The contact felt real. Solid.

"Help them," Chao Gai said. "Help them to stay on the path. You all have so much more ahead of you. Greatness to bring to the world."

Lin Chong wanted to protest that she was nobody, only an arms instructor with humble beginnings. Not a hero.

Except that Liangshan had become larger than herself, now . . .

She looked back up to tell Chao Gai this, but in that blink, the apparition had gone.

A profound sadness filled Lin Chong from the soles of her feet, spilling down all her limbs until she curled her arms around her knees in the clearing in silent grief.

The clearing did not hurry her. Bees zipped merrily past, the nearby stream never ceasing its calming babble. A breeze rustled the leaves up above. It was a fine summer day in the Empire of Song.

Finally, when Lin Chong's legs began to cramp, she unfolded herself and stood. She had a full-body soreness—the self-inflicted wounds from the tattoos still ached, and layered over them came a thousand bone-deep bruises, first from the fight with Gao Qiu and then from the final blast that had taken her all the way out here.

Protected, though. She had protected all of them.

For now. Gao Qiu was still alive—of that she was certain. He had stood at the epicenter of his destruction—it wouldn't have touched him, and it hadn't burned to consume him like the man back in Bianliang. Somehow she knew.

He was still alive, with the power of a god, albeit a power he could not yet master. *Which may make him even more dangerous . . .*

He would no doubt come against the mountain again. Against the mountain, and against her.

He might be mobilizing already.

They would need to prepare. This battle might have only been the first of many. She would get back to Liangshan, and find the others, and they would figure out what to do.

She stood and tried to stretch her abused muscles. When she took a deep breath, her chest spiked in pain, reminding her where Gao Qiu had kicked her.

She began hiking to the south, to find Lu Da and go home.

Lu Junyi woke surrounded by corpses.

She was on the outskirts of the camp. It took her a few turns to recognize it. The tents had been flattened and scattered, the neat military orderliness become a graveyard. What soldiers had been left in the camp during the attack now lay with their limbs flopped at odd angles, like armored plums that had dropped to the ground too ripe, now burst open in rotting death.

Lu Junyi staggered up to her feet. She was, miraculously, unhurt. She remembered a feeling of—of something, as if a hand had hooked into her, pulled her down, and then nothing.

Nothing except the power of Gao Qiu's god's fang.

She had known the god's fangs were strong, but this . . . her mind kept trying to shut itself down in the face of what she had witnessed.

Nobody should have that power.

Now Gao Qiu did, and thanks to the elixir it would not devour him as it had all the others before him. He would become untouchable.

Because of her.

She stepped numbly through the camp. Not all the soldiers lay lifeless. A few moved here or there, a groan or a plea or the spasm of a dying man. Not a single one unharmed, however.

Except for her . . .

Her feet took her back toward where the command tent had been, toward the center and the front of the camp, near the shoreline. The marsh lay gleaming in the sun, debris from the battles dotting its surface. More corpses lay half in the water, finished before they could launch their boats. Other shapes drifted farther out, the marsh reclaiming them.

Lu Junyi found the remains of the command tent.

Gao Qiu was gone. A scorched ring marked where he must have stood. She stared at the spot for a turn or more, wondering what she had expected to see. She hadn't thought him dead, but if his body had lain here it would only have been a relief. He must have fled back to Bianliang or somewhere else, once he understood what he had wrought.

Lin Chong and Lu Da were gone as well. No corpses, but no living sign of them, either.

Had it been they who had—done something? That saved her? Lu Junyi did not understand how that could be possible. Of course, she didn't know how it was possible they had been able to fight him for as long as they had either. Lu Da must have improved with her own god's tooth since they had last met.

A noise made Lu Junyi look around.

Cai Jing twitched against the ground behind her.

Not dead. Not yet. He grasped at nothing with clawed hands, trying to crawl. His legs and arms twisted the wrong way in multiple places, his body become a mass of misarranged parts. A tent spar had driven itself through the lower part of his chest, and blood soaked his fine robes in a great red stain.

His face was still bloody from when she'd kicked him. A century ago.

"Help . . . your Chancellor . . ." he gasped. Red dribbled from his lips. His long white beard tangled across the blood and dirt in a filthy mass. "I shall tell the Emperor, the bandits . . . your duty, Lady Lu . . ."

Lu Junyi found herself dead of any interest in whatever scheme he wished to spin to the Emperor.

He had caused this. All of it.

She stepped over and stared down at him, feeling nothing. Then she grasped the spar that pierced him and wrenched it to the side, leveraging it through his flesh as hard as she could.

Something crunched inside his chest, an ugly, sickening sound. He contorted around the spar, and coughs racked him as he choked on his own fluids. Instead of pain, however, his face registered only shocked betrayal.

He hadn't thought her capable.

She wrenched the spar through him again, and again, mechanically, working the wound wider until his flesh began to pulverize and blood brimmed up out of his mouth and nose and the deepening hole in him, until red drowned his robes and the ground and the hems and sleeves of her clothes. He shuddered and thrashed but could not fight her, his body broken against the ground.

The spar pierced low enough in him that it took a long time for him to die. She should have found a blade and cut his throat instead.

By the time his twitching stilled, by the time she realized that no more breath gurgled through his mouth and that his eyes stared sightless, the spar had become slick with his blood. She let go. Her skin and clothes were soaked sticky as well.

She fell back to sit slumped on her heels, staring at nothing.

The sun had crept over a broad angle of sky before she managed to rouse herself.

She had to check for the god's fangs. They mustn't be left for anyone to find—anyone who might do what Cai Jing had tried to do. Lu Junyi could make sure of that, at least, and prevent tragedy from being multiplied by many times.

She pushed herself to numb feet and moved around the ruined area, searching. The blood of the Chancellor of the Empire had dried stiff and tacky against her. She discovered Cai Jing's carved chest, on its side beneath collapsed wreckage from the tent, but no god's fangs by its side. After heaving aside piles of broken debris and combing the ground until she burned and sweated in the sun, she had to resign her hunt to defeat.

It was possible the extra god's fangs had all been sucked in by Gao Qiu's enormous surge, drained of their power until they shriveled to dust. It was possible.

She didn't think she would ever know.

She gazed around the camp one last time. Only corpses lay close enough to witness anything she had done here.

Lu Junyi turned her feet to the southwest and let her bloody footsteps begin the long walk back toward Bianliang.

She did not look back.

It took five days for Lin Chong and Lu Da to return to the mountain.

Lin Chong was far more injured than she had thought, Lu Da far more fatigued. They leaned on each other, traveling only a handful of li per day. They sold the armor and weapons they'd stolen to sneak their way through the army's camp, and they used the coin to stay in taverns at night.

It took about one full day for Lin Chong to convince Lu Da to stop calling her a god, and maybe to cease bragging so loudly about having bested the Empire where other people might hear.

Oddly, however, Lu Da was not the only person invested in spreading rumors about them. The gossip around the inns . . . Lin Chong started sharply the first time she heard the name *Liangshan*, but told herself news of such a battle would of course be talked about. In fact, she should expect the odd passing of information about what had happened at the mountain. She tried to keep her face down, hustle them through, and not react when she heard their camp's name.

Except then it happened again. And again. And six times more that same day, when Lu Da had made not a peep about where they hailed from.

Lin Chong began trying to listen in without being obvious about it. The whispers were hushed and sounded in awe, and even more peculiar, they mostly *didn't* seem to be talking about the battle. Lin Chong's next assumption was that the news had instilled a general fear of the bandits—until she heard someone use the word "heroes."

"I heard *Song Jiang* is one of them," whispered a woman at the next table, but she and her companion blushed and looked away when they caught Lin Chong's eyes on them.

All mildly unsettling—but Lin Chong had far more important worries to stress her. Gao Qiu would be rallying to return, determined to finish what he had begun. The absence of herself and Lu Da put Liangshan in heavy danger. Not that either of them were in much shape to fight at the moment, but Lin Chong still fretted at not being present.

At least they heard no rumor from the gossiping countryside of another attack. She and Lu Da also meditated together three times a day, and no visions danced through their heads like the premonition they had seen of the massacre at Dongxi. Lin Chong did not know how reliable such a lack of signs was.

She tried to push to a greater hurry, covering the ground as fast as they were able.

When they arrived at the edge of the marsh at last, the remains of the battle still dominated the landscape, shredded debris and then corpses upon corpses. As might have been expected. Except . . .

"I didn't think flowers grew that fast, Elder Sister," Lu Da said in puzzlement.

"Did we lose time?" Lin Chong wondered. She thought she'd woken in the grove the same morning she had been sent there. But here in front of them, the site of the battle had been overtaken by moss and grasses and mound upon mound of wildflowers, growing straight out of the softly collapsing bodies.

The effect was peaceful. Almost beautiful.

They stood and stared for a few long moments. Lin Chong's feet felt like they slipped on unsolid ground. *How many days were we gone from here?* Her wounds were still fresh and unhealed . . .

This was all so far beyond her realm of experience.

It could have been the god's tooth. It might have stimulated the ground even as it destroyed. She wished she could ask Chao Gai . . .

Chao Gai had never visited again, even in her dreams. Lin Chong began to wonder if she'd imagined seeing her at all.

"Come on, Elder Sister, we'd better go on up to the mountain," Lu Da said. Somehow, she'd kept ahold of her heavy metal staff through everything, and now she spun it and plunged the end into the spongy earth as if to make a point. "If we slept a hundred years, best to know now, eh?"

If it had been a hundred years, then it was very unfair that Lin Chong's ribs still hurt.

They hiked over to Zhu Gui's inn, but it was closed tight, with no sign of the Crocodile. Lu Da broke into where the whistling arrows were kept and sent one themselves. Lin Chong supposed they could have tried walking the marsh again, but everything inside her still felt raw and fragile, and she wasn't sure either she or Lu Da was up to the risk.

They had not, in fact, slept a hundred years. When the boat came, it held Second Brother Ruan captaining, and traveling to meet them were a bandaged Song Jiang and Noblewoman Chai.

"We had faith you had not perished," Noblewoman Chai said warmly, clasping their hands.

"What news is there of Gao Qiu?" Lin Chong asked, urgency spilling into rudeness. She suddenly realized the others might not know exactly what had transpired, what she and Lu Da had done. "He has one of Cai Jing's god's teeth now, and he's still alive. If his god's tooth can do *this* . . ."

"You needn't worry about that for the moment," Song Jiang said. "Gao Qiu cannot move without the word of the Emperor."

"The Emperor wants us dead too," Lu Da pointed out.

"Not—anymore." Noblewoman Chai had a queer tone in her voice. "Come. It may be easiest to show you."

They boarded the ferry, and Second Brother took them across. Lin Chong glanced at her as she poled through the reeds, navigating around the sinking detritus of the battle. Second Brother seemed well, but her face was worn and drawn, and she didn't speak much.

Lin Chong wished she had some right words to offer, about the youngest Ruan brother who had died a hero.

They arrived at the shore and Second Brother moored the boat, and then they all hiked up the mountain together. The bandits had been hard at work cleaning up—the well-traveled path to the camp and its guardian watchtowers all looked much like Lin Chong remembered, set to rights with any repairs underway.

"I told them to gather and meet us," Song Jiang said.

"You told who?" asked Lu Da, but Sister Song remained mysterious.

They climbed up into the camp. Lin Chong found that the vision of Chao Gai had been correct. It did feel like coming home. She breathed deep, the wet freshness and tingly pine scents of the mountain filling her lungs. Her ribs barely twinged.

"They'll be in Loyalty Hall," Noblewoman Chai said. She and Song Jiang led the way over.

When Lin Chong and Lu Da stepped through the doorway and out of the sun, they both stopped dead on the threshold.

Stopped and stared.

The hall was filled.

Packed end to end with people—north to south and east to west. Mostly people Lin Chong had never seen before, though she did spot Hu Sanniang with her arm in a sling, Shi Qian leaning against the wall stifling giggles—others of the haojie too, all of them in fact, but mixed up among so many more strangers. The newcomers were mostly women, but not only. Several wore military dress, and several stood with what were clearly their families, including a few young children and infants. Lin Chong even caught one woman sitting to the side with her hands across a stomach that swelled heavy with child.

An intense hush had fallen over the room with their entrance. Next to Lin Chong, Lu Da twirled in a confused spin. "What's going on? Who are all these people, Sister Song?"

"Mothers and wives," Song Jiang answered. "Military officers and hunters and monks and the best archer in the land." She began moving through the aisle that had been left in the middle of the crowd, toward the front of the hall, Lin Chong and Lu Da following.

Everyone's eyes were on them, everyone still unnaturally quiet, except for the occasional squawk of a toddler.

They reached the front, a low platform where Wu Yong lounged, with that sardonic half-smile despite sporting a good deal of splints and bandages. Second Brother had peeled off to join the crowd, leaving Song Jiang and Noblewoman Chai standing in the front with them, plus the Tactician.

Song Jiang turned toward the hall and raised an arm in a gesture that felt weighted and grand.

"Sister Lin, Sister Lu," she announced. "Meet the new heroes of Liangshan."

"How . . ." Lin Chong murmured. She caught at Song Jiang's elbow, leaning in to speak quietly. "Gao Qiu could be coming at any time. We cannot risk taking in more people, especially not families—it may be best if we disband even those who were already here—"

"Gao Qiu is not coming," Song Jiang answered, equally quietly.

Grinning even more broadly, Wu Yong reached out left-handed to offer Lin Chong a leaf of paper.

"What is it?" Lu Da asked, crowding in to see. "Hey, I recognize those characters. It says Liangshan! This is about us!"

Not just about them. It was the story Song Jiang had written for them to distribute in Bianliang, or close enough. The one Lu Junyi had crumpled and refused.

Lu Junyi. She had done this. She must have. The page was printed, shadows visible from the outlines of the press blocks, an all too familiar mark.

"This paper—it says we're heroes," Lin Chong said for Lu Da's benefit, still keeping her voice low. "These people, they came because—they believe it?"

"Not just them," Song Jiang said. "The legend of Liangshan is sweeping the countryside, beyond what we ever hoped. The public has begun to adore us. *Worship* us. The sound of our name is greeted by exultations of dreams and joy."

"The Emperor can no longer move against us," Noblewoman Chai put in. "The wave has come too quickly. Even some in the Imperial Court speak fondly of our names, though they quickly disclaim it. If the Empire marches on Liangshan again, the people will revolt."

"Everyone is Liangshan now," laughed Wu Yong. "The story in Bianliang is that Cai Jing angered the *gods* by trying to take us. Every other official is claiming they disagreed with the attempt from the start. No one even knows what happened to the good Chancellor, or they're saying they don't—he's either dead or racing away with his tail between his legs. To our great good fortune, Sister Song has, with very arduous convincing, agreed to continue as Liangshan's leader for the moment."

Lin Chong swallowed. "And Gao Qiu?"

"The rumors are conflicted," answered Noblewoman Chai. "Many seem to think he suffered some . . . nervous break, but others say he bit off power that he cannot learn to control. He crawled back to the Emperor, who is keeping him hidden. Even Gao Qiu cannot move against us again without a decree, which will not be forthcoming."

"I like to think he stews in anger about that," Wu Yong put in.

"So—all of these people," Lin Chong said again.

"They've come to join us," Song Jiang said. "And more every day."

Lin Chong could feel a slack shock in her face. She could not wrap her mind around any of it.

Song Jiang smiled at them. Then she turned to the gathered room and raised her voice for them all to hear.

"Haojie, friends old and new—we gather here to welcome back Lin Chong, our much valued drill instructor, and Lu Da, the illustrious Flower Monk. Five days ago they acted as heroes to save Liangshan, helped stamp out an unjust crusade against us, and stood against a corrupt oppressor for the sake of us all. Tonight, we celebrate. Let the preparations begin for the first feast of our new era!"

The room erupted in cheers, thundering off the walls and rafters and filling the building with warmth and welcome. Everywhere Lin Chong looked, eyes fell upon her with awestruck love. The noise threatened to burst the whole hall open, a cacophony of excitement, and freedom, and hope.

"How many?" Lin Chong asked Song Jiang, while the cheers continued with no sign of abatement.

"Including those of us who were here before, a hundred and eight. So far."

One hundred and eight.

One hundred and eight.

It stunned her. Overwhelmed.

Chao Gai's voice echoed in her head. *Help them to stay on the path.* "This many people—the responsibility is very great," she said for Song Jiang's ears alone, below the still-echoing cheers.

The Spring Rain turned to meet her eyes, and her face for the first time seemed nakedly sincere, no mask of other motives. "I promise you, Sister Lin. For as long as I am still leader here, I will do my utmost to keep Liangshan directed only toward justice."

"Make sure," Lin Chong said weakly.

Then, slowly, she turned to face her new family.

One hundred and eight people. A hundred and eight bodies and minds with enough strength to change the Empire for the better. A hundred and eight leaders and idealists, iconoclasts and outcasts, victims and criminals . . . all coming to Liangshan for a second chance or to reach for the stars. Or both.

A hundred and eight who had heard the story of Liangshan and decided to leave everything behind for a better life and a better world.

For the first time since that day in White Tiger Hall, Lin Chong felt the liquid, illicit thrill of a power equal to every office of government that had so casually taken her life. Her world teetered with danger and possibility.

A hundred and eight people who could challenge an Empire—who had made the Emperor himself back down.

One hundred and eight heroes. And she was one of them.

EPILOGUE

FOUR MONTHS LATER

Every morning just after dawn, Lin Chong began the day's fight drills for the hundreds of bandits of Mount Liang.

Hundreds, and growing.

She had become a teacher of teachers now as well, entrusting parts of her curriculum to staunch assistants—Hu Sanniang instructing tentative wives and mothers in basic footwork, Lu Da bellowing jolly admonishments in the training of strength, Yang Zhi running precise, disciplined classes on formation combat. And others still, each imparting their own expertise to those who lacked it, all part of Lin Chong's carefully organized school of the fighting arts. The Zhang and Ruan siblings led exercises in swimming and fighting on the water, Shi Qian of the Three Fleas shared practices in acrobatics and balance, and some of the newer recruits had themselves proven wildly distinguished—such as Hua Rong the archer, who had pierced three eagles with a single arrow before their very eyes. Lin Chong had immediately seized upon her skill to help develop the rest of the bandits in ranged weapons.

Others of their new members had never closed a hand on bow or blade before they arrived on the mountain, but that was no matter. Liangshan judged neither past transgressions nor inexperience. All a tentative newcomer needed to succeed in the training Lin Chong had built here was respect and willingness.

Respect, willingness, and a belief in their cause.

The only days Lin Chong did not wake with the light to head down to the fighting ground were the days she was not on the mountain. On those days, she turned over her drills to the hands of some capable assigned lieutenants, while she rode with their kindred into the rocky landscape of Ji Province. Ranging out from the mountain to do what needed to be done.

In a perfect match of more than half a dozen times before now, a remote spill of ridges and valleys had its quiet evening rent asunder. A roar of weapons and horses and righteousness descended upon the rancid opulence of the county magistrate's compound where it stained the autumn forest. Thick and barricaded doors tore from their frames, smashed in by the hooves of a rearing mount or splintered by the fury of a tattooed monk's god's tooth. A raiding party composed of two dozen of Liangshan's finest led that same number in local citizens, bursting apart the compound to pour inside and scour every room and corridor.

Some of those within tried to fight. They failed. Flesh parted sweetly on the blade of halberd or axe or saber. Bodies that were soft with unearned wealth broke against walls and floors, flung by chain or lasso or the scholar's skills of a former arms instructor.

Some tried to flee. They likewise met death—sword and staff and trident licking after them too fast, with arrows driving straight and sure to bury themselves in any who broke through.

Only those who surrendered themselves to Liangshan's mercy were spared.

Today one of these was the magistrate himself, cowering on the polished floor of what had been his hall of judgment. He bobbed on his knees, hands working over themselves, his rich robes and great headpiece askew.

Such repugnance. One man—one *worm*—who had caused such hardship for so many. Who had torn families from each other for no reason beyond imagined insult, confiscated goods until farmers and merchants were starved into poverty, forced more than one young woman into terrified marriage with a friend or crony . . . the bandits of Liangshan had learned of it all, those acts that had been written in blood upon the local villagers.

The bandits of Liangshan let that blood fill their ledgers, and this time it was they who rendered judgment.

It was no accident, either, that the men who had been placed here generation after generation were those both too lazy and troublesome to be trusted, and too entitled to hereditary power to be ignored—the worst type of combination. Like in many counties of northern Ji, this magistrate position was nearly one of punishment, even as it gave a man a title: rural, far from the capital, with no space for advancement or glory. A place for the Empire to shuffle off those it found disgraceful or embarrassing, and let them abuse people who weren't important enough to matter. Where venal men could revel in petty acts of power, and the Court could wash its hands of responsibility.

All too common in these remote county courts. Lin Chong understood that now.

She left Lu Da, Hua Rong, Xie Bao, and four of the locals to finish securing their new prisoners and strode for the compound's cells, while reaching out with her senses in a scan that now took no more thought than breathing. She was pleased—everyone from the mountain had followed her directives and stayed perfectly to form, adhering to the training and discipline she had been molding into Liangshan's methods. Even Li Kui the Iron Whirlwind had gone where she was told this time, which was a most definite improvement. Lin Chong noted all of their successful positions with satisfaction.

The local people Wu Yong had trained were a bit more desultory, rushing in tumultuous overexcitement, but they had done their part admirably, and Lin Chong could make no complaint.

Now those citizens would reap their rewards. This was the part Lin Chong wished to see.

She slipped into the back building where the prison cells packed up against each other and positioned herself in a corner, not stepping in to offer help. She would not take the joy of this from them. Already the residents surged between the barred doors, wielding hammers or hatchets or stones picked up from the ground, any tool they could find to strike against the ancient locks—locks that were rusted through to corruption at their cores. The rotted metal broke easily, and prisoners tumbled into the arms of their loved ones, weeping and laughing.

Wu Yong and Song Jiang had been the ones to devise this lengthy scheme of claiming county courts for the local populace. One or the other of them would travel out and find disgruntled and overtaxed farmers, or stouthearted wives whose husbands had been locked away on a pretense . . . or parents who feared for their daughters, or children who feared for themselves. These first counties were selected with great savvy—ones that sat too far away from any noble landowner for an armed estate to exert convenient dominance; ones that were out of the way of any interest of powerful military governors; ones that the weak provincial government barely acknowledged. Places where the local magistrates' words were law, and no one else cared.

Liangshan came and offered a listening ear. And then they offered resources, and training, and aid, in preparing a fistful of handpicked citizens to take back those same towns and villages.

Take them back—and then oversee them with stability, those citizens' oversight over their fellow villagers supported and coached at every step by chieftains from Liangshan. Respected members of these rural communities would now also become saviors, assuming the mantle of leadership in a way none around them would question.

Liangshan's reputation had begun to glow beyond the brightest sun. The heroes of the people, who descended like beneficent spirits to oust the oppressors and return the land to its rightful citizens . . .

An undeserved reverence. Wu Yong and Song Jiang's methods less returned the land to the people as it did manufacture and install allies to Liangshan in these positions of power over the rural counties. These offices became run by new masters, ones who owed the mountain everything. Ones who would, if asked, swear loyalty to Song Jiang from now until their deaths and beyond.

The bandits fed the legend that they brought freedom, while creating their own outposts across the province.

Lin Chong had not protested it. It was not the worst Liangshan had ever done, and the good they brought to these villages was genuine. The people *would* prosper more under the hand of a local trained by Wu Yong than beneath the crushing power games of these gutless local magistrates. Besides, when the Empire did come for Liangshan . . .

They would need all the strength they could gather.

It would not even be long before they would not have to pick their targets so cleverly. Once Liangshan's allies began to surround the noble landed estates on all sides, those same nobles would hesitate to challenge them, even as they saw the bandits encroaching on the illicit fiefdoms they had claimed. Upcoming winter snows might slow the effort some, but Lin Chong strongly suspected the nobles themselves might fall next in Wu Yong's plans.

Unless those nobles decided to surrender and turn ally.

Liangshan *would* accept, if asked. The mountain was very forgiving of past sins.

Eventually, even the military governors and provincial governments might begin to fear. After that . . .

The future was one of luxurious possibility.

Challenging nobles and governors. The very notion might have seemed absurd to Lin Chong a year ago, unthinkable, but those titles had somehow ceased to inspire their automatic deference. Stripped of a title, such people would become only ordinary men, like any other.

A smile touched her lips as she watched the embracing, weeping families of the county that had been chosen this time. The warmth made her feel whole in a way she never would have expected to find after that day so many months ago in White Tiger Hall. She slipped back out before any of the villagers could find eyes for her again to try to express gratitude.

No matter its other motives, Liangshan had done good here.

Lin Chong had thought, the first time they did this, that she would find the greatest gratification in the justice they would bring to a corrupt and lawless magistrate, a dull echo prickling through her of her own forced confession in the courts. Instead, she found herself . . . indifferent to their fates. It was a powerful sort of indifference—a freeing one—the knowledge that pitiful men like these no longer held sway over her own thoughts, such that even their deaths mattered so little to her.

An oddly shaped victory. But a victory nonetheless.

She left the prison to return to the front of the compound, but ran into Lu Da and Hua Rong escorting the erstwhile jailers, headed to immure them in the same cells those men had used so brazenly as tools of their power. Monk and archer had become fast friends, and their pairing was a study in contrasts: First marched Hua Rong, as short as Hu Sanniang and as dark as Li Kui, her hair a fierce black halo and the slender bow in her hand nearly reaching her own stature. After her came Lu Da, grinning and whistling and poking their prisoners with her staff as she ambled behind. Lu Da was not *quite* twice Hua Rong in both height and girth, but at times it seemed that way.

"Elder Sister!" Lu Da called. "Did you feel me using my tooth? Did you? Were you watching?"

"I was," Lin Chong said.

"Smooth as a baby's cheek, wasn't I?" Lu Da grinned at her drill instructor, waiting expectantly. "Could you feel the difference? Tell me you could!"

Lin Chong relented. "You did very well."

"I did! I did, didn't I?" The Flower Monk twirled her staff from the prisoners to poke Hua Rong in the shoulder—gently, but it almost knocked the archer off her feet. "Did you hear that, Sister Hua?"

"Careful where you point that thing!"

Lin Chong shook her head. Discipline was, apparently, still a work in progress. She gripped her sword hilt just in case any of the prisoners took this opportunity to become rowdy, but they all seemed too cowed.

"Wait," Lin Chong said, her eyes scanning across the bound men. "Where's the magistrate?"

"Oh, him." Lu Da was cheerful. "Sister Li killed him. I told her you'd be mad, but I was a bit late at saying so, as she'd already chopped his head off him."

"He *did* deserve it," Hua Rong put in. "He tried to bribe us to let him go."

"*Are* you mad?" Lu Da asked Lin Chong. "See, I *said* she'd be mad . . ."

Lin Chong sighed. Definitely a work in progress.

She returned to the audience chamber to find it mostly empty, except for two of the local citizenry, a swath of blood in a half-smeared pool on the floor, and Li Kui—who had balanced the magistrate's great wide headdress upon her hair, draped his embroidered robes over her broad shoulders, and taken it upon herself to perch upon the magisterial chair.

"You must make one up, then!" she was demanding of the locals when Lin Chong came in. The ornate and bloodstained robes caught and tore on her battleaxes with every gesticulation. "Make up a fight, and I shall rule on it! One of you will go free, and the other shall be executed."

"Madam?" squeaked one of them.

"Ignore her," Lin Chong cut in. "Sister Li, please get down and go back to only your own clothes. You two may go," she added to the local men, who scurried out of the room as soon as the words left her mouth.

"Sister Li," Lin Chong said more seriously, when they had gone. "We must speak about the magistrate. What have we told you? Time and again."

"But the scurrilous cur, he tried—"

"I heard. You *must* stop killing those who have surrendered. Sister Song will hear of this."

It was, truly, the only punishment the Iron Whirlwind ever seemed to fear. She harrumphed and climbed down from the magistrate's seat to slouch out of the room, tearing off the swooping headdress and letting it tumble to the ground.

Lin Chong followed more sedately, stepping out into the cool forest evening. Her padded coat kept the dropping temperature at bay, but a late-autumn snap burst inside her with every breath in a pleasant chill. They would stay here tonight, and depart the next morning, with Wu Yong's trainees safely ensconced. So far, Bianliang had sent no replacements to these remote wild county courts that Liangshan had targeted. No new magistrates, nor any detachments of the Guard dispatched to remove the competent locals and install new villains chosen by the Empire's ministers.

Either these posts weren't worth it to them, or they had become stiff with panic about what Liangshan might do. Or both.

"That's eight now."

Lin Chong turned slightly.

Wu Yong sidled up with that usual predatory grin, chain dangling from one hand, and leaned against the outside wall next to Lin Chong. "Eight counties, and more to come. A good day."

"Bianliang will have to try to stop us eventually," Lin Chong said. "They must know what they risk letting us continue. One of these will be one too far, when they'll no longer be able to sit back and pretend countryside disputes are beneath notice."

Despite the truth in the words, she felt the tranquility with which she spoke them. Whenever the Empire came, they came.

Liangshan would be ready.

"Ooo, let them try!" Hua Rong tumbled out next to them, having heard Lin Chong's words. The flush of their victory still radiated from her. "The cowards won't have it easy. This whole land is becoming Liangshan!"

She whooped and ran to catch up with Li Kui, who was tearing off bits of the magistrate's robes and leaving them on the path like silken feathers shed from a bird's plumage. The two traded japes and laughed together. Lu Da jogged up to join them, followed by Shi Jin the Nine Dragons and Zhang Qin the Featherless Arrow, who had both joined Liangshan at the same time as Hua Rong.

Backlit by the setting sun and a forest of leaves that had gone aflame with autumn color, the group seemed one of true siblings—embracing each other, cheering each other on, challenging each other. Zhang Qin and Hua Rong had soon begun a friendly contest, in which the Featherless Arrow let fly stone after stone from the sling that had given him his nickname, and she shot them out of the air with her bow. She hadn't missed one yet, and the cheers from the others grew louder every time.

Hu Sanniang eventually came out to join them as well, walking with two of her martial siblings—the former constables Zhu and Lei who had heard the tales of Liangshan and given up their posts to pursue true justice on the mountain. With them also were two of the local citizens, the first of whom Lin Chong recognized: Mistress Gu Dasao, the long club she'd shown her strength with now resting casually against her shoulder. The other, the thin man, must be the husband she had just worked to free from the magistrate's cells.

Stout, jolly, and flush-faced, the fierce Mistress Gu had been an innkeeper here—and would now be Wu Yong's chosen successor to the magistrate who had met his untimely end on the blade of Li Kui's axe.

It was a good choice. Mistress Gu would do well in her new post. The Tactician did have an eye for skill.

The five newcomers joined the growing crowd, adding to the roars every time Zhang Qin sent a stone higher and faster or spun the sling behind his back or released two at once—and every time Hua Rong's arrowheads sped to smack into those stones, arrow meeting rock in the air at all speed for them to pair and fall away, like a mating dance of phoenixes. The small archer's bowstring never stilled, so quick was she in drawing one after the other, the moves overlapping with no space between.

Only a single season ago it had been, when Gao Qiu had failed to best them at Liangshan Marsh, when Hua Rong and so many others had first joined their number. Already the time before that seemed of a different age. Hua Rong and Zhang Qin and Shi Jin and everyone who had come to them then—so quickly had they become embedded in the spirit of Liangshan, and so deeply, that it was difficult to remember what the mountain had been like before them.

Lin Chong did not think she had fully understood what it meant, before, to be haojie. Loyalty, honor, courage—death before betrayal—these were nothing more than words. True heroism was both smaller and bigger: this, here, the young blood of brash idealists; hotheaded, delinquent, imperfect . . . but who took up arms to defend the weak, with no promise of name or credit or reward. Even as it made them criminals. Even as they crossed the lines of law and dared an Empire who could crush them with a thought to turn its ponderous eyes upon them.

Today still more new heroes would follow them back—it always happened so—and their population would continue to swell, both on the mountain and across the land. Such would include those who planned to remain here, like Gu Dasao and her husband—they would maintain their communication with Liangshan, sending reports and receiving advice and requesting aid if needed. In the other direction, the chieftains at Liangshan would range out periodically to return in person, to bring these villages rice or coin or textiles or whatever else they had need of, and if Liangshan ever called them to come ride in defense of others, all of these local citizens would rally to arms with no second thought. Like Noblewoman Chai on her estate, like Zhu Gui at her inn, like in seven other rural counties . . . like so many other allies burgeoning across the land . . .

Hua Rong had spoken truly. Bit by bit, the entire countryside was becoming of Liangshan.

These days, even those who had never met the bandits might well whisper the name *Liangshan* in the dark and promise their hearts to the cause.

"Such noble work we do," Wu Yong murmured next to Lin Chong, gaze also on their compatriots. "Fit to make the heavens smile. Don't you think the Empire would agree, Drill Instructor?"

The tone of the question was sly, a joke meant to be shared. But Lin Chong had a serious answer.

For in a way, it no longer mattered if the Empire came for them tomorrow, or if they never came at all. Liangshan had become more than a few dozen scratching bandits. More even than its expanding web of power, of allies and outposts and recruits and military strength—more than a legend, or an idea.

Liangshan had become *change*. Had become the future.

The future of a changing Empire.

No matter what the Empire did, now or later, no matter how it came at them—such an act would only be an attempt to repress a part of its own self. The marrow of its own tomorrow.

"Didn't you know, Tactician?" Lin Chong said mildly. "We *are* the Empire."

Wu Yong laughed. They stood together until the sun kissed against the mountains, watching the citizen bandits who would change the world.

ACKNOWLEDGMENTS

From afar, writing might seem like a much more solitary endeavor than it is in reality. A very large number of people contributed to the book you hold in your hands.

First, so much gratitude to my editor for *The Water Outlaws*, Ruoxi Chen. From large-scale plotline reassurance to nitty-gritty discussions of province names, Ruoxi not only shepherded this book to publication but has been its most heartfelt cheerleader. She brought so much love for the source material and wider cultural understanding to this project, and it's been a joy to indulge in this journey with her. Also at the top of the list to thank are my agent, Russell Galen, and my film agent, Angela Cheng Caplan, whose unwavering support continues to make my career what it is. It's been a hard time to be a writer, especially through the last few rocky pandemic years—without my agents I would not even be in a position to write or share books with you.

So many other talented professionals have had a part in making *The Water Outlaws* reality. Illustrator Feifei Ruan created the stunning cover art for this book, and I hope she knows that reader reaction to it has been an absolute home run. Cultural consultant Yvonne Ye read for authenticity, language, and history, and commented with such a brilliant level of scholarship that the edit letter threw me into clouds of geeky joy. (And you got my Chinese puns!) I'm additionally grateful to Tor for going the extra mile to hire an authenticity reader so we could give this book's cultural inspirations and source material the respect they deserve—any missteps remaining are my own.

At Tor, it's also been my absolute pleasure to work directly with assistant editor Oliver Dougherty, my publicist Giselle Gonzalez (who has seen me through several books now!), and, previously, assistant editor Sanaa Ali-Virani. *The Water Outlaws* is further indebted to the skills of the following people at all the myriad steps in the run-up to its release: production manager Steven Bucsok; marketer Isa Caban; designer Greg Collins; jacket designer Christine Foltzer; marketing assistant Samantha Friedlander; publisher Irene Gallo; production editor Dakota Griffin; copyeditor Amanda Hong; managing editor Lauren Hougen; proofreader NaNá Stoelzle; cold reader Cassie Gitkin; and operations wranglers Michelle Foytek, Rebecca Naimon, and Erin Robinson.

On the UK side, I'm extremely grateful for the enthusiasm of commissioning editor Michael Rowley at Solaris, and now for my utterly amazing team there of editor Amanda Rutter, editorial assistant Chiara Mestieri, and PR and marketing manager Jess Gofton—your collective excitement for this book has been making the UK release feel straight-up magical!

Finally, I want to give a shoutout to Diana Gill, my prior editor at Tor, for kicking off this whole journey.

Outside of my agency and publishers, I am lucky beyond compare to have had my sister join me for this book every step of the way, from reading every chapter as I drafted to waxing enthusiastic about Wu Yong to decisively acting as a sounding board during my copyedits. Maddox Hahn and Emma Maree Urquhart gave me astute critical feedback on the proposal and initial chapters and helped me solidify my vision for the plot and characters. Jesse Sutanto read an early version of the manuscript and has been an invaluable source of advice. Federica Fedeli did me the favor of proofreading my Italian at the last minute. (*Grazie mille!*) Many more of my author friends and colleagues and my larger writer communities have also offered helping hands in ways too many to list, including but not limited to the members of the Codex Writers' Group, Dream Foundry (and the R3K book club!), and my various deeply wonderful writer chats (you know who you are!)—who answered my research questions, sent me resources, gave me perspective, and helped me brainstorm everything from capitalization schema to pronoun decisions to logline wording ("ungovernable gender"!). I want to particularly highlight the members of my BIPOC and queer communities for their extremely thoughtful support, whether they were giving me feedback on how to address colorism and Li Kui, talking through modern Chinese approaches to nonbinary familial honorifics with me, or holding my hand regarding the intersections of identity, publishing, marketing, and reader expectation. I wish I could mention everyone by name; I only hope I can pay this support back and forward.

Whether or not they gave me direct help with the book, my friends and family—both those who are writers and those who aren't—are invaluable to my life, and I would not be able to write or publish without them. You know what you all do for me. Without you I'd be lost.

Last but not least, I'd be remiss if I didn't credit a few public figures who sculpted the long tradition this book joins. The original, marvelous fourteenth-century classic *Water Margin*—which is the source material that this book reimagines—is attributed to Shi Nai'an. In writing *The Water Outlaws,* I additionally depended on the translations of J. H. Jackson (with updates by Edwin Lowe), Sidney Shapiro, and John and Alex Dent-Young. Though in general I have attempted to create my own versions of any English representations of Shi Nai'an's work, the translations of the Mus' nicknames—"the Unrestrained" and "the Slightly Restrained"—are my favorite decision of Shapiro's and are dropped in as an intended homage to the role of his translation in *Water Margin*'s history. I am also indebted to John Zhu of Chinese Lore Podcasts for his audio retelling of *Water Margin* and its extensive cultural and historical notes—and for answering a research question of mine on air that I couldn't figure out myself for the life of me! (I didn't use the answer, sorry—Wu Yong carrying a chain weapon is just too cool! But I was delighted to know!) If anyone would like to read the original *Water Margin* in English, Zhu's podcast is my recommended version and can be found at outlawsofthemarsh.com.

And though they lived far in the mists of time, I think it right to mention the real historical figures whom Shi Nai'an fictionalized in *Water Margin* and whom I have taken further liberties with here. Song Jiang, Emperor Huizong, Cai Jing, Gao Qiu, Zhou Tong, and Hua Tuo were all real people. (Though perhaps some of them wouldn't be happy to be immortalized this way. . . .) I also brazenly borrowed the names, histories, or work of several other real people on my own—General Han Shizhong, who was husband to the Song Dynasty's most famous female general (General Liang Hongyu); Zeng Gongliang, the Song Dynasty scholar who recorded the earliest known formulas for gunpowder in the *Wujing Zongyao*; Shen Kuo, a polymath scientist of the Song Dynasty; and Qu Yuan, poet and author of the real *Heavenly Questions.* I like to hope they would get a kick out of having a cameo here a millennium or two later!

Read on for an exclusive short story

The River Judge

by

S. L. Huang

The first time Li Li buried a corpse, she was nine years old.

Her father had been shut up inside one of the inn's private dining rooms all day. At such times it was understood that he was never to be disturbed. The rule had been drilled deep in Li Li since she was a small child—whether she had fallen on the riverbank and matted her hair with blood, or a patron of the inn became belligerent with drink and flung wine in her mother's face—knocking to interrupt her father was strictly forbidden.

Such times were for *business,* he always said. Meetings with business associates, planning for the inn's future. How could Li Li's mother expect the place to prosper if she did not respect the undisturbed peace needed for such work?

This time, only one other man had joined him. Li Li hadn't seen the man arrive, but her mother had waited on them with the finest meals and wine, the door always shutting firmly again when she had barely crossed the threshold to leave. Li Li had been ordered to get on with her usual long list of daily chores, gathering the washing and scrubbing dishes and packing out the night soil from the latrine buckets. But some rebellious river current always seemed to draw her into baiting dragons, including tempting her father's fury.

When she snuck close to listen through the wall this time, however, she couldn't hear much of interest. Only her father's voice rising and falling in conversation with the other man's. Then the two of them laughing together, her father much louder and longer.

She was still listening when everything went silent.

Li Li scurried from the door in apprehension of being caught. Her father's temper might be the chief concern, but both her parents disliked her tendency to lurk around corners and in shadows. They disliked a great many things about her—she had once eavesdropped on them telling people she was "strange and cold, like a stone" and "not a proper child at all." After that, she'd sat up on a hill once for half a day, challenging herself to stay perfectly still. It took so much strength that she decided being a stone was a compliment, and had begun testing her muscles with stillness as often as she could. She had always been stocky but small, and the other children in the town tended to be surprised at her strength, when they deigned to notice her.

She had stayed motionless as granite by the door for a long time today, lest a sound give her away. When that sudden silence reverberated so deep and strange, she threw herself back into her chores with an overdone vigor, as if to prove she'd never left them. She had relocated to the kitchen to sweep out the hearth's charcoal and ash when her father's silence bloomed into several loud crashes and thumps audible through the entire inn—which after a short time evolved into shouting at her mother.

That, at least, was very normal.

Li Li's mother kept her voice low, though the front room was empty of patrons this time of the afternoon, especially as travelers through the town had been dribbling off since the new magistrate had arrived. In contrast, Li Li's father never seemed to worry about potential patrons at all, even when the inn wasn't empty. None of the guests ever seemed bothered by his taking his house in hand, anyway.

His voice snapped off in furious declarations, vibrating through the walls about how *"this isn't your concern, the inn would have been ruined, it was the only way . . ."*

Li Li did what she usually did when her parents argued: she made herself scarce and still. As unnoticed as a shadow on the wall. If this argument followed the customary routine, her father would shout at her mother and then her mother would storm through the inn to find Li Li, raining down cruel digs and extra chores as if passing on a bucket of vitriol that was too hot to hold on to for long.

Li Li knew how to navigate such attacks as little as she knew how to handle her mother's interleaved spikes of affection or proclamations of her child's preciousness. In a bid to stay out of sight, she slipped into the back storeroom of the inn, intending to hide out among the earthenware pickling jars and stacked dense heads of winter cabbage.

Until she saw the dead man.

He sat slumped against the great cisterns of wine in the back of the storeroom, his head fallen forward from its own weight. His clothes were finer than any Li Li had seen, his robes spreading in layers of wide, embroidered skirts, and fur-trimmed leather armoring his legs where they stuck out in a stiff sprawl. Crimson stained the luxurious clothes, a shining wetness slowly creeping wider from below the man's collar and across his chest. More blood dripped from his manicured beard and mustache, leaving a spotted pattern upon his lap.

Li Li was so fascinated she momentarily forgot her parents' fighting. She had seen a dead body before, of course, but not like this, in rich clothes dumped in the back of a storeroom. She stared for several long moments, watching for the tells she always tried to squash when staying motionless herself. The rise and fall of breath, the twitch of eyelids, the shift of a cramped muscle . . .

No breath moved the man's lips or chest. His eyes were half-lidded and filmy, and one wrist had folded against the ground at an odd angle. His skin had gone white with a hint of purple, like the inside of a taro root, and the blood was beginning to dry into the color of rust.

Dead. Li Li felt very proud of herself for such a definitive conclusion.

Curious, she crouched down and scooted closer to the body, staying on her knees as if standing too tall might wake the man from wherever he dwelled on the other side. Then she reached out a daring finger and poked it against his cheek.

It was shockingly cold. And soft. And still felt like human skin.

Li Li jerked her hand back.

Only then did she notice something behind the dead man: a fine black hat with long, swooping wings that lay crushed against the floor. She was not old enough to recognize it as a mark of high office, but she would recall it later.

From the front room drifted in the bitter hiss of her mother. "*. . . that kind of business here at the inn . . .*"

Li Li's father snorted back something much louder—a lot of words about "*just think it through,*" and was her head empty, and no good wife would peck at such trivial objections. Then a sudden series of bangs and slams, as if someone moving about in anger. Li Li froze, a nebulous idea cobwebbing through her that she must be violating some rule by finding the corpse, much less touching it, and would be shouted at until her ears rang, and then have mountains of extra chores piled atop her. Like scouring out all the latrine buckets on top of the usual collection of night soil to sell to farmers, until the smell got in her nails and hair and clung for days . . .

After a moment's thought, she crept out of the storeroom as if she'd never been, and in a roundabout fashion snuck back into the front room. Her mother slumped at one of the empty tables, a cold cup of tea untouched before her. Li Li's father was wrapping himself in heavy layers to go outside.

"I have to go downriver and speak to Elder Mu," he said, without looking at his wife. "The investigators might arrive before I return. Make sure they have no cause for questions."

Li Li's mother raised stricken eyes. "But what about—"

"Just take care of it! Must I do everything for this family?" Her father shut the door hard behind him. A gust of cold settled in his wake.

Li Li's mother noticed her daughter then, and Li Li tensed. But to her surprise, her mother only reached out for her.

She came obediently.

Her mother crushed her in with both arms, face pressed against Li Li's hair. As usual when this happened, Li Li stood very still until she was released.

"Go play," her mother told her, sounding sad. "Outside, eh?"

Li Li went.

Outside was frigid. Li Li wrapped her arms tightly around herself and counted out the three thousand steps over to the shipping house on the river where her cousin Li Jun lived, stamping her boots every few paces to keep the numbness at bay. Her father and mother didn't like her playing with Li Jun, but they couldn't stop it on account of being family.

But Li Jun wasn't at home. Only her mother, Auntie Ru, a large and muscular woman who was tearing the hide off a couple of boatmen so loud the paper vibrated in the windows.

"River licenses? Do you think I give three farts for the capital's nonsense about river licenses? You're paid what the ledgers say you're paid!" Her gaze fell heavy on Li Li.

"My elder cousin . . . ?" Li Li asked.

"On the river, most like. *Ai! How dare you turn your back on me!*" Auntie Ru grabbed the case from her counting rods and began to beat the two boatmen around the head with it.

Li Li retreated. She'd heard her parents muttering about her cousin's family—how Li Jun ran wild, and how Auntie Ru didn't act proper in the least. As a widow with no sons Auntie Ru had been permitted to inherit her late husband's shipping brokerage, and Li Li's father made frequent bitter remarks toward the way she ran it. And toward his dead brother for marrying her in the first place. And toward Li Li whenever he paid enough attention to notice her associating with the family more than he liked.

He needn't have worried so much. Li Li didn't like her aunt much, either.

Now she walked back to her family's inn and paced about the yard with gloved hands over her tingling ears. The chickens fluttered about and squawked at her, and she scattered their evening meal early, her fingers becoming stiff sausages. The temperature plummeted until it knifed into her bones and teeth, but she stayed outside until the gray sky became grayer and she stopped feeling the tips of every extremity.

When she went back in, two patrons sat at a table, their rumpled clothes those of merchants off the water, their faces red and bunched with impatience. "Girl! We've been waiting an age. Hot wine and rice, and kill a chicken for us if you have it."

"Yes, Uncles." Li Li went back outside through the kitchen, grabbing the sharpest butchering knife on the way. A single swipe to catch a chicken; she held its warmth tight against her body and sliced with one swift move. The blood drained fast and practiced and red upon the frozen ground.

She took the bird back into the kitchen to prepare and went into the storeroom to get the wine—where she found her mother heaving at the arm of the dead man, tears dribbling down her jaw.

The corpse had collapsed on its side now, but had shifted only a few paces closer to the back door.

Li Li looked at her mother, looked at the corpse, and then back at her mother, who was not scolding or sniping but instead giving the distinct impression that their roles had reversed, and her small daughter of less than ten years had become the authority who had walked in on *her* doing something untoward.

Li Li pointed at the front room. "Guests," she said.

She walked past to ladle out bowls of cloudy yellow wine, then returned to the kitchen to prepare the food. The men ate and she sent them on their way, but by that time another patron had arrived demanding a meal and lodging. Li Li cooked and served, made up a room, and scrubbed out all the plates and bowls and pots once the man had retired.

By then it was full dark, an oppressive pitch aided by the overcast layer smothering any moon and stars. Li Li took a candle to the storeroom.

The room was empty, save for the dead man, who had now been wrapped—badly—in a length of rough cloth. Li Li moved past to where the back door was ajar.

Her mother stood in the patchy grasses behind the inn, shoving a spade against the ground, each motion barely chipping away another sliver of frozen dirt. Her breath huffed out in a gasping sob with every hit.

Li Li went back inside and brought the sole lodger a full hot pitcher of wine, no extra charge, and peeked out to make sure his room only saw the road. Then she listened until she heard his drunken snores and bundled back up in her warmest clothes.

She walked the three thousand steps to her cousin's place. All was dark, the living quarters behind the shipping house shuttered up tight. Li Li carefully lifted the latch of the tool shed where her aunt kept supplies for the vegetable patch. She borrowed a pickaxe and a digging knife and hiked back, stopping every so often to heave the heavy pickaxe from one shoulder to the other.

When she returned, her mother's body formed a curled crescent motionless around the haft of the spade.

Li Li thumped the pickaxe off her shoulder and sent the sharp end into the ground. Then again. And again.

Her mother roused at that. The two of them worked into the deep night, wood hafts blistering their hands. Then Li Li helped her mother drag the man out of the storeroom and into his shallow grave, where they packed the frozen clay tight atop him.

The next day, Li Li's shoulders ached and her hands cracked and bled. She wrapped her fingers in cloth and went to return the pickaxe and knife.

"What did you take those for?" asked Li Jun.

"I had to bury the dead," Li Li said.

Li Jun laughed. She was three years older than Li Li, tall and lithe like the eels that slithered down the river, and her hair stuck out as wild as if she'd not only been out on the frigid water but swimming its depths. Maybe she had. "Make sure you bury them deep," she said. "Otherwise they'll come back as ghosts."

Li Li did not laugh back. She had seen ghosts before, but only of her ancestors, and only in dreams. The idea of the dead man haunting the inn did not scare her, but it did annoy her. He had no right to invade her home.

She resolved to keep a close watch for ghosts.

She was still watching when, two days later, the Empire's investigators arrived.

They stayed at the inn.

They stayed at the inn, and demanded lodging and food without offering coin, and were rude to Li Li's mother, complaining that the food was too dry and the wine too weak. Then they interviewed every man in town and many of the women.

Li Li's father returned at midday but kept himself scarce, leaving his wife to wait on the interlopers. She stayed meek to them and then snapped at Li Li in the kitchen for peeling too much meat off the winter melon.

When the investigators went out to chase down anyone they decided to suspect, a handful of the townspeople congregated in the inn's front room in their place, and Li Li's father emerged to gather with them. Together they hunched over drinks, voices bouncing tense off the wooden walls.

"What will we do? How could they know so fast?"

"Some damned mouth must've talked."

"Even the swiftest boat would take more than a day from Bianliang. I heard it was sorcery; an omen came of the magistrate's death . . ."

"Why would the Imperial augurs be casting their eyes all the way down here?"

As Li Li retreated back to the kitchen, she heard her father grunt. "Same reason they pay just enough attention to send these grasping judges in the first place," he said. "Mark me, our worth to the capital is merely what they can scrape out of our pockets and stomachs . . ."

A weight seemed to hang over the inn all day, a heavy darkness that made the candles gutter and the rafters creak. Until that evening, when the townsfolk returned to the front room but the investigators did not—and all with a sudden roar of good cheer as if an overstretched noodle had finally snapped. The men laughed and shouted and toasted each other in every variety of the inn's wine, and the center of the party seemed to be Li Li's father.

"To Brother Li!" they cried. "A true man of the Empire!"

Wine sloshed and another sloppy cheer went up—until they saw Li Li watching and quieted.

"Eh, it's all right, Brother Li's daughter knows not to yap, don't you, girl?" said a younger one of the Tong brothers. Li Li knew him vaguely—the Tong family did a good deal of business with her aunt, and the eldest Tong brother had two daughters a bit older than her that Li Jun was fast friends with. Sometimes the three deigned to allow the littler cousin to join their group—which Li Li always did, even if they made her take enough bruises to prove her worth. They were bigger, and could always wrestle her down, but she never gave in.

Like a stone.

Elder Tong was staring at her, and Li Li realized he expected an answer. Her parents often scolded her for letting grown-ups' questions linger in the air for a moment too long. "Yes, Uncle," she said.

The men's hands unclenched, their faces relaxing back into easy smiles.

"I'd best be off anyway," Elder Tong said, rising and reaching for his fur-lined cap and outer wraps. "My elder brother thinks setting off for a delivery up in Ying Province might be in order, just in case anyone gets around to asking questions . . ."

"About today, or about your 'deliveries'?" said another of the men, with a tone in his voice that Li Li had come to recognize as a joke. The others guffawed.

"You want to stop benefitting, that's fine with us! Go on!" Elder Tong roared, laughing harder than any of them, while the joker raised his hands and hastily declared his lack of any desire for a change.

"To Brother Tong and Brother Li! Heroes of the Empire!" the

men cried raucously. Elder Tong brushed them off and slapped Li Li's father on the shoulder.

"After today, Brother Li's talents far outstrip those of us lowly boatmen. Shall we do some cleanup for you on the river, Brother? We can take the boats, find a convenient swamp . . ."

"Oh, no, no, I couldn't ask such a thing," Li Li's father said in his booming voice. "The cleaning part is easy, just a trifle. I wish you good hauls and a swift return."

Once the men had all left, Li Li's father staggered to bed sauced with his own drink and fell into a motionless slumber. He might have been mistaken for a dead man himself, but for the snuffling snores reminiscent of a rooting hog.

Li Li went to pick up the scattered wine bowls and to wipe up the drink that sopped tables and benches. She wrung out the wet rags and went into the storeroom for a bucket and mop.

Her mother sat on a stool in the back, staring at two more corpses. Li Li couldn't see their faces, but the hems of their skirts had the silken trim of the two Imperial investigators.

Li Li's mother raised her eyes with something like hopelessness, sweaty hair falling across her face. The spade leaned against her knee, her hands drooped across it like the branches of a shrub that had given up against too harsh a clime, with no willingness left to lift its leaves toward the sun.

Li Li curled her own hands. Her scabbing blisters crackled against themselves.

No men from the government came for some time after that. None of the people in the town had any sort of ear into the capital, or knew any reason the magistrate was not replaced or more investigators sent. Li Li continued working at the inn alongside her parents, although, slowly, her father disappeared more often and returned sodden with wine, and her mother snapped less and retreated into a hollow shell, her skin beginning to shrink tight against her bones.

Over the years, as if now by custom, here and there another body would appear in the storeroom for the women to tidy. A tax collector who had come to raid the residents' pockets. A regular merchant from off the river who'd been suspected of slipping overweighted stones onto the payment scales. A boatman who became sloppy with drink every time he came through and made aggressive attentions on married women. Then another man from the capital who'd proclaimed officiously that he had come to enforce the river's ferry licenses, as he'd had information that many in the area were in violation—and a few weeks later, his cousin from a nearby village whom the gossip reported as having leaked such business about his neighbors. Once, a poor but handsome local man who'd caused trouble for a friend of Li Li's father by competing over a marriage contract.

Sometimes, after a disappearance rid the region of some acknowledged pestilence, Li Li's father would get a few grins or nods from select guests, and he would always smile back and put on a genial act of ignorance. Occasionally more investigators arrived, but they either came and left again or ended up in the storeroom like so many others.

Traveling the river was dangerous, everyone knew. Storms and cutthroats and serpents of the river's wide depths . . . The people of the villages in this bend of the river were well-used to donning a wide-eyed innocence. See nothing, hear nothing, speak nothing of their own, not to some uncaring government official from far away.

And every time, once night fell, Li Li and her mother would drag the bodies out into the dark, heaving a growing collection of digging tools along with their burden. They'd discovered, eventually, that a nearby bog provided the most forgiving ground for grave digging, soft muck that would suck down a buried corpse with no outward sign, and that only froze across the very top layer in winter. It still took half the night to drag a body such a distance, and then to excavate enough mud for even a shallow covering. In cold months it might take the whole night, as they broke through the ice to where the swampiness somehow still churned warm beneath.

The river itself might have provided a more secretive maw, but the inn had been built far back from potential spring floodwaters, and an easy walk for a sailor or merchant was not such for dragging a corpse.

Li Li imagined the men's flesh decaying in the bog until their bones settled into the depths and crisscrossed atop each other. Like chopsticks thrown into the bottom of a basin to wash. Stacks of latticed chaos.

It was not until she was fifteen that the Empire sent another magistrate.

The position had remained vacant for so long that the local magisterial compound had become overgrown with knotweed, its ornate scrollwork broken in places and the tiles of its sweeping roof crumbling or chipped away. The retinue that preceded the new magistrate ordered the men of the town to scrape the weeds free and make every meticulous repair, with no mind paid to the labor that would ordinarily occupy their days—the fish that failed to come fat and fresh to market, the crops struggling untended, the dike walls and building stilts in need of this season's maintenance.

A muttering resentment blackened the town. Li Li was old enough now to comprehend it. The people did not need or want a new magistrate—for any rulings, the military governor in the nearest prefectural city could be appealed to, and conveniently, he was so far away and his attention on so many more important matters that here in this bend of the river they could live their lives without interference. The governor's lack of attention might mean he was also no reliable source of justice, but that was all right, too, because this tiny bustling town and its surrounding tiny sprawl of villages and farms could largely oversee itself. Small squabbles were solved by a clean verdict of fists, larger ones sometimes by a gang of one man's friends banging on the other's door in the dark with the silver flash of a knife, or sometimes more civilly by their neighbors dragging them before a wealthy estate like the Mus' for a judgment. The Mu family were not true nobility of the type who had such heaven-granted judicial authority, and their eccentricities and occasional viciousness were well-known, but a decision with their teeth behind it was one all would respect. Most considered it a fair enough court for these parts, out here on the rural reaches of the Four Great River Deltas.

And sometimes, a person who upset the balance of this bend in the river would simply disappear.

Bones in a chopstick pile.

Li Li did not, at this point, remember the previous magistrate very clearly, although somehow the image of his noble hat smashed against the floor had stuck in her mind with the sharpness of recent detail. She could not recall whether they had buried it with him.

The new magistrate arrived off the river amid a great fanfare of silken banners and golden bells, far beyond anything Li Li remembered seeing in the town. But this part of the river had been burgeoning bit by bit, its vibrancy and traffic flourishing, and perhaps someone thought it merited notice. Certainly the sole local inn had lately been humming through every watch of every day.

Most of that work had been falling on Li Li. Her father had grown increasingly absent, more often than not returning only to raid fistfuls of silver from the inn and depart again . . . Even when home, he intruded so much, while completing so little, that it sometimes seemed questionable whether their workload truly lightened with his presence. Her mother still rose at the same time and moved among the same chores, but over the years had faded to a weary remoteness, and Li Li would frequently find her gripping a door frame or a table and staring at nothing.

The last few months the inn had gained the assistance of Li Li's cousin as well—after Li Jun's mother had succumbed to a hemorrhagic fever in late summer. The shipping business had gone to Li Li's father, who promptly sold it to the Mus for a tidy sum. Li Jun had approached her uncle with a humble but passionate argument not to sell, promising she could do the work of the ledgers and even go out as a helmsman herself and report everything back to him. But Li Li's father would not entertain the notion.

"I shall do my responsibility by my brother," he said to her, "and find you a decent marriage contract. A difficult order, I dare to guess. Of course, you're not to blame for how you were raised—if a plant is allowed to grow to weed it will naturally become hardened to proper pruning."

Li Li, eavesdropping as usual, knew her cousin well enough to see Li Jun's posture knot into the tightness of angry defiance, even if she was wise enough not to challenge the uncle who now held control of her life.

Instead, she unloaded in long monologues to Li Li later about how she was going to go off and join the Tongs on their boats for good, just as soon as they would have her. Li Li did not think it likely. Tong women might be just as brawny as the men, saying all hands were needed when scrubbing down a salt barge, but what was accepted on the river was not the same as the ways of the town, and the Tong elders wouldn't pick a fight with Li Li's father.

Practicality would win out. Li Jun might be older, but she had never been practical enough.

Today Li Li let her cousin's usual complaints fade into the background, drowned behind the day's never-ending duties. Her feet ached and her hands had split in stinging cracks from the washing. Her father had chosen to forego supervising the inn today, as he often did, leaving it to Li Li and her mother and cousin. When Li Li's mother entreated him to please stay and help, this one time—he told her he trusted her, and wasn't that flattering? That he could delegate the family income to her entirely, that it made him proud . . . and she wouldn't prove him wrong, would she?

Li Li's mother flinched and hunched, a hand going to the side of her abdomen. She'd been making that same motion commonly of late.

"Lie down, Auntie," Li Jun said, her face crinkling in concern.

"You don't look well. We'll take care of the guests and then bring you some tea and tonic broth."

Li Li had the distinct feeling *she* ought to have said that first, but she hadn't thought to. A dark scorn spiked as she watched her mother hobble to her room—one that had been biting at Li Li more and more often. Guilt lapped vaguely on its heels: children were to protect and provide service and support to their forebears; it was what children existed for.

But if her own father wouldn't care for her mother's weaknesses, why should she?

She followed Li Jun to fetch wine for the packed front room of guests. Too many guests. The new magistrate's presence certainly hadn't damped the number of travelers, at least not yet. Some of those travelers would have brought their own provisions for her to cook, but the inn wouldn't have enough meat to feed the rest—not until the Tongs returned with more stores for the town.

Li Li was already bracing for the endless complaints sure to pelt down upon them. The inn had better have enough wine.

She didn't want to know how the men might react, if the inn didn't have enough wine.

At the entrance to the storeroom, however, Li Li almost ran into her cousin's back, where Li Jun stopped stock-still in the doorway.

Piled behind the barrels were the familiar stacked limbs of ever more bodies. Rich clothes, limp hands, slack faces. And this time a very large lot of blood, seeping across the floor as if a barrel of dark fruit wine had spilled across it.

The dangling limbs were too many to easily count. More than her father had ever left them to take care of at once before . . . Li Li's scorn at her mother's weakness sharpened into a white-hot anger at her father. *Does he not realize how long this chore takes?*

And now her mother leaving her to it alone . . . !

"Aiya," whispered Li Jun. "Look, it's the new magistrate."

The same swooping black headdress lay a bit apart from the corpse pile. The visceral stamp of the first man, six or seven years ago, had never left Li Li's memory.

"What do we do?" Li Jun asked.

"We clean it up," Li Li said. "That's *our* job. Father does his business, and he says it's his women's job to clean up."

"The other disappearances . . ." Li Jun was clever, which was good, because it saved Li Li time explaining. She had no concern that Li Jun would cause any trouble. Li Jun was of the local populace, and family besides, and everyone knew how the government officials stripped prosperity from the villages and played games with the residents' livelihoods. How pretty women were advised to appear less so when near the eyes of government men, and how their husbands were advised never to step in, lest they lose more than a wife.

"We'll have to deal with it after the guests go to bed," Li Li said, assuming the authority of experience.

As if in response, rowdy shouts erupted from the front room, demanding what was taking so long with the meat and wine. Li Li's eyes crawled over the corpses. A hopelessness wanted to throttle her. How many bodies to drag? How many trenches to dig?

Li Jun seemed to be thinking the same. "Could we get them to the river? I could swim, weight them down in one of the caves . . ."

Li Jun might be older, but she was ignorant of the way dead bodies sagged like sacks of rice in the shape of a man. "We'd need a mule and a cart for that," Li Li said.

They'd need to rid the inn of the bodies the same way they always did. Li Li's fury at her father welled up and up, flooding her. Drowning her.

"Where are those useless wenches?" came a yell from the front room. "Meat, girls, or I'll butcher the lot of you instead!"

Li Li recklessly wondered what would happen if she walked out of the inn and left it all undone. Would her father have to bury his own corpses for a change?

But no, her cousin and her mother would do it, her mother falling and fainting, and though Li Li didn't strictly love her mother, she did feel a familial duty, and the image reeked of an injustice so vast it made her teeth hurt. But the prospect of dragging so many out to bury—and with so many guests who would already keep them up late into the night with demands and complaints, that the wine was too thin or the beds too cold, or that the inn did not have enough meat—

Li Li's eyes flashed wide.

"Cousin?" Li Jun said. "What is it?"

Li Li had begun moving, retrieving the cleavers. Knives in hand, she appraised the body on the top of the pile. It stood to reason a man would not taste different from a goat or a hog.

And she knew how to butcher those.

"You get the wine," she said to Li Jun. "I'll bring the meat."

The guests went to bed full and happy, and the inn even had a surplus of shanks that Li Li placed on hooks as she had been taught. Only this time she took some care to disguise any humanlike foot or hand or expanse of bared and hairy skin.

Once the guests had been calmed and put up, and any repeated whines or calls for yet another cup had been dealt with, Li Jun helped Li Li mop up the blood from the butchering and burn the men's clothes. Tomorrow the guests would not only tell tales of a well-stocked inn, but rhapsodize about how warm the place had been kept on a blustery night. What luxury!

"Your father is a hero," Li Jun said in a hush, as they finished. "I never knew!"

Li Li snorted. "He's not a hero. He only does the easy part."

"Maybe he'd let me help," Li Jun said. She spun the mop to *crack* it against one of the pillars of the back room. "I've done summers with the Tongs keeping ruffians off their boats, and I'm just as good with a knife as them. My mother said she'd marry me to the first boy who could swim longer than me or beat me in a fistfight, and I'm not married, am I? And the Weng boy drowned trying!"

Li Jun loved telling that story.

"You oughtn't be so proud of not being married," Li Li said.

"Your parents are dead. Now you're dependent on charity until you do find a husband."

Li Jun's eyes narrowed. "Why, though? The Tong sisters are going to take over the salt barges eventually, their father said so, and the Mus don't have a son either and they taught their daughters to hunt tigers. We aren't any weaker than them. Besides, you're right, you and your mother run the whole inn, your father doesn't do anything. I bet I could do his other 'business' just fine, too." She made a stabbing gesture in the air. "I've heard of groups of female bandits in the hills. Maybe I'll go join them."

Li Li had heard such tales, too. She wasn't sure she'd like that. Women annoyed her just as much as men, most days. She wasn't even sure she *was* a real woman; she seemed to be cursed in some way—her women's monthly water still had never come, at this point surely backing up its toxins into her blood. Meanwhile, the eyes of the boys in the town skimmed past and through her, which was just as well since she was repulsed by them in turn. She was old enough now that Li Jun and the Tongs bragged openly in front of her of their ever-escalating obscene exploits—Li Li was pretty sure they'd even "done things" with *each other* while out on the boats, which they said didn't count. Li Li was unclear on whether this was because they were all girls, or if because they were all involved then none of them could score anything above the others, but all of it sounded so distinctly unenjoyable that she secretly dreamed of worming her way out of ever sharing a marriage bed.

Sometimes men didn't get married. Rarely, but sometimes. Maybe she could become a man. Gossip said one of the Mu daughters had done that the other way around, but rules were different for rich eccentrics who taught their daughters to fight tigers.

"I could be a bandit," Li Jun was saying. "A hero of the hills. Like your father, but not leaving all the work to the womenfolk. I bet I'd be great at it."

She produced a knife and threw it in one move. The blade buried itself in a doorjamb across the room, the handle vibrating with the force of it.

Li Li walked over and wrenched it out. “You’d better not say such things when the Imperial investigators arrive.”

Her cousin’s expression went shocked and tense. Maybe from nervousness. Maybe eagerness.

Li Li sighed and handed the blade back. “Just don’t say anything, right? They’ll come eat all our food and go away again.”

Unless my father kills them first, she added silently.

Li Li had spent no serious worry over her cousin knowing the truth. But she ought to have remembered a far deeper concern than Li Jun telling tales about what she knew: her cousin was uncontrollable.

Without consulting Li Li at all, she conspired with the Tong sisters, who had just come back downriver with their family. The Tong girls spread wild rumors of a wakening water demon among the surrounding towns, and Li Jun plunged into the deep, gray fathoms of the river and swam below every one of the investigators’ boats during the last days of their approach, holding her breath so long they neither saw a ripple of her arrival nor when she surfaced afterward.

When the investigators disembarked at the inn they jumped at every small sound, dark moons pressed out beneath their eyes and their fine beards and caps awry.

“Something knocking at our boats—”

“A river demon, everyone is saying so!”

“It must have been that which devoured the magistrate and his men, we mustn’t stay long . . .”

“It’s this place, this place is surely cursed!”

Li Jun came back to the inn rather insufferable. “I fixed it all, didn’t I?” she bragged. “See, I *told* you I’d make a good hero.”

“It’s not done yet,” Li Li said. “And you should have asked first. This isn’t some game.”

“Stop being such a mud-stuck clam,” Li Jun said. “They swallowed it like fish bait. They’re going to leave and no one is ever going to come back to bother us, you watch!”

Such a plan might have worked. Even Li Li had to admit it, though she refused to say so aloud.

If only it hadn't been for the ghost.

After so many years of corpses, Li Li had ceased to worry about ghosts. She knew ghosts could enter the world at times, everyone knew such a thing, but they were so rare, and so often mysterious in their methods of manifestation, and as likely to bestow beneficence as to make trouble. More importantly, Li Li's father had been killing people for enough years that Li Li had become jaded to the possibility that one might return.

Until this magistrate did.

He didn't visit in dreams, the way Li Li's ancestors had on brief flickering occasions. He didn't make his presence known through strange events, either cursed or blessed, nor did he return as animal or insect, nor through cold or wind.

He came as a shadow.

The inn was abuzz with it the next day, the day the investigators had been hastening to depart, with their report of the magistrate's demise via river demon. But four of the six investigators had seen the magistrate in the night, along with another three guests.

They talked in hushed voices of his shadow sliding silently out from cracks in the darkness.

Reluctantly, the delegation's leader determined that they must remain longer and seek communication with the apparition. He assigned himself and one of his men to depart to a neighboring town to find a spirit medium, giving his other four unhappy subordinates strict instructions to keep watch for the ghost.

Traveling for a medium would take at least a full day and night. The four remaining investigators lurked sour and white-faced around the inn, and Li Li tried to go about her duties as if she did not feel the weight of a dozen panthers scrambling up her back. Her cousin was even jumpier.

"What if he tells them somehow?" Li Jun whispered while they cleaned out the lodging rooms, no matter how Li Li tried to shush her. "What if he can tell them who killed him?"

"My father's gone again anyway," Li Li said. As had become his habit, he had disappeared up- or downriver before any investigation descended.

But the thought snuck up from her heart, in the greatest of familial betrayals: *No great loss, if they do come for him.* After all, hadn't Li Jun said herself how Li Li and her mother were the ones who truly ran the inn?

If the investigators took her father away . . .

No more long absences while only returning to yell at Li Li and her mother or plunder the inn's savings. No more finding fault with their work while barely moving to help with the inn's chores, only drinking and heckling and reminding them that it all came from him.

No more bodies left in the storeroom for them to clean up at the most inconvenient times, while he alone raked in the whispered adulation of any in the town who knew.

Her prior disrespectful words had been nothing but truth: her father only did the easy part. Any of them could kill a man just as well, couldn't they? It didn't take some great skill to stab into rich soft skin that was sopped with beef and potent rice wine, did it?

She made a retreat into the kitchen and ground tea and cardamom and pepper, too much and too fast until she struck too hard and the pestle cracked.

She stopped. Forced herself to stillness. The spices had scattered across the counter.

Maybe, with her father gone, her mother might cease being so sick and weak all the time. At least her mother worked hard. At least she did what needed doing. A small, fleeting part of Li Li wondered if, with her father gone, her mother might become a figure she would gladly pay daughterly duties toward.

Besides, Li Li was discovering that she despised injustice even more than weakness. Not because of any souls-deep sympathy for her family and neighbors, but because of the way it added up so wrong and out of joint, like a ledger that wouldn't match itself. The world ought to balance.

It ought to, and it never did. The rich government officials took whatever they wanted, and Li Li's father killed whomever he wanted, with Li Li and her mother crunched in the fissures of it all and working their hands to bleeding.

She returned to her chores and allowed herself to imagine a future where her father met some timely end. With his nuisance removed, her mother could gain widow's rights to the inn, the same as Li Jun's mother had. They'd finally be able to run it in peace, doing a hard day's work and then retiring to bed without worry . . .

Thus it was that when Li Li came into the back storeroom to lock everything up for the night, and she saw the great swooping headdress shadowed on the wall by a light that came from nowhere, she stopped cold and still as a rock but did not turn away.

Li Li stared at the shadow. She did not feel afraid.

The inn was quiet. The remaining guests would be in bed, trying to sleep—or failing to sleep, what with word of a ghost about. Most had fled with nervousness at such an interaction, leaving the rooms near-empty for once.

The shadow elongated slightly, the body growing taller and thinner. Somehow, the magisterial headdress simultaneously stretched wider, until its authority yawned to near comical levels.

"Do you speak?" Li Li inquired finally.

The shadow was silent.

"Are you here for vengeance against my father?"

Again, no reply. No movement.

Li Li wondered if the magistrate even knew her father had been the one to assassinate him. When she'd chopped through the grizzle of the body, she'd noted the knife wound that gaped between the back ribs.

If the ghost didn't know who had been responsible for such an end, she supposed she had now told. But the shadow had not extinguished itself.

What else might it be seeking?

With a start, she wondered if her own actions had caused this manifestation. Cooking human flesh . . . could such a thing release a restless ghost? After all, even among the ardent admirers of her father's activities, most would frown on what she had done.

The thought made her angry. *Those* men had not been working their hands raw to help ill mothers defray exhaustion when dumped with such inconvenient corpses, and she was sure how they would judge her nonetheless. But her solution wasn't of some inferior moral character. It was *clever.*

"They won't find your remains," she declared to the ghost. "If it's my father you want to point at, though—is that it? Is that what you're looking for? Well, if he didn't want anything found, he should have done it himself. The old magistrate, the one before you—he's buried in the yard out by the larch tree, and anyone who—"

The shadow winked out.

Li Li stood in the empty night, stood long enough for her feet to grow stiff against the unmoving ground, stood stiller than any rock face on a carven mountain. The strange righteousness that had filled her had burst as suddenly as it appeared, leaving a vague void behind.

She'd told on her father. Her family, her elder. Her *father.* An act against Benevolence, against nature, even more than eating human flesh.

She should be flooded with guilt and shame.

Instead, something had begun to sizzle and bubble within the emptiness like when the river churned with typhoon-fed floods.

Something very like excitement. Or power.

The inn was awoken by screams.

Li Li struggled out of sleep in disorientation, deep dreams still snatching at her. The light had begun to turn, almost at dawn—almost when she would have been rising anyway—

Someone screamed again. Li Li was struck by the sudden instant certainty that the scream belonged to her mother.

She was on her feet without being fully awake, racing outside without proper outerwear or boots, her breath fogging with the late-autumn cold and her ears ringing with the aftermath of those screams. The first edges of dawn cracked weak and watery over the yard.

Others from the inn were stumbling out into these last dregs of night. The few guests who had remained—and Li Jun, too, wrapped hastily in a blanket, the Tong sisters with her, strapping young women who stood with the confidence that they were no longer children. Li Li hadn't known they'd stayed over with Li Jun; they usually lived out of their boats.

Li Li's eyes raked across the yard—and found her mother.

Her mother, who knelt a few paces before the larch tree, her worn thinness suddenly in such sharp relief that her fragility seemed shocking. Someone had chipped up the clay beside her.

The four remaining Imperial investigators surrounded the shallow grave beneath. One leaned a pickaxe haft against his hip, another had discarded a spade upon the ground. In the pitted earth, a half-unburied human skull stared from naked and collapsed sockets. His fine clothes had turned to dust, roots twining through where his flesh had been. But somehow the swooping magistrate's hat was still as broad and black and fine as the day his corpse had appeared in their storeroom.

Within Li Li, the surprise of it warred with smug satisfaction. She'd told the ghost, and the ghost had communicated to them, even with no spirit medium to interpret.

Now the scales will balance. Everyone will get what they deserve.

"Explain this, innkeeper," said one of the investigators to Li Li's mother. He bit the words so sharply that spit flew forth with them.

Li Li's mother hunched over against the ground, shaking her head over and over, not in defiance but desperation. Her breath keened high and hard, so fast she couldn't seem to speak.

Li Li did not feel sympathy. Her mother had always reacted with overly high humors. Once the investigators had taken Li Li's father away, and the inn slipped back to normal, all this frenzy would recede and everything would turn calm.

One of the other men turned to his partners. "The snake cannot move without the head—the husband must also be involved. Bind her and take her to the magistrate's compound. The chief will decide if they face justice here or if it's to be prisoner transport to Bianliang."

The words took many heartbeats to coalesce into meaning, so contrary were they to Li Li's expectations. Why would they—but her mother hadn't—

They *assumed*—

Li Li began to call out—what, she hadn't determined; she only knew that this was not the way she had meant anything to go. Before she could, her mother launched herself at the feet of one of the investigators.

The motion was one of supplication. As if to clutch at their hems and press her face upon their boots in weeping entreaty.

The man's lip lifted in a sneer. In that moment, with a movement that was almost casually slow, he moved the pickaxe from against the side of his leg.

The head of the tool thumped against the ground in front of him. Directly in the path of Li Li's mother as she fell at his feet.

The dirt-clodded spike of the pickaxe plunged through the soft skin just below her jaw.

Her cries cut off with a wet crunch. Her limbs flopped boneless against the ground in the sudden silence.

"Stupid woman," said the investigator. "At least now we won't have to—"

A choked gurgle cut him off as the edge of the spade *thunk*ed straight into his throat.

The investigator struggled against suddenly folding limbs, his eyes casting about in confusion. He hadn't seen Li Li grab the spade off the ground. Hadn't seen her heave it upward with all her strength.

People always underestimated her strength.

She yanked the spade back from his neck, and blood fountained forth, more than she'd ever seen when butchering animal or human. The other three investigators had begun to move by then, hands fumbling for the blades at their sides. Li Jun's knife took one of them in the chest. The Tongs tackled another with a shout, pounding him into the earth. The last man stumbled in his shock, and Li Li heaved the spade again.

Its dull metal rang hard against his skull.

He clattered onto the ground. Li Jun dove in to grab the man's own short sword, and she plunged it through his body as if driving a fence post.

The Tongs stood up. The elder of them pressed a nonchalant hand against a bloody slash that gaped her forearm open. The younger gripped a jagged rock in one hand. Bits of white bone shone through the face of the man unmoving below them.

The elder Tong sister jerked a chin at the inn's few patrons who had braved the haunted night. Three of them, all men, watching with slack jaws and wide eyes—two merchants from off the river and one man from a neighboring village who'd stayed to sleep off his drink.

"We'll have to kill them, too," the elder Tong said. "They saw."

"No—please, we won't—" started one of the merchants, at the same time the other began to shout. "How *dare*—!"

Li Jun's newly retrieved knife found the shouting man in the liver.

The man who had begged broke into a panicked run, but the younger Tong dropped her rock to grab one of the short swords and caught up with him easily. She loped back over to join her sister and Li Jun in surrounding the final man.

"Wait," Li Li said.

The others stopped, their expressions aggressive questions. The only sound came from the still-dying merchant whose gut Li Jun had buried her knife in; he curled on the ground with moans ever more thready and pitiful. One of the cocks crowed suddenly, calling out the start of the day in an unsettling contrast.

Li Li approached the local man. "You're not from off the river," she said. "Do you know what my father did here?"

His chin trembled in a nod, his ragged mustache shaking. "I heard—rumors, miss. Only rumor."

"Would you ever have told men like these?" She pointed back at the dead investigators.

Shock suffused his face. "Of course not! Never."

"Good. Speak nothing of this, either. Remember what protection this place has given you."

"Yes, miss. Of course, miss. We are all loyal to your father, miss."

Li Li tasted bitterness at that, and her hand twitched to complete the violence here, but she held the judgment at bay. Instead, she said, "Go home to your family."

He wasted no time in scrambling away, backing up with jerky bows. By that time the man on the ground had stopped moving.

Everything had stopped moving.

Li Li let the edge of the spade fall to the dirt, let her hand grip tightly against its haft. She didn't want to turn around. Didn't want to look at her mother's body.

She didn't want to look at the rest of the bodies, either. *So much to clean up . . .*

She hadn't meant for anything to go this way.

But she hadn't started any of it, either. That had been the investigator, and the vile officials before him, and most of all—

Li Jun stepped over and rested a hand against her shoulder. "You did right. None of this was your fault."

"I know," Li Li said. "It's my father's."

Rumor said that when the investigators' leader learned his four subordinates had been devoured by the river demon, he and his right-hand man scurried straight back to the capital, convinced they had enough for their report after all.

Rumor said the capital seemed prone to forget the magisterial post existed, after that. Or perhaps they tried to assign men to it and failed, until a harried minister looked at the judiciary lists and decided leaving one remote bend of the river to the military governor was good enough.

Rumor also, however, now knew the name of Li Li's father, and knew embroidered stories of a skeleton found beneath his inn, stories whispered as often in admiration as in judgment. They were carefully never whispered where they might reach the ears of Bianliang—not that they likely would have been deemed important, by those far away whose wish was to ignore such a troublesome rural town. Even so, Li Li sometimes wondered if she'd been wise in sparing the local villager's life. Her generosity was returned to her, however, when still other rumors reported how her father heard the tales being told of his name and how he shook with fear as he ran. He fled toward the western mountains with no glance back at the inn or the living daughter he left behind.

The daughter was just fine with that.

Li Li and Li Jun smartened up the inn with some help from the Tongs, and Li Li made certain to declare to the right ears that her father's other "business" was finished and had disappeared along with him. Most took this to mean that no more skeletons would be buried in the inn's yard, and indeed, none ever were again.

The law technically provided no way for Li Li to come into ownership of the inn, as her father was still alive, and even if he had not been, as an unmarried daughter she would not inherit. In this bend of the river that lacked a magistrate, however, no one was too fussed about each and every stroke of law. Li Li declared that of course she must keep up the inn for her father in his absence, and that was enough for most people not to question.

If any questions did arise, they were not heard for long before mysteriously going silent.

Thus, for the next four years the inn at the bend in the river gradually became even busier and more prosperous, growing into a well-known stop for hungry traders. And if gossip whispered anything else about the inn and its young proprietor, it was wise enough not to whisper too loud.

Four years was how long it took for Li Li's father to decide the law would no longer remember his name, and then to return to claim his wealth.

Li Li was wiping down tables when his shadow loomed up in the door. He stepped inside with his chest puffed out in assumed ownership, then stood in the center of the clean and polished front room, fists on his hips. His eyes crawled over the walls and tables, the customers comfortably tucking in food and wine, the expanded wings that had been added on with their newly carved wooden screens and the delicate brushwork scrolls Li Li had hung upon the walls for both aesthetics and luck.

His shape sucked away the smooth balance of the space more than any shadow from beyond the grave. Cold gripped Li Li's heart, as if another ghost had entered her home.

That's all this man was. A ghost.

She straightened her clothes and approached him. From the way his eyes slid uncertainly she could tell he did not recognize her until she said, "Hello, Father."

His smile slipped, just a touch, before it shuddered back into place. "I see my inn is not as well-kept as it could be, but not ruined. Good girl. I knew you'd handle things until I returned."

Li Li had come to consider her natural lack of expression to be an asset for just such moments as these. No stirrings showed on her face.

"You must be so tired," she said to her father. "Come into a private room. I'll bring you a meal."

He grunted and took what he considered his due. Li Li served him stew and steamed buns and noodles simmered in sauce, along with the inn's most fragrant wine. He rambled on about how he'd returned to sell the property, as innkeeping life no longer fit him.

When did it fit you? thought Li Li. *When have you ever kept the inn?*

"I have a few buyers nibbling about. And I don't want you to worry; I'm only considering the ones who are also willing to bring a bride price. We'll get this business done."

Li Li barely blinked at the casual assumption she would be sold off as a rich man's concubine. This must be what it felt like, to have power.

"I've been doing your business," she said instead.

Her father's wine-glazed eyes wobbled over to her, uncomprehending.

"*Both* your businesses," Li Li added silkily.

She pulled up a chair and sat beside him, leaning in against the table as if they shared secrets in a conspiracy. "Let's be truthful, Father. You never did those businesses yourself anyway. I've been doing both since the beginning. For ten years now."

Her father licked his lips, a quicksilver nervousness darting through his eyes for the first time.

"You're feeling heavy," Li Li said. "That's a mineral sleeping powder in the wine. It's very potent."

And made everything much more tidy and convenient, she'd come to find.

It took a moment for her father's eyes to grow wet and wide, and then he jerked as if to lurch up or swipe at her before falling heavily back in the chair. "Can't. You . . ."

His lips flapped against the words until they were unintelligible.

"None of this was ever yours." Li Li's voice became a slither. "I saw so clearly, by the end. You claimed ownership but left every meaningful task to us. Because this bit now, it's no work at all, is it? To kill a man who's soft with meat and wine, and only full of air and words."

Her father tried to answer. Fear suffused every line of his face.

Li Li's knife moved with the whispering speed borne of four years of practice.

That night, Li Li straightened her inn with great care. She had plenty of meat stored up for the inn's travelers—the ones who would leave to travel onward, rather than those who would best serve by staying on her hooks to fill the bellies of the next . . . those she judged to be too much like magistrates or fathers, or the rude oglers or complainers who demeaned and demanded.

The inn never wanted for traffic, here on this busy bend of the river. If not everyone made it up- or downstream, well, everyone knew the river was dangerous. Full of cutthroats and smugglers and undertows and ghosts and demons.

And Li Li. Who met and judged, just like a magistrate.

Tonight, however, she made a very special soup only for herself.

She waited for Li Jun to come back from the river—to come back from making the river more dangerous, as one of those smugglers and cutthroats who caused so many to hoard their silver in fear. Today she came from accompanying the Tongs upriver, returning with hulls that bulged with silver and salt and spices, dried fish and pickled vegetables . . . all "donations" from choice estates, as Li Jun laughingly liked to say. She and Li Li added her share of the silver to a lockbox below the inn floor, alongside the establishment's own quickly expanding riches.

The inn was becoming impressively flush. Nobody had ever asked how the two cousins had come to run it, or how they had achieved such success. At least, nobody had asked for long.

Li Jun had spoken with great prescience, those years ago: they did a very good job without any husbands at all. Or fathers.

Tonight, Li Li left her cousin in charge, and she carried her freshly made soup up to her mother's grave on a hilltop overlooking the town. The streets and buildings spread out below, multiplying outward in a slow creep every season as the town expanded. Beyond them the river stretched wide and fathomless, a muddy gray-gold snake draped across the landscape, the farms on the other side tiny at this distance.

Li Li sat with her mother, and she leaned against an ash tree and drank her special soup while she watched the sun set.

Her home had never felt so peaceful.

ABOUT THE AUTHOR

Chris Massa Photography

S. L. Huang is a Hollywood stunt performer, firearms expert, and Hugo Award winner with a math degree from MIT and credits in productions like *Battlestar Galactica* and *Top Shot.* The author of the fantasy novella *Burning Roses* as well as the Cas Russell novels, including *Zero Sum Game, Null Set,* and *Critical Point,* Huang's short fiction has also appeared in *Analog Science Fiction and Fact, The Magazine of Fantasy & Science Fiction, Strange Horizons, Nature, Tor.com,* and more, including numerous best-of anthologies.

slhuang.com
Twitter: @sl_huang
Goodreads: S. L. Huang